D1490661

PRAISE FOR LADY BE GOOD

"This finely-crafted gem of a novel holds within it an entire world: Jazz Age New York, with all its vibrancy and thrill. Rich with smart dialogue and period detail, it's a window into a vanished time, bringing historical legends back to life—but more than that, it's a mirror that helps us see our own society more clearly."

—Kermit Roosevelt, award-winning author of *Allegiance*

"In this deeply evocative story, Hamilton beautifully captures the themes of love and betrayal, class and culture, and the price of fame. With stylish prose and clever dialogue, she reveals the fascinating story of Dorothy Hale and her complicated friendship with Clare Boothe Luce—two women of intellect, wit, and beauty who strive to have it all and ultimately transcend societal expectations imposed on women to realize their dreams. Meticulously researched and well told, *Lady be Good* is a magnificent debut novel, taking readers on an enthralling and heartbreaking journey with the famed and feted as they make their mark on American culture."

—Bill Dedman, Pulitzer Prize winner and *New York Times* #1 bestselling author of *Empty Mansions: The Mysterious Life of Huguette Clark and the Spending of a Great American Fortune*

"*Lady Be Good* is a coming-of-age story. It's a love story. It's a story of friendship, grace, and betrayal. Pop open a bottle of Veuve Clicquot and fall into Dorothy Hale's rarified world of glitz, glamour, and grand times during the Jazz Age. Hamilton delivers an astonishing and tender portrait of a captivating woman who is navigating scandals in the highest echelons of society with her outspoken confidante Clare Boothe Luce by her side. Poignant, heartbreaking, and a whole lot of fun, it's filled with snappy dialogue and vivid descriptions of the glitterati of 1930s New York. Written in lyrical prose, this elegant, absorbing tale tells the true story of a misunderstood woman who captured the hearts of all of those who knew her. Irresistible. You'll never see the Frida Kahlo portrait in the same way again."

—Andrea Cagan, *New York Times* and
Los Angeles Times #1 bestselling author

"Did you ever wonder what was going through the mind of an outstandingly beautiful, improbably elegant and gifted woman? Satisfaction? Contempt for ordinary people? Desperate fear of losing one's high status? Dorothy Hale was surely that person, and in *Lady Be Good*, Pamela Hamilton takes us, as only superb fiction can, deep into that mind. Based on meticulous research and with prose as stylish as Hale herself, Hamilton recounts the mystery of the dazzling socialite, whose friends included Frida Kahlo and Clare Booth Luce. *Lady* is a many-layered mystery exploring not only the overt question of how Hale came to die, but also a much deeper and even more fascinating investigation of fame, class, gender, appearance, and the American dream. It's a truly compelling story."

—Dennis McNally, *New York Times* bestselling
author of *A Long Strange Trip*

"An absolute candy dish of luxury, opulence, and grandeur. Every word as delicious as the next. A lens into the upper echelon of the roaring 20s. Delectable, divine, and delightful."

—Ashley Longshore, author and pop artist

Lady Be Good: The Life and Times of Dorothy Hale
by Pamela Hamilton

ISBN   978-1-64663-270-1

Cover design by Richard Ljoenes Design LLC

Published by

◤ köehlerbooks™

3705 Shore Drive
Virginia Beach, VA 23455
800–435–4811
www.koehlerbooks.com

Dorothy Hale by Lee Miller

LADY BE GOOD

THE LIFE AND TIMES OF DOROTHY HALE

A Novel

PAMELA HAMILTON

VIRGINIA BEACH
CAPE CHARLES

For my parents

TABLE OF CONTENTS

PART I

PART II

PART III

PART IV

PART V

PART I

LAST DRESS
FROM BERGDORF'S

Dorothy Hale stood at the window, sixteen floors above Central Park South. Surrounding her were souvenirs from her family and friends, her Broadway shows and movie roles, but they were of no comfort to her now. Nor was the warm October breeze or golden colors of sunrise. She was trembling with fear.

Looking out at the city lights in the distance, the emerald crown of the Carlyle Hotel reached upward in the eastern sky. The American flag at the north end of the park hung motionless. She felt the world was moving in slow motion. At 6:15 a.m., she balanced precariously at the open window in her silver high heel shoes, and in a terrifying last moment, her thoughts turned to her late husband and to prayer, as she tumbled out into the sky under a blanket of rolling clouds.

At 6:16 a.m., moments before O'Brien, the milkman, arrived at the Hampshire House, a loud thump caught the attention of the building's accountant, Thomas Conroy. He dashed outside and found Dorothy on the cement sidewalk, faceup.

Tied around her neck was a black velvet ribbon with the Florentine

Victorian pendant Gardner had given her during their first year of marriage. Dorothy often recounted what he had said as he wrapped his arms around her to tie the ribbon: "We will never miss a sunset together. *Jusqu'à la fin des temps, mon amour." Until the end of time, my love.*

Lying broken on the pavement, her black velvet dress from Bergdorf Goodman, the one she saved for special occasions, draped around her like a widow's veil. The corsage of yellow tea roses that her friend, sculptor Isamu Noguchi, had pinned at her breast just hours before was fastened in place and had begun to wilt. One shoe was still fastened at her ankle, while the other lay on the street beside the wheel of a chauffeured Packard. They were the same silver heels that had carried her so gracefully across the marble floors of her building and into the lounge where she sipped champagne and enchanted aristocrats as the music of Benny Goodman and her friend Fred Astaire played in the background. The accountant and the milkman knelt beside her and cried for help as blood leaked from her body onto the sidewalk. Her soft amber eyes looked through them as if gazing toward the park, and her scarlet lips were moist. They say that even in death, Dorothy Hale was one of the beautiful women of New York.

A gust of wind blew in through the open window, scattering some notes she had left on the desk. The scent of her perfume, Joy by Jean Patou, whom she knew, lingered in the room. There was a strange silence in the air, an eeriness in the breeze that stroked the delicate fabric of the chairs, the mink coat, the photographs—the unremarkable things that now seemed abandoned, even ghostly, in her absence. As the sun began to rise over Central Park, the sky glowed in a shade of queen blue, casting silhouettes on rising towers. The city was not yet awake. The news had not yet spread.

Her glistening eyes were motionless in the glare of the flashbulb. Harold Coldwell, a police photographer, wedged himself between the Packard and Jaguar parked by the curb, mindful not to step on her dress as he looked through the lens. Had it not been for a cascade of blood streaming from her lips, it would have been a photograph worthy of framing, he thought, the last of her storied life. Homicide detectives watched as he took the final snapshot, a close-up of her hand, unadorned. Leaning against the cars, the photographer and policemen kept their gazes fixed on her as the wail of a siren sounded in the distance.

When detectives opened the door to her apartment, 16E, remnants of her party were in clear view—empty bottles of vodka, whiskey and wine were set on a side table, and Baccarat glasses still shined. They examined the narrow frame of the French window and recorded in the police report that she could not have fallen out.

As they searched the apartment for evidence, they found letters from Mrs. William Randolph Hearst and Cole Porter, invitations from the Prince of Wales and Elsa Maxwell, and a playbill from *Oscar Wilde*, the show she had seen the evening before. The detectives knew from the newspapers that she was a socialite, the fiancée of America's hero, Harry Hopkins, and a woman the public adored. As they expected, there was no trace of Hopkins to be found—not his letters of devotion or photographs from the Twenty-One Club. Suited men from the White House had already removed them and innumerable other items when they swept the apartment, the first step in distancing Hopkins from the incident. Dorothy would have loathed the notion of strangers foraging through her personal belongings.

Journalists scrambled to write front-page stories and peppered detectives with questions, yet only a few details were disclosed. They said she wrote letters late into the night. They said she fell or jumped from her suite on the sixteenth floor. They said she dropped 200 feet to the ground. There was no mention of a crime.

The *New York Journal-American* ran a full-page feature by "fat vain little Maury Paul," the most notorious gossip of the Gilded Age, whose simple stroke of the pen could raise one to the apex of the good life as easily as it could destroy a name. And so it went for Dorothy Hale. He said the beauteous glamour girl had been taking sleeping pills. He said she was depressed. He said she was brokenhearted and jinxed from the start. Long gone are the people who would tell you that Dorothy Hale exuded vibrancy throughout her splendid life, that she was not a woman to leap from the ledge. That was the story Maury Paul would have told had it not been for the meddling of the president's men.

· Fifty-Five Years Later ·

"We have a long history of notable residents here at the Hampshire House," said Mr. Lachann, the manager of the building. In the darkened office, his desk surrounded by stacks of leather albums filled with photographs, he swelled with pride as he opened one up to show me the people he wished he had known and the parties he didn't attend. Page after page the images revealed tuxedoed men and their wives, their smiles broad, gowns tasteful, pearls large. Not a mention of Dorothy Hale. The name, of course, would have held no meaning to me then, nor would her picture. More than half a century had passed since she died. I had never heard of her when I signed those papers for an apartment overlooking Central Park and felt a surge of happiness for my incredible good fortune.

If there was some ghostly quality to the place, it was imperceptible to me in those first hours. At twenty-five years of age I was enchanted by the grandeur of the Old New York building, its towering ceilings, intricate Baroque moldings and Art Deco design. It had retained its formality, the uniformed bellman beckoning, "This way, Ms. Harrison," as he ushered me through the gleaming black-and-white marble lobby. Luciano Pavarotti breezed by wearing a bright-red scarf wrapped around his neck. "To keep the tenor's throat warm for his performance at Lincoln Center," I was told. And Rupert Murdoch, exceedingly elegant in a crisp blue suit and Hermès tie, walked past me with a purposeful stride and said nothing as he approached three men standing by the entrance like a diplomatic envoy, then disappeared through the turnstile door into a chauffeured car. The bellman averted his eyes and led me down a long corridor, past Carrera marble busts tucked into niches while Vivaldi's *Four Seasons* played softly in the background.

Turning the corner, my pace slowed as the palatial ballroom opened before me, its gracious ambiance brightened by sunlight streaming in from grand glass doors. Well appointed with ornate ivory furnishings and adorned with jade-colored murals, its centerpiece was a chandelier so large and elaborate in design it was fitting for a palace in nineteenth-century France. There was a strange stillness to the room, yet the uproarious banter of bygone days seemed to come alive.

As I drifted toward the courtyard, a scene of vivid detail intruded on my mind and played like a black-and-white silent film: *A woman entered the cocktail lounge. It was still bustling in the after hours, clouded with cigar smoke and scented with scotch, the corner tables filled with couples huddling together, and elegant women, a dozen or more, their diamonds sparkling under dim lights, drank champagne with suited men.*

The woman walked past the bar, stopped briefly to allow a man to light her cigarette, and went to the far side of the room by the window where she met a man she knew. They spoke. They argued. She left abruptly and ran up the stairwell to the third floor to escape. He followed her. They argued by the window. Now the scene was a blur. She was on a higher floor. She was falling out of a window.

The vision startled me. It was both familiar and profound, like the sudden return of a memory when you catch the scent of a perfume once worn by your mother.

That evening, I searched the history of the building into the wee small hours to find an explanation for the scene I had pictured.

I saw her photograph and the headline "The Suicide of Dorothy Hale," and my heart stopped beating.

The paper called her "a tragic woman, more beautiful than the young Elizabeth Taylor, whom she resembled," one of those evident gifts of God polished off by privilege, ease of confidence, and a good measure of grace. At first glance her beauty was striking—fresh-faced and delicate with large eyes, her little black dress cinched at the waist, her hair pinned in a chignon. At second glance, her deep, intelligent eyes were entrancing, still vivid on newspapers yellowed from light and air and lined with age that Fate didn't offer to her.

"Jilted at age 33, she jumped from the window of her penthouse apartment. . . . She died of a broken heart." The reporter's story was sensational—maybe too sensational. I knew because I too was a journalist, one with a keen eye and without clemency for writers who cobbled together accounts with gossip and grand assumptions to profit from others' pain. But this was the way of rogue newsmen; it was the way it had always been. Dorothy Hale was a curiosity on public view, a thing to write about.

The more I read, the more it became evident the story didn't seem to add up. One sentence contradicted the next. Quotes were clearly contrived. The reasons for her alleged demise would only be said of a woman, an unsurprising lock, stock, and barrel cliché that was an affront to any female, to be sure. "She died of a broken heart and fading career." Indeed.

Perhaps more striking and most impossible to overlook was the hunch, the inescapable instinct that soon became unignorable for there was, with little question, more to this romantic tragedy. Fell, jumped, offed—these were the unfortunate possibilities before me. To know the truth, I would have to know how she fared in adversity and the traits that defined her—what was her circumstance, and who did she trust. Only then could I ascertain the cause of her death in the early-morning hours of October 21, 1938. Thus, with the bright surety of a youthful mind and career journalist, it seemed in that split of a second like a perfectly reasonable proposition to learn everything possible about Dorothy Hale.

Reaching for a cigarette from the French antique silver case on my desk, I considered all that I had read, and then, in a moment that would determine the course of too many others, I remembered strolling through the lobby when Mr. Lachann asked his assistant to tend to the attic, clear out the items, and send personal belongings to descendants. I dropped the cigarette onto a tray, took a flashlight from the drawer, and headed for the stairwell. Because what else was I to do? You see how it was an entirely unavoidable course.

I stole away to the attic, climbing step by step and floor by floor until I reached thirty-six, the end of the line. There was no evidence of a route to the pinnacle, but with further exploration I came upon a single door. I opened it a crack, and soon found myself in a twisted purgatory, a maze of narrow passageways with naked bulbs illuminating the walls painted black and crimson red, rusted wires cut and tangled like vines, and more doors revealing other mazes that brought me finally to a stairwell. As I ascended, the thump of my soles echoed in the silence until I reached the top landing. Standing before the final door, I listened to the quiet, and with deep trepidation, I turned the well-worn knob, gave it a vigorous push, and slinked into the room.

Stacked and strewn across the vast wooden floor, abandoned trunks lay worn under a half-century of dust, dated by colored stickers from luxury steamships and European hotels popular with those who could afford the indulgence in the 1930s. From the pitched ceiling reaching two stories high, a faint light came through a small window, casting shadows on a circular steel staircase winding upward to a hatch. It was there, in the little space at the very peak of the Hampshire House, where I discovered three leather trunks embossed with the initials DDH. With a mixed sense of triumph, unease, and extreme curiosity, I lowered myself to the floor, considered which to open, brushed dust from its latches, and raised the lid, releasing a thick, musty smell that seeped into the ghostly air.

Piles of leather-bound notebooks and typewritten pages, the edges browned and tattered with age, had been placed in chronological order, labeled, and tied with white ribbon finished off in a bow like a gift box at Christmas. Touching the fragile paper, it was strange knowing hers was the last hand to hold them so many years before.

The following day, as the sun lowered in the sky, I stepped into the former cocktail lounge on the second floor, a desolate space with an aged mahogany bar and crystal sconces darkened from neglect. I sensed the unsettling aura, the stillness giving way to silent pandemonium of a crowd that could no longer be seen—the nights of posh black-tie parties, laughter and scandal, champagne and cigarettes long since gone.

I had found the clues Dorothy Hale left behind: the note to her attorney, the entries in her journal, and the memoir she never finished. In her last days she noted it would be important for someone to find them, someday in the future, to show that her life had been grand. It seemed she sensed she would become a talebearer's prey. Surely if she knew she would be referred to as hapless, she would have smiled gently, thought it an idiot's remark, and twisted a long strand of pearls through her diamond-jeweled fingers. Yes, she would have rolled her eyes upward—astounded at how they had missed the point entirely.

And what else is one to do when presented so unexpectedly with such stupefying intrigue but continue turning the pages back in time, a time when a wave of excess carried the American aristocracy and titled Europeans to grand ships and grander estates for extravagant parties never before seen and never seen thereafter. They stumbled onto the laps of married lovers, champagne spilling onto polished marble floors, betrayal and indecency dressed up in custom-made suits and an air of refinement honed since birth. This was the Jazz Age. The Crazy Years. *Les Années Folles,* as she often said.

2.

THE CRAZY YEARS

For God's sake, what would the nuns say now? she thought, strutting across the stage. Dorothy swung her bare hips as she pranced down a sweeping white staircase on the elaborate stage of the Ziegfeld Follies. Her rhythm was smooth, her dance steps synchronized with thirty other chorus girls, their shapely legs kicking high as they balanced enormous headdresses resembling feathers of a peacock, their sequined costumes sparkling under blazing lights. With a playful wink and dazzling smile, she awakened even the most unimpassioned of men.

Wallace Harrington, the Pittsburgh-born heir of the Harrington Steel magnate, stared at Dorothy, muttering under his breath, "Too young to know what you could have had," as she shimmied her shoulders and sang, "With every shake a lucky break . . ."

"I like the one with the dark hair, to the right of the blonde," Wallace said to his wife, who knew, from a friend of a friend, that he was enamored with one of the dancers.

It was 1923 and Dorothy had made it to Broadway, but it was hardly the role she had intended to play. The job was meant to be a stepping-stone, a means to an end, an open door to her dreams.

She extended her leg high in a sweeping arc, tracing the lines of a rainbow, dipping low, shoulders back, smiling to bursts of applause from the audience, who marveled at the beauty and the longing it stirred within them.

"She is something else," Wallace mumbled. He failed to notice the look of disdain on his wife's face as she admitted to herself that his likeable qualities had begun to diminish the moment she said "I do." All she could do now was wait and hope that fate would intervene, be it lightning from the heavens or a long-legged girl. *You can have him*, she thought as she gazed at Dorothy, whose chestnut locks had curled into playful loops in the humid air. She exuded a youthful elegance with her chin held high and a confident come-hither look that for a moment, Mrs. Harrington was sure, said "not on your life" to Wallace, who watched intently. *That showgirl would never do for Wallace*, she thought, startled when Dorothy seemed to look her straight in the eye. Mrs. Harrington nearly melted from Dorothy's stare of sultry innocence.

"I have to admit, Wallace, the girl is lithe," she sighed, straightening her back to accentuate the generous swell of her breasts. "I suppose she is like all those girls, looking for a pot of gold."

Dorothy loathed being judged by those who didn't know her, though she knew it was the inevitable consequence of becoming a showgirl. Others endured the leering men backstage who promised wealth and the talent agents who promised stardom, and they disregarded hostile looks from wives and lovers left behind in the fantasies of their loved ones. Yet, even if they were there to marry rich, Dorothy resented the assumption that she was one of them. For years she had dreamed of making it on her own as a legitimate Broadway actress, though her parents, upon learning of her intentions, had admonished her swiftly.

"Our people do not become show people," her mother had said. Dorothy had inherited her mother's modesty and fine Victorian manners, yet she developed her father's tendency to step blindly into fires of his own creation, and their self-conscious regard for public perception skipped her generation like a gift in a well-planned will.

"Find yourself a more noble pursuit," warned Dorothy's father. That was years ago, long before she joined the show, the tantalizing details of which were unimaginable to her family. On exhibit were the most dazzling girls that Florenz Ziegfeld could find in coffee shops, department stores, airports and elevators, or at auditions where they would appear before his throne seeking approval of their scantily clad physiques. To pass the audition, a girl must possess special talents, among them gliding across the stage in sky-high shoes while balancing a book on her head. Most were cast away to obscurity, into the cities of lost dreams. The Follies was the place for starlets to be discovered, and she had won the coveted role over thousands of others who tried. She left the ballroom soirées and country-club cavorting in Pittsburgh without looking back, for a world far, far, away.

Dorothy made her way through the crowd backstage, the steel floor and narrow width unaccommodating to a chorus of dancers, many of whom lingered to flirt with men who were hoping for a Ziegfeld girl of their own. One by one, each man turned to look at her as she went by. But she said nothing. She looked at no one. She had a habit of looking through people when all eyes were on her. She squeezed between the bloated girths—evidence of drink and steak and other indulgences their lives afforded them. Overhearing the pleasantries, it was clear they had some reverence for the girls and no allegiance to social position, although the scent of their cologne and their lack of restraint in applying it seemed to indicate they were new money, the first of the family to thrive. When one touched her shoulder and another spoke a luring word, she smiled politely, or tried to, brushed them off, and made her way by. *Oh, please*, she thought, quickening her pace, *you have no idea who I am.*

"Nice clavicles, sweetheart," she heard as she opened the door to the dressing room.

To her delight, there stood Maggie Case, the friend with whom she had caroused at the Club Fronton speakeasy the night that Dorothy was informed she would be joining the Follies. Everyone knew they were half seas over from champagne when the famously modest Maggie danced the Charleston on the bar, ripping the seam of her prudish dress a little higher with each kick of her leg while Dorothy clapped along. When others recalled the evening, Maggie and Dorothy would say in unison, "Ahhh, *the Incident*," and redden with regret, but secretly, when they were together, they doubled over in laughter.

"Dorothy, you were marvelous!" Maggie raved as she helped her lift off the headdress. "And who is Georgie? I read the card on those divine flowers. It says, 'We could have a lifetime of evenings as glorious as last night. I intend to marry you within a year.' Do tell me the glorious part, and I want every naughty detail."

"I will tell you he gave me a charming ruby necklace in the shape of a heart. But isn't his note something? He'll marry me within a year—such a vague commitment, as if he's putting a suit on hold at Bergdorf's," she said, slipping into a white silk drop-waist dress.

"Being a Ziegfeld Folly girl doesn't mean you're there for a man's folly."

"Some of these girls would do anything—and, darling, I mean anything—for a chance at stardom, or marriage, or whatever it is the men are promising them," Dorothy said with an expression of incredulity.

"The poor girls. They're in for a rude awakening."

"They're devastated when they're tossed away like a broken Tinkertoy."

"If only the men would behave."

"If only the women would," Dorothy said. "And as you well know, refusing them without making them feel rejected is an impossible feat. The last thing you want is to be alone in a room with an angry man. Let's hope I won't have to play this role for long."

She had been dancing in the show for three months and had come to dislike it. She did not care for the exhibitionism; she felt contempt for the Broadway producer who made advances, then passed her over for a freewheeling buxom blonde; and she was impatient to ascend her role as a Ziegfeld girl, a title she did not wear well.

A bang on the door startled them. Charlie Karmody, the director of the theater, rushed breathlessly into the room.

"Hold on to your hat, honey. Fred Astaire is on the line for you!"

She leapt up with happiness—sure that her prayers had been answered, her dream was about to come true. She hugged Maggie and dashed out to pick up the phone.

The limousine came to an abrupt stop, lurching her body forward. The red lipstick she was applying smeared across her front tooth. Noticing it, one of the blonde dancers beside her leaned over, rubbed it off, and wiped her finger on the seat.

"There, now you look perfect," she said.

Dorothy was taken aback by the casual way in which Mitzy had stuck her hand in her mouth. *At least the girl acknowledged that I look good*, she thought, as she smoothed her hair and hoped her rouge hadn't faded. At times like this, when she was about to make an entrance, she felt anxious, worried that her appearance would be less than what was expected, less captivating than the most beautiful woman in the room. But of all the nights she had dressed and fussed for another night on the town, this was the most momentous, the one that would determine the course of all to come. After the twists and turns, the striving and struggling, the disappointments, discord and dreams, she knew for the first time in her nineteen years that it had been worth it after all. December 1, 1924. The date of her Broadway debut.

With only a few minutes left before she would face the public, her heart was beating very fast, her eyes fixed on the limousine parked in front of hers. Fred Astaire and his sister, Adele, stepped out of the long black car and into the cold December air as they looked up at the entrance of the St. Regis Hotel. Jerome Zerbe, on his first assignment for the *Times Herald*, scuttled to the curb to take their picture. It was a coup, even for a Yale boy, to cover the premiere of the Astaires' Broadway show, *Lady, Be Good*, and the celebration that followed.

Dorothy watched the doorman dash out of the ornate, gold-trimmed booth in front of the hotel to escort the Astaires along the red carpet and into the grand Beaux Arts lobby, then rush back to the sidewalk.

He extended his hand as she emerged from the darkness, his face brightening at the sight of her, a brunette beauty with a slender silhouette, clothed in an ivory satin dress draped seductively low in the back to reveal her porcelain skin.

"Darling," she said over her shoulder to Mitzy, "would you reach to the front seat and hand me my stole?"

Seeing Jerry, her friend and fellow jazz enthusiast, Dorothy smiled with a wave and posed for his camera, catching the attention of a group of tuxedoed men who stopped to whistle.

Standing by the entrance of the King Cole Bar, by now overflowing with guests, she skirted past a large group ogling the Astaires, made her way through a tangle of black silk, and found herself in the embrace of composer George Gershwin and his brother Ira, a lyricist, neither of whom she knew, but they were euphoric on this opening night of their first full musical. They immediately resumed making the rounds. She spotted her friends at a table in the center of the room and made her way toward them, noticing with some amusement that Clare was rhapsodizing—about what, Dorothy did not know.

There was Maggie, listening intently with one high-arched eyebrow raised in a look of disbelief as she smoothed her platinum-blonde hair, tucking the sides behind her ears to reveal pearls of considerable size, a gift from Dorothy and her family when Maggie was hired as the society editor for *Vogue*. Maggie considered style a reflection, and sometimes predictor, of the economy. "Follow the hemlines. When skirts go short, go short on stocks," she was fond of saying.

Seated beside her, looking inquisitive, was Jane Kendall, Dorothy's oldest friend, the athletic, all-American, golden-haired debutante with a taste for adventure and mischievous look in her baby-blue eyes as she elbowed Maggie in the ribs. To her left, Rosamond Pinchot, the ravishing, strawberry-blonde debutante with plump lips stained in red and wide in a winsome smile, leaned toward Jane and whispered, while Jane stifled a laugh. She played the lead role in *The Miracle* on Broadway as a nun who ran away from the convent. Dorothy found this amusing, having run away from home and her Catholic school not so long ago. Holding court was Clare Boothe Brokaw, the striking beauty who chattered away and smiled angelically as she touched her hand to her soft yellow locks. She had a clever wit and grand aspirations of success, having conquered her first goal by marrying the heir of a clothing manufacturing empire. All of society still jabbered about the extravagance of her guest list and custom Vionnet gown.

They turned their heads in unison and looked up at Dorothy, her eyes twinkling and her gown shimmering in the semi-darkness.

"Dorothy," Clare said as she hugged her, "the champagne is flowing in your honor." They raised their glasses in a toast.

"Congratulations on your Broadway debut, my lovely roommate! Santé!" said Rosamond.

"To my wonderful friends," said Dorothy, raising her glass as Fred Astaire approached her from behind.

"How did you enjoy your first opening night?"

"It was a dream, darling. And I owe it all to you for calling me to join the ensemble."

"Shall we dance? Ladies, do you mind if I steal her away?"

When he took her hand she felt lightness in her step and the slowing of time as the room was brought to silence for a brief moment. Their bodies swaying and bending, a crowd formed around them. Fred waved them in to join the dance, and two by two, couples abandoned themselves to the music. Gaillard Thomas II watched Dorothy from across the room, unresponsive to the voices around him as they dimmed into the background.

"One gin on the rocks and one champagne, sir," said the waiter, setting two glasses down on the table. Gaillard excused himself from the group, carried them to Dorothy's table, paid no mind to the others, and waited for the song to end. Her heart raced as she approached him. His looks were pleasing—a warm smile framed by sandy hair and broad, capable shoulders, an elegance in the way he held himself. She hoped he was there for her.

"Glorious performance," he said in greeting her. "Gaillard Thomas. Pleased to meet you." She accepted the glass of champagne and the seat beside him.

As they drifted easily into conversation, Dorothy felt a strange sense of familiarity, unaware of time as it passed, indifferent to the world around them.

"A career is like the building blocks we all played with as children. You assemble it piece by piece until your vision is realized. You're well ahead of the others," he said, making her blush.

"That's kind of you. I've dreamed of dancing on Broadway ever since I was in school. In fact, I spent three weeks in New York when I was sixteen and . . . it was at once imposing and inspiring." Trumpets blared from the twenty-piece orchestra, suddenly drowning out the conversation. Just as well. There was no need to tell him that she was a runaway on that trip to New York; she had snuck out at midnight, the footlights of Broadway beckoning.

It was the day that her father had forbade her from dancing. Imagine what Gaillard would think if he knew about the night of the row with her parents, when she protested their plans to undo her destiny. She shuddered as she recalled the argument, the escape to her room, the tears wetting her pillow. From the hallway, Marjorie, Betty, and James, her younger siblings, knocked lightly on her door, surely overhearing her mutters in French and the thump of her closet door closing. When the clock struck midnight, she looked through her bedroom window, out to the driveway, then tiptoed to the front door and climbed into the black Rolls Royce, amazed that her friend

Jackie had commandeered it without waking her parents. The next day Dorothy was gone. No one knew where.

The memory flashed before her. It seemed like a fine idea at the time. She had considered it for more than a heated moment when she packed her weekender bag with the chicest dresses she owned, long strands of pearls, and $200 from saved allowances. While she didn't expect a red carpet to be rolled out upon her arrival, she intended to place herself firmly upon one before she was through. When the whistle blew and the train started its slow chug out of the Pittsburgh station, the low rumble signaled her freedom. Only sixteen years of age, she reasoned it was the nuns who had roused her independence, especially Sister Mary, a woman ahead of her time, a rebel of rule. Still, Dorothy and her classmates were expected to gain understanding of humility, simplicity, and charity, the words etched in stained glass at the entrance of the school chapel, words forsaken at their coming-out balls when, as debutantes, they returned to the prodigal habits of their kind.

Of course, when she left home, she didn't anticipate facing the fire at auditions, the closed-door meetings with low-down producers forcing themselves upon her, the kicks in the shins and bolts out of the theater, the sheer fright that reached to her core. She didn't expect to run out of money in two months and have to go home. A sense of relief washed over her when she stepped into her bedroom, glanced around, and rested her gaze on a crumpled tissue on the side table, out of place in the meticulous surroundings, an oversight by her mother, who had been distracted, in a tearful daze, worried and worn. Now she was safe under her parents' watch. Her belongings were exactly where she had left them, yet she knew the room had been searched, each sheet of paper read, every drawer carefully combed through by a private investigator who had been hired by her parents to find her.

Dorothy asked God to forgive her for the contentious things she had said to her parents in the weeks before. "A sixteen-year-old runaway," she had said aloud, astonished by the sound of it as she watched a hummingbird hover outside the window, suspended in space by its fast-fluttering wings, so tiny yet unmoved by the shifting wind, determined to make its own course. Then, gone. Almost too fast to follow with the eye. She thought of what her mother had once said: "It's the most delicate creature. Do you know how it survives out there, Dorothy? Inside, they're tough birds. They fight for it."

Running away seemed impetuous to her now as she looked into Gaillard's eyes, deep and blue and serene.

"Tell me about your visit to New York, the inspiration that brought you here tonight," said Gaillard.

"It was a bit daunting but marvelous."

"What was most marvelous?"

"Well," she hesitated, "do you really—"

"Yes, please, I want to hear every word." He smiled, his elbows propped on the table.

"I had been to New York many times with my family, but this particular visit was different. The city took me by surprise with all its temperaments and moods. I drank in its thrilling vibrancy and star-filled nights where only the brightest of the galaxy stood out among the glittering towers. You have to look for them, though. Have you noticed, Gaillard, how starry nights in New York are only discernible to those who break their stride and seek its beauty? And to languid men on stone-carved terraces who look down upon the small people on the street, then glimpse at the sky to thank heavens for their good fortune that they were not invited to that particular party."

He laughed lightly. "Absolutely. Come to think of it, I've gone weeks without noticing the sky."

"Isn't it something when you turn a corner and the city abruptly changes its tone? I saw debauched characters lurking in shadows on lonely streets. But everywhere, on the pathways in Central Park and the bustling sidewalks, the air thickened by soot and dust, I felt its reverberant promise to surrender to the dreams of my own making."

"Fantastic," said Gaillard, sitting back with a sigh, his eyes gleaming. A waiter stepped between them to top off their drinks, drops wetting Gaillard's trousers. He didn't seem to give it much thought. "Where did you attend school?" he asked as he moved his chair closer to hers.

"St. Joseph's Academy in Pittsburgh." She described the foreboding gothic mansion set atop Seton Hill, surrounded by 200 acres of pristine land that was once owned by William Stokes, a major in the Civil War. She thought better than to tell him of the school's modern approach. The battle cry of St. Joseph's Academy was "Hazard Yet Forward" and the sisters' mission was "to fit you for that world in which you are destined to live." Sister Mary frequently said a woman could enter a field dominated by men and not change who she was.

Best to keep quiet, Dorothy thought. *It would make him nervous.* He would know they were taught those lessons in defiance of what they had learned at home. The course of each of their lives was set at birth to become like their mothers', and their mothers' mothers', matriarchs of the home, bred to lead the next generation of the smart set. How could he understand? Her own parents couldn't fathom how something irrepressible had risen up within her when she soared in grand jeté, a feat of grace that made her feel as though she had touched the sky.

"Do tell me more about your work, Gaillard."

"Ah, yes, investing, working the market. Educated guesses, really. There are no guarantees. It can be like pirouettes, spinning in circles."

"You seem cool and collected. I would never guess it," she said, touching his arm and meeting his eyes. She sensed he wanted her to touch him again. "You know," she added, "you're not at all like the other brokers I've met."

"You're not like the dancers I've met. Or debs."

"Much to the dismay of my father, who would prefer that I dedicate myself to more noble pursuits."

"Well," he said, "you're an angel in flight when you dance. Your parents must be proud of you." She smiled sweetly and looked away. *If he only knew,* she thought, imagining the anguish her parents had endured when she ran off to New York. And the disappointment they felt when her sister told them her nickname, Peck's Bad Girl of Pittsburgh Society. Too distraught to say "runaway," her mother had called it a French leave, a more acceptable term to her upper-crust friends who had gotten wind of the incident. "A showgirl. God have mercy," Mrs. Biltmore, their neighbor, had said in disgust. Dorothy was expected to transition seamlessly into a God-fearing wife with a pregnant belly, a pie in the oven, and crisp bills for the collection dish on Sunday.

"You are too kind," she said, wanting to change the subject. "You must be busier than ever. It seems like everyone is in the market."

He swirled the gin in his glass and took a swig. "That's right. Same folks that called it gambling not so long ago."

"I call it calculated risk." She knew the term from her parents. They had once said it was a calculated risk for her to attend drama school at the Carnegie Institute of Technology with the sole intention of becoming an actress. By then her parents had come to realize there was little they could do but try to protect her. She was fearless, confident of her future, ready to conquer the world with lyrical grace. They conceded it was that magic of youth, hard to contain and impossible to recapture in midlife when one looks back wistfully, yearning to ignite that part of them that was burning out like a flickering candle in ceaseless summer storms.

"I suppose we're both in the business of calculated risk," he said. "But you know what they say: no guts, no glory." He could not look away from her or restrain himself from saying she was so unlike the other beauties he had known, more winsome, more self-assured, more vital. His expression showed that he took pleasure in the way she looked at him, her attention unwavering amid the cacophony of the crowd. "My father did well with long-shot investments. He taught me about risk. God rest his soul."

She recognized the heaviness in his heart and understood the distant look that came over him. Two years before, when she was eighteen, she had the same feeling. Her father had called a family meeting. "Well, kids, there is no easy way to say this, but your mother and I feel it's best to tell you." He took a deep breath and then continued with measured words. "We didn't want to worry you, but your mother hasn't been well, and her doctor has finally determined the cause."

The children didn't speak. The steady tick of a grandfather clock ended with an ominous chime as it struck 6 p.m. He turned his head toward the window, covering his mouth with his fingers. Dorothy felt a sickening wave rise from her heart to her eyes, stinging them and breaking into a roll of tears as her legs began to feel numb.

Her mother came to sit beside her. "Now that we know what it is," she said, "the doctors can take good care of me. I'll be fine . . ." Dorothy heard the words in a blur of snippets, as if in a horrible dream. "Fighting spirit . . . still here for you . . . pelvic cancer."

Dorothy snapped back to the present. "I'm sorry to hear that your father passed. It's one of the most difficult trials in life, and no one is spared," she said a little wistfully.

She put her hand over his for a moment, wanting to push away thoughts of her mother, whose health had steadily declined for two and a half years. Every wince of pain, each day that her body had withered from disease and her eyes grew more distant, was agony to Dorothy, who wanted so desperately to help. She maintained a semblance of strength for her family and shouldered the daily chores, making sure the kids and her father were taken care of. Her prayers to God did not return the melody to her mother's weakened voice or vigor to her listless body.

Mrs. Donovan must have known she was nearing the end. As Dorothy fluffed the pillows behind her mother's head one evening, she patted the mattress in a signal for her daughter to sit beside her. Dorothy nestled in until she felt her mother's fragile body beneath the warm blanket. "I want you to remember what I'm going to tell you," she said, taking Dorothy's hand.

"Yes, Mummy. I love you. What is it? I will . . ."

"Promise?"

"Promise. Cross my heart."

"Okay, darling, listen closely. In life's difficult moments, I want you to think of your ballet—how your feet ache with blisters and your legs throb with soreness and you can't turn one more time. But on you go. I've seen with my own eyes how you smile into the pain and you finish the dance beautifully. In the end, you're always glad that you did. Always smile when your heart is breaking, and dance through the pain." Wiping a tear from Dorothy's cheek, she continued in a whisper, water welling up in her eyes. "Last night I had a dream that you were dancing on Broadway. Oh, and how exquisite you were. Go back to New York and follow your heart."

The following night, on August 7, 1922, at 9:55, ashen clouds of a rain shadow lingered in the blackened skies enveloping the family home on Dunmoyle Place when, at age forty-two, Dorothy's mother passed away in her sleep with a tender smile resting on her lips. Dorothy was left without the sparkle, the touch, and the constant loving presence that had breathed life into her world. With her mother's blanket wrapped snugly around her torso, she lifted a shoulder to her cheek to breathe in the familiar scent of jasmine that still lingered on the wool. She reached over to Betty, her sister. Cradling her in her arms, she whispered, "Lamentations 5:15. The joy of our heart is ceased; our dance is turned into mourning." For the funeral, Dorothy covered the casket in a blanket of white crêpe de chine.

Dorothy looked up to see her sadness mirrored in Gaillard's eyes; he too was haunted.

"Would you do me the honor of a dance?" he asked, rising in his seat. "Please." Taking her hand, he led her to the dance floor and reached his arm around her waist. She liked the feeling.

They moved well together and slowed to a waltz as the music staved off their pasts. She looked up and locked eyes with him, falling under his penetrating gaze as one song played to the next. With some hesitation, he leaned toward her, relieved when she lifted her chin in answer to his unspoken bid. Receiving his kiss, she allowed the tender moment to last longer than she might have, had she not lost herself to the pleasure.

"I like that," he whispered, leaning his temple against hers.

The following day, the girls were anxious to hear all the delicious details. Maggie and Clare met Dorothy in the Rose Room of the Algonquin Hotel for their weekly lunch.

"Is that Douglas Fairbanks Jr. who just walked in?" Maggie asked. "I don't have my glasses."

"It is, and he's marvelous," Clare said. Maggie waved him over.

"Miss Case!" he said. "Pleasure to see you here. Usually you're armed with a list of interview questions for *Vogue*."

"You're off the hook today. I have better manners than to ask such personal questions unless it's going to print. Allow me to introduce Mrs. Clare Boothe Brokaw," Maggie said, knowing Clare would smile seductively. "And this, *this* is the beauteous Dorothy Donovan who dances with Fred Astaire in *Lady, Be Good*. Perhaps someday you two will be in a movie together." Dorothy looked to the floor, her lips turned up in a little smile. Douglas took her hand and kissed it softly.

"Enchanté," he said as their eyes met.

"Charmed," Dorothy said in a whisper, suddenly losing all ability to articulate very much else as her thoughts tripped and traipsed and stuttered away in bashful departure. So there she stood, smiling silently in the warmth of his gaze while Clare watched, stroking her pregnant belly.

"Tension of the unwed," she said under her breath as the manager swept Douglas away to a table.

"Clare, are you and George getting on all right now?" asked Dorothy, having regained her composure.

"If I've learned anything from my one year of marriage, it's that a man's home may seem to be his castle on the outside; inside is more often his nursery."

Dorothy laughed. "It probably doesn't help that you're living with your mother-in-law."

"Oh, you mean the outlaw. She is the bane of my existence."

"I have to admit she's an overbearing if elegant woman."

Maggie rolled her eyes. "Well, it's no wonder that George is emotionally stunted. He's still living with his mother, for God's sake."

"But, Clare, now you have the freedom to do whatever you like," said Dorothy. "He is so supportive, after all."

"If by supportive you mean too inebriated and otherwise occupied to discourage me from something I want to do, then yes, he is supportive."

"Good ones are hard to find," said Maggie.

"Gaillard seems like a good one," said Clare. "Maybe not good, but as good as it gets."

"We're going to Rao's tonight for a late supper, but I'm sticking to my rule that until I get married, I'll continue to see other suitors," said Dorothy. "The problem with that is keeping everyone's story straight. I can't remember if Franklin's father is the sixty-eight-year-old writer or if it's Bill's father, and if it's Bill's mother who just died or Andrew's. It does make for awkward moments. But I remember everything Gaillard tells me."

"You should just marry him and call it a day," Clare said, waving her hand dismissively. "Men are so easy. You just have to know where to tickle them. Then take some time away, but not too much time."

"How long is too long?" asked Dorothy, though she was veritably disinterested in strategizing marriage.

"Yes, you have to know that because if it's too long you'll lose him," Maggie said.

"Men don't like to be alone," Dorothy added.

"The hound has to keep the scent or it'll charge off in another direction," Maggie said with a nod.

A loud chuckle came from the next table where Max Reinhardt was seated, listening to their conversation. Dorothy, recognizing the raspy-throated sound, caught a glimpse of him and realized he was taking the afternoon off from his duties as the director of *The Miracle*, Rosamond's Broadway play, to join his friends. *Oh no,* she thought, seeing the others, *it's the Algonquin Wits.* There was Harold Ross, the journalist preparing to launch his magazine, *The New Yorker*; Robert Sherwood, the *Vanity Fair* writer; and Heywood Broun, the *New York World* columnist and founder of the American Newspaper Guild. Dorothy Parker's seat was empty. *Oh good, the Algonquin Twit isn't here,* she thought. Clare couldn't stand to be in the same room with her.

One day at the entrance of the Algonquin, Parker said to Dorothy, "Clare Boothe speaks eighteen languages and can't say *no* in any of them," and Clare, approaching from behind, overheard. Dorothy replied in a hushed voice, "Please stop, darling. Underneath, Clare has a good heart." Soon after, Dorothy and Clare saw Parker again, this time at the entrance of the Waldorf-Astoria Hotel. Clare stepped aside to allow Parker to go first. "Age before beauty, my dear," said Clare. "And pearls before swine," said Parker as she breezed through the revolving door.

"Clare, you were awfully demure with Fairbanks. Are you well?" asked Maggie.

"Usually you're a masterful flirt. You could teach a course," teased Dorothy.

"Well, if you don't play to your audience, what's the point?" said Clare.

In a way, thought Dorothy, *Clare is right.* She realized that was what she had done with Gaillard; she played to her audience. *Oh God,* she thought. The last thing she wanted was to see Clare in herself. She had come to accept her friend's less admirable traits, yet the ease with which extravagant fibs rolled from her tongue remained a source of bewilderment. Clare had explained, "Lying increases the creative faculties, expands the ego, and lessens the frictions of social contacts," and as such, she had renounced her past as an illegitimate daughter raised by her fortune-seeking mother and rewrote her history as an Upper East Side Wasp.

When she married George, she finally scaled the top echelon of society where, to her frustration, she fatigued them, particularly when she told the tale about her coming-out at the debutante cotillion in 1918, which would have made her three years younger than her young age and vastly more comfortable financially. The truth of it was, she grew up poor, so her mother cultivated her marriable qualities—French lessons, smarts, strategy, and the certain je ne sais quois of the femme fatale. The Four Hundred innately knew, of course, for they had a remarkable ability to sniff out birds of a feather with pure blue blood.

The thrill of seeing her name in the Social Register was balanced with her contempt for the Social Registrites with whom she indulged. Dorothy and Clare both wanted more, much more than scoring the latest Patou dress to wear to a weekly charity function that served primarily as a place to gossip about manicurists, hairstyles, and each other—as much as they did love Patou. He was the only designer sensible enough to lower the hemlines that Chanel had made so fashionably short. Patou had Elsa Maxwell to thank for the suggestion, which she had made during an impromptu tête-à-tête at the Paris Ritz. And that was the thing about Elsa. She had this way of showing up at exactly the right time.

3.

BLESSED ARE
THE DEBONAIRE

March 21, 1925. At 2 p.m., Dorothy, Maggie and Clare left the Twenty-One Club with plans to meet that evening at the King Cole Bar. At 5 p.m., Maggie canceled due to work. At 8:30 p.m., Dorothy arrived and saw Clare seated at a table for two. Across from her was the long-faced banker Shelby Whitehouse, listening at full attention when he broke into laughter and slapped his hand to the table, just missing the plate of cold canapés, thus prompting a startled if satisfied smile from Clare. With a breezy sureness, Dorothy crossed the room to fetch a drink from the bar.

"The lovely Miss Dorothy. It's been ages. May I lure you to my table?"

Turning, she found Wallace Harrington eyeing her with an amorous look. Harrington's father may have bequeathed his son an empire, but he had robbed him of self-confidence and thus the requisite social finesse, replacing it with an insatiable need for pomp and praise. Wearing a disarmingly hopeful smile, he pulled out a chair, and, with some hesitation, she sat down.

That's when Elsa Maxwell and Cole Porter saw her. They were

intrigued, wondering who she was, this enchanting newcomer seated beside the eccentric Mr. Harrington.

"Wallace never takes a breath," Elsa said to Cole.

"Delusions of rapt attention," he replied.

Wallace had just proposed marriage to Dorothy. *What nerve,* she thought, *proposing to me in a bar when he's marrying another woman next week. He might be crazy. I think he is.*

Elsa and Cole knew they would like her just by looking at her and had made their way to her side when Brenda Delamore stepped between them, looked at the weathered Wallace Harrington, then at fresh-faced Dorothy, and remarked, "So, you must be the niece."

"So, you must be the witty one," Dorothy replied. Brenda fell silent. Elsa and Cole stole Dorothy away from Wallace and the pernicious Miss Delamore and took her under their wing.

As they sank into a cushiony couch, Elsa raised her finger to signal service.

"Veuve Clicquot and three glasses, if you would," she said. Feeling the silk hem of her dress had slipped up to the top of her thighs, she shifted awkwardly while nudging it down to cover her skin, so pale and plump and generously spread across the soft velvet seat. "I don't want to frighten the children." The waiter nodded politely and trotted off. "These days there's no appreciation for the full-bodied femme. I like to say I'm a Rubens painting come to life. Now, tell me, Dorothy, what are your plans this Monday?"

"I haven't any. It's my evening off from the show."

"Good. You'll join us. I'm hosting a party. No need for a gown," she said with a mischievous smile, pulling an invitation from her purse.

"Come as You Were," Dorothy read, turning to Elsa with her eyebrows raised.

"Yes. All the guests will come as they were when they received the invitation."

"Elsa had them delivered at all hours of the night and god-awful times of the morning," Cole added. "We expect to see it all. Silk lingerie, day dresses, tuxedos—"

"Yes, perhaps some tuxedos with no pants, if I know this crowd," Elsa interrupted.

"Underwear in hand, if I know the Barnaby brothers," Cole said with something of a laugh.

"Lucky for me I received it now," Dorothy said. "What fun! I'll be there."

Elsa nodded contentedly, her cheeks rounding in a frisky smile. "Someone has to unbutton the stuffed shirts of the beau monde. It's time. The war has ended, the mood has lifted, and gaiety reigns!"

For the next two hours, over two bottles of champagne and sour cream–coated blinis with dollops of caviar piled generously on top, she and Cole told stories about the capers of upper-crusters whose roguery made them seem less precious, less inaccessible than the guys at the Irish bars down on Seventh Street. Raising her glass like a conductor with her baton, Elsa smiled at Cole as she recalled their own escapades from the shores of Southern France to Newport, Rhode Island, where he enlivened and in some cases resuscitated grand soirées with piano playing and impromptu songs. One day, she told Dorothy, he called to tell her he was intolerably bored, they needed adventure, and the next thing she knew she was on a ship to Italy. He had used a small fraction of his inheritance to purchase a barge and then transformed it into a nightclub paradise that floated through the canals of Venice "to accommodate his guests, who had a wonderful time eating and drinking off his impeccably starched cuff," Elsa said.

"No doubt he provided a great service to the gentry that marveled at his conspicuous consumption and happily left their ennui behind at their homes in the South of France to join him," Dorothy said with a wink.

They watched as six waiters marched by in a line, proudly holding silver trays of Baked Alaska desserts like the Statue of Liberty holding her torch. And then they marched right back out of the room, having apparently gone off route. Elsa smiled, moved closer to Dorothy, and with a saucy smile she confessed that money and real estate weighed her down until one day she decided she would much prefer to be weighed down by a Baked Alaska. So she gave in and followed her dream to indulge herself and others in guilty pleasures that promised a bigger, sweeter bite out of life.

She didn't mind that she was perpetually broke, the living exemplification of hell to the minds of those around her. "Fat, broke, and unmarried," she declared with pride, for she knew she had transcended the unwritten rules. She had become indispensable, presiding over social affairs for kings and baronesses and French nobility. Describing the people she had befriended and the guests who attended her parties dressed up in costumes and game for treasure hunts, she enjoyed setting a scene to arouse their more devilish nature.

"I rather like how you mix and match classes as if you're pairing a Chanel dress with shoes from the Sixth-Avenue Bazaar," Dorothy said.

"And I applaud the elegant way in which you traverse the bawdy jungle of show business, a perilous place for a woman of your beauty, and the sublime setting of high society where you are safe among your own."

Tears stung Dorothy's eyes. Perhaps the champagne made her particularly sentimental. But that's what she wanted, to feel safe. Who would love and protect her? Who could she trust with her innermost secrets? Of the hundreds of friends she had collected, she counted five. Gaillard might make six.

Three months had passed since she and Gaillard met. Three months of moonlit nights and candlelit dinners under the starry Manhattan sky, of high times with friends and galas with acquaintances, of breakfasts at dawn and outings on Sunday afternoons, and evening strolls in Central Park where they rode the carousel and stole kisses in the Belvedere Castle like teenagers too young for love. While he was given to indecision and known for spontaneity, Gaillard was in many respects predictable, a fundamental quality for easing the inevitable insecurities that rise up in those early days of courtship when the heart softens to a fragile state. Not a day passed without a telephone call or handwritten note or glorious bouquet of flowers from Gaillard. He was charismatic, kind, accomplished, and indisputably the most splendid man in the room, and he had inserted and entwined himself in her life with a boyish charm she hadn't the wherewithal to resist. And why would she?

It was a Monday night in late March. The early days of springtime in New York were reliably fickle with heat rising and cool wind blowing, with shadows and rain and shimmering sunlight falling on blooms, the city one step ahead and setting the rhythm for residents trying to keep its pace. In a topsy-turvy continuous motion, it reminded them they'd somersault and skid and finally turn in the direction they ought to go. As Dorothy gave further consideration to the ivory wool skirt set she had slipped on for a quiet dinner at Gaillard's, her telephone rang.

"Hello, darling. I was just on my way out the door," she said cheerfully.

"How did you know it was me!" Gaillard asked with a light laugh.

His brother popped in from Connecticut, he explained. They would meet him at the Stork Club for dinner and then head downtown for jazz.

As much as she prized schedules, set times, and knowing in advance where, when, and with whom she would spend the evening, she had come to appreciate his more improvisational approach. But then, she had little choice. One evening when she expressed her vague disappointment in the change of plans, he replied in kind with disappointed silence, and with quiet brooding that lasted for days. Thus she learned his distinct methodology and made it a point to prepare for eleventh-hour U-turns, roundabouts, and double-backs of their plans.

He would first plan their evening in much the same way she

would. Precise times for each activity, exact locations, and full guest lists thoughtfully typed on sheets of paper like an agenda for a board of directors. Once that was done, the green light would flash, signaling the whole caboodle would take a turn—to where, she did not know. She was seen in Harlem clubs wearing ivory satin and diamond jewels, at formal dinners in a casual sweater and skirt, in Central Park walking barefoot over the cobblestones while carrying her high heel shoes and trying to keep his stride.

Having seen them by chance on that particular night, Maggie phoned her. "With all due respect, underneath his crisp bespoke suit and calm reserve, Gaillard is an *agent of chaos!*"

"No no no," Dorothy replied, "he is *splendid.*"

In their quiet moments when they lazed about in his townhouse, when they shared stories and a lover's touch, when he serenaded her with songs of love and verse of heroic feats, she saw his soul—and tumbled helplessly into his arms.

It was 2:15 a.m. when she arrived home from the Stork Club, the overindulgence in champagne leaving her more lighthearted than usual. *What a glorious night*, she thought, lying back on the sofa and kicking off her shoes. Seeing a letter she had dropped onto the side table in haste, she reached over to pick it up and was surprised to find her name handwritten on the envelope with no address. Someone had delivered it in person. Carefully ripping it open, she pulled the piece of paper out and immediately looked at the signature. *Gaillard.*

He began with the confession that he could not get her out of his mind. From the time he woke, thoughts of her consumed him: how she glided across the room at the Ritz, and the St. Regis, and Rao's, and tripped into his arms, laughing; how she popped open a bottle of champagne, the cork ricocheting into his head, and she laughed more; how her poetry made him sentimental for days; how she drew him out of his silence with her tender voice; how her touch gave him strength. And she excited him. She was the debutante dancer, the innocent and the showgirl, shy at one moment and baring it all the next. He had lost the fight to suppress the hypnotic attraction—Gaillard Thomas II was in love.

"My place tomorrow, Monday, 7 p.m. Just the two of us. Yours, Gaillard."

Delightful, she mused, holding the letter to her breast as she drifted off to sleep.

At half past six she woke to the morning sunlight streaming through the sheer silk curtains. From the looks of her dress, unwrinkled and draped to her slim ankles, it seemed she hadn't moved but an inch. Setting Gaillard's letter by his photograph on the table, she thought they made a fine pair indeed.

At promptly seven o'clock that evening, Dorothy passed through the wrought iron gate guarding Gaillard's five-story townhouse, and she saw a note the size of a playing card taped to the front door. Holding it under the light, she read, *D - Come right in!* With a quick pinch of her cheeks to brighten her complexion, she stepped inside, and smiled.

A trail of freshly picked rose petals had been laid out like a red carpet and led her through the grand foyer. At its end they were arranged in the shape of an arrow pointing to the right. She followed the path into the wood-paneled library and stopped in front of the mahogany bookcase where a card had been placed on a shelf, propped up against a book by Alfred Lord Tennyson. Taking the card in hand, she wondered what he was up to and managed to decipher the words he had scrawled in uneven lines. *Light, so low in the vale, You flash and lighten afar, For this is the golden morning of love, And you are his morning star.*

She continued along the trail, drifting past the drawing room, climbing up the stairwell, and meandering down the long corridor enclosed by walls covered with family pictures elegantly framed in sterling silver. It led her into the salon where a vase of long-stemmed roses was set beside a glass of champagne on an ornate side table. She took a generous sip. And then another. And a few more as she read the poem again. Returning to the petaled path, she went up the stairs to the fourth floor, turned the corner, and passed through the study in a direct line to the terrace, where Gaillard stood facing her.

He flashed a winning smile and said nothing as he took her arm gently and moved to the railing. Bending on one knee, he lifted his hands and presented her with an asscher cut diamond ring that sparkled and shone in the night.

"Will you marry me, Dorothy? Say you will," he said, his voice soft and sanguine.

In that brief moment, a thousand thoughts rushed forth like an avalanche barreling down a mountainside in the far corners of the Southern Ocean, a surge of doubts, misgivings, resistance, and regret crashing through its placid and icy crust. *How do I know how long this love will be? What if I lose hold of the dreams I've dreamed? Oh,* she thought, *but what about love? That too is my dream . . .*

"Darling?" he said, his royal-blue eyes twinkling brightly.

"Yes," she heard herself saying. "Yes, darling, I will marry you . . ."

After a cool shower and a hot cup of coffee, Dorothy could think of nothing but her sister Betty. Oh, how she wanted to tell her more about Gaillard, but poor sad Betty was alone in Pittsburgh nursing wounds of the heart. Maybe a trip to New York was just what she needed.

She phoned her and proposed a visit. To entice her, she shared her sense of wonderment about the changing times. Cocktails started every evening at dusk. The smoky jazz clubs of Harlem were thriving, packed with patrons succumbing to the mood of Bessie Smith's soul-wrenching songs, and Duke Ellington's layered grooves moved everyone to dance the Charleston night after night. There was a burgeoning creativity in the arts while prosperity sparked a building boom and fattened the wallets of laborers. Yankee Stadium opened for play, and great Art Deco towers soared to the sky. An electrifying sense of optimism and cheer abounded—America was flourishing in the wake of war. Still, she said, if Betty came to New York when her stint with *Lady, Be Good* ended, whenever that may be, they must go on to Paris for its art and architecture and air of romance at every turn.

"It's a dream," Dorothy assured her, hearing ennui in her sister's voice. "We were too young to appreciate it when Mummy and Daddy took us. Writers and artists gather in salons, one as inspiring as the next." Her eyes rested on the cityscape painting of Paris leaning against the wall, reminding her of morning walks along the Seine. It had been a Sunday when she happened upon an aged artist sketching the scenery with a seasoned hand, cigarette smoke encircling his face, swirling up to the pink sky of dawn, then drifting away in the cool breath of the wind.

"I really should come visit, and Paris sounds divine. There's nothing happening here," Betty said with a sigh.

"Tell me how you are. The last time we spoke you were despondent over your breakup."

"Oh, I do want to forget him. Nothing seems to fill the hole in my heart, but I'm getting along just fine. Please tell me more about Paris."

"All right. But promise to telephone me the next time you're blue."

"Promise."

"The best-known salon is that of Gertrude Stein. She always says, 'America is my country and Paris is my hometown.' Hold on, darling," Dorothy said, checking her wristwatch. "I'll tell you all about her later on. I have to go if I'm to make noon mass."

Standing before her closet with her hand on the little curve of her narrow hip, she pondered, finally pulling out the ivory dress she had worn on her visit to Gertrude's two years before. It had been during a summer-long stay with her friend, Estelle Manville, and the entire Manville clan. She and Estelle had studied sculpting and painting and French couture and met Coco Chanel in her atelier. On the night of Estelle's seventeenth birthday, her father led them to a limousine waiting at the entrance of the Hotel George V and instructed the chauffeur, "Twenty-seven rue de Fleurus, sixth arrondissement," then announced to the girls, "We are going to see Gertrude Stein."

When Dorothy stepped inside Gertrude's house, a low melody

of voices filled the hallway like a rambling jazz improvisation setting the scene for out-of-towners in a downtown club. Bellows of laughter drifted through the corridor and grew louder as she drew closer to the salon. There she saw the familiar faces of Hemingway and Scott Fitzgerald. Paintings by Cezanne, Degas, and Matisse covered the walls in no particular arrangement. Then she laid her eyes upon Gertrude, who was giving counsel to a lonely-looking man with haywire curls that reached to his shoulders. Suddenly she glanced up at Dorothy and smiled warmly. Dorothy returned the gesture.

After a grand introduction by Mr. Manville, who espoused Dorothy's talent in the arts, Gertrude took her hand and led her on a tour. There was some truth to the description that Gertrude had "the face of a Roman Emperor on the body of an Irish washerwoman." But when she smiled, she lit up the room like the Rockefeller Center Christmas tree sparkling magnificently on a cold New York night.

"I started the collection a long time ago with my brother Leo," Gertrude had said. "The artists were unknown then. Alice and I— that's Alice standing in front of the Renoir—we invited friends and collectors to see their work, and most scoffed at the canvases. We did everything we could to promote them, and now . . ."

"And now their work is exhibited in museums." Dorothy's attention rested on a painting by the door. "Extraordinary."

"That's Picasso's *Melancholy Woman*."

"It captures a moment we've all been through, doesn't it?" Dorothy said.

"Yes, yes, the emotive quality goes straight to the heart."

"It does. It reminds me of the days that followed my mother's death." It was a rare moment of candor about her loss. Gertrude stretched her arm around Dorothy's back in a signal they were bonded together, both far from their Pittsburgh roots. That night she made it a point to introduce her to Thornton Wilder, who would become Dorothy's friend and remain so for fourteen years, right up until the day she died.

Thinking dreamily about Gertrude and that summer holiday in France, Dorothy checked the time and took a last look in the mirror. The telephone rang, but she couldn't answer it now. With a last glance at the painting of Paris, she turned to go, feeling grateful for the happy times. She fully expected the next chapter would outdo even this.

4.

A LUCKY BREAK

I t was a Friday night in early April. Dorothy and Fred Astaire changed out of their costumes and met on the stage. At last they had the theater to themselves. Stolen moments when the seats were all empty and the cast and crew were gone. A single spotlight hung from the ceiling, casting shadows on their forms, her leg reaching up and bending over his shoulder. She felt his grip on her ankle and the stretch of her taut muscles as he moved her leg outward and smiled with satisfaction.

"Good, good, make sure to keep it straight. Now turn your torso to the left and lower your leg in a sweep, bringing it forward and to the floor en pointe," he said, watching her move. "That's it! You've got it! Bravo."

Twirling, leaping, moving in stride in the silence, they practiced dance steps late into the night, a routine they had developed to work off energy from the performance, from the storm of applause from the crowds. Seven months after the opening of *Lady, Be Good*, it was still a hit, a stroke of luck to Dorothy's mind. After all, the year of 1925 was the year of the Broadway musical. Audiences had no less than forty-six to choose from, though none had the extraordinary panache of Astaire or the sensational music of the Gershwin brothers. When the Astaires and Gershwins met ten years earlier in Tin Pan Alley and concocted a dream to collaborate for Broadway, they never imagined the grand debut would be introduced on stage by Walter Winchell, regarded by the populace as the last word on many matters of which, they did not realize, he knew very little.

"How's that fiancé of yours?" asked Fred, a bit out of breath as they sat beside one another, dangling their legs over the stage.

"Gaillard is fine. He's been traveling the past few weeks," she said softly. When they last spoke she was feeling blue, having spent the morning deeply missing her mother, who would have turned forty-five years old that day. After mentioning this to Gaillard, there was a brief silence, and then he began talking about a painting he had won at auction.

"Darling?" she queried the moment he took a breath. "We must have a bad telephone connection. Did you hear what I said about my mother?"

"Yes, I did," he answered. "So many things on my mind today. A crush of business meetings, more art to acquire, travel planning for the golf trip—should be a grand time with the boys. Sweet what you said about her. Wait until you see the painting. It's a hunting scene. Just magnificent. It will go in the drawing room . . ."

"Just as well," Dorothy said to Fred as she stared out to the seats. "If Gaillard was here, I might have missed that night on the town with you and the Prince of Wales."

"Do you know," Fred said with some surprise, "the old chap has attended ten performances? Ten!"

"He quite likes you, especially after that infamous night at the club," she said teasingly. The prince had taken them to the Stork Club where Fred's seductive performance of the Charleston with Countess Edwina Mountbatten seized the attention of every patron and made headlines the following day. Dorothy was surprised to see Fred in a scandal, if not the countess, whose extramarital affairs had become legend. "I hear the countess and her husband, Lord Louis Mountbatten, who by the way is the mentor of Prince Charles, are the most talked-about couple in London, due in part to her promiscuity."

"So I've heard. The countess is unashamed of the vast number of lovers she took, and then left, in her wake."

"So be it. They say her husband is solely interested in himself," Dorothy mused. "Fred darling," she continued, wrapping her arm around his shoulder, "have I thanked you today for making me a part of the show? It's a dream come true. If there's ever anything you need, call on me. I'm here for you." As he patted her knee, they heard the shuffling of feet behind them and spun around.

Looking bedraggled in a frayed, green corduroy blazer, the manager of the theater stood before them scratching his wiry beard. "Show's over for the night," he said with an anguished tone. When he began skulking away, Dorothy tried to stifle a giggle with little success. "Show's over," he said a little more loudly, turning to face them. "Sorry to break it up, fella, but you gotta go. I gotta get home to the wife."

Fred and Dorothy exchanged rascally glances, gathered their belongings, and exited through the backstage door. He opened his umbrella to shield them both as the first drops of rain began to fall.

"Don't you just adore New York?" Dorothy said with a jounce in her step. "It's everything I dreamed of, all that I ran away for. Would-be actors run to Hollywood to become screen stars, and everyone else comes here."

"It fills me with a sense of extraordinary possibilities." He took her hand in his as they crossed Forty-Eighth Street and she skipped up the curb. "Say, Dee, I think the girls in the show are a little jealous that Adele and I asked you on board. If they give you the cold shoulder at times, that might be part of the reason why."

"What's the other part?"

"They know you're different. You're rich."

"They dislike me? I had no idea."

"They like you. In fact, I heard Gertie and Mitzy talking about how beautiful you are. They said you're dignified, sophisticated; they look up to you. Gertie said you're pretentious in a way that's delightful." Fred chuckled, nudging her with his elbow. "Anna says you're a ton of fun."

"I think there's some gossip about our practice sessions, too."

This he couldn't fathom since they already had their parts in the show. She explained it was what girls did—they talked about other girls. Then she considered what she had said. *I suppose I've been guilty of that on occasion. I think I'll stop.*

Fred told her not to take it to heart. "The more success you have, the more people want to take you down," he said.

"The higher you rise . . ."

"The harder you fall. Now that's the kind of story people like to hear, Dee." They arrived at her apartment building. "Get a good night's rest, now," Fred said as he tipped his hat, tapped his toes rhythmically on the pavement, and turned to go home.

When Dorothy arrived at the theater the following day, she felt uneasy and didn't know why. Then, backstage in the moments before the theater curtains parted, she stood alone in the corner of the hallway trying to catch her breath. *Nerves*, she thought. It hadn't happened since opening night.

"Don't you wonder why we put ourselves through this?" asked Fred, approaching her from behind. A faint smile crossed her lips.

It was clear to her now that her only hope was to escape, run from the theater never to return. What was the worst that could happen? After all, the show would go on. Her legs began to feel numb.

"Come on now, Dee, breathe. Deep in, one-two-three . . . deep out, one-two-three." She followed his breath. The warmth of his smile calmed her. Had it been anyone else, her shame would be heavy at such an exhibit of weakness. She was always the one who was cool. *Nothing ruffles your feathers*, Gaillard had told her. She laughed to herself at the thought. "In, one-two-three. Out, one-two-three," Fred continued, as she focused her mind.

When the curtains began to part, she gasped as if it were exposing the frailty inside. On her last breath counting with Fred, she finally said, "Enough" and stepped into the spotlight.

Dancing brought her back to herself, and the show that evening was tops. When the last crooning note fell into harmony with applause, she felt a palpable thrill, and the burgundy curtain closed. Backstage, she skipped past the other chorus girls so she could change out of her costume before Maggie arrived.

Once through the crowd, she made her way to the towering staircase when Gene Keyes stepped in front of her and held his hand up in a signal for her to stop. She recognized him. One night, the dressing door flung open and Anna, a dancer, ran out in tears while he stood there calmly combing his hair.

"Whoa, whoa, whoa, hold on, honey. I've been waiting for you. Why don't we have a nightcap to discuss your future as a leading lady." Dorothy's skin crawled. She noticed that his belly far exceeded the width of his wrinkled trousers.

"I'm sorry, Mr. Keyes, but I have a date."

"Business first, sweetheart."

"Thank you but *no*. I have to go now or I'll be late."

He grabbed her arm, his fingers pressing into her flesh.

"Come on, pretty."

"Please, *stop*!"

She tugged away from his grip, trying to escape. Turning toward the stairwell, she extended her leg and stepped down, only to feel the open air beneath her. Crying out, she pitched forward, downward, tumbling sideways, banging the edge of each iron step, hitting the wall, rolling all the way to the landing below. She lay silent and broken as the prince, the dancers, Fred and Adele gathered around her in utter shock.

The hospital room was cold and silent when she awoke, unable to move inside the cast that covered her body. Dozens of flower bouquets lined the windowsill. Propped up on the bedside table was Gaillard's card: *When the going gets tough, the tough get flowers.* The doctor came into the room and looked her over.

"How are you feeling? Quite an accident you had. We've been keeping a close eye on you."

"Doctor, how long have I been here? How long will I be in this cast? I'm a dancer; I must get back to the theater."

"I know. I've seen your performance. Excellent. Good show. Mr. Astaire and his sister have been by to see you."

Her eyes softened.

"Fred and I practice together every day. How long will it be until I'm better?" A rush of dizziness overwhelmed her.

"It's the side effects of the medication. I must say you're a fortunate woman, lucky to be alive. Someone must be watching over you." *It was Mother*, she thought. She had come to her in a vision during the fall. As she waited for the doctor to continue, his face came into focus, and she searched for an answer in his impenetrable gray eyes. "Simply put, you have broken your vertebrae."

Fear made the seconds long as she tried to absorb what he said.

"Recovery could take up to a year. And I am sorry to say, you will never dance again."

Her mouth fell open in a gasp. The doctor clenched the chart in his hand, scribbled a note, and didn't think of wiping the tears that wetted her skin. Lying still, her arms were immobilized by hardened plaster and gauze, her swollen fingers stiff. She thought of the hands of Fate, a thief in the night that was stealing her dreams. The doctor said nothing more.

Outside the window, a pigeon pecked on the violet-feathered neck of its mate. Dorothy strained to hear what the doctor was saying in the hallway, but his words became more distant. Tears spilled down her cheeks, covered her lips, and splashed onto the blanket.

"Why, God, did you turn your back on me? What's left for me now?" The answers didn't come.

"Breathe in one-two-three, breathe out . . ." She knew if she gave in now, there would be no way back from the fall into darkness. "Jeremiah 31:4. I will build you up again and you will be rebuilt . . .

Again you will take up your tambourines and go out to dance with the joyful." The words gave her no solace.

Alone in the barren room, she watched the sun rise and set in slow succession. There was no escaping the aches of her body, no relief from her thoughts. Grief crushed her more with each passing hour, day, week, indistinct and blended together, a black hole of time. Doctors checking, nurses prodding, telephones ringing, machines beeping, friends consoling, pain pounding, surgeries, narcotics, needles, vitals, braces, bandages, broth and biscuits—these were the things that filled her empty days. On the tray beside her was a calendar with each day crossed off in a big red *X* and months crossed off in black. August. September. October. November. December . . . soon it would be one year.

On August 1, she stirred at half past ten. With her eyes half open she rolled onto her back and glimpsed the blare of sunlight flooding the room. Fury ripped through her, her cheeks flushed. Crying out for the nurse, her mind spun. She was trapped in this room, this frail body, gripped by Fate and suffocating under its hand. Helpless. Another morning. Another test of resilience that she hadn't the wherewithal to pass. Giving up, she tried to release her tears in surrender, hoping for relief.

"Please, Margaret. Please, close the curtains," she pleaded in a wavering voice to the nurse. Hearing herself, it occurred to her that she was not as far along in acceptance as she had thought.

There. At last. Curtains drawn. Shielded from daybreak's call. Pulling the covers over the top of her head, she was tangled in thoughts as they spun and somersaulted until they tired her to sleep.

On the day that marked four years since her mother's passing, she sat up in bed, staring out the window, and fixed her eyes on a hummingbird suspended in the air by its fast-fluttering wings. In her months of confinement, she had grieved not only the loss of her mother, but the loss of her strength and her dreams. Over time, her weeping had turned to whimpers, her mourning to malaise until she was emptied of emotion.

When Gaillard, Clare, Maggie, and others came for their regular visits bringing bon mots and champagne she didn't drink, she struggled to wear an air of good cheer. When they left, she felt ever more unmoored and fell back into quiet. The overflow of love seemed useless. It disappeared into the bottomless well of her heart. But in the stillness of this day, August 7, 1926, her mind was quiet. She felt the well begin to fill. At high noon, the door to her room swung open.

"Look at you, pumpkin. You're coming along." Her father seemed to know instinctively when she needed him most. "I spoke to the doctor and you're doing well. You're going to be just fine. I know you miss your mother now . . . as do I."

She sensed he wanted to say more, to take her into his arms. Dorothy didn't tell him that she had seen her mother in a vision as she tumbled down the stairs and reached out to hold her. But her mother was unready to welcome her into her arms. *It's not time*, she had said, at the very moment Dorothy hit the floor.

As her father kissed her forehead and moved to the metal chair by the window, old sentiments rushed forth. The moments when she and her mother giggled like girls while he watched in puzzlement and smiled a faint smile like he wanted to be in on the joke. And the heated moments when he forbade her to dance and she stood firm. The moments he shouted and she ran to her bedroom, finally running away to New York. Had she surrendered to his rule, perhaps now . . . Well, perhaps her father had been right after all. Though she was sure the thought was foremost in his mind, they said nothing of it and carried on about family news. But then, at the end of his visit, he came to sit beside her on the bed with a look of deep contemplation.

"You set your mind on becoming a dancer, and by God you did it. Broadway with the Astaires! I'm proud of you, pumpkin. Be good." A nod of the head, another kiss on the forehead, and he was gone.

Tears broke through her amber eyes and poured out the pain that had built up, against her wishes, like the Allegheny River to the Lock and Dam.

After a fitful night's sleep, she awoke in time to see the sun rise over the East River. Her mind was clear and bright as she looked ahead to the flowering trees, the blossoms white and pure as freshly fallen snow. Moving to the edge of her bed, she stretched her body, taking care not to twist her torso, and reached for the silver cane leaning against the wall. Victory. She set its rubber knob on the floor by her foot. It was high time to end her long goodbye to Broadway. If she could walk the hallways and round the nursing station three times on her own, she would be released from the confines of the four white walls that were fencing her in. This would be her call to arms, a battle back to glory.

The very thought triggered imagery that fleeted though her mind in rapid succession. She would see Central Park, speeding cars and smiles of strangers, and the glittering lights of the city skyline. She would snuggle with Gaillard, sculpt with Estelle, and sermonize with Clare, and she would, she was sure, sow new and wonderful dreams. She would at last be free.

Dorothy clenched the handle of her cane and leaned her weight on it, noticing that Rosamond Pinchot seemed strangely hurried as she fiddled with her keys and unlocked the front door of their apartment. Dorothy had waited for this moment for months. As she stepped inside, she looked up and stared in surprise at the veil of red petals before her. Enormous bouquets of roses had been placed everywhere, lined up on bookshelves, arranged on tabletops, set in corners of the room.

"Gaillard?" asked Dorothy.

"He's smitten."

"Beautiful. Quite something, really, isn't it?"

"He was here for two hours moving around the vases to set the scene perfectly. In fact, he was so proud of himself he asked me to take a picture of him with the room in the background. I asked how he liked our 'starter apartment,' and he had a good laugh."

"Yes, I suppose he appreciates that most people wouldn't think of a townhouse at Park Avenue and Sixty-Sixth Street as a starter apartment, but technically it's accurate. It's wonderful to be home."

"It's been horridly dull without you. Come on now, it's late. I'll unpack these things for you in the morning," she said, swinging a small canvas tote bag and leading Dorothy down the hallway.

"Thank you, darling. You know I'm perfectly fine to put my things away. The doctor kept me at the hospital longer than I needed. He wanted to be sure I could take care of myself."

"You deserve some taking care of," Rosamond said, turning on the lights in the bedroom. "I put a bell on the nightstand so you can ring if you need me."

Dorothy smiled as she rested her cane against the wall.

"Goodnight, Rosamond. Thank you."

"Night night, Dorothy. Welcome home."

Glancing around the room, she saw that her belongings were just as she had left them. The framed picture of her family, the one of her and Gaillard nuzzling at the Stork Club, the beach club with Rosamond, Maggie, and Clare. On her bedside table were copies of *The Beautiful and Damned*, Homer's *Odyssey*, and *Vogue* magazine, each with a monogrammed silver bookmark tucked inside. On her dresser, the small silver egg sculpture from her mother that marked the birth of her new life as an actress in New York. She would reacquaint herself with the surroundings and settle in tomorrow. Her eyes grew heavy as she unrobed, turned out the light, and slipped under her silken bed covers.

City lights shone into the room and drew shadows along the walls. The shapes were familiar, nearly unchanged since the last time she was there. *Since Fate's rude interruption*, she thought, drifting off to sleep. *Tomorrow I will see Gaillard. Thank you, God. I have my life back. Please help me find my place in the sun.*

At 6:20 p.m. the following day, the telephone rang. Dorothy looked in the mirror and smoothed her hair, pressing the ends against her neck like the girl at the salon had done earlier in the day. From her purse, she took the gift Maggie had given her in the hospital and dabbed the light apricot color evenly across her lips. The telephone continued to ring.

"Yes, hello? Gaillard?"

"Dorothy, I'm running a little behind," he said with a sober tone she didn't recognize. "Charles Barnaby is here. He was a friend of my father's. We're finishing up some after-hours business. Not to worry—I've sent the car for you."

"Righto," she said.

"Bates should be waiting downstairs."

"Righto," she said and then returned the receiver to its cradle.

"Was that Gaillard changing plans?" asked Rosamond. "You'll have to draw the line if he wants to do something too rigorous."

"I'm feeling remarkably strong. The truth is, I haven't needed the cane for weeks. It's been nothing more than a crutch. I think I was nervous from the fall."

"I know," Rosamond said gently. "So? What did Gaillard tell you?"

"He just called to let me know he's running late and he can't pick me up. Bates is waiting downstairs."

"Bates? Will Bates stand with you at the altar and put the ring on your finger for him too?"

"Would that be so bad? Have you seen Bates's baby blues?"

"Have I ever!"

"Well, darling," Dorothy said with a light laugh, "I'll be home late. See you in the morning."

"Be good," Rosamond said, hugging her. "Oh, your father called when you were dressing. He said the funds were transferred to your account and it should hold you over until you're a gray old grandmother. If you play your cards right."

Waiting for Gaillard to finish up his meeting, Dorothy drifted into the salon. Decorated in traditional style with rich shades of burgundy and blue, it had an unmistakably masculine quality. The polished mahogany furniture was French nineteenth century, the drapes of silk velvet. In the far corner, a shiny black piano displayed sheets of music on which Gaillard had scribbled lyrics.

Gaillard did well as a stockbroker and had inherited a generous sum from his father. Seeing a picture of them on the piano, she took it in her hand and studied it. Father and son standing side by side with a striped tent in the background. Covering the bottom half of his father's face with her palm, she looked closely at his eyes. Gentle. Compassionate. And a little twinkle. This was the world-renowned Dr. Theodore Gaillard Thomas, who had made significant advances in women's health and dedicated himself to the cause. He was a founder of the New York Obstetrical Society and the American Gynecological Society, and a real estate tycoon to boot.

Having joined exclusive social organizations and dedicated himself to cliquish camaraderie, Gaillard had earned the title of "millionaire clubman," eternally deprived of the public praise bestowed upon his father—ennoblement for the sire but not for the son. *Surely*, thought Dorothy, *that must have its consequences.*

"There you are. The hint of your perfume led me to the right place," Gaillard said warmly. Turning, she found him standing in the doorway with a large framed photograph in one hand and his blue blazer in the other. He walked to her side and gave her a light kiss. "Here, this is for you."

Taking the frame in her hand, she consulted the picture of Gaillard looking triumphant, a Winchester rifle raised in the air and his foot firmly on the belly of a doe, its almond hair speckled with red.

"The old girl didn't have a chance," he laughed. "I didn't take her down, though. It was Theodore Walker's doing."

"Ahhh," Dorothy said, nodding slowly. "Still, you're a man with brains *and* brawn. You know, darling, this would go awfully well in the drawing room. It would complete the Gaillard Thomas adventures collection and go nicely with the oil painting, the hunting scene."

"Grand idea. Let's go have a look."

He bounded out of the room as Dorothy followed. A piercing pain in her back made her stop in her tracks, and she lost sight of him. After a few minutes it dissipated as quickly as it came.

"Terrific," he said when she came into the room. Pointing in the direction of the credenza where he had placed the picture, he smiled proudly. "Oh, something is wrong," he said, looking at her.

"Oh, just surprised I got this terrible pain in my back. I think I'm all right now." She wandered over to the sofa and nestled in beside him.

"I have a proposal for you," he said, taking her hand in his.

She sat up with enthusiasm, waiting for him to continue.

"We've been apart for all these months. What do you say we make up for lost time and go to Europe in the fall? We can stay in Paris until December and then go on to St. Moritz to do some Alpine skiing. I hear it's a hell of a sport. Bit of a climb up the mountain, but it's all downhill from there. If you'd like, we can go to the spa in Baden-Baden before we return to Paris."

"Well," she said, considering her words carefully, "a white Christmas in Paris sounds splendid."

As the last days of August wore on and the sweltering heat grew thick in the city air, Dorothy began to feel constricted by the oppressive setting, so tedious and unchanging. At the first mention of it to Clare, Clare said she understood the need for escape too well; she had come to feel asphyxiated by pompous women who sucked the air out of the North Shore of Long Island as effortlessly as they filled their homes with carbon-copy friends. At the end of their conversation, Dorothy agreed to visit Clare and her husband, George, in the country.

She set out for a month's rest at the Lindens, Clare's house in Sands Point, Long Island. The twenty-three room neo-Georgian Colonial was set upon six well-manicured acres with a view of Manhasset Bay, a dock for George's boat *Black Watch*, a bathhouse, tennis court, polo field, and staff of thirty. Bates drove Dorothy along the scenic thirty-minute drive from Manhattan, the view opening up to meadows as they drew closer to Clare's home. The salty air along Plandome Road invigorated her as they crossed between a pond and a bay dotted with sails in the distance. He pointed out the Leeds estate set high on a hill, and Raoul Fleischmann's house on the water in Gulls Cove. He turned north toward Sands Point where the Guggenheim, Astor, and Whitney families resided behind walls of stone adorned with battlements and gargoyles. Those who gained entry to any one of them would find a sprawling mansion mightily hugging the shoreline of Manhasset Bay, its placid waters rolling in and out with the tide in a soft, steady whoosh.

On their first morning together, Dorothy and Clare carried their parasols to the beach where they flipped through pages of *Vogue* with its pretty clothes, remedies for weight loss, and proclamations that women no longer needed to marry unless they wanted to.

"Happy Longhorn was so afraid of her husband divorcing her, she spent three weeks in France at an *institute de beauté* working with trainers, masseuses, and doctors who gave her magic potions," Dorothy said as she took a sip of lemonade, then wedged the glass in the sand.

"I know. She came back with a trunk full of Mexican tea and *anagra dragees*—you know, the thyroid pills—and she was an absolute mess, the poor girl. She had the figure of a twelve-year-old boy, which is exactly what one needs to wear the new dresses."

Perusing the pages of the magazine, Dorothy fixed her eyes on the photograph of Mrs. Wallace Harrington. "Have you tried this lightening cream? Look at the advertisement. She's radiant! Maybe I should have considered marrying Wallace. But there was something odd about him." She closed the magazine and brushed the sand off her legs.

"Dorothy, you're looking for something that doesn't exist—the perfect man." A loud thump caught their attention, and they looked out to the dock to see that George had slammed into it with his boat. "Exhibit A."

"Are you upset with him again?"

"No, today I like George."

"That's good, Clare. He really loves you." Dorothy put on her sunglasses and watched the boat fade into the distance.

"He can be such a child. Still, I'm convinced that somehow we could have a good marriage." She sighed dramatically, looking for a hairbrush in her Provencal straw tote bag.

"It's nice to have someone who's always there for you."

"Darling, it's only nice if *they're* nice. I look at some of these people who become so emotionally vulnerable to their self-centered, self-absorbed, unsympathetic and severely flawed spouses that they accept constant criticism and a stilted life."

"Well, I think when the most significant person in your life criticizes you over a long period of time, you start to believe them. You lose the courage to leave."

"You lose all sense of truth. You're manipulated and made to feel you're in the wrong. Marry one and you're in for a lifetime of guilt."

"Aha, so the key to a lasting marriage is guilt," said Dorothy with a wry smile.

"Of course, the poor souls that stay, they tell themselves it's the right thing to do. How could they survive it otherwise? They say it's better to keep the family intact while they damage the children and pass the nonsense on to the next generation," Clare said with a shake of her head.

"They need to hold on to the dream."

"When I was young, I was sure that I would get married and live happily ever after," Clare said more emphatically. "Now I realize forevermore is shorter than you think."

"And sometimes, darling, that's the good news. At least now women can escape a bad marriage."

"Is Gaillard coming to the party tonight?"

"No, he couldn't make it back from his business trip. He calls every day," Dorothy sighed, drawing his initials in the sand.

"Well, you know what I always say. Love is a verb."

"He's splendid."

"He's impeccably mannered, though he does have a bit of an edge."

"I suppose. There are times I wonder what he's really thinking."

"He's thinking about *assets* of one kind or another. Aren't they all?"

"I hope he's more evolved than the others," Dorothy said, wiping the sand from her finger.

"I hope he'll be a good husband to you."

"I have to admit I was surprised when he asked. But I always say, men don't like to be alone." Dorothy didn't want to talk about it. Or think about it. Or she might begin to worry that giving in to love would mean giving up a part of herself. She would meld and blend into the wife she was expected to be. "What's the final tally for the party tonight?"

"Two hundred, not counting Alva Belmont. She said she's coming by car!" Clare exclaimed with incredulity.

"I know she lives next door, but really, you can't expect Alva to hike here. Your driveway must be a mile long. Hers is twice that."

Clare raised her glass. "Here's to us! The first party we're co-hosting." Their lemonade spilled over the rims and soaked into the sand.

At 7:30 that evening, the party was in full swing, the orchestra playing "Fascinating Rhythm" as Alva, Dorothy, and Clare emerged through the terrace doors.

"We couldn't have timed it better," Clare noted, seeing a kaleidoscope of coiffed heads turn their way.

"Alva, your presence is an event in itself," Dorothy teased. "They worship you." Alva had kept the name of her first husband and then added the name of her second husband to great effect in the world in which she traveled. Alva Vanderbilt Belmont was an empress of international acclaim.

"Those ladies, they are perpetually fatigued trying to outdo and undo one other," Alva said. "They certainly tried it with me."

"But what else would they do? They are so limited, after all," Clare remarked. When she married George, those women of polite society welcomed her into their circle with a lavishly rude reception. They had no idea that one day she would serve retribution with her pen, much to the conspicuous delight of Alva and the public at large.

5.

WOMEN'S INTUITION

As the sun dropped behind the majestic mountains of Alleghany County, Pennsylvania, on a cool September day in 1927, the hidden orchestra played Pachelbel's Canon as Dorothy lowered a white veil to cover her face. Her instinct told her the wedding was a mistake. Something didn't feel right.

Candlelight illuminated the church with a soft glow as the scent of jasmine, lilies, and white roses drifted in the air. The choir from St. Joseph's Academy hummed their first notes to cue the orchestra in *Lohengrin*'s "Wedding March." Everyone turned in unison and gasped when Dorothy appeared, a divine vision in her chiffon dress cinched at the waist, delicately trimmed with seed pearls and finished with a pearl-and-diamond necklace once worn by her mother. Gaillard Thomas II waited at the altar and watched her move toward him ever so slowly—perhaps even too slowly, she realized—escorted by her father, James.

Relieved to have friends and family by her side that weekend to celebrate the nuptials, she relaxed poolside. It was hard to be in the Ligonier Valley unable to do her usual routine of riding horses, skeet shooting, fly-fishing, and piddling about the quaint town, but she had strict orders from the doctor to continue to rest after her recent bouts of pain. A group of fifty wedding guests had checked into the Rolling Rock Club, a members-only retreat on 12,000 acres with white-glove service, mountainous views, and a serene ambiance. Gaillard and the men whiled away the time on the golf course and met the ladies on the terrace at sunset for champagne and a dinner of fresh-caught trout. Dorothy's friend Jane provided the largest of the fish, snagged early in the day from a stream on the property, then prepared by the chef as a meunière dish.

Taking a quiet moment on the terrace of her suite, Dorothy gazed out to the English garden, her legs entwined under the table. She thought she should feel more exuberant, but the diamond ring that Gaillard had slipped on her finger felt odd and constricting, not the feeling she had imagined as a child. To her consolation she had at least begun a career, unlike Clare, who had married at twenty, purely out of fear that she would age poor and alone.

"Your work does not define you," Gaillard said as he sat down and watched her leaf through an old edition of *Dancing Times* magazine.

"Perhaps that's true, but dancing was a part of me," she said as she tossed the magazine onto the table and looked at him. "I'll find something to put the wind back in my sails, darling."

He shifted in his chair, unbuttoned his blazer, loosened his necktie. She sensed that he was overly concerned about losing her to another man, to her independence, to the unpredictable world.

"When we get to Paris, why don't you take the girls to see Jeanne Lanvin? Or even better, go to Poiret's atelier and pick up that dress you like, the one with the sequined bow at the waist," he said. Adept at lulling her into brief contentment, he appealed to the side of her that coveted pretty things.

"Yes, yes, splendid idea," she said, imagining herself in the red-and-gold sequined gown with the scalloped hemline and deep V-neck black bodice. And then she reconsidered, the gold too garish for her taste.

"Just relax. Enjoy yourself. You needn't think about a profession."

They watched golden leaves fall from long limbs and followed their descent as they drifted lazily down to the hood of a black Studebaker Commander parked under the tree. A group of their friends barreled out the front door of the club, balancing martinis not very well, their muddled hollers and laughter echoing up to the terrace. Dorothy looked at her wristwatch. Gaillard checked his pocket watch. They glanced at each other, leaned in for a peck on the lips, and rose from their seats to go. She dressed for the afternoon and left for the plush ladies' lounge.

"Did you know," Dorothy asked the girls, "when all the male doctors prescribed sexual intercourse for women's hysteria, Gaillard's father was the only one who said wait a minute, maybe they don't need more of their husbands; maybe what they need is a week without them by the sea. So he set up his patients at a boarding house in Southampton, near his home." Seated on a vanity stool facing the mirror, she dabbed peach color onto her lips and pressed them to a tissue.

"Well, amen to that," said Maggie. "The rest of the doctors should be imprisoned for malpractice for telling women all you need is a good roll in the hay. I'll admit it's better than a lobotomy. Do you realize how many women are getting lobotomies these days? Have you *seen* what they've done to Carol Ann Mallery? One day she strolled out of the dressing room at Bergdorf's with nothing on but French lace lingerie."

"With that figure?" scoffed Clare.

"Gaillard's father was an angel in the hell of women's medicine," said Jane. "Do you remember when the Women's Hospital refused to admit patients with cancer? He joined the board of directors and led the way by erecting a separate pavilion where they could be treated."

"Let's get back to that point about hysteria. Dorothy, just out of curiosity, what do the doctors prescribe for men with hysteria?" asked Maggie. Dorothy smiled a little.

"A round of golf and scotch on the rocks."

Two weeks later, a cool breeze swept through the car as the Manhattan skyline disappeared in the rear window. En route to their country cottage due east of the city, Dorothy yearned for quiet before their honeymoon in Europe; she and Gaillard hadn't had enough time alone, always in the company of a large group of friends. On this day, he was unusually loquacious, looking out to the changing landscape and vast yellow fields in the distance.

"My father went to the Hamptons fifty-five years ago, in 1870, and he fell in love with the place. He said he had never seen such magnificent beaches and pristine countryside."

"It must have been a wonderful sanctuary for him." Dorothy drew a deep breath to take in the fragrant scent of the wind.

"It was. So much so that he built a cottage called the Dunes in Southampton and later bought forty-seven acres on Gin Lane. He was one of the first to build, named his house Birdcage, and you'll see why. My brother lives there now. The guest cottages are named Sandhurst and Bonito. He was a bloody good investor."

She couldn't decide if Gaillard sounded arrogant or proud. "He was responsible for bringing St. Andrew's Dune Church to the town, is that right?"

"Yes, it was a lifesaving station that he had relocated to the beach, and then he did a full renovation. We can walk there from the house. We're midway between the beach and town. Father had a strong hand in creating Southampton as a summer colony. He implored others to build here, and before you know it—well, you'll see. It's good fun."

"Tell me," she said, looking at him, "does losing a parent get easier over time? Can you ever fill the emptiness in your heart?"

"It's been twenty-two years since my father passed, and I think of him all the time. I can still hear his voice."

They turned onto South Main Street and followed the road to the decorative iron gates that were open for their arrival. Through the gates, at the end of the road with a circular drive as its finish line, there stood Thanet House, a stately Dutch-style home topped by three gabled dormers. It was lovely and just grand enough, a faded red-and-white brick, more worn, more weathered, more old guard than those of new construction. This was the dawn of their days together, and she was entirely sure this moment should be one of sheer content.

"It reaches all the way back to Linden Lane, and our property extends to Lake Agawam where you can set your easel and paint," he suggested. "And, darling, I believe the house is in need of your decorating prowess. Do as you wish. Just don't ever leave me."

The remark unnerved her. In five words, he had made her feel as though he lacked faith in their marriage, in her, perhaps even in himself.

"Why would I leave you?" was all she said.

"Ah, fantastic, there's Benjamin the houseman, right on schedule."

They walked on the beach, bundled up against the cool, invigorating breeze. They huddled under a blanket and gazed at the ocean, at once mysterious and soothing, the whispering waves lulling them into tranquility. When they returned to the house they found a fire blazing in the hearth, the air rich with the scent of baking pie and fresh lobster stew simmering on the burner, the cook standing over it stirring patiently.

They took quiet country drives and stopped in town to visit the shops. First to the Good Ground General Store, and then to the Lyzon Hat Shop to confer with the owner, who lived up to her name as "society's emotional hat designer." In the evenings, they giggled and flirted by the fire and read until their eyes grew tired. Throughout the week, she took copious notes and measurements for decorating as Irving Berlin's new song played over and over on the radio. Gaillard knew all the words. On their last day in the Hamptons, he took her to Gurney's Inn on the water's edge in Montauk, and to the Shinnecock Lighthouse, the tallest point in the East, visible from eighteen nautical miles.

"I had sailing lessons here when I was a young boy," he said, as they made their way down the shoreline toward the red tower in the distance. "One day when I was thirteen, I took my boat too far out in the water. Lost my bearings. The sky darkened quickly, and a storm rolled in. I felt so alone out there at the mercy of the wind and the crash of the waves against the hull. I didn't know which way to turn the jib to get to shore. I didn't know if I would survive." He stopped walking and looked up at the lighthouse. "The glow emanating from this old girl in the distance saved me. Seeing it gave me a sort of calm, like everything would be all right, even though I knew I first had to fight Mother Nature."

"She can be a lofty adversary."

"She taught me a lesson or two. For one thing, I should have paid more attention before charging out into the open sea. I should have seen there was trouble on the horizon."

"The lighthouse must have seemed a symbol of resilience and survival, somehow impervious to the mayhem around it. Noble and beautiful in its light."

"Precisely. Quite like you, the more I think of it. And you've brought me safely ashore . . ." This was, she would learn, unusually expressive for Gaillard. He cupped her face in his hands, leaned down, met her lips with his, and wrapped her tightly, maybe even too tightly, in his arms.

6.

TEMPTATION WALK

Heads turned as Dorothy descended the winding staircase of the Paris Ritz, her skin luminous against natural pearls that dipped to her midriff. A sparkling emerald dress clip brought out a hint of green in her eyes. Passersby watched and wondered who she was, then turned to get a second look. She would have been disappointed and even surprised if they didn't.

"*Mon dieu, tu es belle,*" whispered a tuxedoed gentleman, who slowed his pace as he walked by.

Strolling through Temptation Walk, the corridor connecting the Place Vendome side of the hotel to the Rue Cambon section where Chanel kept an office, she glimpsed at the jewels prominently displayed in glass cases. Waiting in the Salon de Correspondance were Clare and Maggie, bubbling over with outrage that women were still not permitted in Dixies Bar with the men.

"I can guarantee the men are not drinking mimosas, that new drink the bartender came up with last month. It's champagne mixed with orange juice. Sounds like a breakfast drink to me," Maggie said.

She was right about the drink and about the men. Gaillard and George, Clare's husband, knocked back martinis with Ernest

Hemingway until 9 p.m. when they all would meet for dinner at Au Petite Riche. The men were seated at the table when the women arrived. Hemingway stood and pulled out a chair for Dorothy.

"Mrs. Thomas, please, allow me."

She complied and sat down, noting straightaway the wine had already been poured. He immediately turned his attention to her, asked how the Rolling Rock Club compared with the Paris Ritz, described the lush gardens, the moist petals, the Beaujolais and succulent beef bourguignon, and, finally, the two fine silken robes in his suite.

"Dorothy has a good man here," Maggie said as she patted Gaillard on the back.

"As I always say, *j'ai de la chance*," Dorothy said. *I am fortunate.* It drew no response from Hemingway, who was checking his pockets for paper so that he could scribble down his own words.

She recognized that her honeymoon was unconventional, perhaps better described as a holiday with friends, yet she couldn't deny the exhilaration of roaming around Paris with the girls. One day they joined Gertrude Stein on a jaunt to Claude Monet's pink brick house in Giverny. Over lunch in the courtyard on an unseasonably warm October day, he suggested they walk through the gardens and over the bridge where they could pause and reflect on the beauty of God's earth while surrounded by azaleas, wisteria, and a pond brightened with water lilies. They strolled around the property and said little.

"Claude, *j'aime les jardins. Ils sont spectaculaires.* They are as breathtaking as your paintings. You capture the serenity of the natural world," Dorothy said as she sat beside him at a table under the portico. Claude was pleased by her remarks. And Claude wasn't easily pleased.

"You are one of the few that understands art is meant to affect the emotions," he said, his thick accent melodious to her ear. "These literary and news men who critique my work, they see it as something to be analyzed with their great intellect, the stroke of their pen as contemptible as the men themselves. It seems I haven't yet created a canvas that people are pleasantly affected by, myself included."

"*Au contraire*," Dorothy replied with a shake of her head. "Your work is divine, and those critics are untalented bores."

"Ha! *Oui, comme jamerais le faire! Ces scélérats.*"

"You're right, they *are* scoundrels, Claude!"

Time passed quickly in the warmth of the day. As he filled her wineglass, she barely remembered finishing the first, but the effects were delightful. After the third round, it was time for them to go. He watched her walk toward the car.

"*Mignon!*" he called out. She hadn't been referred to as "cute" since her teenage years and found it wonderfully refreshing.

As she and Gertrude made themselves comfortable in the back seat, Claude sauntered over and motioned to lower the window. He reached in, handed Dorothy a small canvas, and turned to go before she could respond. As the driver pulled away, she closed her eyes with the image of his painting—her as a ballerina—clear in her mind.

Back in Paris, Clare and Maggie hopped out of the car in Saint-Germain-des-Prés in front of the bustling café Les Deux Magots. The next stop was L'École des Beaux-Arts where Dorothy inquired about the curriculum for painting and sculpting. The art, the music, the sheer beauty of Paris inspired her. At 5 p.m. they regrouped for tea at Café de Flore and then strolled back to the Ritz.

"Dorothy, Gaillard seemed quiet last night. Is anything wrong?" asked Maggie.

"He gets that way," Dorothy answered, keeping her eyes on the cobblestone street.

"Maybe he's tired? Or outside of his comfort zone with the avant-garde," Clare suggested.

"Why don't we skip Gertrude's tonight and take him to the bar at the George V Hotel? It would better suit his taste," Maggie offered.

"I'll suggest it. You know, I've been thinking about what I can do in the arts, but I . . . I get the feeling he'd rather I didn't think about it." They stopped in front of Maison Boucheron to look at the glittering diamond choker in the window.

"Doesn't he tell you?" asked Maggie, continuing to look at the jewels.

"No. He just says work does not define a person; go to the spa and relax. He could be trying to make me feel better about not being able to dance."

"Well, if what you *do* doesn't define you, what does?" asked Clare. Dorothy turned to look at her and refrained from answering.

Maggie, feeling the tension rise, muttered nervously, "Look at the time. How will we make our salon appointments with Christophe?"

"I think we should be able to make our own choices," Dorothy said, looking at Clare, "and not be judged by any of them."

"I agree, Dorothy, even if the Catholic Church doesn't. Listen, I wish I could be happy just being George's wife, but apparently it's not in my nature."

That evening turned into a roving party in Paris with the girls, Gaillard, George, and others who joined them as the hours wore on. They began at Gertrude's salon where artists and writers gathered in the library. Gaillard was unaccustomed to this sort of crowd. "The Lost Generation looking for freedom in Paris," he said under his breath. As far as he was concerned, freedom was alive and well in America; they just had to learn the stock market and stop playing around with paint and pencils. Dorothy winced when he said it.

Early Friday morning, on October 29, before the others awoke, the newlyweds went for a walk in the Tuileries Gardens. It was Gaillard's last hour in Paris.

"George will meet me tomorrow in Cherbourg. We'll have five days together on the ship—says he wants to do some business." They sat down on the cool stone base that encircled the fountain. A rush of water sprayed high in the air in a rhythmic sculpture and cascaded down.

"I wouldn't try to match him drink for drink."

"Righto."

They watched sparrows gather around an old man on a park bench who whistled softly and sprinkled breadcrumbs over the manicured grass. Birds hopped along his shoulders, twittering about.

"That's Le Pere Pol, the bird charmer," Dorothy giggled. "I remember seeing him here when I was a child. Mother sat beside me, holding my hand, and I wondered what was his secret to attracting hundreds of birds. She said that's what it must be like for public figures. If you ask me, the twittering sounds like a ladies' lunch at the club."

"Indeed," he chuckled. "Darling, I know you'll do a marvelous job of decorating the new place. Take your time, stay in Paris for as long as you like. I'll be waiting for you in New York." He watched the water splash and bubble and blend into the pool.

"Look at the hundreds of coins at the bottom. People make a wish when they toss them in. There's something beautiful about it," she sighed. "Each one holds the promise of a dream coming true."

He reached his arms around her and held on. Stroking the back of his neck, she wished they had spent more time alone, just the two of them.

"I adore you," he said softly. He gave her a light kiss and they bid goodbye.

Sitting alone in the Notre Dame Cathedral, she prayed for him, for her family, and for herself. As she sat back in the pew, she silently asked God, *What is my calling?* and opened the Bible to find the answer. She closed her eyes and put her finger on a random page, a game she had played since childhood. When she looked at the passage she smiled, reading Luke 12:34: "For where your treasure is, there will your heart be also."

The guttural notes of the pipe organ immediately took her back in time to her youthful days at the convent when wishes came easily to her mind. She closed her eyes again and flipped to another page, placing her finger at the top.

"Devout Dance. Exodus 15:20: Miriam the prophet, Aaron's sister, took a tambourine in her hand, and all the women followed her, with tambourines and dancing," she whispered, pleased to know that good days with Elsa Maxwell were ahead.

7.

STAR LIGHT, STAR BRIGHT

Three weeks after bidding goodbye to Gaillard, Dorothy found herself on a train to Venice dressed all in gray to suit her mood. She supposed she was missing him. Outside was a blur of greenery and black rooftops.

"Elsa Maxwell was born to entertain. Shall we get an early start on the festivities and have a drink?" asked Maggie, nodding to the server before Dorothy and Clare had a chance to respond.

While they waited for the sherry to be poured, they chatted about the parties that Elsa had planned for Cole and Linda Porter, otherwise known as the Colporteurs, who had left their flat on Rue Monsieur for a change of scenery with a livelier crowd. They had invited the girls to stay at their home, the Palazzo Rezzonico, in Venice, the majestic eighteenth-century palace on the Grand Canal that they had rented for $4,000 a month for the entire year. They hired fifty gondoliers as footmen and had every intention of filling the grand ballroom, large enough for a thousand guests.

The girls strode into the palace as Vivaldi's concerto *The Four Seasons* rose to crescendo. Uniformed servants lined up in formation while others carried away their luggage in a well-choreographed sweep. The pomp and circumstance was typically Cole, who nearly tripped over himself with enthusiasm when they appeared on the terrace. He rushed to their side.

"Cole, your staff is well trained, and I quite like the way they lined up with men on one side, women on the other," said Clare. "So theatrical."

"So Rockettes," said Dorothy.

Cole grinned boyishly. He apprised the girls of Elsa's plans for the upcoming galas, omitting a few of the finer details in order to allow for the element of surprise. As he gave them a tour of the palazzo, he expounded on its history, pleased when Dorothy asked him to elaborate more. She knew that he would like to; he was a natural showman and had chosen storied surroundings. Besides, she hoped he would reveal the details that would account for its otherworldly air.

"In the late nineteenth century, John Singer Sargent had a studio here. It's where he painted," Cole said. "Robert Barrett Browning lived and painted here too. Browning's father, the poet, died on the premises."

"Ah, Browning, marvelous," Dorothy said. She glanced at Clare with a raised eyebrow and smiled. "'My friend was already too good to lose, And seemed in the way of improvement yet, When she crossed his path with her hunting-noose, And over him drew her net.'"

"'A Light Woman'—I know the poem," Clare said, trying to suppress a full smile to no avail. "Clever. Not that I trapped George with a hunting net."

Following Cole down the corridor, they came upon two tremendous doors which opened to a parlor room ornately furnished and brightened with sunlight streaming in through high-arched windows facing the canal. Stepping inside, Clare and Dorothy walked in a direct line to the painting above the mantle.

"Sargent was twenty-five years old when he painted that work, *Venetian Women*. Spectacular, isn't it?" he marveled.

"It's all so intriguing," Clare said, noting the meticulous condition of the nineteenth-century mahogany chest and the Fabergé eggs on top that were arranged in no recognizable order.

"A nobleman by the name of Filippo Bon started building the palazzo in 1649 and then had to sell it when he suddenly lost all his money. As it happens, Venice was out of money too. It was after the war with Turkey. Turns out, it was a case of bonne chance for Giambattista Rezzonico, a true parvenu. He bought the palazzo, and in so doing he made his way into the Golden Book, Libro d'Oro, the regal version of the Social Register."

"No easy task," said Clare.

Cole led them through a maze of corridors into the chapel and Nuptial Allegory Room where Rezzonico had tied the knot just before he became the procurator of St. Mark's Basilica. That very same year, his son was elected pope. *Imagine,* thought Dorothy. *He became Pope Clement XIII, and one day a long time ago, he lived here, the site of Elsa's fabulous parties and the playground for Coleporteur's friends.* Entranced by the stories and the frescoed ceilings, she lowered herself onto the faded cushion of a Louis XVI chair.

"Glorious," she said, eager to see the sculptures in the courtyard.

"The pièce de résistance is, without a doubt, the throne room," Clare proclaimed.

The throne room was, at one time, the bridal chamber of Rezzonico's wife, and now served as an inspiration to Clare, who desperately wanted to renovate her outmoded Manhattan townhouse to suit her opulent tastes. Dorothy thought, but didn't say, the throne room was befitting of Clare's dynamic with her husband, George, which by all accounts was that of a queen and jester. "He is a dear soul in need of a tender ear and a little direction. Give it time," Dorothy had told her years before on the beach in Sands Point as she watched his boat speed away haphazardly from the dock. But each day Clare's disappointment in him deepened in equal measure to his growing insecurity of her. What she viewed as sheer antics—his insobriety, frat-boy behavior, and workdays on the golf course—Dorothy recognized as an unhappy man. It was always more clear from the outside looking in.

"Clare, is the throne room inspiring you for redecorating your place in New York?" she asked.

"It *is*." She rolled her wedding ring around her finger in circles, unaware of the nervous habit. They strolled to the courtyard while Maggie retired to her room. "If redecorating doesn't relieve my growing restlessness, I don't know what will."

"I understand. You can do so much more than plan menus and masquerade balls. You'll have success once you decide what you want to do. The sisters used to say a woman can enter a field dominated by men and not change who she is."

"Someone recently told me I should stick to my knitting."

"Only a man would say that."

"I'm flattered by your faith in my potential. I daresay it would behoove you to take your own advice," said Clare. They didn't notice Scipione, the gray-haired butler, standing at attention by the door. "Tell me, does Gaillard mind that you travel without him?" asked Clare, eyeing her closely.

"No, in fact he tells me to enjoy myself, take my time," she replied, glad for the sense of freedom, yet wondering if Gaillard missed her at all.

"I see. And do you miss him?"

"Yes. But you know, we're both very independent," she reasoned.

"And does he tell you he misses you?"

"Yes, yes," Dorothy said, thinking how Gaillard always managed to say the appropriate things.

"And do you think he'd prefer if you were with him in New York and not here?"

"Oh, he said to have a wonderful time and he's looking forward to my return. I don't really know. You have to be direct with me. The unspoken subtleties get lost in translation."

"Well, of course they do. A couple has to be able to communicate. You can't be formal in love," said Clare.

That night at the party, drums started beating and spotlights flashed in the sky, the bright glow illuminating three acrobats dancing and leaping on a tightrope high above the ground. Giggles and shrieks came from the women standing by Dorothy as she watched excitedly and then with fright that one of the performers would fall. With every courageous move, she gasped in anticipation; upon every safe landing, she exhaled vigorously into her crystal glass, emptying it with a quick gulp to catch the next perilous maneuver. And without fail, every night of that week, Cole sang clever songs to entertain the guests and himself, no easy assignment for a virtuoso whose mind flipped, turned, and cartwheeled with fancy.

At week's end, the girls departed Cole's palace in need of rest after all the exhaustive leisure, and they checked into the palace of Aix-le-Bain, a wellness resort in the shadow of the French Alps known to the Brits as Aches and Pains. There they would rejuvenate in the warm sulfur springs.

The moment Dorothy stepped into her suite and opened the terrace doors, she felt a sense of extraordinary relief. It was the first time she had been alone since her wedding. The mountain breeze drifted into the room, and she tilted her head toward the sky. *Star light, star bright*, she whispered, *I wish for a marriage with infinite nights.*

Stretching out on the sofa, she began to write in her diary so she would always remember, in her most aged and forgetful years, the joy of these days and the people and places she adored. Aix-le-Bain and the cure towns surrounding it had mountainous views and unspoiled terrain, the residents as warm and refined as the Swiss-style homes that dotted the landscape. The healing waters would hopefully subdue her recurring backaches. And the respite from social engagements would allow her time to think of how she could build a lasting marriage with Gaillard. She wouldn't discuss it with her friends, and Clare didn't understand this at all, always asking meddlesome questions and always assuming the worst. What Clare considered secretive, Dorothy considered private, a couple's personal business. Dorothy realized she'd had enough and was ready to go home, her mission to furnish a Paris pied-a-terre a fait accompli. It was a place she would go, and go often, with or without Gaillard—her home away from home.

8.

IN VOGUE

Gaillard arrived in Southampton on Sunday, October 9, in time for cocktails at sunset. It was the day after his jaunt to Yankee Stadium, where he had watched his home team beat the Pittsburgh Pirates in the 1927 World Series. Still exhilarated from hearing Graham McNamee's play-by-play broadcast on NBC's radio station, and over the guilt of rooting for Pittsburgh, she rushed outside to welcome him home and hear more about Lou Gehrig and Babe Ruth's plays. There hadn't been such ballyhoo since Charles Lindbergh made the first transatlantic flight in his airplane, traveling from New York to Paris. Gaillard gave her the obligatory kiss and of course the usual niceties because Gaillard was a consummate gentleman and, as Dorothy's friends said, unfailingly formal—an oddity in an intimate relationship, according to the girls. "He's splendid," she told them with a dismissive wave of her hand and a smile.

"I can't wait to hear all about the game," she said as they walked into this office.

"I see the new desk has finally arrived," he said, puttering around.

"Yes, darling, Louis XVI. It suits the room, don't you think?"

Pleased the decorating was finally complete, she looked around at the fruits of her labor. She had imported a collection of fine French antique furniture and filled the shelves with leather-bound books that reached high up to the ceiling. The living room too was done, an elegant collection of ivory furnishings complemented by ivory curtains and bouquets of white hydrangeas perfectly arranged in large urn vases. He sat behind the desk, running his hands over its smooth top before looking up to answer.

"It's very much like the one father had. If we ever get a divorce, I would like to keep it. You can have everything else," he said matter-of-factly. "Would that be all right?"

For a minute, she was stunned into silence. "Of course it's all right," she said lightly. "But—"

"Say, I'm taking Charles Norton and Johnny Singleton for a spin on the boat. Why don't you join us? We're heading to Montauk."

"I would love to." She felt reassured. Maybe she had sensed trouble where there was none. Maybe he needed reassurance from her. She went to him, wrapped her arms around his shoulders, kissed him on the neck, and on his lips, in the way that always thrilled him. He pulled back, gave her a peck on the cheek, and sat down.

"I have some papers to read through before they arrive." He shuffled a few folders, tossed them aside, and stood up. "I've got to see a man about a horse."

"I'll pack a few things and have Gabrielle whip up hors d'oeuvres and stock the boat," she said softly, feeling ashamed as she walked to the door.

"Righto."

I won't do that again, she thought. On her way upstairs, she thought of all the signs of trouble that had been there from the start. His reserve that now seemed aloof, his buoyancy with the boys and silence with her, passion for nothing but bets and numbers like a gambler at the track with his last penny on the long shot.

In their bedroom, she pulled a sweater from the drawer in case it was chilly on the water, and she flung it into her tote bag. Then she found herself taking Gaillard's rain hat from the closet. *Habit.* Sitting on the bed, she placed the hat beside her and fixed her eyes on it, deliberating as to whether she should pack it. *Let him get wet.*

So childish, she conceded, slipping it into the tote. Lying back with her head on the pillow, she reflected. Softening, she remembered how he smiled lovingly when she wrapped his hand in a bandage after a rough-and-tumble game of squash. How he held her at the Tuileries Gardens when he had to leave her. And the way his eyes lit up when she emerged from her dressing room decked out for a party and kissed him on the cheek. And all those times they reunited and he waited not a moment to embrace her with all his might, and asked if they could spend the week, just the two of them, in quiet repose. With careful consideration, she began to think it was entirely within the realm of possibility that it was she who had caused their emotional distance, which felt as vast as the ocean that often separated them. And bingo, there it was.

Usually when Gaillard was reserved or curt with her, she demonstrated her love, holding him more closely, stroking his back, canceling plans to stay with him and offer some cheer, and he in turn would usually come around with expressions of adoration. But somewhere along the line, and she didn't know where or when, she had begun taking his moods to heart and reciprocating his remoteness in kind. Moreover, she had on many occasions approached him with reserve, waiting for a sign of affection, the signal it was safe to show hers. And so they went, round and round, one reacting to the other in a love match neither won.

The only way out of the game was to drop the ball, toss her pride, place her heart back in his hands. *Have some understanding. He simply doesn't know how to express his feelings.*

As she packed his rain jacket, she was glad the wives wouldn't be joining them on the boat. She thought back to the last time she had seen them. The conversation was always the same, word for word.

"Charles is so ill tempered," Agnes had announced.

"You should see Walter," Lucille complained. "He stomps around the house in utter misery. Grew up poor, you know. By the end of the weekend I want to stab him with his dessert fork, which is always lodged in a wedge of chocolate cake or his mouth."

"It must be *exhausting* for you, Dorothy, to keep up with the social schedule that's ensued after your wedding," Agnes said. "And one needs to pack dozens of outfits for travel, and you can't remember in which house you left the black Chanel frock, so you must buy four of everything to put in each of your homes and spend hours fitting them all."

"It's an absolute horror traveling with thirteen trunks, but at least they're all Louis Vuitton. I've made it easy for the chauffeurs to recognize them, and they can fetch everything posthaste," Lilian said.

Oh, thank goodness they're not coming along. I'm in no mood for the nonsense, Dorothy thought, recalling that day at Twenty-One. Binky Melon was there. She gulped down four glasses of Veuve Clicquot before they finished the first. Binky had everything in life she could wish for except self-restraint. Moving aside her dish, on which one string of spaghetti remained, she unleashed a profanity-filled rant about the poor, damn, dumb pilot who, for fifteen minutes, held up her private flight to Cuba because he was waiting for his coffee to brew. Speaking very slowly with a slight slur and giving great emphasis to each word, she concluded, "He was too blockheaded to know better."

The others laughed at Binky while Dorothy sat quietly thinking what a half-wit the man must be; no one should have to wait at those prices. Dorothy was something of a spoiled girl—this she had always admitted to herself—but the unseriousness with which she and they carried on suddenly seemed alarming. She felt that something within her was starting to change.

If there was any vindication to the frivolity of it all, it was their philanthropic work and fundraisers. Never mind that it largely served the purpose of putting oneself in the spotlight, each host desperately trying to outdo the others with a formidable guest list and an ingenious theme. Her mind wandered to Cheerio 2nd, the benefit for Southampton Hospital where patrons from across the Hamptons colony put on a spectacular amateur show that opened with the rise of velvet curtains donated by Florenz Ziegfeld, who said to her in the booming timbre of a ringmaster that it was *he* who gave her a start. Gaillard smiled with cool superiority and allowed several moments of silence as Ziegfeld's nose twitched. "Good luck, old chap," Gaillard said, his eyes bright and piercing. With a nod, he turned and led her away.

"You are splendid," Dorothy said, wrapping her arm around his waist and squeezing his side. "Let's have a drink, shall we?"

Having briefly paid their respects to their acquaintances, they explored the carnival on their own, laughing and chatting and finding places to be away from the crowd. Sitting on a bench under an apple tree, he stroked her hair and kissed her softly on the cheek. An inescapable yearning rushed forth, causing her to slide her hand on his knee.

"Shall we go, darling?" she asked, caressing his neck and kissing him gently on the corner of his mouth, indicating he was to take her home, and take her completely. That day they looked at each other like that first night at the St. Regis Hotel. That day there was still an attraction between them and a love they didn't want to lose.

As the captain guided the boat toward Montauk, she stood at the bow and looked out to sea. Hearing them howl with laughter, she made her way back to Gaillard's side and stroked his back for only a moment, but long enough. The men deftly balanced martinis while making dollar bets on horse races at Belmont Park. When the Shinnecock lighthouse came into view, Gaillard turned to her with a loving smile and kept a soft, steady gaze into her eyes. She thought of their first visit to the Hamptons, walking the sandy shore, when he said he wanted her to be his forever. She knew by his expression there was a chance she would be.

Dorothy opened her new diary and scribbled *February 1928,* vowing to write regularly so she could see the arc of her life on paper. She stared at the blank page and hoped to fill it with something wonderful about Gaillard. Glancing out the window, she caught sight of him, his arm around the shoulder of the hotel photographer. She'd seen this before and knew what was to come.

There he was, posing grandly with the ocean in the background, his smile broad. He changed position. Hands on his hips, feet spread, king of the world. Then, the victorious smile. The feigned laugh. The confident smirk. Casual cool, piercing, indifferent, amused. *Absurd.*

Clare didn't bother to knock on the door as she swept into the living room of the suite, her noontime ritual to gather the troops. Maggie and Jane sauntered in, nibbled on grapes from the tray, and chattered away until they all left to toast themselves on the beach.

With a linen cloche shading her eyes, Dorothy leaned back on a red-striped folding chair in the sand and adjusted the skirt of her navy bathing suit. She thought of Gaillard and George.

"I suppose by now the boys are off smoking cigars and looking for balls," Dorothy said with one corner of her lip turned up as she turned to Clare.

"They could use some," Clare lobbed back.

"Apparently it's a champion golf course," Dorothy said, smiling. "So by day's end the boys will either be mad with defeat or elated."

"Or inebriated. George will be," said Clare.

"This will be a good year. I just have that feeling," Dorothy said cheerfully.

"Dorothy darling, you say that every year," Maggie replied, keeping her eyes closed to the brightness of the day.

"Yes, and so far I've been right. Have I mentioned Gaillard and I are moving to the Drake Hotel? Then I'm going to Paris for workshops at L'École des Beaux-Arts. Will any of you be there?"

"Yes," said Clare, "I'm spending the spring and summer in Europe while the Fifth Avenue house is razed to the ground. I suppose I should be worried that George will be sleeping when the wrecking ball takes its mighty swing. But alas . . ."

"I can't go to Paris," Jane said. "I want to get the new house in Jaimanitas in order. I'm going to fill it with a gaggle of animals—flamingos, foxes, peacocks and bears—and a crowd of theater people!" She pulled her hat over her brow and chuckled, enlivened by the idea of living in Cuba with her fiancé.

"Are you all joining me at the Charity Carnival on the second of May at Madison Square Garden?" asked Dorothy.

"I wouldn't miss it," said Maggie.

"They're staging a fashion show, an oriental pageant, music and dancing, and a midnight Follies presentation called *The Streets of Baghdad*. They've gone all out," said Dorothy. She had purchased a box so she could entertain comfortably, away from the circus of the main seating area.

"Bergdorf's just got in some gorgeous dresses with jeweled necklines. Did you see them?" asked Maggie.

"Yes, I had my eye on one." Dorothy sipped her mimosa and was glad that she'd decided to wear something from her wardrobe. Enough was enough.

Then they all considered the matter of attire for the wedding of the year, that of their friend Estelle Manville and Count Folke Bernadotte of Wisborg, the nephew of King Gustaf of Sweden. Estelle was to become a princess. Clare, feeling she had been outdone, suggested Patou dresses for the girls while planning to wear a show-stopping custom gown by Mainbocher, perhaps in a queen-blue color.

Reclined on cotton chairs facing the rolling ocean, their wavy locks thickened by the salty air, the girls had more on their minds than they would say in conversation. Maggie speculated about why Gaillard was leaving a week earlier than Dorothy. Dorothy reflected on why Clare was still married to George. Clare would have given anything to know if Jane was having second thoughts about her impending wedding. Jane was curious if Clare mistakenly thought she'd made a pass at George. Rather than bringing up all the messy business, they talked about *Vogue*.

"Have you noticed how many of these *Vogue* covers resemble you, Dorothy? They're all perfectly timed to your life," Maggie said. "Look at these. January, February, and this one from March, it shows your black, fur-cuffed robe, pearl drop earrings, and flowers in the background of the picture. Glamour and nature. That's you. I think your visits to my office have been noted by the art director of the magazine."

"What about the September issue, the month Dorothy was married?" Jane remembered. "The illustration was the spitting image of her. The brunette bob, the gray frock with long pearls, the black-and-white checkered floor like the one at Rolling Rock."

"Only you would know details like that," Dorothy said with a warm smile. "We're lucky, aren't we? We will always have each other. Love and loyalty!" Certain her loyalty was well placed, she raised her glass in a toast, a snapshot in time that her friends would later recall.

"Love and loyalty. Hear, hear!" they cheered.

April 1, 1928. Dorothy noticed the pages of her diary were nearly full yet void of intimate detail. Just some notes about galas and galleries, favored clubs, memorable spots around the world—it was more about places than moments, save for the entry she made in Bermuda. *His silence is louder than usual* was all she wrote about Gaillard. Placing the diary back in the drawer, she looked out the window to the English garden in the back of her Southampton home and watched him saunter off to the pool.

They had arrived early in the season, long before the mass of friends descended upon the town for the Fourth of July soirée at the Toppers' house overlooking the ocean. This would allow them time to recoup after their annual sojourn to Europe in the spring, which was, as always, rejuvenating. Paris. Deauville. Rome. Baden-Baden. There were grand balls, quiet country walks, and the occasional display of debauchery at artists' parties on the Left Bank. Life in Southampton was simpler. They had settled into a routine of small gatherings, dinners at home, and sailing the pristine waters. When Gaillard played golf, she sculpted in her studio and painted by Lake Agawam in the back of their property where, during those quiet hours, she would assess the state of their union. *No marriage is perfect*, she would inevitably conclude with vague acceptance.

She stood outside the front door waiting for her friends to arrive as the summer sun lowered in the sky. A warm breeze brushed her shoulders. Tulips swayed, the soft pink blossoms the same shade as her cheeks that were brightened from days of leisure. Chin up and head tilted back, she closed her eyes to take in a moment of peace.

"Now stop that, Claude," she chided, the miniature dachshund pawing her dress. Having become the foremost breeder of this pint-sized hound, she forewent the title of esteemed sculptress on one too many occasions when introduced by those who didn't know better. Her twelve other blue-ribbon dachshunds scuttled about as she counted one by one all the way to thirteen. Hearing a car approach, she checked her wristwatch.

Maggie and Clare waved from the windows. They were right on time.

"Hello, darling! This was Clare's idea," Maggie said, sounding a little awkward, as she stepped out of the car and handed Dorothy a large box.

"We couldn't arrive empty-handed, so we stopped at Max and Clara Fortunoff's store," said Clare. "I'm told they have the highest-quality cookware in town. Have you seen the ads? They say, *Live Rich. You Can Afford To!* So we splurged." Her chauffeur took five boxes from the trunk and set them on the ground, then waited for instructions.

"Please, bring them inside to Gabrielle and she'll make you lunch," Dorothy said to him. Eyeing the boxes, she knew that Clare's gift was a thinly veiled commentary that Dorothy had given in to a life of domesticity, save for a pack of champion hounds.

"Darling," she said to Clare, who had no prospects for work, "this is a terrific reminder that we all must have our own accomplishments. Solely being a wife is the diamond-paved road to hell. Isn't that what you said recently?"

"That's right," Clare answered, nodding slowly.

"Now," Dorothy said, opening the front door, "don't mind the man in the sunroom. He's painting frescoes, but he'll be finished tomorrow. *House and Garden* magazine did a feature on the murals in Selma Lewisohn's salon in Paris, and it inspired me."

"And what—or who—inspired this?" asked Clare as she picked up a large sketch pad and regarded the masculine profile on the first page.

"Oh," Dorothy replied, watching Clare turn the pages. "Those are just some drawings I did. I wanted to get the facial features just right before I start to paint. It will be a scene in England. He looks like a prince, wouldn't you say?"

"Actually, he looks like Archibald Leach."

"Who?"

"My old friend Archie. He's a juggler—the best-looking man in vaudeville."

Dorothy called for Gabrielle while the girls settled into their rooms. It was de rigueur for them to travel without their husbands, whether to Dorothy's or to Biarritz, the Riviera, or Deauville where they went every year, leaving behind Prohibition, which made upstanding citizens into outlaws for enjoying a good glass of wine. It was no secret to Dorothy that the estates of the Gold Coast were visited regularly by rumrunners who zipped across the Long Island Sound to make illicit deliveries of liquor, which were then hidden away in haystacks in barns. Astonished when she heard of it, she went straight to the Port Washington Library and listened to audio recordings of local kids like Chappie Miller, who said he and his friends would run down to the docks at night when they saw the boats coming in. Chappie was too young to understand booze but old enough to hope for a quarter if he'd scram, which he inevitably was asked to do. She left the library, went down to the docks, and handed rolls of quarters to the kids, urging them to go home to safety.

Gaillard charmed the girls that evening at dinner. He told them gripping stories about Captain Kidd, who had buried treasures all across the Hamptons, and how World War I torpedoes were tested in Sag Harbor and remained in the waters nearby. When the subject of show business came up, Clare suggested to Dorothy that she should visit Los Angeles and have another whack at acting, causing Gaillard to take a swig of scotch and loosen his necktie.

"Dorothy, if you think the winding roads in Provence make for precarious driving, you would loathe the hills of Hollywood where any aspiring actress might surely end up," he remarked, tension in the air suddenly thick. Clare stole a glance at Maggie and looked tempted to raise her knife of conversation.

"Dorothy, you could always stay in the flats at the Beverly Hills Hotel and get a driver," said Clare, serving herself green peas and onions from the tray that Benjamin held at her side. "Anyway, I must say these gardenias are divine," she continued, looking at the blooms floating in the bowl at the center of the table. "You know, it's said the scent lowers stress."

"Clare, are you still writing that play?" asked Maggie.

"Yes, I hope it makes it to Broadway. Gaillard, it's a black comedy. It's about a wealthy man who fakes his own suicide so that he can escape from his narcissistic wife and elope with his secretary. To hell with the *Bookman Journal*," she said, referring to an article about how people believed that Broadway and the new talkies were the moral decline of America. "Did you read it?"

She excused herself from the table to retrieve it, returning moments later.

"This is what it says about Broadway and Hollywood. 'It is at once an enticement and a hell, a Circe's cavern of lascivious and soul-destroying delights, an unholy place where the producers are the seducers of women, where stars without talent are made meretriciously overnight, where pure girls succumb to rich admirers for diamond brooches, furs, imported automobiles, apartments, and other luxuries.'" With a shake of her head, she flipped the magazine closed. "Is it really any different from the Upper East Side of New York?"

"If morality can be destroyed by the arts, we're all in trouble," said Maggie.

"The rising popularity of tabloid news clearly indicates that the public wants to hear about sex, slaughter and betrayal, and the rich falling from grace," said Clare.

"Nonetheless," Dorothy said, "the *New York Times* is doing well. As a matter of fact, they wrote in an editorial, and I quote, the readers' desire is not to be amused or scandalized; it is to be informed."

Given the expressions on Maggie and Clare's faces, she sensed they had the feeling that her marriage, like Clare's, was not long for this world. It was the feeling she had about Jane, who had married the Pan American Airways executive Grant Mason. No one had the nerve to tell her before the nuptials that it was a colossal mistake and she would quickly tire of the institution. They knew she wouldn't have listened anyway. Girls in love never do.

One of the last girls standing was Rosamond, who was at the pinnacle of her career as the star of *Midsummer Night's Dream*, set to open on Broadway the following month. Dorothy had arranged tickets for herself and Clare, expecting they would watch the play with an irrepressible zeal for theater and an undeniable yearning in their lives, convinced they could somehow have it all if only they understood what "all" exactly meant. To the legions of women who followed their lives in the press, they already did.

Society columnists tracked their every move, their seating at dinners, and the charm they exuded. The most fawning of all the reporters was Maury Paul from the *New York Journal-American*, who wrote under the pen name Cholly Knickerbocker, a man who wielded more power with the upper crust than Alva Belmont herself. For all the women who prided themselves on the most elegant dinner or the most impeccable taste or most successful charity event, debutante ball, or wedding, Maury's public acknowledgement was a seal of approval, and without it, they might as well have stayed home, which they frequently wished they had done when Maury turned his pen on them. But it would all come back to him when *Time* magazine proclaimed him the "fat, vain little Maury Henry Biddle Paul who coined the phrase 'Café Society' and made a fat living insulting it." Dorothy and Clare saw it coming.

As they adjourned to the card room, the conversation turned to their plans for the following day.

"I had to invite Cholly, of course," said Dorothy. "He'd better behave when he writes about it."

"Hats off to you for co-hosting with the vapid Mrs. Littlejohn, who, as you know, has little care for the crippled children the fundraiser will benefit. Although I hear John Bouvier is co-hosting. That certainly makes the trouble worthwhile. And as for Cholly," Clare said with an annunciatory tone, "there won't be a wet eye in the house at his funeral."

"Yes, even though he's ever so clever, that little Maury Paul," Maggie replied, "so very competent at putting two little words together to make such grand statements, words like 'old guard' for blue bloods and 'Lawng Oylanders' for the unfortunate souls on the South Shore of Long Island with those accents and pocket-sized estates."

"Happy told me some women ensure themselves a steady stream of accolades by donating money to the ever-expanding pockets of his custom suits," Clare added.

"Happy has a penchant for acquiring information," said Maggie, smiling. "She told Mabel it's simple. She seduces men who have the answers she wants to know, concluding, 'Information is power.'" Dorothy and Clare laughed.

"I can't imagine women actually pay Cholly for good press or that he would accept it," Dorothy said.

"Well, *you* certainly don't need to," Maggie answered. "Everyone knows he has a thing for you. He's admitted on more than one inebriated occasion that he envies your goodness. You're everything he is not. 'Ahhh, Dorothy. Delicious. She's considerate. Kind. Pure. A light that shines among our people!' he says, while he is catty and cruel." It made Dorothy like him.

After the evening drew to a close and Maggie and Clare had gone to their rooms, Gaillard poured himself a scotch and took a sip as he leaned back in his club chair in the living room. Dorothy dropped onto the sofa feeling pleasantly tipsy.

"Gaillard, darling," she said lightly, "I've been waiting to tell you, I've been invited to manage the Demmette Galleries. Funny how it happened, really. I suggested they introduce French art to the American public, and they insisted I be the one to do so. I could make it the international headquarters of French art."

"Well," he said with pause, "you can work on that, or you can work on this marriage." The words came in a slow and measured tone, which always made her nervous, but less nervous than when he was silent.

With no further thought, she dropped the idea altogether. Certainly this tension between them couldn't go on forever, whatever the cause of his discontent. On some days she was certain she was the cause; he must find her utterly, maddeningly, hopelessly annoying. On others, she wondered what it could possibly be. He was short with his brother, he yelled at the driver, he returned entrées and fired his staff. Thus, she resigned herself to her role as a full-time wife and would endeavor to play it well.

"Darling," she cooed with a tender smile as she rose from the sofa, "you're absolutely right, and besides, there's nothing I want more than to be here with you." And with that sentiment she seated herself on his lap while leaning in to touch his lips with hers, and with a little reluctance he took her into his arms.

In the morning, as she savored her morning coffee, she looked at the calendar. August 25, 1928—the date she had eagerly anticipated.

Finally! Carnival Day! For months she had planned the event, overseeing vendors and guest lists, calling friends and acquaintances, garnering support and hoping to see approval in Gaillard's eyes. His mother had given birth to a crippled boy who was taken by God too young, and Dorothy's fundraiser would raise a substantial amount of money for others with the affliction.

The instant Cholly saw Dorothy graciously tending to her guests, gliding through the crowd with an air of elegance, her soft pink dress clinging to her svelte figure, he turned to Maggie and said, "If I were a woman, she is the woman I would want to be." But Maggie paid little attention, distracted by the sight of Happy Longhorn in a fuchsia sequin skirt.

It was unanimously decided that Happy was the most conspicuous of all the guests, which would have pleased her immensely if only she had known. Midway through the festivities, she asked what organization they were supporting—"Something to do with free camp for kids?"—while accidentally spilling red wine on her blouse, which Dorothy said was just as well because Happy therefore left early, already far too deep in the cups. Besides, she had only attended to make an appearance. As for the others, there was lingering doubt in Dorothy's mind that their contributions were born of humility, simplicity, and charity, the three virtues engrained in her mind as clearly as they were etched on the stained-glass window of the chapel at St. Joseph's Academy.

Carnival Day proved a smashing success and a fine way to end the season in the Hamptons. In the evening, after a light dinner and glass of wine, Dorothy and Gaillard strolled to the back of their property where the pool glistened in the moonlight. Slipping off their robes, they said nothing, and floated into the cool water. He came to her. He pulled her in closely and placed his hand on the top of her head. He pushed down gently.

"Don't do it," she said.

He looked at her with feigned childlike innocence.

"Don't dunk me. I don't like when my head is underwater. It scares me." Looking into his gleaming eyes, she was met with a glazed, blank stare. "I mean it. I nearly drowned in the ocean when I was young. My brother plucked me from the waves just in time."

"Oh, come on," he said sweetly, but dismissively. "Don't you trust me?"

Not entirely, she thought. *There's a side of you I don't understand. What if you snap? No one would believe you did it. Is this instinct or a case of a runaway imagination? How could I think such a thing? He's gentle.*

"Of course I trust you," she said. Now she would have to prove it. "But I don't like my head to be underwater."

She succumbed to the pressure of his hand. As her face plunged below the water's surface, she thought her odds of survival were, perhaps, fifty-fifty.

The frigid air numbed Dorothy's fingers as she stood outside the chapel and looked up at the brick belfry, the steady chime of the church bells calling her to attention. She closed her eyes, asked God for guidance, and thanked Him for His blessed gifts. Her gratitude deepened more when she stepped inside the chapel and heard the boys and girls sing "Amazing Grace," the hymn she still sang on occasion. But even the most hardened of hearts were touched by the angelic voices of the two choirs at Estelle Manville's wedding ceremony in the Episcopal Church of St. John, the chapel exquisitely wrapped in ivy in the tony setting of Pleasantville, New York.

Dorothy and Gaillard took their places in the third pew where Maggie, Clare, George, Jane, and Grant had already been seated. There was barely a whisper among the guests, their jewels and eyes shimmering in the golden hue cast from hundreds of candles. During a saintly rendition of *Lohengrin's* "Wedding March," Dorothy looked up to the cathedral-like ceiling and prayed for Estelle's contentment in her new life in Stockholm, far away from her own familiar world. More than 2,000 people waited outside the church in the frosty December wind, with 2,000 more along the road to Hi-Esmarco, the Manville family home. They eagerly anticipated a glimpse of the bride, once a local girl and now royalty in her velvet-and-lace gown trimmed with seed pearls and aged to a soft ivory. A large brooch of diamonds and pearls was set at her breast. A diamond coronet crowned her veil.

By the time Frederic Lake's holiday supper party rolled around three weeks later at the St. Regis Hotel, Dorothy had been to a dozen events, few of which Gaillard attended. She found her place card on table number two, positioned between Jack Wilson, son of the late John Percy Wilson, founder of one of the largest banks, and James Butler, who was head of a large bank in the South and had led the relief committee of New Orleans after the devastating 1927 flood.

"I hope the people of New Orleans were fairly compensated," Dorothy mentioned as plates of duck à l'orange were served. She knew the answer was that they hadn't been and they should have been. Jack swiftly brought the conversation back around to the country's economy, how the income of the American worker had increased over the last nine years and inflation was low.

"Yes, it's terrific. Workers have seen an eight percent increase in wages and business has increased by sixty-five percent," Dorothy added.

"That's right. But this economy won't last. Its very foundation is on credit," Jack cautioned. He had liked her since the moment they met in 1924 and never could decide if his instinct was to marry or adopt her.

"That's what I hear, but everyone is still in the market, even people who can't afford to lose their investments," she said.

"Dangerous game, dangerous game. They don't know how the traders and bankers manipulate the market. It's not as robust as people think—not even close," said James.

"It will be devastating when it blows up," said Jack, shaking his head at the thought.

"I hope it's not a complete collapse," said Dorothy.

Gulping his wine, James's elephantine forehead shone with perspiration. "New Orleans isn't ready for another catastrophe."

"A collapse would provide excellent opportunities—buy when the stocks are down," Jack advised. "Dorothy, drop by my office tomorrow. I'll give you a list of solid investments, if you can wait it out."

"Yes, I'll stop in." She was curious to see if they were the same as Gaillard's picks. Oh, but it was such a *relief* to finally be talking about something other than Estelle's crown of jewels and eye-popping wedding that everyone at the other end of the table was still a-chatter about because "it was such a *fine* affair," they assured the Smiths of Alabama. "It's a *shame* you didn't see it."

As the evening wore on, she counted the days to her departure for Cuba for the last party of the year. Twenty-four. First, however, there was Christmas with Gaillard. And then, reflecting on his moods, she was struck with a thought. *Socrates said sometimes we put walls up not to keep people out but to see who cares enough to break them down.* She knew just what to do.

At half past five the following evening, Gaillard emerged from his office the moment she was walking by with three bouquets of roses in her arms.

"Dinner at seven? I'm afraid I'll be tied up with work until then, putting out some fires," he said with an unmistakable look of concern.

"Sure, darling," she answered. "Whenever you're ready."

With a nod and a turn, he stepped back into his office and closed the doors behind him. She heard the telephone in his office ring. Then, a loud thwack. He'd smashed the receiver against the desk again.

She hurried to the kitchen, swung open the cabinet, pulled out two tremendous wooden bowls, each of which contained rose petals she had plucked from their stems earlier in the day, and she set them on the counter. With a feeling of excitement, she stepped out of her shoes, picked up a bowl, scurried quietly down the hallway, and stopped in front of Gaillard's office. Bending down, she scattered them in a line and moved carefully backwards, leaving a trail to the library, round the corner, up the stairwell, one flight, two flights, three flights, stopping at four. The bowl was empty. She ran down the stairs, through the corridors, and into the kitchen where she put down the empty bowl and picked up the other, then turned and retraced her steps. At the top of the stairwell, she scattered the petals in the design of an arrow pointing right, in the direction of the study. Just one last thing to do and she would be ready.

Hearing the soft thump of Gaillard's footsteps coming down the hallway, Dorothy rose from the sofa and stood facing the door. On the table behind her were two glasses, one bottle of Dom Pérignon, and a cut of blue silk fabric she had draped over a sculpture nearly three feet high.

He stood in the doorway, looking at her with raised eyebrows and an expression of curiosity.

"Champagne, darling?"

"Please," he said, walking toward her. "Sorry it's so late. I don't know why you put up with me." She took the glass from the table, handed it to him, and led him by the arm to the sofa.

"Because you're splendid, and you put up with me."

"By the looks of things it seems we've retraced our rose-petal steps to the night of my marriage proposal," he acknowledged, looking somewhat uncomfortable.

"Yes," she said, taking a large sip of champagne. And then another. "Now I have a proposal for you. I sense that you've been under some pressure." Looking into his eyes, as bright and blue as an arctic sheet in the rays of the winter sun, the man she knew wasn't there. The moment passed when she wanted to say she'd been feeling distance between them, he must be feeling it too—how or when it began and what had changed, she didn't know. Having drawn no response, she continued. "I've been thinking, how about if we retrace our steps a little farther and go to Paris for an early Christmas, just the two of us?"

"A Paris Christmas! What a nice idea," he said with a lack of enthusiasm, little commitment, and no acknowledgment of anything else she had said. Suddenly she felt so alone.

"And I have a surprise for you," she said, managing a warm smile. Patting his hand, she rose from her seat and stepped over to the table. "Come here, darling."

"What do we have here?" he asked, regarding the blue silk covering.

"Are you ready?" She lifted the fabric in a grand gesture. "Voilà!" It was a marble bust carved in his likeness. He sprang from his chair in delight. "It was done by Isamu Noguchi, the sculptor I introduced you to."

"Why, it's magnificent!" he said, running his hand over its smooth surface. "Aren't you a love," he said softly.

And for the remaining hours of the evening he spoke—in what could only be called soliloquy—of the sculpture, the artistry, and the placement of the piece, of his hectic schedule and his hunting trip, of a new lyric he'd written and old song he'd forgotten, and, at last, of nothing at all, sinking them into a silence from which they could not recover.

Three days passed in silence, save for monosyllabic and empty words from Gaillard. Five days. Seven days. Each day perspiration fell from his brow as he emerged from his office at home. Each other day he gave her a peck on the cheek before bed. Ten days. Fourteen. On her calendar, she crossed off the days in big red Xs and the month in black.

9.

CUPID'S GRAVEYARD

The morning sun warmed Dorothy's delicate face as she strolled through the tropical gardens at Jane and Grant's home in Cuba, the sweet scent of mariposa flowers reawakening her spirit. Her silken peach-colored housedress brushed her leg as a white Persian cat rubbed its head against her and purred with satisfaction. A flock of birds whistled cheerfully in the trees, hopping along branches. She stopped to see how close they would come. *Le Pere Pol*, she remembered, the bird charmer in the Tuileries Gardens. She flinched when a bird fluttered its wings by her cheek before landing on her arm, its feathers intricate swirls of teal and olive. The corners of her lips rose in delight as she drew in a long breath of air and rested her bare shoulder on the sturdy bole of a fern. It would be hours before the others awoke. They had danced too long into the night.

It had been the first New Year's Eve that Dorothy did not pronounce a good year was ahead. She was all too aware of the simmering troubles of her friends, and she had deep concerns of her own. There was no telling what was beneath Gaillard's silence and polite smiles. Would she wake up one day to find out he was through, it was over, she was on her own again? Would it be tomorrow or ten years hence? Ten years, no; she would avail herself a certain period of time to improve the marriage. But how long could she wait for him to come around? How long could she hold on? Stretching her legs on the chaise lounge under a lush banyan, she picked up a magazine that someone had left behind. With no interest in reading, her thoughts drifted to the unknown of her future.

When she looked down at the creased edges of the magazine, she stopped her hands from fidgeting and looked at the cover. The *Vogue* illustration showed a woman playing chess with human figurines as the pawns. It got her thinking—not about using people to win, but about carefully planning her moves.

"*Bel ange*," Clare said, sitting beside her, "you look as though you have something on your mind. I know the look too well."

"I must have been lost in thought. I didn't even hear you approaching. What are you doing awake so early?"

"It must have been the repugnant odor of absinthe coming from George that woke me. I don't know if he drank it or bathed in it," she said as she smoothed Dorothy's hair and sat on the chaise next to hers.

"He was terrifically drunk," said Dorothy. "George doesn't get . . . rough with you, does he? He was awfully riled up last night."

Clare paused before answering. "George? Rough?" she said in an unconvincing tone of surprise.

"You *must* leave him immediately if he is. Absinthe makes people mad. Look what it did to Van Gogh."

"Surely that's what made him cut off his own ear."

"But think of all the nonsense from Paul Gauguin that he didn't have to listen to," Dorothy said with a little smile.

"Good point. I've found a better way—I'm thinking of divorcing George." They looked ahead in silence.

"I can see how unhappy you've become. You look drawn and you've been short tempered."

"I'm melting down from the constant deluge of indignities," Clare said, her voice trembling.

"What is going on?"

Clare couldn't answer. Teardrops fell from her eyes.

"Have you tried talking to him?" asked Dorothy while recognizing her own feeble attempt to do so with Gaillard had failed spectacularly. "You're only twenty-five. There's time to salvage it, unless he's being a brute," she continued, feeling somewhat hopeless about her own marriage. "Does he know you had an affair with what's-his-name, the financier?"

"Yes, and he isn't pleased. I've tried desperately to make our marriage work. I've told him time and again, 'George, love is a verb,' but he doesn't change. This is in confidence, but I met with a lawyer. By the end of the month I'll present him with a separation agreement." She dabbed her eyes with a handkerchief and tucked it in the fold of her cuff.

"I'm here for you," Dorothy said, exercising restraint in telling her of her own troubles, which would reflect poorly on Gaillard and ultimately be a mistake should she decide to stay with him after all. But she had some feeling of envy toward Clare, who invariably exposed her every thought with no caution or concern of a possible consequence. It must be liberating, but surely it was unwise.

"And the worst of it is," Clare continued, "aside from the fact that I may end up with half a million dollars, which is what I spend in a year, I can't come up with a good excuse to be missing the Prince of Wales' gala in March. I don't want everyone to know I'm in Reno for a divorce."

"They'll know," Dorothy said, reassuring herself that there was no cause for her own concern over money, and that there wouldn't be at any time in the future. For Clare, on the other hand, too much was never enough. "The tabloid reporters are just waiting for news, and there are plenty of women who would tip them off. At least now you only need three months' residency in Reno to obtain the divorce. Cornelius Vanderbilt is there. He could give you the lay of the land," Dorothy concluded with a hint of a smile.

"I'm sure he could," Clare lobbed back with a coltish look. "But would it mitigate three months in Cupid's graveyard with dreadfully sad women?"

"It's true, the men don't go. Divorce is a woman's work." And it was. They estimated 80 percent of the visitors were women there for quickie divorces. "For the men," Dorothy said, waving her hand, "it's as easy as a stock trade."

"And sometimes as costly."

Dorothy lay back on her chaise, holding back the tears welling in her eyes. If she were to obtain a divorce, she would be committing an act that was irreversible, that was condemned by the Vatican. But upon further reflection she realized it was widely accepted in the beau monde. Thus the title of divorcée would be of no consequence to her now and wouldn't be later.

They spoke not a word of the subject again for weeks. And then, on the morning of February 14, Dorothy held the telephone to her ear while reaching for the newspaper neatly folded on her desk.

"All right, Clare, I have the paper. What should I be looking for?"

"Take a look at the front page."

"Mob hit ordered by Al Capone," Dorothy read.

"Look at the headline."

"Valentine's Day Massacre," Dorothy read.

"Yes. How fitting. Today I leave George."

She left immediately for Reno, and for the first time in her adulthood, there was no staff to tend to her prodigious needs. On the twentieth of May, 1929, she called Dorothy to say her divorce was finalized. Everyone on board the *Aquitania* for the prince's fundraiser knew why she wasn't there, but they didn't know why Gaillard wasn't with Dorothy. Happy Longhorn had seen them lunching at the Colony the day before.

On the night following the fundraiser, Alva, Elsa, and Dorothy dined in the grand ballroom of the SS *Ile de France*, its massive hull leaving a white spray of foam in its wake. They watched as Dorothy picked at the asparagus tips on her dish. She stole a glance at Happy, who was seated across the room and wearing the same violet gown as the evening before.

"Maggie, Jane, and Estelle all send their regards," Dorothy remembered to say.

"Why didn't they join us?" asked Elsa.

"Maggie is working, Jane and Estelle are traveling, and Clare is still in Reno. Next week she'll go to her mother's house in Sound Beach to recover from the divorce."

"Well, Clare will be fine," said Alva.

As Alva and Elsa discussed the booming business in Reno, Dorothy's thoughts were far away. Upon her return to the States in two weeks' time, she would have much to do to prepare for the new chapter of her life.

"There's a certain *je ne sais quoi* in the air," Alva said, looking at Dorothy.

"Darling, I've been meaning to tell you, Jack Wilson says to avoid stocks and debt. It's only a matter of time before the great bubble bursts," Dorothy said, and then continued a little wistfully. "All good things come to an end. You know that, Elsa. As soon as one of your parties is over, you immediately plan the next."

"We can all learn a life lesson from that," said Alva, while Elsa nodded in agreement. They both turned to Dorothy.

"I'm here for you," Elsa said with a tone of reassurance, "to help with any planning you might have in mind."

The flickering light of morning woke Dorothy as the train chugged along a barren desert landscape. She kept her eyes closed, the low rumble of the engine reminding her of where she was, where she had been for days. Ten hours left to Reno—enough time to finish her book, *The Age of Innocence*—and three months to a divorce. She would take rest in a reserved suite at the Riverside Hotel, the red brick building next to the courthouse, and she would be granted her freedom on the twenty-eighth of September. She was sure to see people she knew who would undoubtedly ask too many questions that she would have to delicately evade in order to retain some privacy, for she loathed the notion of strangers foraging through the foibles of her marriage.

She wouldn't say she had packed her belongings and then asked Gaillard for a divorce. Or that she asked during dinner at a restaurant uptown, where he wouldn't unleash the criticisms that he might have been holding at bay. She wouldn't describe his widened eyes or how he said, "Are you . . . serious?" She wouldn't tell them that he didn't ask her to stay, that he only said, "Is your decision final? Is there anything I can do to change your mind?" *That's Gaillard*, she thought, *too stoic or starkly uncaring.* When they said goodbye, he told her he would always love her, but she didn't believe him. She believed this was what he wanted but couldn't summon up the courage to do.

She knew that her departure would be seen as an impulsive act to those who didn't know the progression of events, but she had planned it for months. *If it's still this way in six months, I will have to leave,* she had promised herself.

She could hardly muster a smile when the hotel clerk handed her the key to her suite and, with it, a note from Cornelius Vanderbilt Jr. that read, "Welcome to the city of broken vows!" It was clipped to his novel that he had named, simply, *Reno,* for no further description was needed. It was the biggest little city in the West, with every temptation imaginable for a lonely heart or those with a tendency toward overindulgence of any kind, be it haute couture, liquor, or ladies of the night. This city of sin had become the epicenter of gossip, and as any gossip worthy of the title would gladly tell you, there was no better place to get it than at the café at the Riverside Hotel. That's where Happy Longhorn cornered Dorothy on a quiet August morning. She marched right over, plopped her brand-new wide-brimmed fuchsia hat on the table in a startling bang, the mammoth stone of her pink sapphire ring smacking the fragile glass, then slid a hand over her immense and exposed breasts to adjust her black lace brassiere, and sat down.

Happy asked Dorothy in one breathless sentence, "The newspapers say you and Gaillard just bought the building at 600 Madison Avenue and I quote, 'with mortgages aggregating six hundred and ten thousand dollars,' *why* would you sign a mortgage when you were planning a divorce, why are you divorcing, anyway?"

Her attention to detail was astonishing. Dorothy knew that Happy considered divorce an appeal to arms, having battled it out with her two ex-husbands. Happy would never understand an amicable parting or why Gaillard had sent flowers to the Riverside Hotel with the message "Yours, Gaillard." No, Happy wouldn't understand this at all, and like the others, she was left to wonder what had gone wrong. Of course, rumors would abound when Dorothy appeared in public with Gardner, the man she had recently met. They would take one look at his stunning smile and blame the divorce on him.

"Come on now, Happy. Introspection is out of vogue. Enough of that boring business. Did you hear about Leonard and Helen Bullock? A shame. I expect we'll see her here any day now."

"I know! But you don't know the latest. I'll tell you . . ."

Dorothy was deft at eluding the questions she had already been asked by people with much sharper minds than Happy, if not with more social grace. People like Cholly Knickerbocker, who got no grist for his mill when he phoned Dorothy and started the conversation by saying, "If ever two people were mis-mated it was you and Gaillard!"

"But we are excellent exes," she replied, for she and Gaillard were of the mind that a couple's personal business should be private.

And while she knew that one could find a sense of relief in sharing these matters with friends, she was well aware it would merely be a temporary balm, the consequences of which could last a lifetime. The friend would mention it to another friend, who would then mention it to someone like Cholly, and the next thing you knew, your marriage was the main course of conversation at a dinner party. Still, she did confide to Maggie, Elsa, and Clare that she asked Gaillard for a divorce, to which they each replied, "I've been expecting this call."

Admittedly, there was a temptation to recount the many moments that added up to this one. But if she couldn't entirely understand the unraveling of her marriage, she surely couldn't explain it in any way other than exasperated confusion. In the telling, she would inevitably sound as though she were carping and criticizing. It was not the woman she wanted to be. Thus, very few details were disclosed. She said there were no dramatics. She said they had grown apart. She said she was dispirited, he was splendid, and they would remain friends.

But with Clare she went further, Clare ever the exception, standing by in friendship with a sword in her hand, ready to slay the beast. She had always dropped the armor with Dorothy, and Dorothy, in her own way, reciprocated in kind.

And so, when Dorothy answered the telephone at half past seven the morning of September 29, 1929, and heard Clare's voice, her guard was down.

"You and I are two fragile hearts," Dorothy confessed.

"Two loyal sisters in arms," Clare said.

"I wouldn't say this to anyone else, but the truth of it is I can't wait to have a normal functional relationship."

"Yes," Clare replied, "and have a normal functional *fight*!" And that was the thing about Clare; she understood completely. "Estelle said she invited you to stay with her. You can sculpt in the studio together like you did that summer in France."

"Yes, as much as I appreciate her offer of refuge, I don't want to be an imposition," Dorothy answered.

"Dorothy, it is exactly what you need. And frankly it's what she needs too. Her husband is in Sweden. She's like Rapunzel in that monster of a townhouse."

"She told me in my next marriage I'll have a love so deep and unconditional that we are forever entwined. The kind where a rush of serenity washes over you from being in the same room. It sounds lovely," she sighed.

"We all want the fairytale. The 'lost kingdom of peace.'"

"Ah, yes, Eugene O'Neill," Dorothy said brightly. "'Obsessed by a fairy tale, we spend our lives searching for a magic door and a lost kingdom of peace.' Well sure, why not!"

One month later, in her bedroom at Estelle's place, Dorothy sipped her morning coffee, heard the telephone ring, and looked at her wristwatch. It was half past seven. Estelle would be sleeping. When she picked up the receiver, Clare didn't wait for her to speak.

"Have you seen the papers?"

"No, but I have it right here," Dorothy said, taking it in her hands and unfolding it. "Huge Losses on Wall Street, Sales Set All Time Record," she read. "It's happened."

"The market crashed. Crashed! I hope Gaillard saw this coming and didn't lose *everything*. You are so fortunate, darling, to have gotten out when you did." She couldn't see that Dorothy was smiling at the other end of the line.

PART II

10.

THE LOST KINGDOM
OF PEACE

The smoldering, dark-haired crooner Nick Lucas serenaded the crowd from the stage, surrounded by royal palm trees swaying in the breeze. Dorothy's dress of white crêpe de chine glimmered in the darkness as her hips moved in rhythm with Gardner's, their eyes fixed on each other. He pressed his hand on the curve of her back and pulled her in closely as trumpets in the orchestra peaked in crescendo. It was the first time she had danced in years. Feeling his firm hold, she sensed he would never let her go.

Gangsters, flappers, and titled ladies rollicked around them on the patio of the Sans Souci in Havana, Cuba, far from the shores of America and the law of Prohibition, the floor wet with champagne from the unruly crowd. Gardner whispered in Dorothy's ear and led her by the hand to the water's edge where he kissed her in the glow of the fingernail moon. Tall and strapping with a chiseled jawline, he was impossibly handsome and had the added distinctions of being a world-renowned muralist and a Harvard man. Dorothy touched her finger to the corner of his lips.

"You've swept into my life like a gale force and uprooted any notions I've ever had about love."

"Mrs. Hale, Mrs. Dorothy Donovan Hale. What we have together is beyond what I even hoped love could be," said Gardner, wrapping her in his arms as the tide rolled in.

Three days after their Christmas celebration at the Breakers in Palm Beach, three months to the day after her divorce, they had, to everyone's surprise, married in New York at dusk. The ivory silk of her Schiaparelli dress hugged her frame and draped gracefully to the floor as she walked down the aisle with her father, who paced her steps more slowly than her body wanted to move. The sorrow of her divorce washed away in the beatitude of divine intervention. Elsa Maxwell had a hand in it, too.

Three months earlier, Elsa had left the chateaux of England for a discounted suite at the Ritz Carlton in New York, where she was to throw a party. "Will Gardner Hale be there?" asked Dorothy in a casual tone, to which Elsa replied, "He accepted immediately when I said you'll be attending." With regard to attire, guests were asked to "Come As Your Opposite." George Gershwin showed up as Groucho Marx, Cole Porter as a football player, Fanny Brice as Tosca, Mrs. Vincent Astor as a bad woman, Mrs. Harold E. Talbott as a madam, and Wallace Harrington as the pope. Her eyes twinkling, Dorothy dashed to Gardner's side and slipped her arm through his. When he turned to embrace her, looking absurd as Albert Einstein, she giggled and threw her arms around him.

"*Ahem*," she heard, and spun around to find Cholly stifling a laugh at the sight of her, the spitting image of Clare, her wig blond, short, and styled conservatively, her gown cut low, her diamonds large. Elsa came to his side. "They're ideal mates, wouldn't you agree?" Cholly said, glancing at Elsa, and then he did a double take at her astonishing resemblance to President Hoover and her remarkable fit in Alexander Woollcott's suit. Cholly and Elsa exchanged another glance, both wondering if the other knew that Dorothy and Gardner had fallen for each other long before the night of the party.

They had met by chance at the Art Students League on West Fifty-Seventh Street, on a night that Gaillard was in a mood and wanted to stay home with his scotch. Dorothy had only just arrived at the exhibition when, on the stairwell, distracted by her thoughts, feeling guilty for leaving Gaillard to his own devices, she looked up to see Gardner looking at her. She liked his warm smile, though falling in love was far from her thoughts when she slipped out of the party to go with him for a walk through Central Park.

They lolled away the evening under a silver linden, looking east. There was magic between them. He gave words to her feelings, the contemplation and imagination when composing art, the decisions, predictions, and interpretations one made with colors and forms, the feeling of connecting with oneself and others in a way more profound than words. It was, he said, the ultimate expression of the soul. There were tales of her past as a runaway and his as a Harvard rebel, daydreams about their future and hopes for today, and somehow, in the most unlikely of meetings under the silver linden in Central Park, she found herself fused and fascinated with this Gardner Hale.

"You know, it will always be like this with us," he said in a deep, silky voice, looking at her with a soft and somewhat helpless expression: *There's nothing we can do about it.* She sat perfectly still. In his gaze, so clear and bright, time seemed to stop.

"I know," she sighed with an inward smile and a longing for him to kiss her with those magnificent lips that turned up so readily, wondering how he would love her, when he took her—if he would be tender.

"*Happy days are hhhere again, the sssskies are clear . . .*" slurred a band of nighttime revelers as they sauntered unsteadily toward them, passing around a pocket-sized bottle of liquor and howling between verses. With a light laugh, she touched his shoulder.

"Gardner, have you ever noticed the emerald crown of the Carlyle Hotel?" she marveled, looking beyond the treetops. "I'm entranced by it. It's majestic!"

"I'll think of you whenever I see it aglow in the night."

She giggled, thoroughly pleased at the notion and wanting time to skip ahead to when they'd long since fallen in love.

In the light of morning, Dorothy recognized the extent to which she had exposed herself. Perhaps she should have given more consideration to the consequences of being seen with a man other than Gaillard, particularly on a midnight walk. Perhaps Gardner would reconsider his feelings if he was the sort who acted on a whim. With an exasperated shake of her head, she sprang from the sofa, hurried down the hallway, rushed up the stairwell, into her bedroom, and sank onto the chair.

Tapping her fingernails on the desk, she stared out the window as the telephone slipped a little from her shoulder and rang and rang in a low, stuttered pitch.

"Elsa! I hope I didn't wake you."

"Not at all. I was just on the other line," she said warmly.

"So sorry I missed you at the exhibit. I didn't stay long, but I thank you for inviting me," Dorothy said.

"Yes, I thought I caught a glimpse of you on the stairwell, but that Wallace Harrington character was bending my ear."

"Oh!" Dorothy said with some curiosity as to whether she saw her with Gardner. "Well, the exhibit was terrific. I met a *wonderful* artist—"

"Gardner Hale, by chance?"

"Yes, how did you know?"

"Because he called me right before you did."

"What did he s—"

"He said he met a *wonderful* artist last night. *You.* He's a good man with a big heart and complete integrity. Now go to Reno next week as planned and hurry back."

Before they had parted ways at the corner of Central Park South and Fifty-Eighth Street where he hailed a taxicab for her, Gardner said they should meet the following day at high noon. And so at precisely that hour, she walked along the sidewalk and looked up from the cobblestones to search for him in the crowd, feeling a little concerned he wouldn't be there, that he was given to indecision and change of plans. But there he was. Standing at the Artist's Gate entrance of Central Park, he twirled the stem of a single white rose in his fingers and suddenly turned toward her, smiling magnificently when he caught her eye. And every morning that week, the moment she awoke, she counted the hours to their late-afternoon tryst when they would stroll along the paths until the sky turned dark. Then one day he detected her unease.

"You seem subdued. Is anything wrong?" His observation took her by surprise; she couldn't remember Gaillard asking that question in all the years of their marriage. She had grown accustomed to silence. And then, reaching his arm around her shoulders, he swayed side to side and sang in gravelly baritone, "Though things may not look bright, they all turn out all right, if I keep painting the clouds with sunshine," drawing a smile from Dorothy as she turned to face him.

"I'm okay," she said.

"Just okay? Let's talk about it."

"You're a darling. I do feel a bit off today. Nerves, I think. I leave tomorrow for Reno."

"Ah, of course, I understand. Ending a marriage is painful." He sat in quiet contemplation and slowly turned to her. "You know, I never expected to find love again, and then you . . . well, you swept in, just like that," he said, snapping his fingers. "I want us to share everything. If you'll have me," he continued, taking her hand in his, "we'll be married by New Year's Day." And for the first time since she could remember, she felt she was home.

She left for Reno and reluctantly vowed not to see him until the appropriate time had passed after the divorce. It would spark a firestorm of scuttlebutt if he were to visit Reno. Thus, over the course of ninety days, they wrote letters pages long and practically in sonnet. Her daily routine began with a slow stroll past the front desk and a casual "Any mail?" to the bell captain, who would smile courteously and hand it over. But when she returned to New York, there was no word from Gardner.

Lying on the bed, staring blankly at the telephone in her room at Estelle's, a whole day passed. Then two. Then she regretted writing in her last letter to Gardner they couldn't be seen together for a month so he wouldn't be blamed for causing the divorce. *A mistake*, she thought, longing to see him and wishing he would insist. She had hurt his feelings, made it seem she was perfectly fine being apart, but she didn't know what to do. Call him? And then, on the third day, Elsa stepped in, reunited them at her party, and three months later they were married.

Dorothy and Gardner felt like the luckiest people in the world as they danced the tango and the Charleston and waltzed well into the wee hours at the Sans Souci before returning to their villa at Jane and Grant's estate. Jane had told Dorothy that a house full of guests was a welcome distraction from her domestic routine. Grant told Dorothy that he liked having companionship while Jane took center stage, their friends thrilled and amused by her free spirit as she loaded her shotgun to hunt. Grant could easily have whiled away his time with a free spirit too, at any number of clubs: the Knickerbocker, Harvard, New York Yacht Club, the Metropolitan, the Friar's, the places he said were filled with far too many men afflicted by a nagging emptiness because their wives had little capacity for love.

Gardner was a member of all the requisite clubs, having been listed in the Social Register from the time he was a boy. But the trappings of social prominence were of considerably less importance to him than exhibiting at the Art Institute of Chicago or finding the right grain of sand to blend his own colors of paint. His lifestyle was a departure from the course he had been groomed to take. His father, a preeminent scholar, wrote the book on Latin grammar and ran the department at the University of Chicago before founding the American School of Classical Studies in Rome. He hoped his son would become more serious with age. Then came dashed hopes with the unfortunate foofaraw at Harvard when Gardner was expelled and his father tried to repair the situation, which, by then, he was well accustomed to doing.

The following day they decided to explore the city and set off on their own. "I'll drive," Gardner said, as he always did.

Dorothy grabbed the edge of her seat, her shoulder bumping the door of the shiny red Duesenberg as it swerved into the left lane to avoid oncoming cars. Gardner straightened the wheel and looked ahead intently.

"Well, that was a near miss! This stretch of beach is magnificent. I want to remember the detail so I can paint a seascape," he said.

"I worry about your driving, darling. Promise me you'll pull over when you see something you want to paint." He held her hand as they drove through Old Havana toward the capitol, an architectural wonder with carved archways around its crown.

"This sort of detail is completely lost in the modern designs you'll see in other parts of the city."

"Darling, promise me . . ."

He squeezed her hand twice and said nothing.

"Not a day goes by when I don't think of Elsa and feel grateful for her bringing us together the night of the party," Dorothy sighed. "There was no need to be apart."

"Sweetheart, I told her to be sure you were there. I wanted to surprise you with the news that our wedding date was set, and all the arrangements were finalized."

They made it to the Almendares Hotel in time for high tea. At the entrance stood Happy Longhorn, who was scowling at the man beside her while tugging at the hem of her dress—a short, sequined number that squeezed her curvaceous behind. She seemed distracted when they greeted her. Moments later, Dorothy looked over her shoulder and saw her across the lobby placing a call. That was one of Happy's more irritating habits; she tried ingratiating herself to society columnists by tipping them off about who was where, with whom, and when, in the hopes that her name would also appear in the paper. With full attention on her fuchsia sapphire ring, she tilted her hand from side to side as if admiring its absolute loudness, which she herself was given to at the very moment Dorothy and Gardner walked by.

"Well, let me tell you," she said with a tone of excitement, "just an hour ago, Jane and Grant Mason were rolling the dice at the casino between nips of royal highball cocktails, and Dorothy Hale—you know her, the pretty one who jilted Gaillard Thomas—well, she declined Jane's invitation to join them. She said, 'I've already had excessive luck in finding Gardner. I quit while I'm ahead.'"

"And I'm glad we declined," Gardner said to Dorothy with a laugh as they headed toward the courtyard. "It's our last night in Cuba, and I want it to be ours."

At dusk, they meandered the streets, slowing their pace by a saxophonist, the wailing sounds as haunting as his forlorn eyes. A few paces beyond sat an aged man sketching a portrait of a young American girl. As they rounded a corner, they came upon Bodeguita del Medio, an overpriced and well-liked restaurant with the best mojitos in town. They sat side by side at a table in the back of the room, nuzzling and whispering, anticipating the rapture they soon would feel entwined in each other's arms. The world around her dissolved.

The moment they arrived at their villa, he took her in his arms, their bodies fitting together like two pieces in a puzzle.

"All the guards are down," she confessed. "You have a straight channel into my heart. It's in your hands."

"Do you feel that?" he asked, his voice raspy as he held her more tightly, his arms moving across her back, sending ripples of warmth through her body. Minutes went by, maybe five. She wanted the moment to last forever.

"Yes, I feel it." *It's powerful, extraordinary, wondrous, magical, pure— No*, she thought, *it is more, more than words or sonnets or songs could say.*

"It's love." He slipped off the straps of her dress, allowing it to fall to the floor. "Look at you. You're beautiful . . . and you're smart . . . you're funny . . . you're talented . . ." She unbuttoned his shirt, brushing her lips across his chest, unbuckling his belt.

He lifted her up, her legs wrapping around his waist as he made his way to the bedroom.

"I want you, all of you. I can't get enough of you," he whispered, his hand pressing firmly on the back of her thigh.

"I'm yours." A rush of vulnerability washed over her. She looked up at him. His face glowing, his body heavy on hers, she felt safe. "Beautiful boy," she purred, her eyes gleaming with tears, her love for him too deep, too vast, too much, overflowing and spilling onto his skin. "Tell me."

"I love you. So much."

She ran her finger along the curve of his upper lip, the curve of his shoulder, sculpted and strong, and down his back to his leg.

"Beautiful mind," she said, her lips touching his ear as she ran her finger lightly across his chest. "Beautiful heart. When I'm with you, everything in the world seems right and full of color."

"*Dorothy*," he whispered, the call of trumpets and drums beating wildly in the distance as they held on to each other, fused and forever entwined.

January 11, 1930. Gardner had arranged their travel to coincide with Dorothy's birthday, her twenty-fifth. He ordered twenty-five white roses, purchased a bracelet with twenty-five sapphires and one large diamond, for good luck, and acquired a signed first edition of Alfred

Lord Tennyson's *Works* in which she would find her favorite poems. He undoubtedly knew she would light up with joy and say, "The only thing I need is your love." They celebrated under the midnight glow of the moon on the top deck of the SS *Caronia* luxury steamship.

"Can you see those three bright stars in a line?" he asked, pointing to the sky. There was a wonderment and awe in his tone that came naturally and often and made her fall in love with him over and again. *Beautiful man*, she thought as she glanced at his profile, and his aristocratic nose, realizing she had been painting him all her life. Those sketches in Southampton, the portrait with Leeds Castle in the background, the figure walking on the stones of Hadrian's Wall. *What a strange and wonderful coincidence.*

"Yes, I see them."

"That's Orion's Belt. The people of Spain and South America call it the Three Marys."

"The English call it the Three Kings. And Clare calls it the Three Heirs."

"So that's what she prays to when she looks up to the heavens. She's a pip, that girl," said Gardner.

"She is. Deep down she's kind; she's just scared to death of being poor again."

"I see. And you? What are you most afraid of?"

"I'm afraid of being afraid. Sometimes I think the more you fear something, the more likely it is to happen. Every night after my performance in *Lady, Be Good*, I went down that staircase terrified that I would fall. But I think now I'm most afraid of being forgotten someday. We all want to bring light into the world in some special way, don't we? We hope to do something wonderful, something worthwhile."

Gardner touched her hip, stroked the curve of her back. Her eyes, a light-gold color, were lighter than usual. Brushing the strands away from her eyes, he kissed her, and her love for him felt deeper than the sea that swelled and subsided in drowsy rolling billows.

Had it not been for the passengers who became increasingly intrusive during their private moments, Dorothy could have stayed aboard the ship indefinitely, she so loved the sea. Instead they returned to New York and settled into their sprawling apartment at 240 East Seventy-Ninth Street, the building with the Art Deco façade painted in bright green, and they paid $300 a month for a place they would rarely use. They decided to sell Gardner's apartment at 19 Fifth Avenue, near the artists' club, the Salmagundi, and they would keep the brownstone he owned and had worked in for years. After spending several contented weeks together without the company of friends, they began the whirl of parties at the East Side apartment of Mrs. Benjamin Caruso, who was hosting a dinner in honor of Great Britain's first high commissioner. It was the following day when Gardner brought Dorothy to his studio.

"I wanted you to see the neighborhood at this time of day when the lowering sun casts shadows from trees and you can hear those hand organs, and the mothers calling their children inside for dinner."

Dorothy could see why he was drawn here. It must have felt like a refuge after living in France where he witnessed the ravages of war from the edge of the battlefield. She admired him for organizing and carrying out relief efforts, something she didn't think she could do.

"When I bought the place," he said as they turned a corner, "the newspapers wrote that I was the first artist to reside in Greenwich Village. Now you're the second." He stopped in front of a red brick nineteenth-century townhouse. "Well, this is it. Welcome to our second Manhattan home." Holding open the wrought iron gate, he kissed her cheek as she took in the setting. She liked the way it was set back from the sidewalk.

"Oh, darling, it's lovely."

"Come on, I'll show you around."

In the entrance hall, she glanced at the photographs of his parents, prominently displayed on a nineteenth-century English chestnut console, as they followed the line of the softly faded Persian runner that ran the length of the corridor. The moment she stepped into the living room, she stood in awe of the intricately detailed frescoes that he had painted on the walls. The sky, the billowy clouds, the landscape in the distance were sublime.

"It's breathtaking. It's as though a divine light is coming through the colors. I've never seen anything like it."

"There's more. Let's go upstairs. I'll show you the view."

From the second-floor terrace, she took in the loveliness of the garden, the sculptures and trees, and the stone pathway to the studio where brass lanterns hung on either side of the door, illuminating his mural of the Madonna painted in light gold and white over a background of sky blue. She knew she would be comfortable here.

"I have something else to show you," he said, taking her hand as they bounded down the stairs and exited through the back door, entwining his fingers in hers until they stepped inside the studio and stood before two easels, from which he lifted white cloths to reveal his paintings *Kitchenend* and *Two Trees*.

"This one is a representation of us," he said. "Like the trees, we'll grow side by side, strongly rooted in the pureness of God's earth. An enduring love that will remain unchanged by blowing wind or rain upon our leaves."

"Two trees standing strong," she said, turning to look in his eyes. "I love you." For several minutes, she examined the graceful strokes on the canvas and admired his prodigious talent. He allowed the silence. They did not need words to understand the feelings between them.

"Here, I've cleared this area for you," he said, walking to the far end of the room where an easel and paint had been placed by the window. "And here, this is where you can sculpt," he said, turning the corner into a smaller room filled with light and all the supplies she would need. "Someday we can exhibit our work together."

At 7:30 that evening, Clare arrived. She roamed around the living room looking at the frescoes before easing herself in a black leather-upholstered chair by the blazing fire where she chatted pleasantly while observing Dorothy's attentiveness to her husband.

"Dorothy, what are you going to do in the French countryside while Gardner looks for sand?" she asked, clearing her throat and smiling with a raised eyebrow as she tapped her scarlet nails on her knee.

"She'll be right alongside me," said Gardner, a wide grin filling out his narrow face. He turned on the radio. The station always played Cole Porter's songs one after the other. "What Is This Thing Called Love," "You're the Top," "I'm Getting Ready for You."

"Gardner asked me to be his manager, so if I'm not on expedition with him, I'll be arranging for commissions and exhibits," Dorothy said cheerfully. He kissed her forehead and sauntered away with Clare watching until he turned the corner and disappeared. She placed her elbows on the arms of the chair, clasped her hands in front of her, tapped her forefingers, and looked straight at Dorothy.

"There's a growing chorus of people who would like to know what you're doing. Where's Dorothy? Where's the Dorothy I know?"

It caught Dorothy by surprise, like a slap in the face.

"I'm right here," she answered, considering for a moment that Clare could be a tireless twit. She was doing precisely what she wanted, and besides, who was Clare to think she was losing her way? She would paint and sculpt and work with galleries to introduce artists to the public. And whatever else she might decide.

"Do something for yourself. Exhibit your own work."

"Well, I am going t—"

"Look what happened to me. My ex-husband married Frances Seymour, and what do I have post-divorce but a penthouse, a governess, three servants and nothing to do?"

"And you have your wonderful daughter," Dorothy reminded her with a tilt of her head to make the point, which prompted a dumbstruck expression from Clare.

"Dorothy, a woman's best protection is a little money of her own. And moreover, a life of her own. I know, I know, by the grace of your father and the good fortune of Gaillard you have more money than you can spend in your lifetime, but there's a sense of accomplishment in making your own way."

"Of course, darling," Dorothy said, understanding that Clare had never experienced this herself. "Anyway," she continued curtly to signal the end of the conversation, "we so enjoy being together. We're infinitely happy." There was no point in telling Clare a thing when she was on one of her rips.

"Well, now that I have that tedious business of marriage behind me, I'm going to work as a writer."

"You're talented, Clare."

"I still have a few good years to find a husband I love."

"Precisely. Now is the time to exercise your mind, not your patience."

Sifting through photographs of Gardner's work, they recognized three large frescoes from their visit to Viscountess of Rancougne's home in Paris. "The technique the artist used is so brilliant, they'll out-survive mankind," the viscountess had told them.

"Perhaps they will. If they out-survive the next owners of your house," Clare had replied. What she hadn't seen was Gardner's decoration of a tomb that housed the family of Madame J. Ramon Fernandez in the Cemetery of Montparnasse. The picture intrigued her.

"I should like to have an equally impressive resting place."

"Clare, look, Gardner is taking me to the spots where he painted these. *San Gimignano, Roofs in Italy, The Olive Grove—*"

"You'll be missing Rosamond's dinner."

"Yes, I know." She ignored Clare's chiding.

"I've seen Gardner's work many times, Dorothy—the frescoes at the home of Walter Spalding, the one at Edward Shearson's, which I saw on holiday in Palm Beach. May I suggest he paint something that doesn't require lifting a wall out of the house so you can show it on exhibit." Her eyes were sharp under heavy blonde brows plucked in a straight line.

"Darling, don't be silly. Many of them are removable. Anyway, he has a big project coming up for the new Chrysler Building."

"And who, pray tell, is *this*?" asked Clare as she studied a picture of one of Gardner's portraits.

"Isn't she divine? It's Gardner's mother. She passed away last year."

"I see. Well, that explains a few things."

"Oh, Clare. You—"

"Well, ladies, what do you say we go for a cocktail?" asked Gardner as he stepped into the room, his buoyancy deflating when he looked at Dorothy, and then at Clare, and nodded in acknowledgment there was tension between them. "Should be great fun. Come on, what do you say!"

"Don't you look handsome," Dorothy said, rising from her seat and expecting Clare to make a remark, but instead she hummed to the music playing on the radio. Gardner stood still while Dorothy tucked his collar into his jacket. He slipped their coats over their shoulders, and they left for Romany Marie's on Minetta Street, where they would meet sculptor Isamu Noguchi and his chum Buckminster Fuller, both of whom were indebted to Romany for serving them dinner free of charge as the Depression deepened.

"Congratulations on the nuptials," said Isamu, hugging Dorothy when they arrived. "You both look remarkably happy."

"*Ca a été le coup de foudre.* Love at first sight," said Gardner with a bright smile.

"O'Neill says we're all looking for the fairytale, expecting to find the lost kingdom of peace," said Clare. "Maybe they've actually found it." She smiled, sat down, and picked up the newspaper. "Let's see now," she said, skimming the front page. "President Hoover reassures Americans by saying we've passed the worst of the Depression, the market will recover on its own from its thirty-billion-dollar loss. Thirty billion!"

"Meantime, Al Capone—a gangster, for God's sake!—has actually opened soup kitchens to feed the poor who, as we all know, are living on Hoover Stew," Dorothy said. "Just devastating."

It called up images of the changing Manhattan landscape, where she felt at times like a stranger in her own city, the parks overgrown with handmade tents and shanty towns where the streets had no name, where a small blonde girl and her mother, their eyes desolate and clothes soiled, wandered aimlessly asking for a dime, where drunken men as still as statues slept on the pavement with only a weather-worn suitcase to spare. And when Dorothy rolled by in a limousine one night and saw them, she asked the driver to pull over, stepped out to the sidewalk, slipped bills into their hands, and felt them clench the paper tightly. "The crash has caused a ripple of destruction. It flows through the financial district, up the East Side, and across the country. People just can't bear it. They're empty of all hope."

"They leap out of windows high above the city streets. Imagine?" said Clare. "Things can only get better. I heard that in the days following the crash, hotel clerks asked people if they wanted the room for sleeping or jumping."

"I once considered suicide," said Bucky rather matter-of-factly. "After great contemplation about my place in this world, this spaceship that is Planet Earth, I understood that was not an option. Once you recognize that your purpose on this planet is to advance the human condition, you find dynamic synergy and value in life. Aheh," he concluded, with what seemed like a stilted laugh and moment of joy, yet Dorothy knew it was futile to calculate what could possibly be in his erudite mind. She had told Gardner about him earlier in the day, how he had spent the previous two years in seclusion, depressed from the failure of his company, and then he invented the Dymaxion House, a design for mass production that could be airlifted to any community in need. Gardner quite liked the idea, and Dorothy's friends, and he invited them all for drinks at Twenty-One.

On their way uptown in Clare's limousine, Isamu ran his hand along the leather seat and looked her over, beginning with her fair ankles, continuing upward with a few long pauses along the way, and landing his gaze on her eyes.

"Tell me, Clare," he asked, "what did your husband do to make you leave him?"

"Well," Clare answered, sounding as though it were obvious. "He breathed."

Dorothy laughed and told Gardner the story about the night she, Clare, and Maggie snuck out at dawn with the two owners of Twenty-One. It was the last day of the year. They helped remove the wrought iron gate from their former establishment, then secured it to the entrance of their new place for opening night. In order to avoid rows with policemen looking for liquor, the owners installed a peephole on the front door, which was kept locked, and made an elaborate contraption inside that had something to do with levers, tilting shelves, chutes and sewers to swiftly eighty-six the booze. "No one has to worry about getting busted at Jack and Charlie's speak."

Laughing, they stepped out to the sidewalk on West Fifty-Second Street, opened the gate, knocked on the door, stood before the peephole, and swept inside. They were greeted enthusiastically by Jimmy Coslove, who ushered them to the dining room.

There, Frank "Crownie" Crowninshield sat in a corner appreciating the wood panels decorated with signed pictures of famous guests, the ceiling adorned with toy airplanes and dollar bills. The atmosphere was cozy and elegant with elegant customers at every table. None more so than Crownie, who was meticulously dressed from his French tie to his polished English shoes. He spotted Dorothy by the doorway and waved his arm to catch her attention. As she made her way toward him, she told Gardner how Crownie had taken over Condé Nast's magazine *Dress & Vanity Fair*, changed the title to *Vanity Fair*, and took it in a new direction.

"I recently met Condé Nast and he told me you once lived together in a Park Avenue duplex. What an intriguing arrangement," Clare said to Crownie after settling into a seat beside him. Without acknowledgment that he had heard what she said, he sniffed and turned to Dorothy.

"Maggie tells me you're going to Venice. Be sure to photograph the Modigliani exhibit and send my regards to Onorato Carlandi if you see him. His work is poetry on paper, as if he sees the natural world through a soft lens from the heavens," Crownie said, holding Gardner's full attention.

"I studied under Carlandi—good man," Gardner said.

"Brilliant. I acquired his watercolor of Vallambrosa. You may know the place, the eleventh-century monastery in Tuscany."

"Yes, I'm planning on taking Dorothy to see it. Carlandi was inspired to go there after reading about it in Milton's *Paradise Lost*."

"Extraordinary place. Said to be a life-giver more potent than all the resources of pharmacy. Drop by my flat tomorrow and I'll show you the painting."

"Will do."

"Send Carlandi my best too," Isamu added, stealing a glance at Dorothy. His admiring eyes did not go without notice. Knowing that Isamu was trying to make a name for himself as an artist, Gardner suggested they go see the sculptor's work.

"My new studio is a short walk from here. I have the top floor of the Carnegie Hall building," Isamu said with a slight tilt of his chin in the upward direction. Clare looked at Dorothy with an expression of curiosity that said she was wondering which libidinous lady of polite society had agreed to pay his rent. Regardless of his inability to give lavish gifts or anything of importance to those of the material world in which they lived, he did possess youth, strapping good looks, shiny jet-black hair, and a gifted mind.

Once there, he showed them his work, and the friends gathered around a chrome-plated bronze sculpture of Bucky. They stood and stared, gaping at their distorted reflections in its mirrored finish.

"Incredible," said Dorothy. "There's a hint of who we are, but we are, basically, unrecognizable. It's like the sculptural form of a Cholly Knickerbocker column."

"It's a shame no one responded to your work last year when you exhibited at Eugene Shoen's gallery, Isamu. How terribly disappointing for you," said Clare.

"People will come to appreciate his talent. It takes time," said Gardner. "There are few exceptions, like Modigliani. He died too young, but he left a legacy of inspired work for which he'll always be remembered."

"Either that or he'll be remembered for his debauchery," Clare said. "We'll see which narrative stands the test of time."

"I urged him to lay off the absinthe and hashish, but it didn't do any good. We all saw it coming," said Gardner, taking Dorothy's hand.

"Yes, yes, it masked his pain from tuberculosis, which of course none of us knew he had," Crownie said. "Then he convinced himself that he needed narcotics to create his best work."

"Yes, which caused him to strip off his clothes at parties," Clare added.

"Of course, he remained on every guest list in Montmartre," Dorothy said with a light smile.

"A shame that Modigliani died penniless," Clare said, "and then his girlfriend jumped out a window to her death with their unborn child in her womb. They left their fourteen-month-old daughter orphaned. Can you imagine?"

"In fifty years we'll see what he's remembered for," said Dorothy. "You know how easy it is to rewrite history or even forget it altogether."

"And let's face it," Clare said with a nod, "we all want to be remembered for something."

"Only if it's something wonderful," Dorothy replied.

At half past eight on a Saturday morning, Dorothy pulled the bedcovers down to her chin and turned to Gardner, considering for several moments the big prolonged baritone notes and frequent fermatas that composed the remarkable resonance of his snore, which suddenly fell in harmony with the low-octave wail of the steam whistle signaling their arrival in Le Havre, France. Climbing out of bed, she took care not to wake him. He didn't move but an inch as his symphony of snortled sounds continued, his head nestled comfortably at the peak of a pyramid of pillows. A light three knocks on the door of their suite roused her attention.

She took Gardener's white dress shirt from the floor and put it on, buttoning it up as she ambled through the sitting room, her eyes still blurry from sleep. An envelope slipped under the door and stopped at her feet. With great curiosity she took it in her hand, immediately ripped it open, sauntered to the sofa, and sat down to read.

"Dorothy, I am writing to you from my office at *Vogue*. Yes, darling, *Vogue*! Last week I dropped in unannounced to see Condé Nast, and as luck would have it, he was out of town. So what else was I to do but commandeer a desk and allow the staff to believe he had already hired me? The pretty and petulant little things gave me a warm if curious welcome and had me write some captions. Maggie, of course, has been a doll. Needless to say, when Condé returned, his first thought was that the editor gave me the job, and upon learning what really happened, his second thought—which admittedly was spoken to me at increasing volume—was to request that I slam the door softly on my way out. Imagine? So I suggested dinner instead, and by the time we left Twenty-One he was charmed into submission. A fine finish. Love, Clare."

"Bravo!" Dorothy giggled. She looked over at Gardner and out to the ocean. "'Where the rainbows play in the flying spray, 'mid the keen salt kiss of the waves.' You said it, O'Neill," she said as the dock in the distance came into view.

The cool breeze tousled her hair as she strolled along the Promenade des Planches, holding Gardner's hand while listening to nature's symphony—the crying melody of seagulls, waves cresting and rumbling to shore, then softening to a whoosh and rolling back home to the infinite sea. It was early in the season, before the crowds descended upon the beachside town for horse races, parties, and gambling at the Deauville Casino, still popular with the au courant who had tired of Biarritz. Dorothy was glad to have arrived before the circus began; the boutiques of Van Cleef and Arpels and Jean Patou were quiet, the outdoor cafés empty. She treasured its tranquility after five days at sea where each of the day's activities necessitated a change of clothes and continuous chatter with acquaintances.

Buttoning up her sweater, the jersey fabric too light for early spring, she gave thanks to Chanel for designing high-waist palazzo pants with women's comfort in mind, and delivering on the vision. They wandered down the boardwalk to Ciro's and chose the table closest to shore.

"When we get back to the hotel, I'll show you the sketch I've done for the mural in the Chrysler Building," Gardner said as he eased into his chair.

"Wonderful! Did you hear, the Cloud Club will have three floors with a Renaissance-style staircase."

"Sounds terrific, doesn't it? Well, our expedition to Italy and the Luberon will forever mark the walls of the Chrysler. We'll collect sand and make paint in the colors of the earth, sky, and sea."

"Whatever you don't use for the mural we can bring to Maine. We can relax and work by the lake. By the time we leave, we'll have enough new paintings for a show," Dorothy mused. "You may want to do more cityscapes if you're so inspired. There will be a lot of interest after the Chrysler opening."

"You know, darling," he said affectionately, squeezing her hand, "you're a wonder."

"I love you," she said, looping her finger around his.

"And I love you."

After a week in Deauville, the days began blending together, days of dust spraying from the wheels as they drove through vacant villages and past blooms of the landscape en route to Northern France where they were to visit a seventeenth-century chapel. With fifteen miles of open road between towns, Gardner couldn't resist the power of the Bugatti and tested its might around turns. The wind blew Dorothy's headscarf away, and she spun around, watching it sail through the air and float to the ground. Ahead in the distance, fields of red poppies lay before clusters of old stone homes, the silhouette of town in the distance.

Shifting the car into low gear without a hint of a glitch, Gardner turned to her with a roguish expression, prompting a smile and a shake of her head. They came upon the village, passed a boulangerie, a bustling café, and a salon de coiffure, then rounded a corner and pulled up to the chapel on the banks of the River Jeaux.

They found the entrance door slightly ajar. With one hand on the well-worn knob, Gardner gave it a light push and they stepped inside, the faint scent of smoke still lingering from candles that were burned at mass. Then, Dorothy stood motionless. Rays of light reached through the stained-glass windows and shined onto the murals Gardner had painted so many years before. Scenes from the life of St. Louis came alive in vivid color with 600 handsome characters, depictions of brave crusades, and massive ships on the stormy sea. She dashed up the center aisle to the nave and choir, running her hands over the murals and marveling at his work, which was unmistakably reminiscent of nineteenth-century masters.

As they continued their journey south with stops along the way to see each of his works, she found herself reflecting on the feelings they evoked, from the ethereal murals in the chapel in Sovereign Mill, to the chapel in Pau where he painted *Descent from the Cross*, so lyrical and celestial in effect. She would never see the world in the same way again.

Medieval villages rested high atop the mountains of the Luberon, the open landscape of lavender fields as vast as the soft blue sky. Pine scented the air in Roussillon where they gathered sand colored in shades of the sunrise. He looked over at her and saw that her hair was disheveled, her cheeks spotted with dirt.

"What's so funny?" she asked, wiping her hands with a towel before smoothing out her hair, which had curled into unruly loops.

"You. You're beautiful. You're such a girl," he said adoringly with no evident concern over his hair, which was standing up at the top and sprinkled with sand.

"You're such a boy." *A wonderful, brilliant, sweet, rugged boy,* she thought.

"You know, you're following in a long tradition of artists who have used the earth of the Ochre Trail since the eighteenth century."

"And who am I to break tradition?" she said with a laugh. "Say, I was thinking we should go to Apt or Menerbes today and go to one of the outdoor markets. Avignon will be more crowded."

"Apt or Menerbes it is. We'll take a basket and a bottle of wine to the castle in Lacoste and have ourselves a French toast."

"Imagine what it was like in the seventeenth century, its glory days? It goes to show, all it takes is one coup d'état to turn a treasure to ruins."

"I'll say. How about if we leave Thursday for Italy?" asked Gardner.

"*Sì, meraviglioso.* Wonderful."

When they arrived at Château de Lacoste, Gardner spread a blanket over the time-smoothed surface of an eighteenth-century stone ruin wall and set out thick cuts of salami and soft cheese, placing them alongside golden bruschetta and vines of plumpish grapes. In the distance, an aged man stroked his violin in a stirring ballad that suggested halcyon days of yore.

As Gardner poured the last drops of Amarone into Dorothy's glass, the music shifted into a sweeping tempo of Brahms. He emptied his glass in one gulp, sprang to his feet, and extended his hand to her. And in the empty halls of the castle now abandoned and silenced by time, they waltzed cheek to cheek over the ancient floor of dust with unknown stories buried deep in the soil below.

"If I could have wished for the man I would spend my life with," she said, "I would have wished for you."

Once in Venice, with Gardner by her side, Dorothy discovered the city anew. At half past six a few days into their stay, Gardner shifted in his seat in the gondola and reached for his leather satchel.

"I have a surprise for you," he said. "I know you've been to Venice, but there's something you should see."

"How intriguing! Is it a spectacular sculpture in the piazza?" asked Dorothy.

"You'll never guess."

"Or an awe-inspiring fresco?"

"Giovanni!" he called out to the gondolier. "*Vai al canale con il Ponte dei Sospiri, Rio di Palazzo, si prega di.*"

"You know I love when you speak Italian," Dorothy said playfully.

"*Sì,*" said Giovanni, "*non è un problema. Che è dietro la curva, signore.*" He started paddling with a skilled stroke.

"*Sì, sì, lo so, grazie,*" Gardner replied.

"*Prego.*"

"You've seen the Doge Palace, this building," Gardner said as they floated by.

"Yes, I find the medieval architecture so imposing. Seventeenth-century Venetian buildings are works of art. Extraordinary. It was once a prison. Imagine?" They rounded the palace and glided into a narrow canal where a sculptural white limestone bridge came into view.

"Take a look at the bridge," he said, handing her the binoculars. "Italian Renaissance architecture, nothing like it in the world."

"Oh, it's remarkable," she said, squinting through the lens. "I see sculptures of faces. Some look sad, some angry. Ah, but one is smiling. And there are two windows at the top with steel bars."

"As the story goes, guards would take convicts from the palace courthouse and walk them across the bridge to the new prison for their execution. The poor chaps stood on the bridge, took in their last view of Venice, and sighed. Thus . . ."

"The Bridge of Sighs, of course! There's a Bridge of Sighs at St. Joseph's Academy and at the Alleghany County Courthouse."

"I remember you telling me. Now, the legend here is that lovers who kiss under the bridge during sunset will share eternal love." She giggled as she leaned toward him. Their lips met long enough for

Giovanni to watch the sun lower on the horizon in a kaleidoscope of orange and red, and with a final green flash, it dipped out of view. *"Portarci al ristorante, per favore,"* Gardner directed him.

When they arrived at the Trattoria Antiche Cipranatto restaurant, they found Onorato Carlandi seated at a table outside. Breaking bread under the bright stars, he urged them to return for the Venice Bienniale, which was to be dedicated to the memory of Modigliani. Moved by their stories of his kindhearted ways, Dorothy suggested hosting a fundraiser for the Modigliani Fund. Onorato nodded approvingly while placing his paper napkin on the table and drawing a map that would lead them to the fountain of Vallambrosa. Turning to Gardner, he raised his glass and made a remark in Italian.

"Dorothy," Gardner laughed, "Onorato said, 'I'm relieved to see that you've settled down with a woman whose savvy is as striking as her beauty. Your last girl was as bad as she was good.'" He looked at Onorato, who was savoring his wine. *"Ah, sì, Ava, sì sì, caro Dio in cielo."*

Dorothy knew all about her, the formidable Ava Fiona Volatilli of the Volatilli family of Oyster Bay. She had come into his life like a glorious rainbow and tore through their romance like a hurricane. Onorato had met her only once. It was the night of Felicity Farucci's dinner party. Ava became increasingly agitated that Gardner was talking to Colette Moreau until finally she swigged her wine, threw the glass to the ground, grabbed her dish, and promptly unloaded linguini Genovese onto his lap. That was the last time Onorato and Gardner saw Ava.

"E lei è più vivo di quanto la tua ex moglie, Marie. You know how, eh, those writers can be," Onorato muttered with some amusement.

"He said you are more vibrant than my ex-wife. I can't deny that." Dorothy knew about her too. Marice Rutledge, married thrice, never fully satisfied. It was two years since their divorce, and Onorato said he was sure her next was only a matter of time.

In the morning, a heavy fog lifted as the friends boarded a train to go to Père Lachaise Cemetery, the largest of Paris. When they reached the entrance, they stood in awed silence at the towering white stone walls and grand gateway. A cobblestone road led them to an open landscape, hundreds of acres dotted with mausoleums and tombs that were well tended and shaded by thousands of trees. Sunlight shined on a polished black stone, highlighting its inscription, *Marcel Proust 1871–1922*, for there would be at no time in the future the need for further description. Nearby were Oscar Wilde and Frédéric Chopin.

They found their way to the single stone tomb that housed Amedeo Modigliani and Jeanne Hebuterne. Kneeling down in the moist soil, Dorothy placed a bouquet of chrysanthemums beside the carved epitaph.

"Amadeo Modigliani. Struck down by Death at the moment of glory. Jeanne Hebuterne. Devoted companion to the extreme sacrifice," she read. Silence hung in the air.

Onorato asked for a moment alone with his friend; there were things he wanted to say. His voice became more distant as they ambled through the cemetery toward a flock of singing goldcrests.

"Are you all right, sweetheart?" asked Gardner.

"Yes, fine, darling. I was thinking what a tragedy it is that Hebuterne ended her own life. It's against God's will, and it's just such an unimaginable thing to do. Darkness always turns to light. It's the simple law of nature." She drifted away from the sunlight and into the shadow of a tree. Gardner came to her side and leaned against its trunk. "It reminds me of Strauss's *Also Sprach Zarathustra*. I mean, you wouldn't turn off the song in the middle of doom and apocalypse or you'd miss the payoff of divine ascendency and triumph!"

He laughed lightly and embraced her. Morning dew dripped from the tree onto their skin.

"It might interest you to know, my love, this chestnut tree symbolizes a very long life."

When the hour passed, they parted ways with Onorato and set off to Bologna where they stayed the week, and then they moved on to Florence. There they lunched with Mrs. Spelman at her home, Villa Rozzini, where Gardner had painted murals of St. Julian. She had been waiting to tell him that she decided to bequeath the villa to Johns Hopkins University, with a binding agreement to keep his artwork intact. This made Dorothy like her.

Once settled into their villa nearby, Dorothy adjourned to the terrace. Tracing the lip of her champagne glass, their wedding vows echoed in her mind: *To laugh with you and cry with you, to love you and to cherish you, for as long as we both shall live. I promise you this from my heart, for all the days of my life.* She watched the sky turn shades of crimson.

Gardner came to her, enfolded her in his arms, and brushed his cheek against hers, knowing she liked the feel of bristle on her skin. Pulling away, he reached his hands to the back of her neck and tied a black velvet ribbon in a bow. Attached was a gold Florentine Victorian pendant that lay solidly on her chest.

"We will never miss a sunset together. *Jusqu'à la fin des temps, mon amour."* *Until the end of time, my love.* Smiling, she touched her lips to his, and they remained one as she led him to the bedroom, her robe slipping off her shoulders and onto the floor. A light breeze swept open the sheer white curtains as the light clang of church bells faded into the background, his quickening breath the only sound she could hear.

Vallambrosa. They had finally arrived. Dorothy took in the view of the river Arno while Gardner studied the hand-drawn map. They set off to the woods, taking note of the rock cairns, and followed the course for a mile. There they found the circular ruins burrowed deep in the forest floor and surrounded by a spiritual aura that Carlandi had managed to capture on canvas.

Lowering themselves onto a crumbled wall, they heard the crackling of leaves from deer leaping through the forest, Mother

Nature's psalm breaking the silence. A monk stood in front of a stone fountain, patiently waiting for his jug to fill.

"Listen," Gardner said, taking a moment of pause. "There's something I want to share with you." She waited for him to continue. "Our life together already feels complete, but I've been thinking we should have a child. You would be a wonderful mother."

"Oh, darling." She took his hand and felt the sting of tears in her eyes. "I'd all but given up on the idea until I met you, and then . . . well, even then I thought I was lucky enough to have found love, I would be okay missing motherhood. In the last several weeks, though, I can't explain it, but I've been getting this *feeling* inside of me when I see a child. You know, the doctor warned me after the accident that a pregnancy could be too much for my body to bear. But we could get a second opinion. I'd like to." They sat quietly as the monk ambled away into the forest.

"You know of course that I am happier than I've ever been and will remain so if it's just the two of us forevermore."

She tried pushing away the thought of Clare's remark: "Forevermore is shorter than you think."

"Gardner, you look like a movie star," Clare said as she kissed him on each of his cheeks. It was July 18, 1930. It was a night to celebrate. And so they did, on the observation deck of the Chrysler Building, once the tallest building in the world, soaring 1,046 feet into the sky. In the distance, the silver spire on the Empire State Building, which had claimed victory over the Chrysler at 1,250 feet, gleamed in the night and rose high above the rooftops, the city lights twinkling from steel columns, thousands of them, clustered together and lining the edge of the river. Billowing clouds floated over the shrunken cityscape, the very scene featured in the mural that Gardner had painted in the Cloud Club a few stories down. To create the ethereal colors, he used the sand that he and Dorothy had collected in Europe.

"You are such a striking pair. Imagine what your children will look like one day," said Maggie, approaching them. Dressed in a white satin Schiaparelli gown and pearls that dipped low on her back, Dorothy was more beautiful than ever before. "Edward Steichen would like to photograph you," Maggie remembered to say as she accepted a glass of champagne from the server. "I seemed to have lost count, so I'll call this my second."

"Steichen mentioned that to me as well," said Crownie. "It will be a fine addition to the pages of *Vogue*. By the way, Gardner, Paul Hanson's photograph of you in the June issue of *Vanity Fair* was *exceptional*."

"The girls are still talking about your chiseled jawline and chocolate-brown eyes," Maggie added while straightening Crownie's bowtie. Satisfied, she patted his arm. "Crownie, this month's *Vanity Fair* cover is so apropos to this evening. The American flag with stripes in the shape of the city skyline. It's even better than the cover you did of Roosevelt holding a beer mug to appeal to blue-collar men. That trick is older than me."

"Let's adjourn to the Cloud Club, shall we?" suggested Crownie.

And so went the evening of celebration among friends when everything was right and full of color. When the buzz of their chatter reached to crescendo in uproarious laughter and pats on the back. When others around them stumbled onto the laps of married lovers, champagne spilling onto the polished marble floor, betrayal and indecency dressed up in custom-made suits and an air of refinement honed since birth.

When the clock struck midnight, Crownie made a final toast to Gardner's moment of glory. Clare had cause to celebrate as well. After a few months working at *Vogue*, she had abandoned ship to take a job down the hall in the Graybar Building and was now the assistant editor of *Vanity Fair*.

"Well, I have money, a career, a twenty-eight-inch waist, and all of you. Now all I need is a man who looks at me the way Gardner looks at Dorothy," she said, emptying her glass in one skilled swallow. Maggie looked at them.

"You two have the unmistakable glow that John Barrymore called 'that lovely, lost look, that roseleaf cheek that is not quite a blush, that brightness in the yes that is not yet a tear.'"

11

IN THE PINK

"The definition of Hale is strong and healthy, alive and kicking, in the pink," Dorothy said. She closed the dictionary and set it on the desk. "I think you live up to your name quite nicely."

Gardner looked up from his notebook and blew her a kiss. "So do you, sweetheart."

Rain pounded on the windows, and thick fog enveloped their rustic cabin, Aguiden Lodge, nestled in the wooded landscape of Kineo, Maine, on Moosehead Lake, thus named for the shape of land that jutted up from the fickle waters. Dorothy could attest to its likeness, having seen a moose on a leisurely walk. She looked up from the dirt path and right into its eyes as it stared her down, prompting her to sprint away, thinking not that she had escaped an attack, but how the obituary would read. It would be such an inelegant end, a moose mauling! The headline would be worse than the death.

Gardner let out a deep sigh and continued writing furiously, trying to make headway on his book.

"Art simply refuses to be rushed, whether it's painting or prose," he said with evident frustration.

"Take your time, darling. You're the only person who can write it, and it will ensure the craft endures for centuries. It was your fate to become the artist that single-handedly revived fresco painting in America. Even the newspapers say so," she said. "Speaking of, I asked Danny to pick up a copy of the *New York Times* tomorrow when he's buying supplies. It's the only thing I can't live without. Except you."

The very thought that he discovered the secrets of fresco painting purely by chance imbued her with a strange glee, for it was unquestionably one of those signs that you were headed in the direction you ought to go. One day when he was walking along the river Seine, rain started to pour, so he ducked into an old bookshop for cover. Waiting for the storm to pass, he lingered by the window and perused the books stacked high on a worn wooden table. He plucked one from the pile, brushed off the dust, and stared in rapturous disbelief. To his astonishment, it was *The Craftsman's Handbook* by Cennino Cennini, a rare, out-of-print copy that held the answers to questions he had been asking artists for years.

Dorothy watched as he wrote with speed, and realized he probably didn't notice he was on the last pages of the notebook. *We must have more*, she thought, opening the table drawer. It was jammed. Pulling harder, it gave way to reveal letters scattered about, and the disorder bothered her.

Gardner looked up to ponder the perfect word for a particular sentence as though it were written on the wood-paneled wall. He stared for several maddening minutes, then heard the sound of papers shuffling.

"You should read some of those letters, sweetheart. You'll see what you've gotten yourself into with the lot of us as your family."

She hummed the melody of Pachelbel's Canon as she sifted through them, and noticed three from Mary Fanton Roberts, Gardner's friend who attended the cocktail party at their apartment on the twenty-eighth of April. When Mary called to accept, she told Dorothy that Gardner wrote to her to say that he was exceedingly happy, and she must come to the party to meet the girl of his dreams.

Upon their introduction, Mary rhapsodized over Gardner's gifted hands ("as pertains to his art, of course!" she said, turning white), his pure approach to his craft, and his idealism. At that very moment, Gardner, with a commanding presence and deep, impassioned voice, told a cluster of guests, "It's glorious to feel that one holds every thread, is a master of every detail, controls equally the perfection of the materials and the idea. And there is a feeling of particular jubilation in rising to a day of physical as well as mental labor."

Dorothy found a note clipped to the letter and read: "Gardner, I thought you'd like to read these notes. They're from your old friend A.S.S. Sincerely yours, Mary." *Who's A.S.S.?* Dorothy wondered, giggling to herself at the sound of it. She unfolded the card. The signature was illegible in its scribble, but it looked to be written in a woman's hand. She read on.

"People have spoken to us; have asked for photographs, have asked to sketch G's aristocratic nose (!) . . . How droll people ARE when cooped up in a boat for ten days! We are known as the 'lovers,' and women get me in corners to tell me how lucky I am. I tell them back that, exceptional as it may seem to our 1921 civilization, I consider any relationship to G. the normal god-given state of man and woman, and refuse to take it as a sordid exception."

Dorothy's heart started to beat fast. She suspected that Gardner wouldn't wed the girl, so the girl convinced herself she was a modern woman who didn't need a ring to prove their love was true. *Poor, damn, dumb girl*, she said to herself. Immediately regretting the thought, she skimmed over the next letter. "He has the spirit of the craftsman . . . it takes every bit of vitality he has . . . In March we're off to Florence to set up the Panels, and the gods are being good to us for the Spelmans who have most wonderfully lent us their Villa during our stay there. No plans after that. Everything depending on G. He has an idea that he wants to settle in some quiet beautiful Italian spot—perhaps San Gimignano . . . and just . . . paint!"

"What are you reading, sweetheart? Anything interesting?"

asked Gardner with a tone of vague curiosity as he glanced up from his notebook. She smiled sweetly, veiling her sudden discomfort.

"I'm reading the letters from your flapper friend, from the Twenties," she answered, her cheeks flushed.

"Oh, those. I don't know why Mary gave them to me. Why don't you use them for the fire? It's burning out." This pleased Dorothy immensely.

She remembered Gardner telling her, "Whatever happened in the past doesn't matter now." It was why she didn't mention that Gaillard had written her father a letter, wherein he expressed his disappointment over the divorce, it wasn't what he wanted, it wasn't his choice, and he would love her always. By then she had met Gardner and wanted to forget the whole unfortunate matter, but on occasion, in quiet moments alone, she felt a sense of guilt for not trying harder to reach him.

"Here's a letter from your father to your brother Bob. It's dated 1914," she said.

"That's when I got kicked out of Harvard. Papa also wrote to Dean Hulbut to get me readmitted. Unfortunate incident with the fraternity brothers, I think I've told you." His voice rose in a tone of conspicuous amusement. "I was a bit swacked. As luck would have it, my inebriation peaked out-of-doors where I shouted at the night and then at the watchman who tried to calm me down to no avail. I was swiftly expelled."

All boy, she thought, refraining from the delicious urge to touch him. "Your father wrote, 'This is ominous for the future. Poor Mama! She will feel this last blast keenly.'"

There was a gleam in his eyes as he tapped his pen on the desktop. "Mother was an angel. She told me, 'Boys will be boys. Just don't get caught.'" He broke out in a splendid grin. "She was delighted when I got the Harvard degree, of course."

"You wrote this one from the Twenty Rue Jacob Salon on May 17, 1916."

"That was just before I came back to America. What did I say?"

"You wrote, 'My dear bully brother, Mother is writing you about our scheme for a studio, so I shant go into details, but I do want to ask you myself what your feeling is about your old campground. A studio large enough for my work would be necessarily a permanent affair . . . the place is ideal for me in that I can really get away from my client! And his constant visits and suggestions.'"

"Ah, Shelby Whitehouse," Gardner remembered. "The man was relentless, couldn't help himself. He was accustomed to running things. I'm afraid the painting would have been bungled if I didn't escape to the cabin."

"One must always have an escape route," Dorothy said.

She eyed a letter that was curiously folded into a small square, and she opened it. The date at the top said 1912. It was signed by his sister Virginia. Dorothy read: "I wish so often that I were a man, who could be independent in spirit. I hate the limitations of a girl." Dorothy surmised that Virginia simply gave up. She had seen it before: exquisite dreams lifting girls to the sky like balloons at a carnival, then *Pop!*—a long fall down from hope. She had seen the faces of shattered dreams, the zippy Ziegfeld girls, the doll-faced divorcées, the wellborn wives in opulent ivory towers, knocked down and knocked right out.

The sun broke through the clouds in time for her appointment with Millicent Hearst, who awaited her arrival at Mt. Kineo House, the luxurious resort on the water's edge with a golf course, parlor, and card room, and a house orchestra for the pleasure of guests who stayed the summer. Striped canopies covered the porches where ladies gathered for midday gossip and high tea. Dorothy clipped her hair back and pulled a jade dress from the closet.

"The last time I had quiet time with Millicent was on Palm Sunday, at the Greenbrier Resort. Do you remember?"

"Of course, darling. I found you two on the terrace overlooking the mountains. A serene setting, save for the photographer who popped up out of nowhere to take your picture."

"Ha! That's right. I saw cigarette smoke rising from behind a bush, but I had no idea someone was watching us. How unnerving!"

"Well, you girls have a good time. Good woman, that Millicent."

She found Millicent on the porch admiring *Vanity Fair*'s cover illustration that showed three women depicting the commandments See No Evil, Hear No Evil, Speak No Evil, with three monkeys behind them doing the same.

"We should pass around copies at the next luncheon," Dorothy said, hugging her.

"I like the jade color on you—very chic. By the way, I meant to tell you at the Greenbrier, the Steichen photo of you in the December issue of *Vogue* was divine. Such a *novelty* to be wearing clothes for pictures!" said Millicent, with a tinkle of laughter.

They were bonded by their past as showgirls. Well over ten years Dorothy's senior, Millicent had at one time dazzled the crowds at vaudeville shows, where William Hearst first laid his pale-blue eyes on her.

"Speaking of unclothed women, how is Jane Mason? I heard she's still with Hemingway," Millicent asked as a server poured them tea.

"They're madly infatuated with each other."

"I never did hear the story of how they met."

"They met on a ship, coming back from Le Havre. It wasn't long after that when he went to see her in Havana where she introduced him to the Cuban culture and the adventurous side of her nature," Dorothy said, smiling.

"The ladies all say they're glad that she's busy with him and her husband. No one can compete with Jane. She's a daredevil by day and glamour girl by night." They looked out to the rippling water.

"Jane doesn't recognize her potential. She always says she has talents too many, not enough of any." They gasped in awe of an eagle diving off a treetop and soaring through the air.

"What about you, Dorothy? Have you found time for sculpting? Crownie says you're gifted. Really gifted."

"Yes, a bit. I'm quite enjoying the work I've been doing with Gardner."

"Do you ever pine for the theater? Sometimes I think of that moment when the curtains part and you enter stage right to a storm of applause."

"I yearned for it when I saw the Ballets Russes. I thought of how different my life would be if I didn't have the accident. But I wouldn't trade my life with Gardner for anything."

"Did you hear that Fred and Adele Astaire just finished their run in *The Band Wagon* and he's on his way out to Hollywood to make pictures?"

"Yes, and Adele was practically in tears when she told me she's retiring. I'm sending her a leather-bound diary. It will be therapeutic for her to write. That's what I do," said Dorothy.

"Adele had the good sense to get married and avoid the depraved life of an actress. You'd be amazed at the stories I hear. At Mae Lambert's audition, the director chased her in circles around his desk until he finally caught her."

"That sounds terrifying! And a little familiar."

"Well," continued Millicent, "he pushed her against the wall and licked her eyelids. Full tongue. Can you imagine? Best to stay in our world with people like us."

"Yes. Speaking of, Kermit Roosevelt commissioned a painting from Gardner after you introduced us. What a darling man! He has the mind of a scholar and the soul of a poet," said Dorothy, drifting off in her own thoughts.

She caught sight of a bluebird gliding toward her and watched as it swooped down, landing on the arm of her chair. But her mind stayed on Kermit; he had recently sent her a letter about his harrowing adventure in the wilds: "I'm coming in on a wing and prayer. Save a dance for me on August twenty-fifth."

"Kermit was so pleased with his painting, he introduced me to Percy Pyne Jr., who wants Gardner to paint a mural in his country home."

"Percy is a gem. A chip off the old block."

"You get the feeling he'll never divorce, he's so agreeable and grounded. And why would he anyway?"

"His wife is an absolute wonder of kindness," said Millicent. "Remind me of your rule of marriage?"

"Marry a man who loves his mother and has attained success equal to that of his father or you'll pay the piper somewhere down the line," Dorothy said. "It doesn't leave many to choose from, does it?"

"You chose well," Millicent replied.

Dorothy and Gardner stayed at the cabin long after the summer revelers had gone. By mid-November, bitter storms rolled in, cracking limbs of the birch trees surrounding their cabin. In the wintry air of the mornings, they strolled past Gardner's studio and sat on the dock where they watched the glow of the rising sun. In the afternoons, heavy mist engulfed Moosehead Lake.

On a Tuesday morning, she awoke to the sound of unfamiliar voices in the distance and bounded out of bed. Pushing the curtains to the side of the window, she peered out to find four burly figures, all in matching black-and-red checked shirts, hauling a totem pole toward the lake, the occasional groan breaking the silence of the morning. Gardner emerged from the studio and ushered them inside. He had labored for weeks to carve the totem, the last of the series, and had finished the last of twenty paintings, *November Birches*, for Percy Pyne. It was the week before Thanksgiving, and they would ferry back to the mainland in twenty-four hours, not to return to Maine until the following summer.

With only a few days to spend in New York, their schedules filled quickly. They finalized details of the Modigliani memorial exhibit at Demette Galleries, for which they had designed a hardcover catalogue. Cecil Beaton photographed Dorothy for *Vogue*, and others came to the studio to photograph Gardner's work, the latest of which was a portrait of her. Flashbulbs went off, the pictures were

published, and with that bit of business complete, they bade goodbye
to their friends at Twenty-One and Romany Marie's and prepared to
leave for the open skies of California where they were expected to
arrive on the first of December.

"Shall we?" suggested Dorothy Swinburne McNamee, Gardner's
aunt, as she gestured to the abundant platters of Dover sole meunière,
roasted tenderloin, and local vegetables topped with a mustard
hollandaise sauce. She had prepared the east wing of her house in
Long Beach, California, for their two-month stay. Her husband,
Luke, was away on duty as commander of the US Navy battleships
of the United States fleet, one step closer to full admiral after an
already distinguished career.

"He was on the naval advisory board at the Paris Peace
Conference," she told Dorothy, who sensed that she missed him.

"Auntie," Gardner said, "from here on out we'll call you Dotty
because two Dorothys in the same house can get confusing, don't
you think?"

"Indeed. Besides, I always liked that nickname when I was a child."

They spoke of their plans for the upcoming months. Gardner
would paint for clients and visit local artists, and Dorothy would go
to Hollywood for Elsa's parties, but more than anything, she looked
forward to painting in the studio with Dotty. A prominent artist,
Dotty had gained notoriety from her exhibitions at the Knoedler
Galleries in New York and the Metropolitan Museum of Art. She
mostly made pictures of children, of which she had none.

The holiday week was sublime in the warmth of the California sun.
In the afternoons by the swimming pool, Gardner painted pictures of
Dorothy, her skin tanned, her eyes vibrant, her lips red. On the twenty-
seventh of December, they walked the trails between the mountains
and ocean, breathed in the scent of eucalyptus and jasmine in bloom,
and found repose in the tranquil gardens of the San Ysidro Ranch

where they capped off their visit at the Stonehouse, dining on steak Diane flambéed tableside and spinach souffle, followed by a 1907 bottle of Madeira to celebrate their two-year wedding anniversary.

The next day, Dorothy awoke to the tenderness of his lips on her cheeks, the tip of her nose, and her temple, and her face filled out in a smile. She liked their morning ritual.

"Do you remember where we were two years ago today?" he asked.

"Saying our wedding vows with the excitement of our future."

"Our future has turned out even better than I could have wished for."

"By the by, Dotty and I are planning something marvelous for your birthday. You don't look like a man about to turn thirty-eight, but you do have the wisdom."

"Well, it's not until the first of February, so I have a good couple of months before this starts to fill out," he chuckled, patting his slim waist. "But you, you're twenty-eight. You don't have a worry in the world about that sort of thing." With a breezy smile, he gathered papers from the desk and placed them neatly on top of a V-neck sweater in his suitcase. "Say, did you send in the census forms?"

"Yes. I wrote 'none' as my occupation for the first time in my life!"

"But you're an artist and my manager. You should claim it."

"I used to write 'artist.' My work is a labor of love, darling. In any case, everyone knows what I do."

"I want you to always be recognized for your accomplishments, on the record, that's all." He slipped on a sports coat and checked his appearance in the mirror. Catching a glimpse of her in its reflection, he looked as though he regretted their parting, however brief. "I should make it to Barnaby's place in San Francisco by one o'clock. I'm sorry to leave on the day of our anniversary—no choice, I'm afraid—but we did have a marvelous celebration yesterday, wouldn't you say?"

"Marvelous. I love you, darling. Drive carefully. And don't forget your wallet. It's on the dresser."

"I love you. You are a wonder."

Drops of rain rolled down the window of the studio where Dorothy and Dotty painted and giggled and gossiped about the goings-on in the art world. Dorothy's spirits were high, save for a nagging feeling that she couldn't explain. Her thoughts kept turning to Gardner. Perhaps it was due to his absence. They had spent so very few nights apart, and she had become accustomed to his constant presence. With no way to focus on the canvas in front of her, she took a break to look at *Vogue*. The cover illustration depicted a woman's hands releasing butterflies into the air to their freedom.

"Do you know the poem 'In Time of Silver Rain'?" she asked as she searched the pages for Maggie's latest article.

"Langston Hughes! Ah, I hear the telephone ringing. I'll recite my favorite verse when I return."

Perched outside the window, a pink-footed bird whistled in song as the sound of heels clicking on marble caught Dorothy's attention, the echo growing louder, the speed getting faster. It stopped. She looked up. Dotty was standing in the doorway, staring at her with a ghastly expression.

Dorothy froze, the floor falling out from under her. She couldn't breathe. Her mind shut down. A sharp blow to the stomach. The impact too hard, too deep, too overwhelming. Gasping for air, numbness spread through her. The magazine fell to the floor. Her guttural cry echoed to the heavens as Dotty enfolded her in her arms.

"Tell me," whispered Dorothy.

"It was the police. They found Gardner's wallet," Dotty said, gripping Dorothy's hand. "His car plunged over a five-hundred-foot cliff. He was killed on impact."

He had made it only twenty miles to the winding road of Nojoqui Grade in the mountains of Santa Ana, where majestic oak trees soared to the sky, their branches draped with glistening moss like a widow's veil.

12.

REFUGE BY THE SEA

D orothy lay still. Her head felt heavy on the pillow. She saw blackness. At first, she did not know where she was. There was a strange silence she was not accustomed to. A cold wind brushed her bare shoulder as images came into her mind. She thought for a moment she had awakened from a nightmare, and then, she remembered. She pulled the bedcovers around her and closed her eyes to sleep in order to forget.

The town of Newport, Rhode Island, was desolate, restaurants closed for the winter season. Grand mansions were locked, the furniture covered, striped tents stored away until the first ball signaled the start of summer. Not a light shined from the seaside homes; when night fell, they appeared as obscure silhouettes looming over the shoreline.

Dorothy lay awake in the darkness on a pillow wet from tears. She did not care. Nor did she care that tissues encircled her body or that she had lost her sense of hours and weeks as they passed slowly by. She knew by the light peering in from the side of the curtain the sun had begun its ascent, again. A bowl of soup on a silver tray by her bed remained untouched. She did not care about this either.

The scent of espresso suggested another morning had come. Opening her eyes reluctantly, she saw the newspaper on the bedside table and looked at the date. February 1. Gardner's birthday. Thinking of him, she promised he would never fade from her memory like a master painting in centuries of sun. The need to be near him stirred her from bed.

As raindrops fell into puddles by the steps, she gave it no thought, her feet wet and body listless as she opened the front door and stood quietly for a moment in the foyer.

"Where were you, Dorothy? There's a rainstorm out there." Dotty had not seen her out of bed since they arrived at her summer home. "Did you go back to Gardner's old family estate? Darling, it's been years since they sold it."

"It's dangerous. The roads are washed out." Maggie had not seen Dorothy in dress clothes since the funeral. They hung loosely on her diminutive body.

Dorothy lifted the black lace veil from her sallow face and folded her coat over her arm. It trickled water onto the marble floor where two umbrellas lay at her feet.

"That's why I went to Gardner. He's there, in the ground, in this rainstorm," she said, the heartache bringing her to her knees. "Right beside his mother and father . . ."

Dotty and Maggie had no idea what to say.

"Let it out, let it out, darling. I promise you'll be okay," Maggie said as she wrapped her arms around her. But if Dorothy said more, she would open the floodgates, spiral, and tumble into the sea from which there would be no return.

This was not her home. It was a refuge by the sea, yet she had no interest in the moving tide or the solace it tendered. The haunting wail of her own cry was unfamiliar to her ear, rising from uncharted depths within her. Her heart felt broken and it could not be mended.

Her legs felt weak and they could not be strengthened. She lay under the bedcovers and wept, and turned her cheek to rest on the pillow.

Early the following morning, she stood in the dew-covered grass beside Gardner's tombstone. When stripes of powder blue and white colored the empty sky and the sun had fully risen, she knew it was time to go. She would return when the sun began its descent into darkness. To begin and end the day with Gardner was a ritual she wouldn't forsake, the longing to hold him a feeling she couldn't shake at any moment of any hour as she slipped through the cracks of her heart into a lonely abyss.

Kneeling in the soil that evening, tears wetted the rose petals that she placed on his grave. She delayed a final goodbye until twilight faded to black, the stars veiled by filigree clouds. As she tried to find her way out of the cemetery, she wondered if she would ever find her way anywhere again.

PART III

13

THE GOLDEN AGE
OF HOLLYWOOD

Hollywood producer Samuel Goldwyn and his wife, Frances, stood on the promenade deck of the SS *Mariposa* ocean liner and watched the Manhattan skyline fade in the distance. Hundreds of passengers milled about smartly after a festive goodbye to their families, who had waved from the dock under a shower of multicolored confetti. By the time Dorothy reached the pier in a chauffeured car with eleven trunks in tow, the ship was well on its way.

"Can't you go any faster, Marco!" she cried into the wind, the speedboat bouncing over the current as they chased the massive vessel. She gripped the edge of the seat and wrapped her arm around the two dachshunds beside her.

"Signorina, you makin' me crazy," he shouted as he veered left to avoid the ship's wake. At full throttle, he sped along the port side, thrashing around his arms to catch the attention of someone on board. Six hundred and thirty-two feet in length and seventy-nine feet across, the SS *Mariposa* cruised powerfully onward, its hull rising high above the waves with hundreds of crew busy at work on deck. The speedboat circled three times around until, finally, the two steam turbines of the grand dame of the sea stopped and Marco raised his fist in victory.

"I wonder what happened. I think I'll go see," said Frances Goldwyn as she rose from her lounge chair on the second deck. Straightening her scarlet cloche, she waited for Sam to respond.

"Include me out," he said with a smile as she turned to go.

The speedboat rocked vigorously while Dorothy stood upright, anxiously watching two shipmates lifting the dogs onto the deck. The poor little pups. She felt a bit of regret for leaving them with her housekeeper most of the time and determined she should entrust them to William Beauchamp, the kindest breeder of champion hounds, who had taken in her other dachshunds. With a sigh of relief, she held her skirt in place, a gust of wind blowing the oversized bow on her blouse to the side of her blazer that was tailored snuggly to her petite frame. She smiled thankfully at Marco and extended her hand, knowing he would be pleased to feel the weight of bills in his palm. He watched as she climbed precariously up the rope ladder in T-strap heels and stepped on board to a round of applause. Why the captain didn't open the hatch door by the water's surface, she couldn't imagine, but it was of no consequence now. She'd triumphed. Soon enough, she would arrive at the Palace of the Legion of Honor to exhibit Gardner's work.

She settled into her suite, smoothed her hand over the silk bedding, and perused the furnishings—the modern, streamlined, cherrywood desk with rounded sides, the lamps slick and tall with a steel-like finish in the manner of a locomotive. Little Oscar and Claude sniffed around the floor, their long leashes dragging behind them. She took the ends and tied them to the leg of a weighty table. Then, turning toward the balcony, she sighed deeply and gave the door a vigorous push, stepping out into the salty air. There she found two chairs facing the ocean with a yellow rose on the table between them. Easing into the seat, she took the stem in her hand and twirled it round, looking up at the empty sky and waiting for the rhythm of the waves to soothe her.

"'I know that I shall find surcease, the rest my spirit craves, where the rainbows play in the flying spray, 'mid the keen salt kiss of the waves,'" she said, leaning back with her eyes closed. "Bravo, O'Neill." Three loud knocks interrupted her reverie.

Tempted to ignore the intrusion, she instead returned to the suite where she saw a card appear from under the doorway. Curious, she picked it up, ripped open the envelope, slipped out a telegram, and looked at the signature first. Clare. "Courage is the ladder on which all other virtues mount. CB." In that spirit, Dorothy slipped into her white satin Mainbocher bustle dress and left for the grand ballroom, noting she was twenty-five minutes late for the eight o'clock dinner seating.

She saw him the moment she emerged through the doors. Sam Goldwyn scanned the room and suddenly turned his gaze, following that of dozens who were turning toward the entrance where Dorothy stood alone.

"Everyone is looking at her. Fantastic, just fantastic," he said to his wife and rose to his feet, waving Dorothy over.

"I think if you put her in a movie, you would sell plenty of tickets," said Frances.

"That's the plan," replied Sam, his smile spreading as she approached them with a dazzling smile of her own.

Over an abundant meal of sole vin blanc, lobster cutlets, and canopère, with empress pudding on the menu for dessert, Sam pressed Dorothy about her personal history and professional pursuits, when he wasn't pontificating. By the way in which he leaned his elbows on the table, his torso angled at forty-five degrees, he looked genuinely interested in what she had to say.

"I confess," said Sam, "I did a little homework, spoke to a few people about you after we met at Jane's, and the words most attributed to you are vivacious, daring, adventurous, and indomitable."

"And 'fresh and youthful,'" Frances interrupted.

"Rightly so," Sam continued. "I'll admit what interested me very much was what a broad from Pittsburgh said. She said you have more than indisputable charm and vitality; you have a certain *disciplined intention* in your eye."

"And that it *augurs* definite achievement," Frances interrupted again. "I know because I'm the one who called."

"The old girl nailed it," Sam said, raising his glass in gesture to Dorothy and swallowing the last of his vodka.

"What's more, your voice is *wonderful*, so buttery and deep—but not too deep. Womanly deep. Just right," added Frances.

"Ah, you're too kind," Dorothy said with a full smile and slight bow of her head. She raised her glass, took a sip of her wine, and remembered her mother saying with regret that her expressions revealed her every emotion. Yet in this particular instance it seemed to serve her well.

"Why don't you come to Hollywood? I see you in the starring role of Cynara. You'll have terrific chemistry with Ronald Colman, the leading man. Terrific."

"The starring role? Well, that is an intriguing proposal, Sam!" Dorothy said brightly, tempted to return to the stage though she had taken a job as the executive manager of Demotte Galleries in New York.

"Meet me in Los Angeles after the exhibit and we'll do a screen test—just a formality."

"Dorothy, you've already done stage work. You'll be marvelous. Sam has a good eye," Frances reassured her.

"What can I do to prepare? This is such a surprise," she said, watching Sam stroke his head, which she knew at one time was adorned with hair.

"We'll send a script to your hotel and give you a little time to look it over," he said with a casual wave of his hand.

She agreed to meet him in Los Angeles in three weeks. *What a serendipitous turn of events*, thought Dorothy, calling up the image of the night she first met him. Jane had prodded her out of the Plaza Hotel, her deepening grief, and her somber seclusion after Gardner's death by insisting Dorothy come to Cuba for the party she had been planning for weeks. Admitting it was a well-advised antidote to the darkness of her days, Dorothy acquiesced, and the moment she arrived she was introduced to Sam. They laughed and talked and drank well into the night, amused by the pandemonium around them, the glittering guests running wild in drunken celebration of their own splendor.

"Empress pudding," announced the waiter in a deep timbre as he placed the dish on the table in front of Dorothy. Taking a cigarette from her silver case, she held it between her fingers. Sam turned to light it, and, as if on cue, the twenty-piece orchestra of the SS *Mariposa* struck the first chords of "Oh, Lady Be Good!"

"So, here's the story," Sam said. "Colman plays the role of a London barrister and you'll play the wife. You go out of town, he has an affair with a shop girl, and she falls for him head over heels. When you return home he jilts her. She's heartbroken and commits suicide."

"She dies from a broken heart. Only in Hollywood, Sam."

"Terrifically dramatic, isn't it? Anyway, the whole scandal gets out and ruins him. At the end of the film you forgive him, and together you sail into the sunset. Cue the music. There won't be a dry eye in the house. The only woman I know who wouldn't go for it is Dorothy Parker."

"Dorothy Parker, ahhh yes," Dorothy said, slowly nodding.

"Yes, I see you must know the old girl. Impossible."

"I've heard," Dorothy said, continuing to nod.

"Told her to change the end of a script, and you know what the old girl said? She said, 'I *know* this will come as a *shock* to you, Mr. Goldwyn, but in all history, which has held billions and billions of human beings, not a single one ever had a happy ending.'"

Dorothy stifled a laugh.

At half past midnight, she returned to her suite only to find she had forgotten to untie the leashes from the leg of the table. Oscar and Claude sprang from the floor and into the air, bouncing on their tiny paws like two tykes on a trampoline. Rubbing their heads and cooing, she released them and watched as they scurried around the room stealing occasional glances at her with audible disdainful sniffs, much in the manner of Crownie when conversing with Clare.

After some difficulty unzipping her gown as she walked to the bedroom, she slipped on her satin robe. The Modigliani exhibition book peeked out from her satchel. She opened it to the page where she had tucked newspaper clippings and considered for a moment whether now was the time to read them.

Feeling particularly buoyant about Sam's proposal, she felt she could handle anything, and so she walked to the balcony, sat down, looked up at Orion's Belt, and took a deep breath. She had put off reading Gardner's obituaries for too long. Detectives in Santa Barbara had told her the grim details when she was in shock, unable to absorb the words. Gardner swerved off the highway over a cliff and plunged 500 feet down the canyon. The impact of the crash on the canyon floor catapulted him thirty feet from his car, where his body lay broken for six hours before it was found. As she began to read, her eyes blurred with tears, she strained to make out the words. "Examination of the highway paralleling the canyon indicated he had missed a turn in the road made more dangerous by current rains. He'd left Long Beach to drive to San Francisco . . ." Unable to bring herself to read more, she covered her face with her hands and lowered her head, a wave of pain cresting and crashing into her heart.

In his last months, he had been so impatient with nightfall's intrusion, determined to finish his book as though he knew that time was not on his side. "I'll finish it for you," she whispered.

Two months before she boarded the ship, she had hired a writer to complete Gardner's manuscript. Then, in the course of her mourning, she had traveled alone to all corners of Europe and the States, searching for his paintings, determined to find each and every one. To arrange shows for Gardner was a ritual she wouldn't forsake, the longing to hold him a feeling she couldn't shake at any moment of any hour.

When at last she arrived in New York, she drank in its thrilling vibrancy as the black car rolled up to the corner of Fifty-Ninth Street and Fifth Avenue, turned right into the drive, and stopped. The bell captain swept to the car to tend the luggage, leashes, and little hounds while she looked up at the star-filled night, drew in a breath, then stepped onto the red carpet and disappeared through the turnstile door.

At half past eleven that evening, she moved to Gardner's side of the bed, pulled the soft sheet to her chin, and stared out the window at the Carlyle Hotel in the distance, the serene glow of its emerald crown slowing her tears as she gazed at its noble beauty. Looking east, she drifted off to sleep on the uppermost floor of the Plaza Hotel.

The next morning, she followed the red carpet down the front steps of the hotel and set off on a leisurely walk. She crossed Fifty-Eighth Street, turned right onto Fifth Avenue, and slowed her pace in front of Bergdorf Goodman's to see the fashions in the window. A glimpse of her reflection surprised her with its melancholy. Continuing along Fifth Avenue, she felt her mourning was in sync with the city as it sank deeper into the Depression. Crossing Forty-Fifth Street, she glanced to the right and saw young children waiting on a breadline for morsels of food for their families, their parents undoubtedly too ashamed to be one step away from moving to Hoovervilles, the shantytowns that housed the homeless.

Sitting on the pavement at the corner of Forty-Fourth, a ragged man in a crumpled suit leaned listlessly against a storefront and stared ahead. On the other side of the street there were others like him. Men who once were titans of business now were unrecognizable to their friends, friends that found refuge at their homes in Newport and the Gold Coast, places with vodka and rare art and pretty dresses. She felt a heavy pall cast over Manhattan and found some relief in knowing she would return to the comfort of her coterie that evening. They said they were anxious to hear of her forthcoming Hollywood escapades after tracking the news in the papers.

Crownie and Maggie were the first to arrive at Twenty-One where they sat contentedly in the lounge, perusing an album that had been assembled by Gertie, the manager's secretary, who had always admired Dorothy from afar.

"Famed Pennsylvania Woman Is to Enter the Movies . . . Society Matron Signs Contract for Films," read Maggie with dramatic cadence. She took a generous sip of French rosé and continued. "Gardner Hale's widow, who never faced a camera in her life, except to have her picture taken, wins out over other experienced actresses for the coveted role of leading lady opposite Ronald Colman in Cynara."

"Here, here, allow me to take a look at that," said Crownie, fiddling with his bow tie.

"Read aloud, if you wouldn't mind," Maggie insisted as she passed him the book.

"Ah, yes, the *Boston Globe* and the *LA Times*. 'Goldwyn suddenly saw Mrs. Hale as a calmly assured, sophisticated young wife of Cynara. . . . Dorothy Hale registers in person as one of the colony's most interesting acquisitions.'"

"Acquisitions! As if she's a work of art on the auction block."

"It goes on to say, 'She has much of the wit and some of the irony of Aileen Pringle.'" Crownie paused for a moment to look at the photographs of her posing in front of movie cameras, and then continued to read with vague amusement. "'Miss Hale is a widow, one of the first real ones to my knowledge that has ever appeared on the colony horizon. She also has had much to do with modern art.'"

"Ah, here she is," said Maggie, smiling as Dorothy and Clare made their way toward her. "Shall we, Crownie?" He closed the book with a look of puzzlement on his fine-featured face, fingering his mustache as he rose from the chair.

"What does that mean, she has had much to do with modern art?" Crownie asked as they climbed the steps to be seated at their regular table.

"Crownie, you're always editing," Maggie said as she pulled the tips of her gloves, slipped them off, and sat down.

"The usual cocktails and canapés?" asked the waiter who suddenly appeared. Dorothy nodded with a smile and watched him pivot on his feet and trot away.

"Donald did the same thing," Clare said, referring to her former mentor and lover, the man who crashed his car into a tree after she spurned his proposal of marriage. She called it a suicide, then took his job as managing editor of *Vanity Fair*.

"Dorothy transformed Demotte Galleries into the international headquarters for French art," Maggie sniffed.

"'She has much to do with modern art' is a throwaway line. For all anyone knows, it's your job to make sure the work isn't hung upside down," Clare said amusedly.

"Someone needs to," Dorothy laughed. "The National Academy of Design awarded second prize to Dickinson only to find out the work was hung sideways!"

The waiter returned with three others in matching white coats, and in a choreographed sweep, they placed the drinks and platters on the table.

"I can assure you the mistake won't be made at the Museum of Modern Art," Crownie chuckled.

"A toast to Crownie," Dorothy said, raising her glass, "a founding member of one of the great cultural treasures of Manhattan."

"Do you remember Gardner's incredulous expression at the opening when patrons nearly cried with enthusiasm for the artists they had disparaged only days before," Clare recalled. Dorothy looked at her, feeling the sharp punch in her stomach.

"Right right," Crownie said, nodding. "They had called Van Gogh a lunatic and Gauguin a libertine, and that was when they could even bring themselves to discuss them."

Clare stared blankly into her glass of merlot and took a slow sip.

"I know you. What's going on?" Dorothy asked in a hush as she pulled her chair a little closer to Clare's.

"Where to begin?"

Dorothy could guess precisely where to begin—his name was Bernie Baruch, with whom Clare was having an *affaire de coeur*. Clare had told her they had fallen into an impossibly perfect union, one of the rarest kind, a selfless love that strengthened every day, one the champion of the other. But for all his power and might as the president's advisor, Bernie couldn't face the fire with his wife. It was a source of deepening sadness for Clare, who could see the toll his marriage was taking on him, even if he couldn't.

"Is it Bernie? He will never leave his wife," Dorothy said.

"He said we are soul mates," Clare replied wistfully, prompting an expression of disbelief from Dorothy. "He said it two months after we met. And what, may I ask, is the thought that accompanies your expressive face?"

"Darling, don't you know?" asked Dorothy incredulously. "That soon? It's the red flag that your white knight is the prince of darkness and he'll make Narcissus look like an amateur. If I could count the times I've heard those very words . . ."

"God, everything seems meaningless anyway. I am loathsome, barren of virtue. Sometimes I just want to end it all. Do you know, I heard that someone said of me I'm a beautiful, well-constructed façade, but without central heating. Can you imagine?"

"Well, pay no mind to it," Dorothy said. "I know you have the dismals, and I'm here for you. We all are. You must stop drinking so much wine and caffeine, darling. It's rattling your nerves." Crownie, ensconced in conversation with Maggie, turned to Dorothy to light her cigarette as she continued. "This affair with Bernie is draining you. I know you feel you don't have the emotional capacity to take on anything else, and it's been exhausting for you trying to get *Vanity Fair* back on its feet. What you need is some time away to write. That's what you most enjoy. After I finish the Cynara shoot, I'm going to stay with Gardner's sister in New Mexico so that I can start writing a book, which will be much more fulfilling than the articles I've been doing. Why don't you join me?"

"A change of scenery—yes, I think I will. This past year I've come to realize I shall never be quite happy until New York becomes a place to which I go often, rather than leave seldom." She lowered her voice to a softer whisper. "Don't tell Crownie, but as soon as I find something better to do, I'm leaving the magazine. It's a sinking ship. You know what I always say: Down to Gehenna or up to the Throne, he travels fastest who travels alone." She sat back in her chair and sighed, rustling through her purse. "I'm out of cigarettes."

"I have some," Dorothy said, handing her a silver case. Crownie noticed Clare raising the stick of tobacco to her lips.

"You know, it wouldn't kill you two to stop smoking," he said, flicking open his lighter.

The friends left Twenty-One before midnight, notably earlier than usual, anxious to rest up for the demands of the days ahead. While Clare struggled to find solid ground, Dorothy set off to Los Angeles to begin rehearsals for Cynara. By the time she arrived at the Château Élysée, she had been written about, talked about, and interviewed by writers to such a degree that she was unabashed about a few of the finer details of her life. Louella Parsons, Hedda Hopper of Hollywood, Walter Winchell, and their gossip-column comrades in arms left no personal stone unturned. Thus, everyone in the business was well informed of her age, her two marriages, and her past, and they didn't know what to expect. And as Dorothy would soon discover, neither did she.

It was seven o'clock on a Monday evening when she opened the door to her suite and, upon entering, smiled at the sight of the bouquet of blond begonias blooming from a crystal vase on the cocktail table. Beside it, she found a silver folder as thick as Wilde's collected works. Without further ado, she slipped out of her silver car coat, took the folder in her hands, lowered herself onto the sofa with her feet resting on the gold-embroidered pillow, and ripped off the Goldwyn label with the zeal of a child on her first Christmas morning.

A note was clipped to the front of the stack. "To The Indomitable Dorothy Hale, Welcome to Hollywood! Read the script, learn the scene as indicated. You'll be terrific. Best Regards, Sam. p.s. See you next week at the screen test." She looked at the title page. "CYNARA. Inspired by Ernest Dowson's immortal lines 'I have been faithful to thee, Cynara, in my fashion.'" *It sounds like something Clare would have said to George,* she mused as she turned to page one and began to read.

Ten minutes later, as she pored over the dialogue in the section marked "Screen Test," she thought with some surprise, *This sounds like something I should have said to Gaillard.* That it resonated with her made her believe the marriage to him had its purpose after all. *Remarkable,* she reflected, positively sure she would play the role of Clemency perfectly, and thus she began the reading of her lines aloud.

CLEMENCY:
"Jim, if I could only understand. If you could tell me something more. You know, you never really told me."

[She turns her gaze to the floor, her eyebrows furrowed.]

"I have to imagine everything. And that's so much worse."

JIM:
What do you want to know, Clemency?

CLEMENCY:
"Just what happened, that's all. What happened to you. Inside you, I mean . . ."

Continuing to read her lines over and again until her eyes grew heavy, she resolved to resume her practice promptly at half past six the following morning and each and every one thereafter, and so she did, rehearsing various intonations and pitches with absolute assuredness that her expressions were coming naturally.

With acute determination to ace the test, she allowed little distraction from the outside world, keeping her focus on this material, which consumed her completely, save for evening cocktail parties she was obligated to attend. Then, at high noon on the seventh morning, a black car whisked her away to the Samuel Goldwyn Studio in Studio City—only a ten-minute drive to meet her destiny.

Escorted by a sprightly young man with starch in his shirt and spring in his step, she strode into the studio and stopped, a cadre of crew looking at her with curiosity for only a moment before going on about their business. As did she. After quick introductions and a few pleasantries, she met the actor standing in for Ronald Colman, Eugene Nagy, a droopy fellow grievously in want of good looks, and then was directed to the set where a single chair had been placed. Seated, she looked into the lens, finding immediately that it gave her a sense of ease and the epiphany that she was more comfortable surrounded by cameras than a catty crowd at a cocktail party, and certainly would be more forthcoming.

"Lights! Camera!" bellowed King Vidor. And then, in a deep, velvety hush, "*Action*."

"My things are gone. I'll have to leave soon myself," said Eugene, timidly.

"Do you really want to go to this place? South Africa will be so strange for you," said Dorothy in a soft, yearning voice, her expression sorrowful.

"Well, what else is there to do?" Eugene said, his voice a little shaky.

"Well, you're . . . you're sure that your career is absolutely over at home? That . . . that there wouldn't be any chance?" she said with vague hope.

"I don't want to try alone. It would be all right with you, but—"

"Jim, I . . ." She leaned her elbow on the back of her chair and turned to him. "Jim, if I could only understand. If you could tell me something more. You know, you never really told me." Lowering her melancholy gaze to the floor, her eyebrows furrowed. "I have to imagine everything. And that's so much worse."

"What do you want to know? You've heard all the things."

"Just what happened, that's all. What happened to you. Inside you, I mean . . ."

"Oh, my dear, don't you see I wanted to spare you?" Eugene's voice lilted up in an unfortunate attempt at dramatic flair. As she looked into his eyes, her wistful, woebegone expression caused Eugene to draw a blank, thus missing his cue.

Under the spotlight she melded and dissolved into the character of Clemency and felt the moments as if they were hers. After the last line was spoken, a minute went by in silence.

"Cut!" said King Vidor as he stood very still. "That's a wrap."

Dorothy looked up to find the crew standing at attention, looking at her. One stagehand began to clap. Another followed. Then they all burst out in applause. As it grew louder with increased exuberance, whistles were whistled and her cheeks flushed more. Sam stepped forward from behind one of the cameras.

"Bravo. Brilliant. Brilliant!"

"Thank you, Sam!" Dorothy said, striding swiftly to his side.

"Just terrific," he said as he took her gently by the arm, gestured to the exit, and led her away. "We have a garden table reserved at the Beverly Hills Hotel." When they passed through the gargantuan, black steel door, he tilted his head toward hers. "If you can pull that off with Eugene—the boy is a friend's nephew, hasn't acted a day in his life—imagine the chemistry and performance you'll have with Colman."

There was no better spot in town than the Polo Lounge at the Beverly Hills Hotel, the outdoor ambiance as glorious as the Garden of Eden with its trellises and vines and violet flowers fussed over and fixed to look as though they had grown quite naturally in elegant composition. Had it not been for the continuous interruptions by those seeking something from Sam, not the least of which was giving oglers the impression they actually knew him, their late lunch might well have ended earlier than dinner hour. In the course of their conversation, however, she was pleased to learn the news that he had hired a team of acting coaches to school her in technique so she would master the marriage of verbal and physical expression as written on the page and perfect the art of playing to the camera. Aside from the pure emotion and grace she would bring to the role, she would learn to master the craft.

And yet, in the subsequent days, even with all the enthusiasm she brought to these daily lessons, she found herself a tinch overwhelmed by the rapid pace of instruction coupled with the confusion of coaches' concepts, while trying to manage the deluge of shiny new friends, each of whom would call at every hour to invite her to dinner, lunch, or a party simply to earn their way into her good graces before anyone else. Their sparkly, white-toothed smiles were as conspicuously artificial as their surgically enhanced noses, and breasts, and even, in one case, derrière.

On one evening, having spent the preceding hours practicing what she had been taught, she poured herself a tall glass of ice water, stared at the pretty view of the mountains, and pondered not a moment over whom she could call.

"You can't imagine the vast number of directions I'm given by these coaches. There are four, *four* coaches, Maggie. They say, 'Don't move your hand now; wait for your second line and then place it on his. Use your sense memory. Think of a heartbreaking moment and convey the emotion. Hit your mark. Look to your right for a better camera angle. Don't project the way you do in theater. Be subtle. Give us more of a doe-eyed look, lower your eyes to the floor, then turn quickly to face him and pause before your next line.' It goes on and on, and then they say, 'Look natural.'"

"You'll be terrific. I know it," said Maggie.

"Terrific, terrific, yes," she said, hearing Sam's voice in her mind. "You know, yesterday I was practicing in my suite, and there's a scene at the end of the movie when Clemency is brokenhearted and then she imagines life without her husband, and all the grief of losing

Gardner came back. I miss him s—" She held her breath. Maggie understood the silence.

"I know. Breathe."

"Well, I can't do this now," said Dorothy, regaining her composure. "I have only two hours to go through my lines. When I'm not rehearsing in the room I'm spending hours in wardrobe fittings. The costume designer's assistants tell me how pleased they are that I've kept my lithe dancer's physique. They ask, 'How do you do it?' I smile and think, well, I don't eat. Widowhood, girls."

In September, the moment finally arrived when she would appear before the cameras, Sam Goldwyn, the director, King Vidor, and the cast and crew for rehearsal. Things did not go as planned.

All was well and fine in the beginning. She arrived at the studio lot, stepped out of the car, and was immediately ushered to the costume department. Makeup, hair, a high-neck flower-print dress that would read well on black-and-white film. Once done she was ushered to the set where she scanned the room for the star of the picture. Seeing a few stagehands turn toward the door behind her, she too turned her head, and there, with his jet-black hair and mustache trimmed to a narrow line, his gray suit fitted immaculately to his handsome physique, in all the grand elegance of his statuesque bearing, there stood the exquisite Ronald Colman, one of Hollywood's great leading men. And to think she would have the rare and remarkable pleasure of looking into those bewitching brown eyes with a gaze that spelled *take me*. It would not, she decided, be a stretch.

Seeing her standing there, he strode toward her wearing a magnificent grin and holding his arms wide, finally greeting her with an embrace which lasted perhaps a moment longer than was typical in such a circumstance.

"Look at you, more beautiful than I even imagined," he said, his voice a low pitch with confident projection and perfect pronunciation rarely heard except on the silver screen. "This should be great fun. Let's give it a whirl, shall we?"

As they walked to the set chatting about one of their first scenes, wherein Clemency knows of his affair and his mistress's suicide, Dorothy began to notice the cameras wheeling by, the lights turning on, the director's booming baritone, the studio suits in cross-legged chairs, and she felt the excitement of it all. The sets were designed as she had imagined, the bedroom opulent yet tasteful, the fireplace topped with ornate silver accessories, two Bergere chairs, and a white satin covering on the king-sized bed where Ronald would sit, and she, standing before him, would embrace him, his head nuzzled on her chest, his cheek and nose feeling her skin so generously exposed from the wide white V-neck silk blouse cut impossibly low for that purpose.

Their first scene, however, would be shot in the understated room with two chairs and shuttered doors opening to a courtyard. That's where they took their places. But when she looked up in the moments before they were to begin, she saw them. The gaggle of acting coaches gathered by the wall, wagging and nodding their heads, prompting nervous contemplation. *Breathe in one-two-three, breathe out . . .*

Lights. Camera. Action.

"And . . . you say that you still loved me . . . all the time . . ." Sad, worried, Dorothy looked toward the floor, remembering to rub her right hand on her left arm slowly.

"It made no difference." Ronald was looking at her, leaning toward her with his arm resting on his knee.

"No difference?" inquired Dorothy, turning her head away from the camera and into his eyes. "You can't really mean that." She could hear the tension and feigned sincerity in each of her lines.

"But it's true. It's true, Clemency." His voice intense, he clenched his fist.

"Yet . . ." She quickly got up from the bed and turned toward the camera, exiting the frame to the left. He looked upset.

"You . . . you risked everything. All we built up," she said, turning to look at him, remembering what her coach had said about looking more doe-eyed. She rested her hands on the chair between them. "Didn't all that mean anything to you?" she asked, hoping her voice and expression were now subtly intense but still vulnerable like the coach had instructed.

"It meant everything. It does mean everything. More than I knew." He looked at the floor, and she remembered to turn her head away to the left. Then she turned to her right, away from him, and looked out to the courtyard.

"Things that make amusing conversation aren't so funny when it's your own life." That line she knew she delivered magnificently. He stood and walked to her side by the shuttered doors, their backs to the camera.

"I'm afraid it hasn't helped very much, my telling you," he said.

"Yes, it has." She turned to her right so the camera could see her profile. Then she looked down at her hands, holding a tissue and waited for him to look at her. "I'm glad you did."

"CUT!" howled King Vidor.

Acting against her instinct on how to play the scenes, she had employed each of the tactics she had been taught. With the self-critical thoughts that ensued after each word and movement, she had no spark of chemistry with her co-star or her usual luminosity in the lens. Each time King Vidor groaned "Cut," her face flushed, and her coaches' deprecatory voices thundered in her mind.

It was a long several days of silence from Sam as she waited nervously for news. Surely, she thought, this city of second chances would live up to its rightful name and she would be granted one from him. On Friday afternoon, the call finally came in.

A strand of pearls hung listlessly down her slim torso, twisted and weaved through her delicate fingers. She sat upright at attention in a plush chair in the living room of her suite and held the telephone close to her ear, listening to Sam explain.

"You've got promise, and with a few weeks in front of the camera I know you'd be fantastic. I haven't been wrong yet." Knowing what was coming, her mind was too distracted by disappointment to assimilate his words. "We just don't have time; we're on a tight budget, you do understand. King Vidor wants to keep you on and so do I, but we need to wrap on schedule. The role will go to Kay Francis, and you will play a swimmer."

She breathed deeply, in one-two-three, out one-two-three, and graciously agreed to dine with him that very evening, her wide eyes glistening as she purred goodbye and gently hung up the receiver. It was a perfect performance.

She picked up her jewel-encrusted case, pulled out a cigarette, and paced around the high-pile rug in shamed silence. Finally, she sidled up to the plump pillows on the sofa, lit a cigarette, and blew a light cloud of smoke into the perfumed air. Flicking the ashes restlessly, she thought, *Of all the humiliating things, Sam. Well, I've had harder punches than this!*

The morning after her dinner with Sam, Dorothy thumbed through the newspapers until she found her name in the headlines. She read. "For the graceful, tasteful, sophisticated stunner Dorothy Hale, too many hands in the movie-making pie crippled her extraordinary natural acting ability." The next paper. "Miss Hale's stunning performance in her screen test displayed her natural talent as a leading lady. The exquisite beauty lit up the screen, playing the part with such sincerity and magnetism, she was sure to become one of the greats of the silver screen." The next. "Then why, you may wonder, did she lose the role? She had followed the direction of too many acting teachers and forgot about her prodigious natural skills." One writer ended his story saying, "With her ability, intellect, and breathtaking allure, there is no doubt she will enthrall audiences in her next role."

Fair enough, she said to herself. Quite more flattering than she expected, yet still delicious fodder for gossip that she knew she couldn't avoid. It was high noon at Twenty-One, and by this time it would be, without question, abuzz with the news.

The next morning, seated in the back of a black car that the concierge at the Château Élysée had arranged for her, she passed through the gate of Samuel Goldwyn Productions where she found no one waiting to escort her. Thus, she pulled her sunglasses from her purse, put them on, and roamed the lot until she found building number seventeen. There she was greeted warmly by a staff of three sprightly girls who showed her to the dressing area.

"Your derrière is superb," said the fawning costume designer, Milo, as he held Dorothy's waist from behind. "You should see some of the dreadful shapes that stand before me. It's such a trouble to my work." Smiling pleasantly, Dorothy stood in front of the mirror and eyed the little swimsuit she was to wear for her big-screen debut.

"Ah, but I know your talents. You can make anyone look divine," she said with exaggerated verve to veil the embarrassment of her long fall down from the starring role.

"Listen, honey, it's none of my business, but let me tell you, I've seen a lot of girls come and go. Sam does this all the time. One minute it's one girl, the next minute she's out. But I never saw him give a girl like you the lead role. Why, you never did a movie in your life. No, Sam sees something in you, but he has a lot of dough riding on this. You're pretty lucky, as I see it."

"Thank you, Milo," Dorothy said as she stepped away from the mirror.

"Of course, I don't know why you'd want this kind of life. Everyone in this town always has something to say about someone, and it's usually not very nice."

Thinking that over, she slipped into a flowing silken dress and left for the tranquility of the hotel where she would find more reports of her very public travails.

Not even Milo's subtle caution had prepared her for the mighty wallop that was delivered in bold black print. Fanning perspiration from her brow with great swoops of a Chinese fan clenched in her hand, her glossed lips dropped open and her sad eyes enlarged as she read each wicked word. "One wondered how any astute producer could have looked across a dinner table and chosen a refined woman merely because she knew which fork to use."

The walls surrounding her heart that had formed over time came tumbling down in a burst of water and wails. Oh, it did feel good to let go of the pain that had weighed her down for so long. She dropped her head back on the couch, feeling nothing but two last teardrops swelling up in her eyes and ending finally in a soft plop on her cheeks.

She tossed the newspaper to the other side of the sofa, fingered the elephantine stone of her blue sapphire ring, and stared at the blank gray wall for a good many minutes to mull it all over. As she reviewed the ways in which she could appease her muddle of emotions, there seemed to be but one suitable option, barring a lifetime in satin bed covers pulled up to her mascara-smeared eyes, and that was to smile and dance through the pain. Her mother's parting wisdom, the warmth of her touch in her last days, came into her mind as she breathed in the crisp California air and pondered more cheerfully. In due time, she decided, that very same writer would retreat to her sullied cage where she would open the newspapers and meet Dorothy's twinkling eyes, her name sandwiched between superlative phrases, while the writer stewed in her own dissipating creative juices.

Keeping her emotions to a low simmer, she stretched the telephone wire to the balcony where she took in the picturesque vista of the city and placed a call to Clare. Waiting for her to answer, she twisted her necklace in vexed silence. Away with the usual diplomacy; it was time for her to vent.

She did not wait for Clare to say hello.

"*La Remarque de un idiot. Elle est un imbécile complet. Méchant.* Did you read Mayme Peak's article, what she said?" asked Dorothy.

"Ah, the rare unleashing of the French barbs. You must be annoyed. And yes, of course, it *is* an idiot's remark. As one would expect from her. They say we ultimately fulfill the meaning of our given names. She should change the spelling," Clare said, drawing laughter from

Dorothy, who went on to tell her about her plans to return home.

"Have you met Kay Francis yet?" asked Clare.

"Not yet, but I'm told she'll be coming to the set tomorrow. The truth is, I can't wait to meet her. She seems divine."

"She took your role. You're a better man than I am, Gunga Din."

"Well, that was Sam's doing. Or mine. I'll ask her to dinner to break the ice."

The next day Dorothy found herself in a group of twenty bouncy girls wearing low-back bathing suits and caps, milling about smartly, waiting for filming to begin. She smiled pleasantly and was a little embarrassed to be cast among them, so what else was she to do but slip away to the powder room? When she walked in, no one was there, leaving her to her thoughts about what the girls must be saying about her. She went into the nearest stall. And that's when it happened.

At the very moment she was finishing up, the door swung wide open, jolting Dorothy to attention. She looked up.

Kay Francis. Good God! Dorothy flushed feverishly. And what did Kay do but step right in. They stared at each other for less than a moment before Kay said, "Dorothy Hale!" and shrieked enthusiastically. "I heard your screen test was *wonderful*. I've been waiting to meet you. Say, you know you didn't lock the door!"

"I know, I—"

"I've heard so much about you," she interrupted gregariously, entirely unphased while Dorothy, her bottoms lowered, looked at her in astonishment. "Sam said we look and sound alike. I think—"

"Look away, Kay!" Dorothy pleaded, her eyes large and lips upturned at the ludicrousness of it all, which launched Kay into a giggle. "Look away, please, Kay!" Dorothy repeated, erupting in a giggle too. With tears in their eyes, the conversation continued until the suit was on, the lipstick was applied, and they made their exit together stage right. Needless to say there was no point to having dinner to break the ice, but they went nevertheless.

When filming concluded, Dorothy hung her swimsuit out to dry, immediately left for New York, and checked into the Plaza Hotel. With little time to ready for Elsa's party, a treasure hunt, not a moment was wasted. She flung open her trunk, pulled out an armful of clothes, laid them out on the bed, took her toiletries and makeup case and placed them on the vanity, and hopped into the shower where she contemplated which of her dresses would be suitable for this particular moment. Yes, she knew exactly what to do.

With a swipe of petal-pink lipstick, her hair already styled, she slipped out of her robe and stepped into her fringed pink-and-white Patou dress, pulling it up with a quick zip, a clasp at the top, and checked its fit in the mirror. Perfect. Looking herself over, pleased, she slid her feet into a pair of silver high heel shoes, which she noticed in her reflection accentuated the definition of her legs and gave her a more imposing appearance. Then, to complete the armor, she pulled on custom Chanel evening gloves with frilled feather borders and draped a sequined cape by Lanvin over her shoulders. There. Now she felt like herself. With an air of confidence, she dashed out the door with five minutes to make it to the St. Regis, or she would miss the window to arrive fashionably late.

All eyes turned to her as she made her entrance through the ornate gold-trimmed doors. With a big smile, she greeted acquaintances and air-kissed friends, swiftly drifting across the room to Clare, only to find her in a state of depression so severe she was conspicuously disinterested in everything but her own circle of thoughts. At the first opportune moment, she whisked Dorothy away from the throng of guests giddily embarking on the treasure hunt, their booze splashing about. Dorothy and Clare maintained a wide berth around them, keeping their eyes on the moving mass of silk, satin, and suits. Once out of earshot, they pulled two chairs back from the table and sat down. Clare sighed deeply and drew in a deep breath before speaking.

"I have to confess I have the dismals. I am simply unable to climb out of my bottomless well of gloom. I drop farther and farther down, and the only thought that consoles me is suicide."

"Dear God, Clare. Please come stay with me. Things will fall into place." Clare shook her head repeatedly with a thousand-mile stare. "I know you're ready for a change. So am I. Whatever we do, it will be something wonderful."

"I would settle for something unforgettable," said Clare.

"I know. That's what concerns me."

14.

HAZARD YET FORWARD

Three black limousines rolled up to the entrance of the Knoedler Galleries on East Fifty-Seventh Street where a small crowd was waiting—for the arrival of whom, they did not know. One by one, the passengers emerged. Clare Boothe Brokaw, Elsa Maxwell, Buckminster "Bucky" Fuller, Isamu Noguchi, Maggie Case, Frank "Crownie" Crowninshield, Jane Mason, and Rosamond Pinchot. They swiftly disappeared through the doors. Millicent Hearst had already arrived with the Condé Nasts, the Herbert Bayard Swopes, and the Pierpont Morgan Hamiltons. Inside, Jerry Zerbe snapped Dorothy's picture as she welcomed her friends to the Gardner Hale Memorial Exhibit, which she had painstakingly organized to coincide with the publication of his book, *Fresco Painting*. The Florentine Victorian pendant adorned her chest and drew admiring glances as she scanned the crowd. Diego Rivera and Frida Kahlo, in the far corner of the room, gestured furiously as they argued in Spanish. Dorothy went over to interrupt.

"My darlings," she cooed, trying to soothe them. "There are thirty paintings on exhibit." Taking Frida's arm and leading her away, she continued, "Frida, I'll show you the ones he painted in New York."

"You're a savior."

"Well, I know that look of yours," said Dorothy, stopping in front of Gardner's painting *Two Trees*. Frida observed her closely. "Gardner painted this at the studio downtown right after we were married. When he showed it to me, he said the trees symbolize the two of us, how we're strongly rooted in the pureness of God's earth, and we have an enduring love that will remain unchanged by blowing wind and rain that will fall upon their leaves. Beautiful, isn't it?" She thought, but didn't say, how the rain had made the winding roads more dangerous on the day he died, how the roaring winds carried him over the cliff.

"I'm told his book is the bible of fresco painting." Frida ran her fingers over the gold-gilt lettering and opened to page one as Isamu sidled up beside her.

"I didn't know before this evening that Gardner's work is in the Metropolitan Museum of Art, the Whitney, and the Brooklyn Museum," he said, his eyes gleaming with envy.

"Yes, and did you know he's a descendant of Swinburne, the poet?" asked Frida, sensing it would provoke him. "And three of his direct ancestors signed the Declaration of Independence." Shelby Whitehouse swept over to Dorothy, and she excused herself, leading him through the crowd to make introductions.

She gave rapt attention to each and every person, touching a shoulder here, listening intently there, graciously thanking them for attending. Making her way over to Crownie and Clare, she saw they were reading the catalogue of the exhibition.

"Crownie, you did a superb job of writing this," Clare acknowledged.

"It's a beautiful tribute to Gardner's work," Dorothy said as Frida approached. "He would be pleased."

"Some would say he *is* pleased, watching from the heavens," Frida said, sweeping her arm upward as her silver bangles chimed.

"Do you believe in that? In the afterlife? In . . . I don't know, in spirits?" asked Dorothy.

Frida touched her arm gently. "Yes, and they can be tormenting if they had no time to say goodbye."

"Do you mean to say ghosts?" Dorothy was surprised to see the others nod in confirmation, as if there were no question in the very debatable matter.

"Well, well, well," said Cholly Knickerbocker as he stepped between Dorothy and Frida. "I do love this, the cream of the Café Society crop all in one room with the very man who created Café Society in America, Mr. Francis Boardman Crowninshield of the esteemed Crowninshield clan of Boston Brahmin repute."

"I suppose since you coined the term Café Society," Crownie said, "you should be permitted to use it incessantly, like you do."

Cholly turned to face Dorothy, and with an air of drama, he took her hands in his. "It must be hard for you, darling—such a shock to lose your one great love. I haven't found mine yet, but I do hope he looks like Gardner." Dorothy noticed Millicent standing behind him looking pleased as a server handed her a glass of champagne.

"Millicent, please, join us," she said with a subtle sidelong glance at Cholly.

"Darling!" cooed Millicent, taking the cue. "Gardner's artwork is brilliant, and we're absolutely delighted to have you back from the grips of Hollywood."

"Dorothy, you took up an entire half page of the *New York Times* the other day. Did you see it?" asked Rebecca Hamilton.

"Not yet . . ."

"My God, it's fabulous. They listed this exhibit right next to a picture of the gorgeous portrait of you by Barnard. Millicent and I are going to the Reinhardt Gallery tomorrow to see it."

"I'll come along," said Maggie, kissing Dorothy on the cheek.

"Maggie, just the person I've been waiting to see," said Cholly, pitching his voice in delight. "A little bird told me that when you and Clare shared an office at *Vanity Fair*, she stole your secretary. Is that true?" Cholly never could help himself.

"Isn't it fantastic? The girl is making more money working for Clare than she would ever make from working with me."

"Yes, well, Condé Nast is a bit miserly. *Isn't* he?"

"Oh, Cholly," chided Maggie.

Cholly looked at her with a blank stare of stupefied boredom and darted his eyes to three lilting ladies whose whispering huddle spelled gossip with a capital *G*. And off went Cholly with nary a farewell. Once gone, the Hamiltons came over to say their goodbyes and offered Dorothy a lift home, insisting the party would continue without her. It was a relief; the evening had flooded her with emotion.

"We're so looking forward to going to the tropics with you," said Rebecca as they were driving along. "It's quite a group we've put together. Isamu and Cole will be there, as you know. I hear the SS *Colombia* is divine, and it will be good for you to get away. If a trip into the wilds of Haiti doesn't take your mind off of things, nothing will!" She looked at Dorothy as the car came to a stop. "Are you all right?"

"Sometimes I feel like my heart keeps breaking in different places and I wonder if there are any strong parts left," Dorothy sighed. "I have to keep mending it or it will break once and for all."

"Oh, darling," said Rebecca. "I'm sorry. I know this opened the wound. How did you recover from heartbreak before?"

"Faith, I suppose. By giving in and not giving up."

"I'll remember that," said Millicent, glancing out the window. "We all have our moments."

Dorothy leaned in to hug her, then stepped out to the sidewalk. She knew it was time to turn the page. It was, after all, 1933, two years since Gardner had died.

Fluffing her two pillows and the three on Gardner's side of the bed, she tried to get comfortable and settle her mind. Hazard yet forward, as they said at St. Joseph's, she reminded herself over and over until drifting off to sleep. When suddenly she awoke in the middle of the night, his image was clear in her mind. He had seemed so real in her dream. He was sitting by her side on a bench in Central

Park, squeezing her hand, and she felt calm with him beside her. He said, "When I left, there was no time to say goodbye. I love you more than there are stars in the sky. We will never miss a sunset together." He was a part of her, she realized. She decided then to allow herself the joy of memory untainted by the darkness of grief.

Dorothy felt change in the air. By the time she set sail to New York in April, President Roosevelt had roused the country with new hope for prosperous times. In the first 100 days of his presidency, he repealed Prohibition and set in motion the New Deal that Harry Hopkins had designed to ensure the survival of the working man. Upon arrival home, she organized her belongings and left to meet Clare for lunch at Twenty-One where she listened to her rattle on, not about politics but about love.

Bernie looked out for her. Bernie's love was unwavering. Bernie wished circumstances were different. Bernie's wife was perpetually unhappy. Bernie couldn't find the courage to leave. Bernie knew his marriage was long on principle and short on anything else.

"I don't need to remind you that Bernie is not going to leave his wife," said Dorothy.

"You might be right. The wife knows exactly what strings to pull. Maybe one day he'll see that she's tethering him to a sinking ship. She wants company on her miserable, dark descent."

"Yes, but he told you quite clearly that he won't get a divorce. Darling, I just don't want to see you hurt any more than you are. And of course, you know that it's no secret anymore."

"Speaking of secrets, have you been seeing George?" asked Clare.

"Do you mean the lovely Lazard Frères George?"

"Yes, darling. I might also add, Isamu's crush on you has become a bit of a tedious topic at luncheons."

"It's funny, really. No one says a word about Bucky, and he's at my apartment all the time, laying out plans for his inventions. The boys just need encouragement, someone in their corner until their talents pay off."

"Yes, they do," Clare said softly. But she was likely thinking of herself. Her success at *Vanity Fair* was, to her mind, barely a step on the ladder she was anxious to ascend. Dorothy watched her stare at the steam rising from the black coffee and sensed her self-doubt. Thus far it had infused her raging drive to succeed, but where it would lead, Dorothy couldn't be sure. All she could do was be there for Clare in all her darkness and light.

To escape the last days of the long, cold winter, she set off to warmer climes. The swaying palm trees in Bermuda reminded her of those at the Sans Souci, where she and Gardner had danced. In the months that followed, memories of him would be clear, his voice a presence in her mind. At times, she whirled around to see him, sure that she had heard him calling her name. In September, on the SS *Berengaria* from Cherbourg, France, to New York, the stars above recalled evenings with him in the moonlight. He was everywhere if she allowed him to be.

15.

HAPPY TIMES

"You know, you'll always have the memory of a perfect marriage with Gardner, and in that sense you're fortunate. It ended on a high note," said Clare. Dorothy twisted the telephone cord tightly around her fingers.

"Darling, I must go to get ready. I'll be in the lobby at eleven o'clock. À bientôt." There wasn't much time to dash off the letter to her father that she had been meaning to write for weeks.

These are fine days, Father. Ones to remember, she began. The page filled quickly with stories of travels and kindness of friends. Her jollity seemed out of step with the world around her, she explained. An air of malaise had spread through Café Society and quite acutely in her coterie, friends impatient to find their way to the lightness, their place in the sun. The Great Depression cast shadows on the city. The roar of the Twenties had quieted to a soulful cry of the blues. Even the Empire State Building had come to be known as the Empty State Building, the same name bestowed upon Agnes Emerson, but that was another story, and it wasn't particularly kind. Dorothy admitted only to herself that it was a fairly accurate reference to the girl's vacuous mind and stocky physique clothed in masculine, eye-catching suits.

A road trip seemed a perfect antidote to the prevailing mood, particularly Clare's, so they were off to Connecticut in Bucky Fuller's car, his latest invention, a teardrop-shaped contraption he named the Dymaxion—short for "dynamic-maximum-tension." Signing off with love, she sealed the envelope and left it on the console for her maid, Mary, to send.

Swathed in a full-length mink, Dorothy climbed into the back seat of Bucky's car and wedged herself between Isamu and Constantin Alajalov, the handsome *Vanity Fair* illustrator. Constantin and Clare were singing along to "Sophisticated Lady" playing on the radio as Bucky pulled away from the curb, their voices echoing out the windows as they set off for Hamden, Connecticut, to see Thornton Wilder, who was still basking in the glory of his Pulitzer Prize. Then they would attend the much-awaited opening of Gertrude's play in Hartford. Oblivious to the assemblage of people on the sidewalk who had stopped to stare at the Dymaxion as it made a U-turn in its own twenty-foot length, Dorothy joined in the chorus of Fred's song.

"Those lyrics get me every time," she sighed.

"Well, who hasn't cried over lost love and then gone out smoking and drinking to try to forget about it? Futile as it may be," Clare said. "There is no such thing as incurable, there are only things for which man has not found a cure." She leaned over to lower the volume on the radio.

"That's Bernie's line," said Dorothy.

"Yes, but he said it in a completely different context, not about love. Anyway, I quite like it. I think I'll take it as my own."

"How is your play coming along?" asked Dorothy, who had tried to discourage Clare from working out her hatred for her ex-husband by writing a production for the public.

"Well, I've decided it will be about a murder that is covered up as a suicide. The wife kills the husband. Inspired by my marriage to George, of course. The working title is *Abide with Me*, and you should star in it. You could use it after that disastrous stint in Hollywood, darling."

Now she was trying Dorothy's patience. Nevertheless, she thought, *one must take the bad with the good*, and she had become deft at dodging the swats from Clare's lashing tongue. The fact remained there were times she appreciated her frankness, however unpalatable it was. As Dorothy remained quiet, she took a little pleasure in recalling catty comments she had overhead about Clare from a group of women lunching at Twenty-One, each astounded to learn they had the same experience when, prior to Clare's dinner party, she assured them it was a casual get-together, just a few friends, no need to dress, only for them to gape in contempt when she emerged from the salon in a glimmering ray of diamonds and white satin couture cut provocatively low at her well-rounded breasts.

Bucky and Constantin kept silent, knowing better than to try to stave off the girls' debates.

"Clare," Dorothy offered, "I was wondering if perhaps your play is too dark, especially in times like these. Besides, it isn't good for you to preoccupy yourself with writing stories about murders that are covered up as suicides. Especially your ex-husband's."

"It's true, Clare. I noticed you're preoccupied with that storyline. This is the second time you're using it," said Isamu.

"I write what people think but won't say. I'm exposing the dark side of human nature, the fantasies no one admits to," Clare said. She was met with silence. "George's new wife would understand."

"Well," Isamu said, shifting in his seat, "maybe writing will help you work through your feelings about him."

"That's what Hemingway does," Dorothy said.

"Hemingway. Jane made the mistake of falling in love with her lover. She should feel fortunate it ended."

"Well, try to show some sensitivity the next time you see her. She's better now, but she did jump off the balcony at her home."

"Who tries to end their life by jumping from a second-floor balcony? It's so terrifically farcical. I don't know why you're upset that I told her so."

"Oh, Clare."

"Did you hear that Rosamond was dropped from the Social Register?" asked Clare.

"You'll all be coming to the opening of my movie, I hope," Dorothy said, as a reminder to Clare that her disastrous stint in Hollywood was followed by a fine success. Playing the role of Countess Olga in the new film *The Rise of Catherine the Great*, she had received sterling reviews. "It's on February 9. Douglas Fairbanks Jr. is a love. You'll quite enjoy him." She felt for a moment that she could rise up no matter what the unruly universe hurled at her next. "Clare, Bernie said he's going to the movie premiere, so it might be awkward if you bring your new beau."

"He is going. I already told him about it. Unlike Bernie, he is determined to leave his wife. Just don't tell anyone, especially Cholly. He would waste no time printing it in his column."

Clare had met Henry "Harry" Luce the year before at Elsa Maxwell's ball, the one to celebrate Cole Porter's new Broadway show, *Anything Goes*. The second time they met, he told her that someday he would marry her, someday after his divorce, which had not yet been proposed to his wife. A handsome man with sandy-brown, slicked-back hair and well-toned abdominals, he reigned over a publishing empire and, as such, met Clare's requirements. But even he couldn't lessen her love for Bernie.

"As long as you're at the movie premiere, Clare, that's all that matters to me. I suppose Bernie will eventually get used to the idea of you and Harry."

"Well, I certainly hope not. I wouldn't want that."

Dorothy smiled a little bit.

"He told me adamantly," Clare continued, "that once I'm married, our affair is over. He breaks my heart."

"We'll see, Clare. They always come back for Coca-Cola."

They saw in the distance the fanfare outside the Wadsworth Atheneum Theatre. They had expected the extravagant turnout for the most highly anticipated event of the season, Gertrude Stein and

Virgil Thomson's play, *Four Saints in Three Acts*, planned to coincide with opening night of Pablo Picasso's exhibition in the newly opened Avery Memorial Wing.

"Dorothy, why don't you spend some time with Wallace tonight? You need to get over Gardner once and for all and move on," said Clare, casting a sidelong glance as the Dymaxion came to an abrupt halt. While she couldn't hear what Isamu was whispering in Dorothy's ear, she heard him chortle at his own comment. Dorothy gazed ahead with a look of amused satisfaction when a flashbulb went off outside the window of the car and blurred her vision. When her eyes cleared she saw Jerry Zerbe and waved. She hadn't been to lunch with him in too long. She would see to it that they made up for lost time.

Heads whirled and eyes popped incredulously at the sight of Bucky's futuristic car and then at Dorothy and Clare as they stepped out in shimmering dresses.

Folk, blues, and spirituals filled the theater as the cast's stirring performance brought the audience to tears, men handing handkerchiefs to their wives, who wiped black smudges from under their eyes. Dorothy was enraptured, her emotions beautifully raw as she gave in to the soulfulness of song.

"It's the closest to God I've ever felt," whispered Clare. "Let's go to the powder room before we go to the party." Then, the final notes, the curtain closing, the bows of the cast and applause.

When they arrived at the Avery Memorial Wing, Archibald MacLeish was leading a chorus in Russian folk songs, Nicolas Nabokov's swift fingers setting the tone on ivory keys. Clare and Dorothy listened as they strolled to the center of the museum-sized space, then tilted their heads upward.

"Extraordinary. A feat of architectural genius," Dorothy marveled, looking at the upper-floor balconies and glass ceiling.

"Modernism at its best. Everett is ahead of his time."

"Let's find Gertrude," Dorothy said, leading them deeper into the crowd where she turned to Clare, caught her eye, and gestured toward

Salvador Dali, who was sheathed in a black velvet cape and seemed to be pontificating to Mrs. Oliver Adley, a well-known Hartford art collector. As Dorothy drew closer, she watched Dali gape gleefully at her shapely breasts, which were swathed elegantly in a dress with mother-of-pearl buttons. He said, *"Madame, ces boutons, sont-ils comestibles?"*

"Am I mistaken, or did Dali just inquire if her buttons are edible?" Dorothy asked with a laugh, drawing a laugh from Clare and John Houseman, the director of the play, who was caught in a tangle of guests.

"Dorothy Hale, it's been ages. Say, I'm headed out of town tomorrow, due back in a week. Why don't you come see me if you're in New York? That is, if you're willing to give a starring role a second shot."

Two days later, on February 9, 1934, at half past six in the evening, Dorothy sat at her vanity table looking herself over and was pleased to see the sparkle was still in her eyes. She wouldn't have the onerous task of looking cheerful. She hummed the melody of "Oh, Lady Be Good!" while scanning bottles of perfume, and chose Joy, then dabbed the sweet scent on her slim wrists and her nape. The final touches were a swathe of red gloss, a pucker of her lips, and a turn to the mirror to tweak the sashed bow tied at the curve of her back. Sorry to miss the end of Fred's song, she turned off the radio and slipped into a mink cape, hoping it would shield her from the cold. Taking her keys from the console by the front door, she remembered to say a prayer of thanks and closed her eyes.

"There she is. My God she is divine," Maggie said, exhaling gently. Clare and Bucky turned to look from inside the theater door. Walking along the red carpet, onlookers on either side, photographers snapped her picture. Seeing Jerry, she gestured toward the marquis, which glowed brightly in the night with the pronouncement *Premiere! Catherine the Great Starring Douglas Fairbanks, Jr.!* She posed below it to give him his shot. At the curb behind him, the window of a limousine lowered slowly to reveal Fairbanks watching her, allowing her a moment in the spotlight. Dorothy flashed him a smile. Hearing

Jerry call her name, she turned to face the lens again before meeting her friends inside.

"It means the world to me to have you here," Dorothy said warmly. "It's only a small role, but it's a thrill nevertheless."

"Please, how could we miss it?" Maggie said and then cleared her throat. "Isamu is late, as usual, but he'll be along soon."

They took their seats, the theater went dark, and the movie rolled. Clare waited for Dorothy to appear and held her breath in defeat, wanting her own moment of triumph and feeling so very far from her goals. The power and success she enjoyed reigning over *Vanity Fair* and New York's social scene wasn't enough. She thought of Bucky's triumph the year before at the Chicago World's Fair when he exhibited his Dymaxion car.

"This is your Dymaxion moment. It's a *hale* of a comeback," she whispered to Dorothy, patting her hand and musing that she would plan one like Dorothy did after losing her mother, her dream, her two husbands, and her first starring role.

"If I know you, Clare, your next is soon to come."

And that was the night they hatched a plan that would lead them to exactly where they wanted to be. They would sojourn to Europe in the spring, summer, and fall, and spend several months thereafter seeing to it that their checklist was checked off sufficiently by next summer, at which time it would all come to fruition.

June 21, 1935. Summer solstice. Alone in her living room, Dorothy stood by the window and watched a group of schoolgirls go by. She moved into ballet third position, fourth position, then arabesque as Puccini played on the radio. Seeing her diary open on the side table, she nestled into the wing chair to write. She had completed two hundred pages of her book, ten columns for magazines, and zero entries in her journal. *Fine days*, she penned. *Well worth spending the summer in New York.*

Her friends had long since left in mass exodus for Newport, Rhode Island, and Deauville, France, miffed by her decision to stay behind for summer stock theater in Scarborough-on-Hudson, the bucolic Westchester town just outside the city. There she would perform in three plays, *Mars Tarquin*, *Man Proposes*, and *Abide with Me*, Clare's dark comedy for which Dorothy had a starring role and Rosamond, a favorite among the theater crowd, had the lead. Yes, Clare's fantasy of offing a drunken George and covering it up as a suicide would play to the public, thus parading his poltroonery and buffoonery for all to see, for it was no secret the script was based on him.

By the first week of August, Dorothy and Clare had checked off most of the items on their list: Dorothy reveled in the spotlight onstage, having completed three roles in succession, and Clare, having resigned from *Vanity Fair* the year before to pursue playwriting, was rewarded with critical acclaim for her play and an offer to take it to Broadway.

Seven days after Clare's show closed and three days after celebrations in New York, Dorothy set off for northern France where Alva and Elsa were throwing a party, mistaken by the guests as an invitation to pepper her with questions about Clare.

"I read Cholly's article. It said Clare would soon marry a man 'sufficiently rich to indulge any and all extravagant whims' the clever Clare may have. Who is it?" Happy Longhorn pleaded, swigging her champagne.

"Cholly is so ill bred," said Jane, taking a sip from her glass.

"I think it's Thomas Needleman or Harry Luce," Happy said, an expression of confidence flitting across her face.

"Oh, Dorothy, do tell us," Muffy implored, rocking a little bit in her shoes.

"She so wants to give you the news herself, I wouldn't want to ruin it for her," Dorothy answered with a tone of regret and unmistakable finality to keep them from pressing her further. At Alva's behest, she decided to stay on in France well after the others had left, so she could spend the remaining days of summer sculpting and painting and perfecting her hand at prose.

Midway through the sail from Cherbourg to New York on the SS *Bremen*, the most favored and grand girl of the sea, thoughts of the material world dissipated from her mind. In the afternoons, she lazed on the deck and listened to the steady whoosh of the hull gliding mightily over the ripples, the sound a lullaby, a life force that strengthened her soul. Here God was everywhere, in weightless clouds and the infinite horizon and the enchanting ocean below. Her wants and needs drifted away in the cool Atlantic breeze.

When she arrived home on the fifth of August, she was glad it was a quiet time in the city, the sidewalks cleared for daily walks that lasted for hours. With no particular destination in mind, she made her way around Central Park and down Fifth Avenue where shopkeepers knew her by name. A thought kept following her. In a few months she would be back at the theater, this time as a spectator.

On November 21, 1935, throngs of people weathered the bone-chilling cold of Manhattan to attend the opening night of *Abide with Me* on Broadway. They filled the cushy seats of the Ritz Theatre, removed their hats, wrapped their coats around their shivering shoulders, and prepared to be entertained. Behind the velvet curtain, the cast and crew scurried around in choreographed chaos while Dorothy took it all in. She observed the actors as they powdered their faces, muttered lines of the script, feigned an ironic look and a hysterical laugh, practicing, practicing, practicing. Nerves ran high, spirits ran high, panic set in. In the moments before the curtains parted, she took her seat, hoping for Clare's success.

But no award-winning performance could save the play from the critics' scathing reviews of the script, which was written and rewritten and revised again by Clare in her greatest effort at success. The new dialogue didn't lessen the darkness of the melodrama, but she got a few laughs with quips she often said to her friends.

"The critics are so harsh, so cutting, so dreadfully unforgiving," she lamented, reading the reviews, unable to show expressions on her face with the hardened mud mask that covered it. The lounge at the Elizabeth Arden salon was desolate on this Monday morning.

"It was your first play and well worth the effort. You have to take risks, lay yourself bare, abandon yourself completely for the chance to rise or to fall," Dorothy said. She touched her face to see if her mask had hardened and wiped her fingers on a towel.

"You can be so courageous when you're encouraging others to step into the fire. I've always admired that about you. Admittedly, you go in leaps and bounds."

After thirty-six performances and more bad reviews, the show closed. But there was something to soften the blow. Two days after the premiere, in a private ceremony in Greenwich, Connecticut, Clare married Harry Luce. Few people saw it coming; she had managed to keep the affair under wraps and out of the press. The post-ceremony news of the nuptials prompted a collective shrill of outrage and sigh of relief that swept through the salons of Fifth Avenue and the penthouses of Park Avenue—praise be to God, Clare was off the market.

Thus, six days after the wedding, amid a deafening din of whispers and a covey of craned necks at the Colony during a little lunch celebration with Dorothy, Crownie, and Maggie, Clare leaned back in her chair with a triumphant smile.

"I couldn't seduce him with charm, so I slayed him with intellect," she sighed happily.

And that's when Mabel Mortimer appeared at her side with a copy of the *Washington Post* tucked under her plump, jeweled arm and promptly extended it inches from Clare's angelic face, reaching around her to hand it to Dorothy.

"Congratulations, Dorothy. The votes have been cast and the winners have been announced."

"Pardon?" asked Dorothy.

"The international designers have crowned you the best-dressed woman of America. Imagine, darling? You are listed as one of the ten top style-setters of the world. The *world*! For the second year in a row, no less," Mabel said with a sly smile, a sniff at Clare, and a prompt departure.

"To be expected," Clare said with a roll of her eyes. "She's a friend of Lila, Harry's ex."

"Allow me," Crownie said, reaching for the paper. As he read the article, Maggie raised her glass in a toast.

"Congratulations, darling! That's the only list you can't buy or marry your way onto. And here I thought the rubbernecking was caused by Clare!"

"What are you up to, Clare?" Dorothy asked, looking at Clare's expression of amused satisfaction as she scribbled down some notes.

"Oh, just a few ideas for my next play," she said cheerfully.

"Ah, mark your calendars," Dorothy remembered to say. "My next play opens on January 16."

"Ah, yes, *Russet Mantle*. I hear the costumes are fabulous. And that's five days after your thirty-first birthday. We'll have plenty to celebrate," Maggie said.

The night of the Broadway premiere, and each night to follow, Dorothy departed the Theatre Masque through the backstage door and crossed the street to look at the marquis; then she would smile and turn to go home. After a three-month run of the production, Dorothy, Clare, and Maggie returned to the healing springs of Aix-le-Bain where Dorothy was greeted by the desk clerk with a letter from her attorney, John Vincent.

Once in her suite, she went out to the balcony, reclined on a chaise, and, holding her breath, she ripped open the envelope. He wrote to let her know that the appraisal of Gardner's estate was finally complete. Closing her eyes, she allowed her mind to drift to the past and the tenderness of Gardner's voice. "Until the end of time, my love," she said softly, recalling his words. Contentedness washed over her as she gave thanks to God for the time they shared, and the grace of good fortune in an uncertain world. Some people, many of whom she knew, had never been to the lost kingdom of peace. Perhaps she would find it again. It seemed not far away.

The somber wail of a pipe organ caught Dorothy's attention as she walked down West Sixty-Ninth Street, shivering in the frigid New York wind, puffy flakes of snow drifting sideways and dotting her sable hat. As she drew closer to the music, she saw the jewel-colored stained-glass windows of Saint Stephen's Church and realized how long it had been since she attended a service. She entered quietly, sat in the back pew, and lowered herself to the hassock to have a chat with the man upstairs. With her head lowered and eyes closed, she began her ritual of prayer. *Our Father who art in Heaven . . .* She then expressed gratitude for His abundant gifts and remembered to ask for the continuing valor of President Roosevelt, who had just been re-elected in the 1936 campaign. With that bit of business out of the way, she prayed for Clare's success and asked for divine intervention. In the meantime, Clare braced herself for the opening of her second Broadway show, *The Women*. She was about to face the fire again.

A vast number of society matrons returned from Europe for the debut and pranced through the aisles of the Ethel Barrymore Theatre with full-length furs and no idea of the lashing they were about to endure. As the curtains parted and the play began, Dorothy, Isamu, Bucky, Crownie, and Maggie raised their eyebrows with a smile and a knowing look. They had read the script and realized retribution would soon be served to certain people who had not the wherewithal to appreciate their more farcical features.

Booming howls of laughter rang out in the theater, women shifted uncomfortably in their seats, theater critics scribbled notes excitedly. Reviews went to press, and Clare savored each praising word. Night after night, a glittering mass of ticketholders were astonished and amused by the stinging satire, a scathing comedic commentary about the very women Clare knew—the grand dames of society who chose their clothes as carefully as their men and considered both of equal importance.

"It sent lightning strikes through the Colony and El Morocco and nearly popped the buttons off the ladies' Chanel suits," Dorothy said to Maggie over lunch at the Pierre. "As you well know, the extravagant gossip in the play hits a little too close to home for this crowd."

"I know a lot of women who see it as a betrayal by one of their own. And they see Clare as the real-life Sylvia," Maggie added.

"Yes, Sylvia, whose meddling and gossip knocks debutantes off their T-strap heels and right out of the Social Register."

"She said she culled material from a variety of women. You're not using the mignonette sauce for the oysters, are you?"

"No," said Dorothy, passing her the porcelain dish. "Everyone wants to know who inspired the characters. Except Eleanor Roosevelt. She said in her column that the characters in the play have no character whatsoever. I can't imagine whom Clare was thinking of when she wrote Sylvia. She exposes her best friend's secret to the press and ruins the girl. The girl was so trusting and faithful."

"And then after ruining her, Sylvia says it was harmless." Maggie dipped a plump oyster into the sauce and slipped it into her mouth.

"Right," Dorothy said. "Sylvia says the news will peak, vanish, and soon be forgotten, just like the story about the girl who jumped out of a window to her death.'"

"It does make me wonder about Clare. I mean, it's a window into her mind. I wouldn't feel too sorry for her that everyone is angry. While it caused a rift with some of the girls, all the magazines want to do stories on her."

"That interview she did for *Stage* magazine caused a real commotion. I tried to tell the girls it's all in good fun, Clare is good at heart, but she did level them as masterfully as Mother Nature in a bad mood."

"Oh God," Maggie said with an audible sigh. "She said the women she wrote about are nymphomaniacs, dipsomaniacs, egomaniacs, and schizophrenic lice."

"You see why I can mend only so many fences." Pushing her plate to the side, Dorothy shook her head in exasperation and laughed.

"Did you know that she's in Los Angeles to see Norman Krasna at Metro-Goldwyn-Mayer? He wants her to work on a screenplay."

"Yes, and she's doing a screen test for Zanuck at Twentieth Century Fox," Dorothy said with a nod. "I hope it goes well. It's always been her dream to be in the movies."

Exhilarated by the idea of greater fame, Clare did her best to seduce the movie cameras, to no avail and to her profound disappointment, an all too familiar feeling from failed attempts as an actress in her younger years. Lounging on the terrace of her suite at the Beverly Wilshire Hotel, she flicked through the pages of the *Los Angeles Times* while recalling the praise lavished upon Dorothy after her screen test. Feeling agitated, she ignored the call of the telephone ringing. She didn't want to speak to anyone. But then she realized it might be good news.

"Darling! I'm glad you answered."

"I was just thinking about you, when you came here for your screen test," Clare said.

"I understand how you must feel," said Dorothy. "Try not to be too disappointed. Hollywood is just a cruel town with a pretty façade. Your new title should be of some consolation. The press has crowned you the most beautiful playwright in the world." She knew that Clare was smiling at the other end of the line.

"I'm leaving tomorrow for Hawaii. I'll see you and Crownie next month at Claremont. Benjamin Wolf is coming. You know him—the political advisor who ingratiates himself with presidents, regardless of which side of the aisle they're on. He'll call you to coordinate travel plans."

"Happy Longhorn was just talking about him. She said he was born to wealth and bred by governesses who came and went like cookies on a conveyor belt."

"Ah yes, the governesses' exposé of the government advisor. I've heard the backlash. As a child Ben developed no bond or inner need to appease their requests, having long been broken-spirited by the back of his father's hand and the absenteeism of his unsentimental mother."

"Right, and Poppy told him his old governesses talked to other governesses, one of whom was in her employment, and he was upset she had betrayed him."

"Thus prompting a small fit in which he huffed loudly and threw his fat pale fist right through the wall. Broke every one of his metacarpal bones. Obviously his real power is in politics."

Dorothy, Crownie, and Ben Wolf made the trip to Claremont together. A short, wide-framed man with a pint-sized head and little eyes, he had deftly maneuvered his way into a cushy office in Washington. This would be their first visit to Clare and Harry's new home in the Lowcountry of South Carolina, a 7,000-acre plantation with a large manse, three guesthouses, and staff. They arrived in time for a tour of the house before settling into their accommodations and joining their hosts for dinner. As soon as the entrée was served, a Beaufort stew of which the women ate very little, Clare didn't hesitate in discussing the new government programs.

"The New Deal simultaneously provides money to the poor and lessens my wealth, and it makes the unemployed too comfortable to work. Have you any idea how difficult it is to find servants around here? Harry Hopkins might be America's hero to some, but he is a thorn in the side of businessmen, bankers, and all the rest of us." She looked intently at Ben for a response.

"They're not his only detractors. Plenty of people in his own party resent him for the power he wields with the president," Ben said.

"That reminds me," said Clare. "Dorothy, why don't you join me next month at the Republican fundraising dinner that Alfred and Edna Lahnbacher are hosting?"

"Darling, you know I'm all for Roosevelt and the New Deal. I can join you, but please don't think I'll have a change of loyalty."

Clare set down her glass and took a dramatic pause.

"Under certain extenuating circumstances, one must have a change of loyalty, mustn't one? Loyalty might seem like a noble trait, but in my experience it's usually undeserved by those it benefits."

"Agreed," said Ben with smug assurance. "There's nothing admirable about loyalty when someone is testing it. That's poor judgment."

"That's what I call tragically loyal. We must always know who has our best interests at heart," said Clare in a more reflective tone.

The words lingered in Dorothy's mind as she looked at Clare and began to wonder if she and the girls would ever be on the opposing side of their friend—if *The Women* might foreshadow some unexpected circumstance. *Well, of course not*, she quickly concluded. Clare was really good at heart.

PART IV

16

A DAMSEL IN DISTRESS

On the first days of spring in New York, Dorothy strolled along the paths of Central Park, gazing at the trees now filling out in emerald-colored leaves, and magnolias blooming. There were other new beginnings as well. Fred won the starring role in the film *A Damsel in Distress*, and James Roosevelt, her friend, was appointed secretary to the president, having already earned the unofficial title of assistant president of the United States. She would return to Broadway for the production of *Red Harvest*, listed in the playbill under the stage name Malan Cullen, an idea she adopted from Clare, who frequently used a nom de plume.

The play premiered on the thirtieth of May, a success marked by the thousand ticket buyers who sprang to their feet in thunderous applause as the curtains closed. The cast set off to celebrate at the Stork Club, New York's "New Yorkiest place," named such by Walter Winchell—and the meddlesome gossip columnist ought to know since he hosted his radio show from table fifty. Maggie was there chatting with the director Brock Pemberton when Dorothy finally arrived.

"Splendid show, wouldn't you say!" Brock said enthusiastically as she took a seat beside Maggie. "Fine turnout, not an empty seat in the house. I saw Jane Mason in the second row. How's the girl doing these days?" he asked. "The last time I saw her was in Cuba. Terrific party." Dorothy looked at Brock to reply and couldn't help but think that it was true what an actress once said: "He has a face like that of a new baby, all bald and screwed-up into a frown."

"Jane is doing just fine," she said, slipping off her stole.

"If only she had realized sooner that Hemingway was just being the Goodtime Charlie that he tends to be, she wouldn't have fallen for him," Maggie said, and then whispered in Dorothy's ear, "If only Rosamond realized she was better off without Jed."

Rosamond came to Dorothy's mind in a swirl of memories. She had reeled from a series of disappointments, not the least of which was being cast away by Jed Harris, the breakup of her marriage to Big Bill Gaston, and the split from many a friend when her name was expunged from the Social Register in '34. Dorothy had offered support, but Rosamond became increasingly ungenerous with her innermost thoughts. No one would ever know what really happened with her; it was all very complicated, as these things tended to be. On a cold January morning, Rosamond closed the door of her silver Rolls Royce in the garage of her estate in Old Brookville on the North Shore of Long Island, turned on the ignition, and waited. She was found inside her car by the cook.

"Imagine, champagne corks are popping, fine cigar smoke is billowing, the boisterous crowd is dancing and necking, and here I am thinking of funerals," said Maggie, taking an unusually generous sip of champagne.

"Of course you are. Rosamond was a darling woman and a dear friend. I'm devastated about it. We all are," Dorothy said, and suddenly Mat Pemberton's face was upside down and smiling broadly in front of her as her husband, Brock, dipped her in a tango. He swung her upright and led her gliding across the dance floor.

"I was just thinking of what Clare said in the car on the way back from Rosamond's funeral," said Maggie. "It's straight out of *The*

Women. She's quoting her own characters."

"You mean when she said, 'Rosamond has erased her name from history. That's what happens with suicides; people want to forget the tragic end. There's a blast of press followed by eternal silence.' As if all the light she shined on the world was forgotten. Just like that. *Fini.*" Dorothy took a cigarette from her purse.

"You know of course that Clare's tears at the funeral were also for her own mother, having buried her only weeks before. I can still picture you standing beside her at her mother's gravesite with your arm wrapped around her waist for support as they lowered the casket into the ground."

"She was a little unsteady on her feet when she poured the scoop of earth on top of it."

"And then," said Maggie, "she had to wait for every last person to do the same thing. It seemed like it would never end, didn't it? Clare finally said, 'Do you think we can get another shovel and move this thing along?'"

Dorothy laughed lightly, shaking her head. Brock suddenly appeared at the table and took her hand, leading her onto the crowded dance floor, the blaring music of the orchestra drowning out the buzz of chatter in the room. He twirled her around, dipped her low in his arms, her steps fluid and precise. Maggie watched, seated contentedly at the table. "That's Dorothy," she said to no one in particular, "the girl who dances with life."

17.

WHITE HOUSE WEDDING

"Well, isn't it just a shame that a girl of such beauty died so young," said a fifty-something woman fiddling with her gray pompadour coif as she stood in the cramped entryway of Nickolas Muray's apartment.

"Shush, she killed herself, you know," said the woman's friend, who looked bearish in her mahogany mink. "It was a long time coming from what I hear. *Pills.* And so soon after Rosamond Pinchot's suicide over *man* troubles, for goodness sake."

"At least they knew their ending. The rest of us have to play along with God's little game of Russian roulette, His eternal lesson to live it up while you can. And far be it for me to turn away from God—let's get a drink."

Typical, thought Dorothy, feeling particularly pleased that Clare wrote *The Women* about these pitiless Park Avenuites who considered others' calamities nothing more than good material for gossip. She looked at Nickolas's *Vogue* photographs covering the wall in the foyer and was delighted to see one of her. He swept to her side and greeted her with an enthusiastic kiss on each of her cheeks.

"Your photo in the February issue was fabulous," he said approvingly. "Every bit as good as Cecil Beaton's. I think 1938 is your year. You have a particular glow about you. We'll have to do some pictures."

"Whenever you like," she replied, seeing Clare making her way toward her.

"The shots of you in the blue silk floor-length dress and the simple black sleeveless gown were regal."

"Both from Bergdorf's."

"And the jewels?"

"Van Cleef and Arpels."

Clare showed up at Dorothy's side, and Nickolas turned to greet a guest. "I thought he would never leave. I saw the articles about Gaillard. Is it true?" She didn't wait for an answer. "Imagine, suspended from the Stock Exchange for misusing customers' securities among other *illegal* actions. One more reason to be glad you divorced him."

Dorothy was in no mood to discuss it, having read and reread the article in disbelief. "The Ivy League heir, weakened like a beggar in a sure bet" was all Maggie said when she called the morning it was printed in the papers. Dozens of calls had followed. It made her think of his strange silence and sweat-covered cheeks after closed-door telephone calls during their marriage.

"I'm sure his name will be cleared. You'll see. Anyway, tell me how your play is coming along," Dorothy inquired, her jaw tightening.

"Ah, swimmingly. The title is *Kiss the Boys Goodbye*, and it is not about our exes. Tell me, do you think Gaillard has it in him to do such a thing?"

"You know Gaillard. He's an intelligent, philanthropic man. You'd have to be an unprincipled self-centered fool to do such a thing."

"You certainly wouldn't have to worry about that with Harry. Have you been seeing him?" asked Clare.

"Yes, and I'm to meet him in Washington DC tomorrow."

"You're a brilliant match . . . practically speaking."

"Practically speaking?" asked Dorothy, waiting for it.

"The prince of politics and the glamour girl with the grace of a goddess. And, I might add, you would be a good mother to his young daughter. In some respects you're just what he needs. And for you . . . darling, there's something to be said for marrying into that kind of power. It eludes even the most plundering patricians of Park Avenue. Sure, I've said 'one's checkbook is one's *real* autobiography,' but one's power is one's crown."

With a vague shake of her head, Dorothy considered Clare for a moment as she took two glasses of wine from the server's tray and handed one to her. They exchanged glances.

"You've built your little fortune and you've had your great love. There are other things to be had now."

At seven o'clock the following evening, Dorothy stoked a fire in the hearth in the library of Harry Hopkin's home in Georgetown. She felt at ease, watching him as he sat back and lit another cigarette.

"Did you see the report about how we met?" she asked, somewhat amused.

"Which one? They all say different things. Ludicrous, isn't it?" With an adoring smile filling out his long, sunken cheeks, he looked at her with no sign of concern, which was, for Harry, a rarity. She was accustomed to his usual look, his piercing eyes and perpetually solemn face, an expression that he had perfected to simultaneously unnerve and draw confidence from statesmen and foreign leaders alike. Privately, he exuded magnificent charm. Lounged on a brown leather-upholstered sofa sizable enough to accommodate the impressive height of his spindly frame, he watched intently as she threw a log onto the flames.

"The one that said we met at the horse races in Southampton, how I finagled a dinner date with you," she said with a laugh.

"Well. They turned that around, didn't they? Whoever wrote that doesn't know you."

"Cholly wrote that we're a brilliant match."

"Perhaps I should reconsider my opinion of him," said Harry.

"At least he corrected the record quite clearly. He made it a point to explain how James Roosevelt introduced us at a party in New York, and we didn't meet at the horse races in Southampton." She took a sip of champagne and sat beside him, smoothing the sparse black hair high atop the vast field of his forehead.

"You're one of a kind, angel."

"So are you, Harry," she said, nestling her head on his shoulder.

"I don't want you to worry about the press, anything that might come up. I'll take care of it." He stroked her hair and looked toward the red glow of the flames. Loud crackling and pops cut into the tranquility of their moment. She spun around to see if sparks had shot into the room, and he pulled her back in, holding her closely.

"When do you think we should announce our engagement?" asked Dorothy. "I think you're right that we should wait a bit. You're the president's advisor. It might seem an impetuous act to be engaged so quickly. How about in November, just after your confirmation hearings?"

"Yes, yes," Harry said with a slow nod. "Six months from our meeting would be a reasonable amount of time in the public view."

"I'm sure the announcement that you've been confirmed as the next United States secretary of commerce will overshadow our news. I certainly wouldn't mind that!"

"Neither would I. Listen, why don't you stay the week, join me for the dinner at Ben Wolf's, and if I can get away for a few days, we'll go to the Greenbriar on Friday?"

And so they did. They shared the news of their engagement with only a few trusted friends, and with a bounce in her step, she returned to New York eight days later. Sleep came easily. Then, at half past seven the next morning, she awoke to the telephone blaring.

But she ignored it. There was too much to do tout de suite to prepare for the wedding. Sketch gowns to show to Mainbocher, inquire about Lee Miller's schedule—she should do the portraits—and, most importantly, find a place to store her diaries, her manuscript, and other personal items in the unlikely event someone started snooping around. She was too hopeful, too excited about her future with Harry to allow for any mistakes.

As the coffee brewed, she started thinking about certain friends who would surely feel piqued they were not privy to the news sooner. *Yes, Harry, Harry Hopkins*, she said to herself, imagining the inevitable conversations ahead. *I was bursting at the seams wanting to tell you, of course, but we simply didn't want the news to get out. His political detractors would only muddy things up before the hearings.* The telephone rang again. And again. And yet again. And so it continued incessantly throughout the morning.

Taking small sips of coffee, she eased into the Queen Anne walnut chair at her desk, ran her hands over its carved arms, opened a new journal, wrote the date, *May 17 1938*, at the top and *To Do* underneath, and began making a list. At ten o'clock, she sauntered to the front door while tying the white satin belt of her robe, picked up the morning papers, and looked at page one in outright astonishment. Eyes wide, she flung the door closed, rushed to the living room, and collapsed onto the chintz sofa. Cholly broke the story, and that's when the trouble began.

Cholly Knickerbocker's Exclusive Story of Washington Romance Confirmed. She well knew at this very moment shockwaves were spreading across the Upper East Side and through the West Wing of the White House.

Another call came in and she picked up the receiver.

"Is it true?" shrieked Binky. "Like the rest of the free world, I had barely ingested the first jolt of freshly brewed French press when I unfolded the newspaper and was shocked into sudden alertness."

The next call came in.

"I mean I couldn't believe my *eyes*," cried Mitzy. "There I saw your name, and your photograph, and an impressively lengthy announcement in very large, very bold print, smack center of page one." Dorothy stared at the headline: *Harry Hopkins Engaged to Dorothy Hale, Beauteous Socialite.* He calls you a beauteous socialite, actress, and glamour girl."

"Well," said the next caller, Millicent, "you can be sure the moment the papers were delivered this morning, switchboards lit up like Paris at Christmas."

"The *headline*, darling, is it *true*?" asked Muffy. "I won't tell a *soul*, of course. You *know* how people can *be*."

At half past eleven, Happy called.

"I heard someone betrayed you, someone tipped Cholly off to the news," Happy said in a conspiratorial hush, "and I heard that someone is your friend, Clare Boothe Luce. And get this, I heard Clare did it because she was *indebted* to Cholly. He *embargoed* the story of her engagement to Harry until after Harry's divorce. Matter of fact, he agreed not to go to press until way after Clare and Harry's wedding day! And *then*, in return, she promised to give Cholly one delectable scoop of front-page news at some time in the future, and, *honey*, let me tell you, there's no question there's no better scoop than the White House wedding of a statesman and a showgirl!"

Wiping tears away from her cheeks, Dorothy didn't want to believe that Clare would betray her, nor was she pleased the story was out. She offered the same light laugh and vague answer she had given to everyone else.

"Why, we've only just met. You know how Cholly can be. *So*, darling, have you heard the latest about Poppy and Ludlow Pettipiece? No? She'll be checking into Cupid's graveyard any day now . . . Yes, darling, *Reno*."

She decided to take one last call before leaving the telephone off the hook. To her relief, it was Rebecca Hamilton.

"Darling, you saw *The Women*. One of the characters gave up her best friend to those god-awful gossip columnists and ruined the girl. Pushed her to the limit and off the balcony of her high-rise building. Don't think your friend Clare wouldn't do the same."

By evening, an avalanche of news coverage tumbled down. From Oshkosh to Rome, her stunning photograph by Lee Miller appeared on page one of the papers, the headlines announcing *Hopkins and Actress Plan Marriage in July! Beautiful Widow Fiancée of WPA Administrator!* For Dorothy, the headlines triggered elation, surprise, and sheer dread of scrutiny by Harry's political foes, who would be willing to sully her name in order to ruin his.

In the late hours of the night, staying away from the din of gossip and whispers, she found solace in prayer. *Dear God, thank you for giving me so many wonderful gifts. Thank you for the chance to play a role in Fred's next movie. Thank you for bringing Harry into my life. He's a good man. Please heal his stomach cancer. Don't take him away like you took Mummy. Mummy, watch over us . . .*

The next morning, she held her breath as she unfolded the papers. "Hopkins and Hale are surprised by the leak," she read, skimming over the article where she found a quote from him: "I'm always glad to discuss public matters with anyone, but when it comes to private and personal matters, I am disinclined to talk to anyone about them." *Well done, darling*, she thought.

It only troubled her more that Cholly said the wedding was planned for December, a significant fact that few people knew. In a letter to her father, she wrote with disappointment that satin-gloved fingers pointed to Clare as the sole source of the news. *This is how Happy told the story. I'll be profoundly hurt if it's true*, Dorothy wrote. She quickly signed off to answer the telephone. It was 9 a.m., and she knew who it would be.

"Good morning, my darling friend Maggie. Brilliant idea to tell me the time you would be calling."

"I just want to make sure you don't give this press business a second thought. This is your time. Enjoy it."

"I just can't believe Clare would do it," Dorothy said with a sigh, lowering herself onto the velvet vanity stool and looking at her reflection. "She's in Europe now. I expect I'll see her when she's back in a few days."

"I think you should put it out of your mind altogether. This should be a joyous time."

"Oh, but it is. Harry is wonderful," she cooed, glancing at the photograph of him on the table. "He's so dedicated to helping people, even now after the surgery. They removed two-thirds of his stomach, you know."

"I know how important it is for you to be with someone who has integrity. It seems he's got that. Doesn't have a pressed suit in his closet. And he doesn't have much money, but you have more than you need."

"I don't have a lot of time to plan for the wedding. It's set for December. He says time is precious. He's been that way since his wife died, I think."

"You're a good couple."

"I only hope the press doesn't take an unpleasant turn. The stakes are high for him. He's considered a dark-horse candidate for the Democratic presidential nomination if Roosevelt doesn't run, and—"

"And even more pressing is his upcoming confirmation hearing to become secretary of commerce. I know."

Dorothy dabbed a floral-scented French parfum behind her ears, between her breasts, on the inside of her ankles and wrists, and set the bottle down with a thump.

"The last thing his supporters want is for him to marry a divorced showgirl. That's sure ammunition. The administration must be beside themselves imagining newsies on the street shouting, 'Read all about it! Peck's Bad Girl of Pittsburgh Society Goes to the White House!'" Maggie laughed. "Anyway, I have to go, darling, or I'll be late. I'm due at El Morocco for drinks with Jerry Zerbe."

Again, the ringing of the telephone, like a siren wailing in the early-morning hours. The moment she heard John Vincent's voice at the other end of the line, she was worried; rarely did lawyers call before business hours. He told her the cabin in Moosehead Lake, Maine, had been burglarized, and the table knives were missing. He said someone invaded her upstairs bedroom and forced open a trunk, in which she stored mementos. He said her personal effects and the photograph of her in a red leather frame, the one that Gardner had placed on the mantel, were strewn across the room. She had a feeling she knew what the robber was looking for: her diaries and photographs. Her lawyer agreed it could be the motive.

"Well, John, it seems the gloves are off," she said, ending the call.

What if I had been there? thought Dorothy. She hurried to the closet to fetch two weekend trunks, her diaries, unfinished memoir, photographs, labels, scissors, and white satin ribbon. Back and forth she went until everything was laid out on the worn, French antique rug in the living room. There she sat, her heart racing a little bit, as she organized her writings chronologically, put a label on each, separated the stacks by year, and tied them with white satin ribbon like a gift box at Christmas. And then she stopped, suddenly still, looking at what she had done while considering for a moment what had compelled her.

Yes, of course it was indisputably an absolute necessity to hide things away, given the circumstances, but there was more. Washington was for her an uncharted territory, and for many as perilous as the Rio Roosevelt. Well, maybe someday someone would see that her life had been grand, she reflected, lowering the top of the trunks and forcibly snapping the latches closed with a clack.

The next morning she would call Jack Wilson at the bank, open a second account under an alias, transfer money, and ask to use one of the safety lockers downstairs. They were as big as a small house. Then at lunch she would tell Harry about the break-in.

The telephone rang. Isamu. He said Clare was arriving in New York that afternoon. They were planning dinner with Bucky and she should join. She declined regretfully and suggested a rain check, though she didn't say she wasn't ready to see Clare. They chatted for a few minutes, and she returned to her seat by the window. The telephone began to ring again.

Bucky. He insisted Dorothy join them all for dinner that evening. Still she declined and explained she was a bit under the weather, perhaps a rain check—how about Thursday, she suggested. She was off the hook for another two days.

At half past twelve the following afternoon, the maître d' at Twenty-One whisked Dorothy to the dining room where she found Harry surrounded by three suited men who, with a smile, handshake, and slight nod of the head, departed immediately. She eased into the hardwood chair and into conversation with him, which began with the whispered telling of the break-in, prompting sudden silence and a solemn expression on his already serious face.

"I'll look into it," he said calmly.

"Tea and oysters, Miss Hale?" interrupted the waiter. Dorothy nodded in confirmation. "With lemon, of course. And what may I bring you, Mr. Hopkins?"

"Bring us a dozen, if you will," Harry answered. The waiter nodded and galloped away. "Not to worry, Dorothy. I'll make sure it's taken care of. You can be sure of that." He reached his hand across the table and cupped it over hers.

Watching curiously from across the room was Clare, whom Dorothy hadn't noticed when she came in.

"You know," Clare whispered loudly to Harry Luce, "I wondered why Dorothy used a stage name for her last play. She told me she always liked when I used a nom de plume, and besides, she didn't want the press showing up. Happy thinks it's because Dorothy wanted to make it seem like she gave up performing so when people found out about Harry, they wouldn't say she *is* an actress. Rather, it was a thing of the past. Happy said Dorothy and Harry met last year, before the play, when he was still seeing Roosevelt's daughter, Anna. I can't believe she would have kept it from me."

"Hopkins is too politically ambitious to risk getting on Roosevelt's wrong side, and I'm afraid jilting his daughter for Dorothy, or for any woman, could do that, absurd as it is."

"That's what *I* said," Clare said with a relieved expression. "Excuse me for a moment while I drop by their table to arrange a lunch with her."

As she approached the table, Dorothy saw in Clare's bright eyes a flicker of unease. If Clare had leaked the news, it was likely a look of regret, Dorothy supposed. But there remained a lingering possibility that Clare was loyal. The notion of giving Clare the benefit of the doubt brought her a deep sense of comfort. It was awfully good to see the girl.

In the months ahead, Dorothy assembled her trousseau while Mainbocher designed her wedding gown. Most weekends she traveled to Washington DC where she and Harry dined with friends, attended parties, and planned their future in the privacy of his home. In New York, they were oft seen at Herbert Bayard Swope's home, Land's End, the one on the water on Holffstot Lane in Sands Point, the one said to be Gatsby's house. It was there she overheard a private conversation between Harry and their gracious host.

"My personal life is off the table for debate," Harry said with a cool stare.

"Listen, I'm with you," said Swope. "In all sincerity, I like her—wouldn't mind marrying the girl myself. But it's my responsibility to tell you what Ben Wolf told me, and he said, in no uncertain terms, the public doesn't want to see you married to a divorced showgirl. They'll use whatever they find on her to get to you. He thinks you should lose the girl."

Glad to hear Harry emphatically dismiss the remark, Dorothy turned her attention to a group that had gathered near, whispering, "She's Hopkins' girl." "That's Harry's fiancée." She turned to look for Jerry Zerbe, ever the friendly face in the crowd, and instead saw Cholly sashaying purposefully in her direction to tell her with his usual exuberance that she was the talk of the town.

One week later, after seeing Dorothy and Harry lunching at the Colony, he wrote in his column that he frequently saw them in a tête-à-tête, as he sharpened his pen for the wedding of the year.

In mid-July, Dorothy escaped to a secluded house in Lake Erie where the skies were clear and the breeze warm, perhaps her last opportunity for a while to enjoy repose with her family. The manicured blades of grass felt cool on her feet as she crossed the lawn and looked at the view of the sandy shore. She sat beside her father and immediately sensed his mood. He would say less than usual, perhaps a few words. Still, now seemed like a good moment for her to speak from the heart.

"Father, I've wanted to tell you for some time that I know you didn't want me to dance because you were trying to protect me, and I understand. I appreciate that now. I'm sorry, I did give you a bit of a run for your money." He nodded slowly and remained silent. "Harry is a good man."

He patted her hand. "I hope you're right. You know, pumpkin, I have always been proud of you." They sat quietly and watched a flock of birds dive to the water, then take off in flight. The conversation was over.

Watching them from the veranda, Betty knew instinctively that Dorothy would want to be saved from the silence, and she bounded down the hill. Speaking very quickly with exceeding enthusiasm, she insisted they go for a ride on their bicycles to explore. Dorothy kissed her father on the cheek and skittered away, having always had the impression that he utterly enjoyed having his children around him when they talked amongst themselves or with their mother.

For all her years, Dorothy considered Betty too shy to develop a life with more excitement, and varied interests, and interesting friends, and a home someplace less provincial than Pittsburgh where she would inevitably grow old. As the days passed, however, Dorothy began to notice with some envy the quiet content of her sister and wished she too could settle for less. Perhaps Betty was better off. There were no columnists or cunning acquaintances to think of.

There were no producers or cologne-covered men to fend off. There were no political battles threatening to ruin her, no worries that her life was about to explode. *Yes*, thought Dorothy, *perhaps it is Betty who got it right after all.*

Betty allowed the days to pass with nary a word about the concerns that were brewing, yet her regretful expression showed that she felt remiss in her sisterly duties. At half past five on the last evening of their visit, they sat, just the two of them in the sunroom, the screens allowing fresh air and occasional wafts of their father's cigar smoke to drift in as they discussed the details of the wedding. She took one look at Dorothy, who didn't hide the tension rising within her, and so began the conversation she knew they must have.

"Dorothy, why do you want to keep the wedding quiet? What are you afraid of? You haven't done anything wrong."

"No, I haven't done anything too terribly wrong." She looked out to the rippling water and sighed heavily. "Pictures do exist, of course, from my years as a showgirl. I suppose they're more than a bit provocative, but that was the Follies. The trouble is, some of these tabloid writers have no mercy. What if someone finds the photographer and gets hold of those pictures, or what if they get hold of my diaries? I can't dispose of them because I need them for my book. *Ils sont honteux.*"

"Yes, they are disgraceful. Twits."

"There's also the matter of Gaillard, who was in the papers for just the sort of crime that would enrage the public, and there's Gardner's brother, who was a lawyer to Communists on the verge of deportation. It can't be any reflection on me, can it?"

"Well, it shouldn't be."

Leaning back in a floral cotton-upholstered chair on the veranda, her father, having overheard their exchange, turned his head a tinch, raised his eyes from the newspaper, and paused reflectively as he relit the stubby tip of his fine cigar. Once sufficiently enveloped in a pungent fog of nocuous smoke, he took a mouth-filling swig of

Irish whiskey and, with a look of mixed emotions and foreboding, continued to read.

"I can see how concerned you are," said Betty, "but you're a darling of the press. They've only written the most wonderful things about you."

"It's true. I just can't reason why that man . . ." Her voice drifted off.

"What man?" asked Betty. Dorothy kept her gaze on the sheltering limbs of a black willow in the distance. "Darling, what man?"

"I'm almost sure a man has been following me," she said, turning to look at her. "A man in a hat."

Betty raised her eyebrow.

"It's a beige fedora with a black band."

"Aha, like Roosevelt's."

Manhattan greeted her return with a quiet buzz of curiosity. Whether at Twenty-One, Lily Dache's hat shop, or Bergdorf Goodman, women stole glances and Dorothy wondered why. She was the last to hear the rumor that had sparked and spread far and wide—her wedding to Harry was off. Happy heard that Ben Wolf had planted the story with ease: one call to a middleman, who then called a middlewoman, who tipped off Cholly to the news. Cholly took the bait and sent it to press, then announced his disappointment in losing the front-page story. "Anyone who is au courant knows it is over. It is the *end* of the affair," he said assuredly and with no further detail.

Yet it wasn't the end of the story which proved utterly unignorable. Speculation abounded on the cause of the split. Maggie kept Dorothy abreast of the gossip, one explanation contradicting the next. First there was Clare, who told Maggie that Roosevelt ordered Harry to break the engagement. Then there was the writer Johnson Adams, who said that Harry broke it off because of her rumored romantic dalliance with "a Japanese," namely Isamu. And John Orsini, a newsman, said their engagement was called off after somebody leaked the news to a gossip columnist. Happy said the president ordered Harry to break the engagement at the behest of his daughter, Anna, whom Harry had courted, to which Muffy Baker replied, "Harry ended it with Anna and with Dorothy in order to avoid complications with the president." Still yet, Washington insider William Clayton said that Harry ended the relationship to avoid confronting his inability to perform his manly duties, due to his surgery. And for the remaining weeks in the summer of 1938, there was not a moment of silence at the Colony, Twenty-One, or the most tedious of dinner parties, for this was the most sensational and whispered story of the year.

At seven o'clock the evening of July 29, Dorothy followed the red carpet up the steps of the Plaza Hotel, greeted the bell captain in passing, and strode directly to the elevator. Exiting on the seventh floor, she pinched her cheeks and looked for room 703. Three light knocks, and the door opened to reveal Harry's adoring smile.

"Stunning as always," he said, showing her in. "Champagne?"

"Yes, thanks, Harry," Dorothy said as she floated to the sofa and propped a pillow behind her.

"Baruch has quieted the press," he said, handing her a glass emblazoned with the gold Plaza Hotel crest. "You know this about me—I don't like details about my private life in the gossip pages. We won't confirm or deny the marriage until we're ready. The public will forget about it in no time."

"Good of Bernie to do that," Dorothy replied with relief.

"Needless to say, we'll go on about our business." He sat beside her and stroked her hair. "You can tell your pal Jerry Zerbe to refrain from taking photos of us when we're out on the town. And you can rest easy about any further break-ins. We're looking into it," he said as he reached for a sheet of paper on the cocktail table and handed it to her. It occurred to her to mention the man in the hat. "My secretary typed up the schedule of dinners planned through September. I know you like to be prepared," he said, prompting an appreciative smile from her.

"Thank you."

"She'll tend to the wedding plans after the announcement in November. Shouldn't take long. The White House staff is well accustomed to last-minute requests."

The telephone rang.

"El Morocco? Sure, sure, we're on our way," Harry said cheerfully, holding the receiver to his ear while looking at Dorothy. "Tell them to cue up the music."

Dorothy rose to her feet and went to the mirror to freshen her lipstick, thinking Jerry would undoubtedly be at the club. She would ask him not to take pictures and explain she wanted to stay out of the papers for a while. He would abide by her wishes. And until the hearings were over, she and Harry would dodge questions from columnists writing features on him, one of the most easily recognizable, applauded, hated, and revered men of his time.

"Shall we dance?" he suggested with an outstretched arm, a hand on the doorknob, and a look of keen anticipation.

At ten o'clock the next morning, she arrived at the Pierre Hotel and was shown to her table in the Rotunda where Clare was waiting, looking at the cover of *Time*, which featured an impossibly close-up picture of a haggard-looking Harry with a cigarette hanging from his lips.

"Right on cue," she said with a smile as Dorothy was seated, and then she glanced at the waiter. "Another coffee, if you would, and sliced melon for two."

"Ah, coffee. He may as well leave the carafe on the table. How are you, darling?" asked Dorothy, as the waiter placed a white linen napkin on her lap.

"Just fine. It sounds to me like you might have joined Harry in his legendary tangos and sambos last night. Did you read the article?"

"Not yet," Dorothy said, watching steam rise from the coffee as the porcelain cup was filled.

"It makes him sound quite likeable. They say he's as comfortable in the slums planning improvements as he is at swanky affairs with his wealthy friends like Joe Kennedy, or playing poker with a gang of boys in the back room of broken-down bars. You see? You're the perfect mate for him. He won't find another valiant, benevolent, well-bred woman with your looks. You can be sure of that."

"I'm sure my father has read it by now," Dorothy said.

"I know what it's like to want a parent's approval. To this day I imagine what my mother would think. Of course, it's likely she would *only* be thinking my five-digit checks to her aren't sufficient."

"Father called asking if there's anything that might be printed about Harry that he should know. I said there's nothing to be concerned about, but there are, perhaps, a few things that could make a parent uneasy," said Dorothy, taking a sip of coffee. "He said, '*Such* as?'"

"And what did you tell him?" asked Clare, taking a miniscule bite of melon.

"I said Harry is known as one of America's most eligible bachelors."

"And he said?"

"He said 'Fair enough.'"

"And you said?"

"I said Harry's tangos and sambas at El Morocco and Twenty-One are legendary, to which Father replied, 'Unusual conduct for a man of his position.' And then I mentioned that Harry dated Paulette Goddard, the screen actress who divorced Charlie Chaplin, but that didn't last; it was a brief affair."

"Oh, that did it, no doubt."

"Yes," Dorothy laughed. "I was greeted with loud silence." Clare laughed too, putting her coffee cup down with a loud clink. "Now tell me, Clare, how is the play coming along?"

It was half past twelve, after copious cups of caffeine, conversation, and air kisses goodbye, when Dorothy stepped onto Fifth Avenue and headed downtown. At times like this, she resented New York—the exhaust of passing cars, the wind messing her hair, the uneven sidewalk. Sensing someone following her, she quickened her pace.

At the strip of shops between Fifty-Fourth and Fifty-Fifth Street, she slowed to a stop in front of a window where she could catch the reflection of passersby. A group of men passed. A woman came up beside her to peer into the store. A boy rode by on a bicycle. She would be late if she waited any longer. Then, glancing around, she saw a man idling in front of the shop next door. He was only a few feet away.

His hat tipped low in the front, she couldn't see his face, only the cigarette dangling from his lips and his hand moving around in the pocket of his blazer. *That's him*, she thought anxiously as he pulled out a gold lighter, held it up in the sunlight admiringly, turned it around, flicked it open, and raised it to the tobacco stick, all the while inadvertently allowing her a glimpse at the giant-sized initial *W* on one side and the outline of an animal on the other, both in blazing diamonds. It seemed an unlikely accessory for a man in a Paul Stuart suit. Turning quickly, she began walking toward Fifty-Second Street where she made a right turn. Still sensing he was behind her, she stopped in her tracks and spun around to face him.

"If you don't stop following me, I will call the police."

He said nothing as he stood there, smoke rising above his fedora. Suddenly he threw his cigarette to the pavement and scurried away. Once he was out of sight, she hurried the few steps to Twenty-One where she found her lunch date, James Roosevelt, standing outside the gate puffing on a cigar.

"What was that all about?" he asked, leaning toward her with a kiss on her left cheek.

"Ah, you saw that. I'll tell you as soon as we're inside." She noticed his eyes were encircled with shadows and dim with concern.

Per their request, they were seated upstairs at a quiet table in the corner where they both had a view of the room. A waiter appeared, splashed water into their glasses, asked if they were having their usual orders, and trotted away.

"Was he following you?" said James in an uninflected tone.

"Yes, how did you know?" asked Dorothy with genuine surprise.

"I don't know, but I did hear about the burglary at your cabin, and there's some speculation as to who's behind it. Better we leave it there. Sorry I've gotten you tangled up in this, introducing you to Harry. I knew he'd find you irresistibly charming. Of course, you'd be no better off with me the way things have been unfolding this month."

"Well, you and I never had a chance," she said lightly and was really surprised.

"I married too young and met you too late," he said, patting her hand. She returned the gesture. "Now, listen. Does Harry know about the fellow that's following you?" She shook her head. "Just as well. Interesting development, though. It brings me to the conclusion that it's—"

"A dozen oysters for the table," announced the waiter with dramatic pause before he stretched his large, white-sleeved arm between their heads and placed the platter on the table. Dorothy glanced at him and turned to James when out came the arm once again. "Mignonette sauce for the gentleman and freshly cut lemon for the lady."

"That will be all, thanks very much," James said politely.

"You were saying . . ."

"Look, if Republicans had something indecorous on you—or planted something in the news—sure, it could hurt Harry. But it could only hurt him if the public thought he was engaged to you. And they don't. I don't think many people in Washington know."

"Probably just Harry's inner circle. So it's someone in the brain trust?" Dorothy asked nervously. "Should I be worried?"

"Just be cautious until we're sure who it is. Have an escort when you're out—that sort of thing."

"That's why I'm staying at Jerry Zerbe's apartment temporarily. It seems safer there. He has three bedrooms and he travels a lot, so . . ."

"Zerbe, good sport. Yale '28, right?" asked James.

"Yes, the Yale heir gone astray into the art world."

James laughed lightly and lit up the room, his smile so big and friendly, his cheeks wide and eyes squinted.

"I know him a bit," he said. Dorothy watched as he took three oysters and two lemon wedges from the ice and placed them on her dish, then served himself.

"Now, most importantly, James, let's discuss what's going on with you. I've been following it closely."

"Where to begin," James said, smoothing his sandy-brown hair with his palm.

"I know about the allegations, and I know it isn't true, of course—ludicrous to even suggest that you would use your political position to steer business to your insurance firm. They're brutes. For God's sake, you're helping this country, and you oversee, what, eighteen federal agencies?"

"I'm afraid it's hurt the credibility of the administration as much as my own, at least in the public eye. Republicans are set on upending our popularity and they're agitating the public."

"I expect your interview on NBC helped. It was essential for you to deny the allegations publicly. But turning over your income tax returns seems like a bridge too far."

"Yes, never imagined I'd have to do that," he said, leaning back in his chair and scanning the room with a nod to a couple of acquaintances. "What's more," he said, as he tilted his head closer to hers, and folded his hands on his lap, "my resignation from the White House seems to be the only way to quickly restore integrity to the White House. Not to mention, Wolf says they'll come after me harder if I don't go."

"Who is 'they'? Are they the same people going after Harry?"

"That's what Wolf says. They're coming after the people closest to the president." They sat quietly for a minute until he signaled for service.

"Sir?" asked the waiter.

"Two glasses of champagne."

"Right away."

"That sounds like a grand idea," Dorothy said. James leaned forward and paused for a moment, then turned to face her.

"I say, old friend, it seems we've changed the course of each other's lives."

"I know how you've changed mine, but what have I done?"

"It was you who introduced me to Sam Goldwyn and—"

"Your champagne," said the waiter, the white-sleeved arm appearing between them as he placed the glasses on the table, snapped the arm back, and pivoted on his heels. James took a sip of his drink.

"This is in confidence," he said.

"Of course."

"I'm leaving the White House and moving to Hollywood. Goldwyn is hiring me." Clinking their glasses, she sat in stunned silence. "He'll show me the ropes, and then I'll set up my own production company somewhere down the line."

"James! I'm happy for you but . . . you play a critical role in the White House. Was it your decision to leave?"

"Unanimous vote. We're announcing in November. Before the confirmation hearings."

"But why? You're more important to the president than Harry."

"I took my hit. Now I have to do what's best for my family."

"You always do the right thing, James."

"Why don't you come to Los Angeles with me in November? Visit your Hollywood pals. I hear Astaire asked you to be in his next film."

"Yes, it's an autobiographical musical about a dancer. I think it's the last film he's doing with Gingers Rogers."

"You know, Goldwyn's producing it. He said you're a magnificent dancer."

"How does he know?"

"He mentioned something about a party in Cuba."

"My God, that's right—the night we met at Jane's. Listen, I haven't mentioned the movie to Harry yet. There's plenty of time."

"Understood. I haven't mentioned my new job to Betsey yet, so . . ."

"Understood. Oh, so I don't forget to tell you, did you hear about Cole?"

"Cole Porter?

"Yes," answered Dorothy.

"No, I'm afraid I haven't seen or spoken to him in a while," James said with a look of interest.

"Well, it isn't terrific news, I'm afraid. Alva told me all about it. She was there when it happened. She said—"

The white-sleeved arm reached between them to remove the platter and dishes and immediately replaced them with entrées. "Roasted vegetables for the lady," he said, the arm brushing her shoulder as he placed the plate in front of her. "And roasted chicken *au jus* for the gentleman. May I bring you anything else?" he asked, standing as straight as a toy soldier and in no particular rush to go.

"That's all for now, thanks very much," James answered. "You were saying?"

"Alva said Cole was thrown from a horse named Fireaway."

The white-sleeved arm appeared between them and was accompanied by a large peppermill. "Salt and pepper?" asked the waiter. Dorothy shook her head.

"That's all for now, thanks very much," James answered. "You were saying, Cole was bucked off a horse?"

"Yes. Alva said the horse chewed the grass while Cole lay *unconscious*."

"Goodness, is he all right?" asked James.

"She said his leg might have to be amputated. It's just a complete shock."

Their conversation continued for another hour as the tables closest to them filled. At 2:30, standing at the curb, James hailed a taxicab for her, and they agreed to meet at the same time and place the following week. After seeing her off, she headed to Jerry's apartment to call Cole.

"I hear you're doing well. Tell me," Dorothy said, twisting her strand of pearls through her fingers. "How are you feeling?"

"Good to hear your voice. Doing fine now, just fine. Seems they won't have to cut off my leg, so things are looking up," he said with an awkward chuckle.

"Oh, thank goodness, Cole. What can I bring you?"

"Just you. Come visit next month when I'm better company," he said. "Listen, it's a little tedious talking about myself. It's all I do all day every day. Let's talk about you for a minute, shall we? I like the Dorothy Wilder photos of you that were in the papers," he said.

"They're not too bad. Thank you."

"I'm curious, Dorothy. Why are you staying at Jerry's apartment?"

"He's traveling most of the time. The location is on East Fifty-Sixth Street, so it's ideal. It's only temporary."

"But why didn't you get a place suited to your taste? Never mind that—how about I set you up with Cameron Jackson? He's a Brit, ready to settle down. Just as a backup. I know you're still seeing Hopkins, but you're not married yet, so why not? What's going on with you two, anyway?"

"Darling, did you receive the pillow I sent?"

"I did indeed. In fact, I had a good laugh as soon as I opened the box. Nicely embroidered with the words *Never Complain, Never Explain*. Got it. Tell me when you can. Or surprise me with the invitation. I've never been to a White House wedding, and I wouldn't miss it for the world."

"You're the tops, Cole."

"Listen, the nurse just showed up. She doesn't let me alone for a minute!" Dorothy could hear the nurse giggling in the background.

"I send you love. See you soon, okay?"

She placed the receiver on its cradle and went to her room where she sat in bed thinking over everything James had told her. Someone wanted him out of the administration. It might be the same someone who was after Harry and looking to ruin his name in part by ruining hers. It was all about public perception. *But then again, what if it isn't someone who wants to hurt the Democrats?* she thought. *What could it be? And what if it's someone on the inside? Someone in Roosevelt's brain trust.* It made no sense; her mind was spinning. She lay down to rest.

At seven o'clock that evening, she rushed to the front door to leave, knowing the driver was waiting. The telephone rang. She rushed back to the living room and answered. Harry.

"I'm sorry I couldn't make it tonight. As I said earlier, I've been putting out some fires," he said. "It looks like I'll be staying at Hyde Park overnight, probably through the weekend."

"I understand, Harry. Mary Rinehart is my fill-in date. You know of Mary. She's the American Agatha Christie who came up with the idea 'The butler did it.' Mary writes the kind of stories Clare likes to write when she's particularly peeved," Dorothy said, trying to lighten Harry's mood for a moment.

"I'll keep that in mind," Harry said with a laugh. "Mary sounds like a fine escort. Send my best to Sarnoff, if you would."

"Of course. Take care of yourself, Harry. À bientôt."

"Be good."

The telephone call made her late to pick up Mary, who was waiting at the curb when she arrived still thinking about Harry staying at President Roosevelt's home in Hyde Park through the weekend. En route to David Sarnoff's home, she explained to Mary that Sarnoff helped form the NBC network, that he was the "Father of Television," that he was gregarious and charming, and best of all he was Mary's biggest fan. Mary looked thrilled when he greeted her accordingly.

"When is your next book release, Mary? The world is waiting with great anticipation," said David.

"It is in the works!" she said, extending her arm in a theatrical sweep.

"And I heard you on the radio last week, Dorothy. What a voice, that low, silky pitch. I'd like you to do more shows."

"Of course, I would be delighted, David."

She is dazzling, thought Thomas Ellsworth, an editor at *Fortune* magazine, who watched Dorothy from across the room. She smiled brightly, laughed with abandon. Her eyes emanated warmth. Captivating.

"She's Hopkins' girl," said the man beside him. "Lucky bastard."

Thomas deflated. He trudged over to the dinner table to find his place card, and he sank into a chair. After several minutes twirling his wedding band around his finger while hearing Mary explain the elements of a good murder mystery, there was a delicate touch on his shoulder.

"Dorothy Hale. Pleased to meet you," she said, leaning around his slender torso to meet his eyes. He looked up and stared.

"The pleasure is mi—" He choked on his words. "Thomas Ellsworth. Please, have a seat." And for the remainder of the supper party, Thomas exhibited his considerable skill in intellectual acrobatics, discussing news and art and the people they knew. Dorothy rather enjoyed it until questions about Harry came rolling in. Out went Thomas along with the desire to talk with people she didn't know. For now, she would stay within her circle of trusted friends.

She invited Bucky, Isamu, and Jane to dinner at Twenty-One that weekend. After a few cocktails at her place, she suggested they go by foot to enjoy the splendor of the balmy August night. As they strolled down Fifth Avenue, Dorothy held Isamu's arm while Jane took Bucky's hand in hers. Once at the corner of Fifty-Fifth Street and Fifth, they stopped, surprised to see more than a dozen people crowded together, staring at something on the street. Curious, Dorothy and her friends weaved their way to the front. A man's body lay broken and bloody on the pavement; he had crashed on the ground only moments before. Dorothy gasped and turned away. None of them spoke.

"He was perched on the ledge of that building for hours, threatening to jump. I heard about it on the radio! Why didn't someone do something!" a woman shrieked.

"Dear God in heaven," Dorothy whispered. "How could anyone—" She covered her ashen face as Jane led her away.

"Are you all right?"

"Yes, yes, it's just . . . I can't think of a more terrifying way to die. I remember my accident as if it happened yesterday. When I tumbled down the stairs, I felt like I was moving in slow motion. And do you know what I thought?"

"My God, what?"

"I thought I wasn't finished. I wonder if that man thought the same thing. And then I saw my mother. I know how this must sound. I've never told anyone . . ."

"Go on, darling."

"Mother said, 'It's not time.' Oh, Jane, I know it sounds silly."

"It doesn't sound silly. Life throws us a right hook every now and then. You have a stronger will than anyone I know; you always rise up. And if your mother has something to do with it, so be it."

Dorothy was grateful for the comforting words. She thought of that man, and her mother, and Gardner, still and dead and out of her reach. Jane held her hand.

"I'm only sorry that it wasn't Hemingway on the street," Jane said. "The SOB didn't even visit me after I dove off my balcony. And it was his fault to begin with."

"Hemingway has an unquenchable thirst for women and war. You can feel satisfied knowing you're the only one who gave him both," said Dorothy. Jane smiled as they walked into Twenty-One.

Dorothy felt more at ease sitting with friends at their usual table, but their incessant conversation about the jumper was disturbing. It took ten minutes after the first round of drinks for her to steer them in another direction. *Thank goodness*, she thought, when Jane mentioned Sam Goldwyn's movie and opened the door.

"Did I tell you that Fred called and asked me if I'd like a role in his next film? I'm terrifically excited about it. And I'm not getting any younger. I don't know how many years I have left for stage work."

"I've been fighting Father Time since my thirtieth birthday, the son of a— Anyway, your youthful appearance belies your age," Jane said. Isamu turned to Dorothy.

"The fortunate outcome of good genes and easy living. It's hard to believe you're thirty-three," he said.

"Isamu," said Dorothy, "tell Bucky about the project you're working on. Oh, it's wonderful, Bucky—the first of its kind." The moment the men began to talk, Jane turned to Dorothy.

"Have you been sleeping any better?" asked Jane, lowering her voice to a whisper.

"No. Trying to elude gossip columnists is unnerving."

"I'm amazed you've been able to throw everyone off the scent. You're with Harry every weekend and by his side at all those dinners. I mean, everyone who's anyone knows you're still together. Someone must be keeping the press quiet."

"Absolutely, but that man in the hat is still following me. But remember, *c'est entre nous*. It's between us."

"Watch what you say on the telephone," Jane cautioned.

"Why?"

"What if it's to do with politics? They would be listening to every word, and they could take something out of context."

"Oh, for goodness sake," Dorothy said as Jane followed her sidelong glance toward the staircase.

"Could it be some jealous man that's hired someone to follow you? Happens all the time. I heard Shelby Whitehouse hired a private detective to follow his dog walker. His *dog walker*! Can you imagine! He couldn't understand why the dogs were so full of energy when he got home every day, and he concluded the walker wasn't running them."

Dorothy and Jane burst out laughing.

"That takes the cake," Dorothy said, wiping tears from her cheeks with her napkin.

"Could it be that man Harrison? Or Harrington? I don't remember his name."

"Ah," said Dorothy, "Wallace the widower. He still shows up at events knowing I'll be there. Silly man."

"Or what about the other one that bought you the Rolls Royce,

Edgar Kopelman? I still think you should have kept it."

"No, why would they bother?"

"Because they're hunters. Listen, Dorothy, another thing Shelby Whitehouse did, and I know this because Mabel Mortimer told me after she divorced him, he made a secret storage space in a baseboard and a built-in bookcase. Thin wall, easy to do, Mabel says. Think about it."

"I had no idea Shelby was so resourceful."

"By the by," Jane said, "I saw the new article about Harry. I'm sure he sees the condemnation of the Workers Project Association as a condemnation of him. Pretty tough stuff. It sounds like things are about to get messy."

And so they continued through the evening, with Dorothy somewhat distracted by all the news. Bucky escorted her home and suggested she join him and his family for a jaunt to Coney Island the first Saturday she was free.

"Come on," he said, "when was the last time you shot a toy gun to dunk a clown?"

"It's a deal," she answered giddily. "I haven't been there in years, but you'll see. I have skills—center of the target every time!"

As soon as she stepped into the apartment, she picked up the newspaper, went straight to the bedroom, flipped on the light, changed into her nightgown, and slipped under the covers.

"Now let's see what interesting tidbit I might find here," she said, turning the pages to find the article Jane had mentioned. "Ah, yes, Hamilton Fish, taking direct aim at the WPA, suggesting there's something fishy about it. Aren't you a clever one, Mr. Fish. Mmm-hmm, and Harry pulling the gun out of the holster warning him to stand down. Interesting but not terribly helpful." Still, she was curious what exactly Fish was referring to. She closed the paper and reached for the telephone to call Harry. Then she remembered he was in Hyde Park. Bucky answered her call.

"How about Coney Island this Saturday?" she said.

"Splendid! We'll pick you up at noon."

And splendid it was, completely carefree, losing count of the hours as they wandered around the grounds like kids at a carnival, game for the games, cotton candy, rides, and toys, available at every turn. And Bucky, so easy and agreeable and interested, like an old friend from school she'd lost track of along the years. It made her yearn to escape the city and all of its complexities.

After readying for bed, she decided to go to Maine. It was the height of the summer season in the northern woods—when Mother Nature turned her rascally scorn elsewhere and allowed the sun to shine on the rocky coast for more than three consecutive days. She would walk among the trees, dream new dreams, paddle about on the lake with Poppy Pettipiece, who was staying at Mt. Kineo House, and she would be free of any concerns. In the evenings she would read a novel and write poetry in front of the fire and wake to the song of birds.

And so it went, as she had imagined. Her caretaker had put her belongings in order, and she found nothing else missing. Her time at Moosehead Lake was always unpredictable only with regard to the elements. In every other respect it was invariably unchanging, and grounding, which pleased her. On the morning of her return, she stopped at the post office in Greenville before boarding the train to New York and looked at the postcard she had made for Maggie. She smiled a little, looking at her watercolor of the lake with mist rising from its surface. Her note on the back simply said, "I love this life, this world. D."

The lobby of the Hampshire House hotel buzzed with activity as bell captains assisted guests, giving careful attention to those who were staying the season for the ballet and Broadway shows, all of which were conveniently located minutes away from Central Park South. On the sixteenth floor, Dorothy looked around her suite and was filled with excitement. She had moved in the day before with the assistance of Tommie, the building's young handyman, who accepted a weight of bills to keep her confidence and help with a project which entailed a saw, hammer, nails, white paint, wooden boards, and an assortment of other items that were somewhat foreign to her. Within an hour he had cut into the thin wall of the bookcase, made quite a bit of noise with his tools, and completed his masterpiece, a hidden storage space wherein one simply pushed the wall by the bottom shelf and it swung open from the top.

She placed her framed photographs on the desk and lined the shelves with books while Tommie hammered a nail into the wall and hung her painting by Monet. Wondering if she had put too many of her clothes in storage, she opened her suitcases and asked the house girl to arrange the items by color when she hung them in the closet. Here she would be cared for, she thought, as she looked over the pocket-sized kitchen and saw the menu for room service, available at her whim. Hearing a knock on the door, she skipped up the two steps to the small foyer to answer and was greeted by a blooming bouquet of white roses.

The bell captain, poking his head out from behind, handed them over. Dorothy set the vase on the wide windowsill, looked at the card from Harry, and gazed out to the trees. Two blackbirds soared past the window, headed toward the street below. Looking east to the Carlyle Hotel, she decided it was time to throw a party.

18.

LABYRINTH OF BETRAYAL

Dorothy was radiant in her black velvet cocktail dress and silver high heels, her natural beauty every bit as enchanting as the sweeping view of Central Park. The sun lowered on the horizon as brilliant hues of gold and blue enveloped the skyline, a sunset she knew would go unnoticed by millions of people struggling through the Depression. Feeling a deep sense of gratitude for her incredible good fortune, an image of Paris came into her mind. She and Clare were watching the sun go down in the summer of '33 when Clare said, "People like us must always remember that fortunes can crumble and luck can change in an instant." It was a common story in the years leading up to this night, October 20, 1938.

Downstairs, her guests began to arrive, taking in the refined ambiance and chic design that Dorothy Draper had conceived to make the Hampshire House hotel the swankiest in town. Mink-caped women and bow-tied men breezed through the turnstile door as boisterous laughter rang out from the intimate cocktail lounge where "Blue Skies" played in the background. Palatial doors opened to corridors where a crystal chandelier caught the light in prisms, casting glittering rainbows on the mural-painted walls.

Perched on the windowsill, she watched taxicabs and Studebakers roll by the bustling crowds on the street far below. Men out of work wandered by couples headed toward the park, their children playing games with the pavement, running, jumping, and trying not to step on any lines in the cement. The clip-clop of the horse-drawn carriages sounded muffled. Pigeons landed on the ledge outside her window and suddenly soared outward in unison, cooing loudly and making sweeping arcs above the treetops. A gust of wind swept leaves into the air like confetti, spinning around and drifting up to the clouds where they disappeared out of view. She stopped herself from tearing up at its beauty; soon her guests would arrive for the party she had planned for weeks. The invitations promised celebratory cocktails at sunset to honor the newly appointed ambassador to Peru, Lawrence Steinhardt.

A loud clank broke her reverie. Turning quickly, she saw her housekeeper, Mary, bend to the floor, her plump cheeks flushed as she picked up a gilt-framed photograph. Dorothy slipped off the windowsill and touched Mary's shoulder gently as she placed the frame on the bookshelf, then stood beaming at the picture of her and Clare. It evoked the pleasures of summer, their floral silk dresses, their hands gripping ping-pong paddles and their smiles sunny. Underneath, the caption said, "The much-photographed Clare Boothe Luce turns the tables on her friend Dorothy Hale. At the top is a picture she snapped of Mrs. Hale making a smash at the ping-pong table." Rebecca Hamilton had given the framed magazine clipping to Dorothy, cautioning, "The irony of the caption 'turns the tables on a friend' is remarkable. Always remember what they say about her at *Vogue*. 'Anyone close to Clare will eventually feel they have been dynamited by an angel cake.'"

Turning away from the picture, Dorothy decided she would tell Clare about her forthcoming role in Fred's movie when they met for lunch the following day, but she would refrain from sharing the news that her trip to see Harry in Washington DC at the end of the week would be an extended visit. And she would be sure to deflect the questions about him that Clare would inevitably ask in her exceedingly intrusive way.

With one last check in the mirror, she turned sideways, admiring her black Madame X dress and the style of her upswept coiffure, especially the way it drew attention to her Florentine Victorian pendant. She made a last pass through her apartment, pleased that Mary had put everything in meticulous order.

"I'll see you tomorrow morning at 10:30, Mary. The place looks perfect."

One by one her guests arrived, gathering by the window to behold the changing colors of the pastel sky. Seeing everyone together pleased her immensely. Clare, Maggie, Dotty McNamee, Brock and Mat Pemberton, Rebecca and Pierpont Morgan Hamilton, Prince del Drago—all but two had made it on time.

"Front row center of Central Park!" Clare exclaimed. She raised one plucked eyebrow in an arch when she saw the framed photograph of Harry on the desk.

Clare took a glass of white wine from the tray that Alberto, the butler, held unsteadily on the palm of his hand. He then approached each guest, asked their preference of cocktail, bowed slightly, and fetched their requests. The vodka, whiskey, and wine flowed freely as they bantered about art and music, theater and politics, and the future of the American dream. Three taps on the door caught Dorothy's attention.

Ambassador Reinhardt made his entrance at last, well after the second round of drinks and first round of lobster toast canapés had been consumed. With Clare's growing interest in politics, she had every intention of seating him beside her at the first opportune moment. She admired the ambassador for his skills; he was a self-made man who had used his wealth to support the president's campaign in order to ensure his own political future, and it was, indisputably, a fait accompli.

"You know Prince del Drago of the Italian embassy, of course," Dorothy said, standing before the prince and the ambassador.

"Nice to see you," Ambassador Reinhardt said curtly to the prince, and the prince, from one of the oldest families in Rome, knew that it was due to his unfortunate incident in January when a reporter from *Life* magazine had gotten wind of his private appointment with the number one striptease dancer in the country, Ann Corie. When it hit the press, it caused a stir within the diplomatic community. The Europeans didn't bat an eye. Maggie watched, undoubtedly thinking of the entire affair and how wonderfully amusing it really was. If she didn't have such a fondness for the prince, she would write about him in the society pages, but unlike Cholly, Maggie knew the appropriate times to put down her pen.

Brock sat beside his wife, Mat, watching the exchange and looking as though he appreciated the silent dramatics. After his play *Red Harvest* closed, the play in which Dorothy gave a splendid performance, he had turned his attention to Clare's production, *Kiss the Boys Goodbye*, which had opened the previous month at the Henry Miller Theatre. Mat, who designed the costumes, stared out the window, mulling over the tiff she had earlier with a few of the cast members. She turned to Dotty, who was looking at the portrait of Dorothy that Gardner had painted by the pool during their visit.

"You made a wise choice to be an artist, without the worry of a mutiny," Mat told her.

"Mat, perhaps you can design a dress for Dotty's upcoming exhibition at the Metropolitan Museum," Dorothy suggested.

"It's the first time my husband will be able to attend to one of my exhibits," said Dotty. "He retired as admiral and now he's running McKay Radio and Telegraph, so to my delight he is back on a civilian's schedule."

Clare was intrigued, having read about the company's lawsuit with the federal government.

"Mat will make something fabulous," Dorothy said.

"Miss Hale," interrupted Alberto, as he stepped to her side, "you have a long-distance telephone call from Poughkeepsie."

"Excuse me," Dorothy said, curious as to who would be calling, for whenever Harry phoned from the president's home in Hyde Park, the telephone switchboard operators announced "long distance from Poughkeepsie," the town only a few miles away. But Harry was expected at her apartment any minute now. Perhaps it was James. He was just back from the Mayo Clinic where he had been treated for an ulcer.

"Yes, hello?" she said, holding the receiver to her ear. *Ah, Ben Wolf.* Hearing his voice immediately gave her concern. He said Harry had to go see the president, he couldn't make it to her party, he sent his regrets. But there was more—nothing to be concerned about. He would explain later. She should meet him at the second-floor bar in her hotel, 1:30, when she was back from the evening festivities. She listened quietly and said only, "Of course, thanks for calling," and hung up.

"It seems one of my guests can't make it," she said with a cheerful expression and notable awkwardness in her tone as she sat beside Rebecca and patted her knee with an imperceptible squeeze before reaching for her glass of wine. Dorothy crossed her legs and subtly kicked Maggie's ankle, and, having both taken the cue, they immediately carried on a conversation.

Still, everyone assumed it was Harry calling because everyone who was anyone knew that a call from Hyde Park would be announced as Poughkeepsie, and while Dorothy had innumerable friends from Poughkeepsie who might have called at this hour, they'd have put their money on him.

At 5:45 p.m. Alberto announced the time, and in a little swarm, all the guests moved to the foyer where they were assisted with their overcoats and readied to leave, for Dorothy, the Hamiltons, and Maggie were expected at the Colony for a pre-theater dinner. On the way out the door, Mat looked at Dorothy, then turned to face Maggie.

"I think Dorothy has something on her mind," Mat whispered.

Once in the car, the chauffeur winded his way through traffic on Central Park South and turned left onto Madison Avenue, finally delivering them at the corner of Sixty-Sixth Street. Inside the Colony restaurant, they found Mark Hanna, their dinner host, standing at the Vanderbilts' table and then moving on to shake hands with the Whitneys, Elsie de Wolfe, and Marlene Dietrich. All eyes turned to Dorothy as she made her way to the luxurious red banquette strategically positioned across from mirrors to allow patrons a view of their own adoring reflections.

By the wall, waiters stood at attention like a chorus line before their cue, then glided to the table to pour wine and top off champagne glasses, the crystal glowing from sparkling chandeliers above. As the repartee of Dorothy and her friends brought life to the otherwise sedate room, she scanned the crowd for any familiar faces, nodding a few times before mentioning that Isamu would join them later in the evening, which prompted the Hamiltons to reminisce fondly about their travels together to Haiti.

"To think he was still a struggling artist then. Well, he has certainly paid his dues," said Rebecca.

"He's finally made a name for himself. Isn't it grand? Have you all seen his *News* sculpture?" asked Dorothy.

"Not yet. I've been meaning to make my way down to Rockefeller Center to see it," answered Mark, who was finally taking his seat. And then he saw Walter Williams arriving and popped back out of his chair to say hello.

"It's a ten-ton stainless-steel bas-relief, the largest in the world," Dorothy said. "It's right above the entrance of the Associated Press Building."

"Hard not to make news when you plaster it on the company building," Maggie remarked with a small roll of her eyes.

"The boy is well on his way. I remember when he could hardly get a client and you rounded up your friends to buy sculpture busts in their likeness," said Rebecca.

"Dorothy, as I recall, he was working on one for you," said Maggie with an almost imperceptible shake of her head. Dorothy looked at her knowingly. She could practically read her thoughts. She had heard before Maggie's commentary about Isamu's pursuit to be known as a lone-cowboy Casanova craftsman who left a dusty trail of dazzling women in his wake, when really only half of his stories were true.

"Oh, he never did finish it," Dorothy said with a vague wave of her hand.

"Well, it goes without saying that he should. He should be grateful for all you've done. No one gave him the time of day until now," Maggie said, smiling in conclusion.

Suddenly surrounding the table were four waiters who swooped in and served entrées of chicken hash served inside a box of toasted bread, and soft-shell crab, little of which Maggie allowed herself to enjoy. Falling back into familiar banter, Dorothy watched Mark as he worked the room, displaying his interest in the masses, in the possibility of new introductions to people of some importance, people he would name by name to meet others of their position, for it was far more interesting to Mark than what he considered the mundanity of tending to friends he had already added to his ever-growing list. The hour passed quickly.

At seven o'clock, Dorothy mentioned the time to remind everyone they were due at the theater in thirty minutes. The bill was paid, the overcoats put on, and the conversation continued as they strolled through the lobby of the building where glass cases displayed twinkling gems and mother-of-pearl necklaces. Maggie took Dorothy's arm and slowed her pace, seemingly to admire the jewels.

"Don't forget to give me your telephone number in Washington," Maggie whispered. "Who called you? I can tell something's wrong."

"It was Ben Wolf. You've met him."

"Yes, but why would he call? You know, Happy says he's taking payoffs, and I wouldn't be surprised if it's true. He's a twitchy one."

"Harry would know if there was any cause for suspicion, and Ben is held in high regard by the administration."

"What did he say?"

"He said Harry couldn't make it because he had to go see the president. And besides, he advised Harry not to join us tonight because Clare would be there and she might have been the one to tip off the press about the engagement. It wouldn't be wise when they're a month away from the confirmation hearings." Lowering her voice even more, she continued. "He said he needed to talk to me and he would meet me at the Hampshire House at 1:30. Maybe they've found out who's been following me."

"For God's sake, Dorothy. What if Ben is the one who's been having you followed? Maybe he's taking payoffs from the Manzzino crime family or the Pesci brothers. I heard they're in cahoots to take control of the labor unions, and since Harry has a lot of sway with the unions, he could easily put Manzzino's thugs in charge."

"The Pesci brothers. They're probably the most successful businessmen in the country."

"Apparently they aren't just corporate suits with influence in Washington. Word has it, Mark Dedmann is investigating their connection to the Manzzinos."

Dorothy had heard Harry mention the unions on telephone calls. Occasionally she heard some names, none of which she remembered now.

"What are you saying?" asked Dorothy.

"I'm saying be careful. They might want some dirt on Harry to force his hand."

"You think Ben wants to blackmail Harry? No, it's impossible."

"Yes. Harry can't afford a scandal now."

Dorothy stared ahead. "Who told you about this? Happy?"

On the drive to the Fulton Theatre in Times Square, she didn't know how she could possibly pay attention to the play. She had her own melodrama to contend with. If only Harry weren't with the president, she could speak with him.

Robert Morley broke down onstage and wept, playing the role of a jailed man and broken alcoholic, the script drawn from Oscar Wilde's personal story. Mesmerized, Dorothy dabbed the corners of her eyes with a tissue, having lost herself in the drama unfolding in front of her. At the end of the final scene, she leapt to her feet for the standing ovation.

The cold breeze stung her eyes on their walk to Twenty-One. Passing through the black iron gates, she caught herself from tripping down the three steps at the entrance of the old brownstone mansion. It startled her; she was always so careful to avoid falling.

She breezed in with her friends. Jimmy greeted her with marked enthusiasm, then ushered them through the clubby lounge and past the Oak Bar, the air thick with the scent of cigars. They climbed the staircase to the second-floor dining room where Brock and Mat were chatting pleasantly with Mrs. Winston and her husband, Norman, who was closely aligned with New Deal policies. Seated beside him was Isamu, laughing loudly with Fred McEvoy, Erol Flynn's thrill-seeking, racecar-driving pal, who was best known as Suicide Freddie.

The moment Isamu saw Dorothy, he rose from his seat. She kissed him on each of his cheeks and stood very still as he pinned a corsage of yellow tea roses to her dress. He didn't mention that his gesture was in celebration of the new chapter she was about to begin with Harry in Washington DC, but when he winked at her, she got the sense that he knew. Maggie, noticeably unimpressed, bit her lip in tactful restraint while consoling herself with the thought that Dorothy was finally minding her own matters rather than helping Isamu with his. Phillipe stood at the head of the table waiting patiently for their attention.

"May I bring you the usual? Fresh oysters and pâté de foie gras?"

"Thank you, Phillipe," Dorothy answered. "And please let Bill know that I would like a vodka, twist of lime."

"Well, this looks like a choice party. I think I'll pull up a chair." Dorothy and Isamu turned to find Finch Fecken, the London theatrical producer known for his dramatics. "You should see my show when you're in London. It's the best in all of Europe. The best! In fact, it's the greatest show on earth! The girls are extraordinary. They drive the men mad, just mad!" he boasted as he sat down and took a swig of Isamu's drink.

"So I've heard, Finch." Dorothy knew that his productions were nothing more than expensively costumed striptease.

"What about you, baby doll? What are your upcoming plans? Any dancing in your future?" he asked with a lascivious wink. She couldn't help but stare at the pimpled skin of his hopeful, misshapen face.

"No, Finch. I'm going to try something entirely different than I've ever tried before," she answered, blinking several times on the last word as she turned to Maggie, who knew the look too well and kicked Dorothy lightly under the table, trying not to giggle.

"Tell me, wherever do you find those girls?" asked Maggie.

The dying rose boutonniere on Finch's lapel seemed somehow apropos to the man, thought Dorothy, as she turned her attention to her friends. As the evening progressed in an atmosphere of tipsy jubilance, she grew distracted. Awaiting her at home was a list of preparations to complete before her departure for Washington DC, and she was anxious to meet with Ben. At 1 a.m., she finished her drink.

"Well, that's it for the vodka. There isn't anymore," she said to Isamu. "Couldn't have timed it better."

"I'll escort you home," Finch insisted. How could she politely decline his offer? He too was staying at the Hampshire House.

Bidding her friends goodnight, her hugs lingered a moment longer than usual. If only she could explain the labyrinth of betrayal she seemed to suddenly be caught in.

"Might I suggest we take the scenic route up Fifth Avenue?" Dorothy said as they stepped outside. Considering the seven-block walk home, she felt a sense of dread that she would have to listen to his incessant pigheaded nonsense, worsened by the conspicuous bottles of alcohol he had consumed.

Once at the Plaza Hotel, she tuned out Finch completely, and they turned left into the sudden chill of Central Park South, the wind whipping her face as she lifted her sable high on her neck for warmth. When they arrived at the Hampshire House, he asked the elevator operator, Patrick, to stop on the sixth floor to let him off.

"Come on, baby doll. Join me for a nightcap in the lounge. The night is young," said Finch, taking her by the waist.

"Oh, stop," she said, pushing him away. "Behave. I couldn't possibly."

"Just one drink. Come on, baby, how about it?" he said, clasping her shoulders. "I'll have you home within the hour."

"Stop it, Finch," said Dorothy as she pulled away from his grip and moved to the corner. She didn't know him well enough to know if she should be afraid, but she knew he was drunk.

Suddenly he lurched toward her. He pressed on her neck and held firmly while putting his thin little lips on her nape, wetting her skin with his tongue. Crushing his face with her hands, she pushed him away. He reached for her. Patrick jumped between them, slammed Finch against the wall using all the force of his muscular frame, and forcibly held his chest, keeping him in place. Finch reddened with rage.

"Nobody does that to F-F-F-Finch F-F-Fecken!" he shouted angrily as the door opened and he stumbled out. Neither Dorothy nor Patrick knew whom he was threatening. Her heart was beating fast. She remained silent, turning her thoughts to Ben Wolf as the deep rumble of the elevator came to a stop at the sixteenth floor. Patrick tipped his hat.

"Goodnight, Mrs. Hale. Call if you have any more trouble with that creep."

"Oh, Patrick. You're the tops. Thank you," she said, turning to look at him. His eyes met hers. To let him know that she was all right, she flashed a smile, and the door closed behind her. It was 1:15 a.m. Just in time to meet Ben.

When she entered her apartment, the remnants of her cocktail party were still in plain view. She had no time to put things away; she had but a few moments to pray. Standing by the window, she looked out to the glittering lights in Central Park, the glow of the Carlyle in the distance. She closed her eyes and whispered, "Matthew 6:34: Do not be anxious about tomorrow, for tomorrow will be anxious for itself." Checking herself in the mirror above the console, she coated her lips with scarlet color and suddenly realized she might run into Finch in the elevator or bar. She would take the stairwell and survey the room from the entrance to make sure he wasn't there. It would be a long and dark descent from the sixteenth floor.

The cocktail lounge bustled with late-night revelers, ladies dragging on cigarettes and men getting deep in the cups. She took a cigarette from her purse and placed it between her lips. A gentleman standing beside her flicked open his lighter, and with some degree of difficulty, he found the tip of her tobacco stick. Thanking him, she looked nervously around the smoke-filled room. Couples were huddled together, and elegant women, a dozen or more, their diamonds sparkling under dim lights, drank champagne and flirted with men. There was Wallace Harrington, alone at a corner table, staring into a glass of whiskey. And there was Ben lurking by the window in the far corner, peering out to the horse-drawn carriages below.

"Ben, it's good to see you," she said as she approached him. "Is Harry all right?"

"Look, this isn't a social call," he said, putting a cigarette in his mouth and flipping open his lighter. Dorothy stared at it. It was the gold one with the diamond-encrusted initial and the profile of a wolf. "I'm afraid I need something from you." For the first time she noticed his burly shoulders were strangely disproportionate to his diminutive head, on which his eyes twitched nervously. "I need the pictures. The ones of Harry with Trotsky, Siqueiros, and the Pesci brothers."

"The Pesci brothers?"

"Yeah, Pesci, as in fish. And the ones of you—you know what I'm talking about. The Ziegfeld days." Maggie was right. The Manzzino crime family must have paid him off to get dirt on Harry so they could blackmail him and gain control of the labor unions. Maybe the Manzzinos were double-crossing the Pescis.

"I would never give you anything, Ben, even if I did have them."
She turned to go and felt her knees go numb. He took her by the arm.

"This isn't a game. You have until seven o'clock this morning."

"Get your hands off me." She tugged her arm away.

Wallace rushed over, looking incensed.

"What's going on here? Dorothy, are you with this man?"

"Wallace, darling. I was just leaving." He stood silently and stared down Ben, who seemed not to notice.

"I'll see you at seven o'clock," Ben said impassively.

She walked out, her heart racing as she climbed up the darkened stairwell. The sound of his footsteps echoed behind, getting louder, closer. Once on the third floor, she ran to the library in hopes of finding someone there. The lights were off. He appeared behind her. She ran to the window at the far end of the room. There he cornered her.

"I won't do it, any of it. I don't have the pictures. You're a brute. Leave me al—" Her throat closed, the tight squeeze of his fingers on her neck. She gave him a hard kick in the shin. He stepped back. In one swift movement, she leaned against the wall, bent her leg up in front of her, and with all her might she slammed him in the stomach with her foot, digging in with her spiked heel.

"Seven—*aaugh*—o'clock," he groaned, his torso curled forward.

She walked to the door, unable to move more quickly. Once at the stairwell, she paused, trembling: *Breathe in one-two-three, out one-two-three.* If she took the elevator, Ben would see where it stopped. She hastily made her way up to the sixteenth floor, out of breath when she finally reached the top of the landing. She clutched the receiver of the in-house telephone on the wall and frantically pressed the button over and over again. The security guard would answer. She would get help. She could tell them to call her when Ben left the building.

"Hello! Is anyone there! Please, is anyone there? Hello?" Then she saw it. The wire swung lightly against her dress and dangled straight down, cut like a rope from its anchor. She raced to her apartment and locked the door behind her. The wire on her telephone also had been cut. Pacing around her living room, she didn't know where to turn until finally, distraught and jittery, she collapsed onto the bed. The hours passed in a blur. Cries. Confusion. She took her diary and wrote hurriedly. As she slipped it through the swinging wall of the bookcase, she decided what she would do. At the first light of dawn she would go to Maggie's. There she would phone Harry at Hyde Park and tell him everything.

Soon it would be daylight, and she must tend to the matter of her affairs. She had already hidden her wedding gown, photographs, and diaries in Damier trunks; no one would find them in the attic of her building. Sitting at her desk facing the window, she wrote several notes, the first to Mary, her housekeeper, to keep her from entering the apartment and seeing the others. She pinned the message to the outside of the door. Written on paper inscribed at the top DON'T FORGET, it said: *Mary, Will not need you today. D. H.*

She locked the door and hurried to her desk to type a note to her sister. She wished her an enriching life. Then she looked over the letter she had written to her lawyer. "Dear John, I would appreciate your keeping this on file in case anything happens to me . . ." He would have the names of important contacts. Realizing she had forgotten to include the secret bank account and safety deposit box that she kept under an assumed name, she added it to the note in pen and placed it next to the typewriter, moving aside invitations to elegant affairs she hadn't yet accepted.

Then, the sound of someone jiggling the lock on the door. Her breath stopped and her hand fell open, releasing the pen to the floor, where it struck the hardwood and rolled under the sofa. She looked at her wristwatch—6:09 a.m. It must be Ben. Or maybe it was her neighbor again, lost in a blur of drunkenness, trying to fit his key in all the locks until he found a fit for his own. Or it could be Finch. And then she surmised it could be the man in the hat. Immobilized by fear, she kept her back to the door, and listened intently.

The rolling rattle of the knob turning. The soft thud of the door closing. The click of footsteps behind her. Her gaze fixed on the reflection in the window, his silhouette grew larger as he came closer. She spun around to face him.

"It's you," she whispered.

The sounds were muddled from the hallway outside her door. Voices, words, "will . . . date . . . Harry," the sound of a clunk, something sliding on the floor.

Prayers raced through her mind: *Even though I walk through the valley of the shadow of death, I fear not . . . Psalm 31:24: Be strong, and let your heart take courage . . .* She stood at the window high above the city street, shaking with fear, her chin tilted upward, inches away from the stubby hand gripping the knife, its silver spire gleaming.

Then, the sound of three loud knocks on the door.

"Dorothy? It's Wallace. Is everything all right?"

"Wal—"

The tip of the knife touched her neck.

"Say a word and he'll meet the same end as you."

In the distance, the emerald crown of the Carlyle hotel reached upward in the eastern sky as a beacon of hope in her darkest hour. In the park, golden leaves of the oak trees were still, as a red-winged blackbird dove past her window. At 6:15 a.m., as the sun began to rise, she stood precariously at the open window in her silver high heel shoes, and in a terrifying last moment, her thoughts turned to Gardner, and to prayer, as she tumbled out into the air under a blanket of rolling clouds.

PART V

ABIDE WITH ME

A gust of wind blew in through the open window, scattering some notes on her desk. The scent of her perfume, Joy, lingered in the room. There was a strange silence in the air, an eeriness in the breeze that stroked the delicate fabric of the chairs, the mink coat, the photographs—the unremarkable things that now seemed abandoned, even ghostly, in her absence. As the sun began to rise over Central Park, the sky glowed in a shade of queen blue, casting silhouettes on rising towers. The city was not yet awake. Homicide detectives watched the photographer take the final snapshot of her as the wail of a siren sounded in the distance.

Dorothy would have loathed the notion of detectives rustling through her personal belongings. The photograph of Harry was not on her desk when they arrived. Suited men from the White House had removed it when they swept her apartment. Remnants of her party were left in clear view; empty bottles of vodka, whiskey and wine were set on a side table, and Baccarat glasses still shined. Her notes were scattered about. The detectives gathered them as evidence and surveyed the scene. They made note of the narrow width of the French window, concluding in the report that she could not have fallen out by accident.

At half past ten, Maggie strolled down Lexington Avenue on her way to the office and noticed a small crowd gathered at the corner.

"Read all about it! Read all about it!" shouted a newspaper boy as he waved Dorothy's picture in the air, her eyes leaping from the front page. Maggie drew closer. "Harry Hopkins' Fiancée, Dorothy Hale, Actress and Socialite, Dead! Fell or Jumped! Get your paper here!" Her knees buckling, she grabbed the arm of the man standing beside her to keep from falling to the pavement.

Inside the West Wing of the White House, members of the administration passed around the newspapers and grumbled they couldn't afford the scandal now. One headline was worse than the next. "Dorothy Hale Dies in Plunge, Reported Engaged to Hopkins." "Pretty Widow, Engaged to WPA Administrator Hopkins, Plunges To Death."

Word spread like wildfire, matrons of society shaken to the core by the news, wondering what could have gone so wrong as they read the chronicles of Fate: "She was cheerful . . ." "She was apparently depressed . . ." "She was planning an extended stay in Washington, DC." Undeniably contradictory, but it made page one. They read "she fell or jumped"—this according to homicide detectives James Leech and James Sheehy, good Irish cops who got their names in the papers.

Clare's name was kept out of the news, omitted from the list of guests at Dorothy's party. Her friends were aghast, overtaken by sorrow. Maggie and the Hamiltons assured the press that Dorothy was in good spirits, not of the mind to take her own life. Her lawyer said the same. He rushed to the precinct and gave her letter to detectives, drawing their attention to the date at the top of the page, October 19, 1938, and the postmark on the envelope, October 22, 1938, the day after she died. It began, "I would appreciate your keeping this on file in case anything happens to me." The brief note gave directives on distributing her possessions. A clue?

"The case is closed," said the police chief as he walked into the room.

In the barren courtyard of the West Forty-Seventh Street police station, Dorothy's body lay covered in her dress of black velvet, charcoal clouds looming above. Streams of policemen came to see her before their meeting at noon. At 12:15 p.m., a cub reporter from the *Middletown Times Herald* leapt out from behind a tree and scurried toward her.

"Scram!" barked the chief as he went to her side. He eyed the crimson marks on her neck with a look of suspicion. And then, with a confident nod that he had solved the mystery, he gripped the Florentine Victorian pendant and slid it around the ribbon, centering it on her décolletage, beside the corsage of yellow tea roses still pinned in place. A *Herald* columnist watched from behind a cluster of shrubs and noted, "Many patrolmen stopped to look at the body, for even in death, Dorothy Hale retained the striking attraction that made her one of the beautiful women of New York."

Evelyn Gould barreled through the front door of the police station in a borrowed expensive dress that squeezed her figure and claimed she was Dorothy's friend, there to identify the body. While she was escorted to the courtyard, an officer wrote her name on a scrap of paper, finished off a bologna sandwich, then filled out the paperwork. After a cup of coffee, he brought the document to the chief.

"Evelyn Gould?" he shouted. "She's press! Get her outta here!"

Dorothy's body had been taken away and Evelyn was gone. She had managed to elicit details about the service and tipped off a reporter friend at the *New York World Telegram*, who emerged through the gold-trimmed doors of the Plaza Funeral Home at 2:30 in the afternoon the following day, just when the first somber note of the pipe organ signaled the start of the proceedings. Clare had made the arrangements.

The Reverend Nathan Seagal of St. Stephen's Protestant Episcopal Church stood before her father, her brother and sister, Clare, and Luke and Dotty McNamee. Dorothy's sister Marjorie couldn't make it in time to say goodbye. "Simply, swiftly, secretly, final religious rites were bestowed," a *Herald* reporter scribbled on his notepad from behind a potted plant. He noted her dress was white crêpe de chine with a corsage of lilies of the valley, and the blooming pink roses from Harry Hopkins that were set beside the casket.

Harry told the press he was "deeply shocked" and went into seclusion at the president's home in Hyde Park, while Cholly sat at his desk at the *New York Journal-American* and proceeded to write his column: "She was too young, too beautiful, and too talented to come to such a shocking and tragic end." It ran in the evening edition. But it wouldn't be long before Cholly penned a much different story, unaware that he would bury his own name with hers.

A coffee-stained copy of the *New York Journal-American* lay open on the porch table, beside a stack of other newspapers. Bernie Baruch glanced at Cholly's article and let out a groan as he picked up his worn copy of *Extraordinary Popular Delusions and the Madness of Crowds* and flipped through the bookmarked pages to find the line he had read the evening before. "Millions of people become simultaneously impressed with one delusion, and run after it, till their attention is caught by some new folly more captivating than the first." Looking out at the marsh on his South Carolina property, he decided to call Clare.

"I saw the papers. And I saw your quotes in the papers."

"Oh?" said Clare.

"Yes, the ones where you say Dorothy had an estate, so she had plenty of money. And that she had new work to look forward to and no man troubles whatsoever."

"Well, yes, yes that sounds right. It's an absolute mystery how this happened . . . *Isn't* it?" asked Clare, waiting a moment for Bernie to respond. "Did you see Maggie's quote? She said that Dorothy was planning an extended stay in Washington DC, intimating a long stay with Harry."

"I hear the marriage was on." Bernie looked at the *Washington Post* headline, "Dorothy Hale, Beauteous Actress Engaged to Hopkins, Is

Killed in New York Plunge," and cleared his throat. "Harry needs to get his name and picture off the front page. It's too much of a scandal. Someone needs to quiet the press."

"Richard Reede knows all the publishers. He says there are too many unanswered questions, the details don't add up, and it won't go away until someone writes a definitive story. It's just devastating, the whole matter."

Daylight came with an unwelcoming gloom the morning Cholly's follow-up story ran. White fog enveloped the Manhattan skyline. Raindrops fell from the sky. The somber pall of the city suited the mood of Dorothy's friends as they opened the paper in horror of what Cholly had done.

A variety of large photographs appeared on the page, showing Dorothy in portrait, in the movies, as a socialite. The full-page spread featured Cholly's tale of her demise: "Dorothy Hale committed suicide from a broken heart and fading career."

"How wonderfully dramatic. You've done it again, old boy," Cholly said aloud, to himself, seeing his own words in print. He leaned back in a worn leather-upholstered chair and put his feet on the desk in smug satisfaction. His article claimed she took her own life, she was a woman in despair, a pretty face bankrupt of happiness, talent, and money. He peered at his column from five days before, "She was too young, too beautiful, too talented to come to such a shocking end," and tossed it into the wastebasket. With a vague sigh, he ignored the telephone call coming in, expecting it was the president of the Deadline Club, who would undoubtedly tell him, again, how the organization advocated for ethical reporting as strongly as it promoted freedom of the press. Cholly yawned at the very thought. No cause for concern. And he was well accustomed to cold shoulders, unanswered calls, and scorn from those of high society, the very women he wrote about—the ladies he embraced, insulted, built up, and destroyed.

By the time of Binky Melon's dinner party that evening, all the papers had run with the new angle on the story. The moment the crystal wineglasses were filled, Alva Belmont rose from her seat and made a toast in honor of Dorothy.

"People like us take care of one another," she said as a seal of approval to the guests, all of whom had continued to stand by Dorothy. Happy waited impatiently for the speech to end and the glasses to clink so Alva would sit back down beside her, a seating arrangement she happily viewed as a signal they had accepted her as one of their own.

"Alva," Happy said in a hush, "I heard Cholly was told to write a *definitive* story so there's no question about what happened and the story would go away. But Dorothy was a practicing Catholic, she would not have taken her own life, and she would not have requested cremation, to be done 'immediately' no less. And what do you make of those quotes in the papers from Clare, Isamu, and Bernie?"

"I'm not sure that I understand the question, darling."

"Well, they're all the exact same. See here," Happy said as she pulled newspaper clippings from her purse. "This is what Clare said. 'Dorothy Hale was one of the most beautiful women I have ever known. For weeks she was taking sleeping pills for insomnia. Perhaps she couldn't bare it anymore. It was such a waste. She was so beautiful and so vulnerable.'"

"Disgraceful," Alva said, her cheeks flushed with anger.

"And see here, Isamu Noguchi said the same thing, word for word. He said, 'Dorothy Hale was one of the most beautiful women I have ever known. It was such a waste. She was so beautiful and so vulnerable.'"

"What are you trying to say, Happy?"

"And get this, Bernie Baruch said it too. 'Dorothy Hale was one of the most beautiful women I have ever known. It was such a waste. She was so beautiful and so vulnerable.'"

Alva took a large sip of wine. And then another. And then she drank until the last drop dripped onto her tongue.

"What I'm saying is they obviously got together and came up with that statement for the press for a *reason*. They made Dorothy sound *vulnerable*. But why, Alva? *Why*?"

Sitting at her office desk, Maggie found it impossible to focus on work, so she called Crownie.

"Just astonishing," Maggie said. "Only a few months ago, her picture appeared on page one of the newspapers, a storybook life captured in print. Hapless, they now declare—just an unfortunate woman with exceptional beauty and a fabulous circle of friends. And they're the very friends who are betraying her, abiding with the story of suicide, denying her the dignity she deserves. They consider themselves too important, too revered in the public mind to be associated with scandal. You, Jane, Bucky, the Hamiltons, Alva— these are the good people."

Crownie glanced at the pile of newspapers on his desk.

"Finch Fecken told the *Times Mirror* that she eagerly anticipated the drama of death—just astonishing," he said.

"It's all so very wrong." Maggie nervously flicked cigarette ashes into an empty teacup and took another vigorous puff. "Walter Winchell is the only one who got his story right. He said, 'Dorothy Hale, the Pittsburgh beauty, did not die of man troubles.' And Clare in her *first* interview with the press said Dorothy had no troubles, she had money, and they were to have lunch the day after the party where Dorothy was to tell her about the job she was getting."

"Well, it seems everyone's passed over that news," Crownie said.

"Can you imagine people said it was an impulsive act because she had insomnia and took a sleeping pill? Good God, what kind of ludicrous statement is that? What can we do?" asked Maggie, with a forcible exhale that enveloped her in a little gray cloud.

"Are you smoking, Maggie? You don't smoke."

"God, yes, they're Dorothy's cigarettes. Listen, I know Happy Longhorn is seen as a floozy, but the fact is, her gossip is always true, and she said a reporter got it wrong when he claimed that Dorothy wrote a letter that absolved everyone of any blame in connection with her death. Not true. Captain Mullins told the press she wrote a suicide letter last month, and she'd been planning it for weeks. Not true."

"Clare says it will all die down soon and no one will even remember. I'm afraid she's right," Crownie said, choking up on the last word.

"Frida says Dorothy is seeing this from somewhere up in the sky. And there isn't a thing she can do about it."

The avalanche of press peaked and vanished. All in all, everyone at the White House was pleased at the neat tie-up of her death. Harry had Ben Wolf give Bernie a letter in which he expressed his appreciation for silencing the press and handling it with the utmost discretion. They thought they could rest assured that the story would fade out and expire once and for all. But they didn't know Clare Boothe Luce.

Frida Kahlo, El suicidio de Dorothy Hale (The Suicide of Dorothy Hale), 1939. Oil on Masonite with painted frame. Collection of Phoenix Art Museum, Gift of an anonymous donor, 1960.20. Copyright © 2020 Banco de México Diego Rivera Frida Kahlo Museums Trust, Mexico, D.F. / Artists Rights Society (ARS), New York

THE PORTRAIT OF DOROTHY HALE

I t was the first of November, eleven days after Dorothy died, when a flock of patrons swept into the Julian Levy Gallery on West Fifty-Seventh Street to celebrate the first New York art exhibition of Frida Kahlo's work. It was evident from their fresh-faced enthusiasm that in Café Society the fête must go on. Exhilarated by the momentous occasion, yet deeply troubled by the sudden death of her friend, Frida wanted to see Clare. Thus, she weaved her way through an assemblage of elbows and wineglasses until she found her standing before a painting.

Frida knew how the mere presence of Clare, who was wealthy enough to buy the paintings on display, powerful enough to place stories in the press, and famous enough to generate buzz, intoxicated the setting. That was not to say she was well liked. Yes, yes, she was envied for her beauty and talent, both of which were remarkable, and she was admired for the success she had achieved at *Vogue* and *Vanity Fair*, and for penning a Broadway hit—but the prevailing thought about Clare Boothe Luce was that she was heartless. And so, it was to Frida's surprise that Clare commissioned a *recuerdo* of Dorothy for $400.

"Her life must not be forgotten," said Frida.

"Precisely. Dorothy always said the greatest honor you can bestow on a loved one is to keep their memory alive," said Clare. "I'll gift the painting to her mother."

Word spread quickly that she commissioned the portrait for Dorothy's mother, earning Clare a modicum of esteem from detractors, from the inner circle of the Four Hundred to the inner sanctum of mahogany-lined boardrooms, who had long loathed her scoundrelly nature. It did seem a kindhearted gesture except that Frida Kahlo was known for brushstrokes of pain and Dorothy's mother was dead.

Seven months later when Clare opened the crate to see the finished painting, she could not believe her own steel-blue eyes. She nearly passed out from shock at the horrific scene. On the canvas, Dorothy was falling from the window of her high-rise building. She was soaring through the air, facedown. She was lying on the street, clothed in her black Madame X dress, with blood dripping from her delicate face and onto the frame. Yet somehow there was glamour. There was strength in her expression that belied the title *The Suicide of Dorothy Hale*. There was an inscription stating it was a gift to Dorothy's mother from Clare Boothe Luce. And there was Dorothy's angel, looming in the clouds, somewhere between here and heaven. Whether Frida Kahlo had a prescient moment or intended to induce guilt in Clare, for whom she had little fondness, was a matter of some debate.

Dorothy's leg reached to the edge of the canvas, her bare, stiffened foot painted on the frame, making it feel as though she were in the very room with you. Her arm curved upward over her head in the pose of ballet fourth position or, perhaps, in the moment before a final bow. Underneath, Frida wrote a legend in blood-red script:

"In the city of New York on the twenty-first day of OCTOBER, 1938, at six o'clock in the morning, Mrs. Dorothy Hale committed suicide by throwing herself out of a very high window of the Hampshire

House building. In her memory Mrs. CLARE BOOTHE LUCE commissioned this retablo for Dorothy's mother, executed by FRIDA KAHLO."

An absolute horror to Clare, who thought it could only be mended with a pair of library scissors and a thousand cuts to the canvas. But she resisted the urge and devised another plan, which she plainly outlined in a letter to Nickolas Muray.

"I intend to have Noguchi, a great friend of both Dorothy Hale and Frida (Kahlo) Rivera, paint out the legend—that is to say, the actual name of the unfortunate girl and my name. I hope Frida Rivera will understand why I have taken this liberty. The painting will then be put in storage for a number of years, after which I will send it to some museum. May I please ask you . . . not to speak of the incident to anyone."

She didn't say she asked Isamu to paint over the image of Dorothy's angel (or ghost, depending on whom you asked). Isamu complied with her wishes, as one did, and proceeded to take a wet brush to the canvas. He covered up the angel by recreating Frida's ominous gray clouds, and crossed out the words "Commissioned by Clare Boothe Luce for Dorothy's mother." But he took one stand against Clare that would prove to be a fateful decision. He refused to remove Dorothy's name from the inscription.

Clare then recruited Crownie to keep the painting hidden away, only to find it in her possession once again eight years later when he died. Then, in 1987, after serving as a war correspondent, congresswoman, and US ambassador, and after concealing the painting's existence for five decades, she donated it to the Phoenix Art Museum in Arizona with the agreement she would be listed as "Anonymous Donor." *Oh, Clare*, one might ask, *surely you must know better?* Before long, someone inadvertently tipped off a reporter that it was she who was the donor, and the story went to press. And so it went. Clare was back in the spotlight, and the calls came rolling in.

"Well, this whole episode led me to pen a phrase which has since been widely quoted. 'No good deed goes unpunished,'" she said. Exceedingly unsentimental and still very much a splendid storyteller, Clare explained the unfortunate details of her old friend's fate—how she made the mistake of spreading the news of her engagement to all of Café Society and was jilted, and so on and so forth. The dress? The famous Madame X dress, yes, of course. She wore it that night, Clare told a reporter. She would be glad to tell him about it; it just so happened it was her idea, but there was more to the story.

She explained very pleasantly that in the months before Dorothy died they had a falling-out over men, money, and clothes, as girls do. But first, the dress—yes, well, Dorothy called and asked, "Darling, what do you think I should wear at my farewell party?" And naturally by farewell, Clare said, she thought Dorothy must have meant she was off to Hollywood or Washington, so Clare replied, "I always like you best in your old black Madame X velvet," but what she really wanted to say was, "How about that gorgeous Bergdorf dress you bought with the money I gave you?"

Yes, she explained, she gave Dorothy money, just helping an old friend in a pinch, as friends do. You see, in 1937, Dorothy asked for a loan of $1,000 to be repaid in six months, so Clare told her she would loan her half the amount, since she believed very strongly that "all urgent demands are highly exaggerated." Then, of all the things, Clare said, she was in Bergdorf Goodman's made-to-order department admiring an expensive gown when the saleswoman told her that Mrs. Hale had just ordered one. And what was Clare to do but think that was how Dorothy spent the money she had lent her? Well, Clare explained, it came to her attention that Bernie Baruch had paid for it, advising Dorothy to buy a dress so beautiful she would capture a husband.

"Oh, come on. Baruch said that?" asked the reporter, chuckling in disbelief. "The same Baruch who advised Woodrow Wilson and FDR? I hope he gave the presidents more practical advice."

Clare eyed him closely. With an exceedingly erudite tone, she concluded, "We all believed that a girl of such extraordinary beauty and charm could not be long in either developing a career or finding another husband. Dorothy had very little talent and no luck."

And thus, the legend of Dorothy Hale was born again.

Reading the interview, Happy Longhorn, by this time an aged woman on her fourth marriage, yet no less excitable than at the time of her first, flounced into her husband's office on the top floor of their Fifth Avenue duplex, her fuchsia silk dress shouting among the dark, staid mahogany furnishings, and exclaimed, "It's poppycock!" as she dropped a thick folder of newspaper clippings onto his Chippendale desk with a loud thump.

"Look here," she said, pulling out an article. "Clare Boothe Luce said, and I quote, 'Dorothy had no money troubles. She was left an estate.' Matter of fact, honey, that doesn't account for her investments, which I know were overseen by Mr. Jack Wilson himself. That's right, Jack Wilson. Sure, she could have been short on *liquid* funds, I guess. And see here, Phinnie, Dorothy's 'farewell party' was in fact a party for the ambassador."

Phineus removed his eyeglasses, folded his hands on the desk, cleared his throat, and looked at her, dumbfounded.

"And who, may I ask, is this *Dorothy* you speak of?"

"*The* Dorothy Hale in the Frida Kahlo painting. My old friend. You know, Phinnie, two years after she died, Clare bumped into Harry Hopkins and he said to her, 'I know you don't like me,' and *she* said, 'That's right, I don't, and you know the reason why,' and *he* said, 'Well, it's not the slightest bit of importance; there's nothing you can do for or against me.' Boy oh boy, was he a heartless brute. Why, I should have—"

"*Ahem.*" Phineus dabbed perspiration from his brow with his handkerchief.

"See here, Phinnie," Happy said, placing a sheet of paper on his desk and sliding it in front of him. "Years after she died they stuck to their old script, but they made it even *better.* Clare told a writer, 'Dorothy Hale was one of the most beautiful women I have ever known. *Not even the young Elizabeth Taylor, whom she resembled, was more beautiful.*

It was such a waste. She was so beautiful and so vulnerable.'"

"Aha, yes, sad indeed," said Phineus, looking at the telephone with a longing, hopeful expression. It did not ring. "Perhaps—"

"And look," she continued, knowing precisely where to place her finger on the page. Her nail, polished in Jungle Red, swept from side to side. "Isamu Noguchi told her the same thing: 'Dorothy Hale was one of the most beautiful women I have ever known. Not even the young Elizabeth Taylor, whom she resembled, was more beautiful. It was such a waste. She was so beautiful and so vulnerable.' And Bernie Baruch—Phinnie, you knew old Bernie—he said, 'Dorothy Hale was one of the most beautiful women I have ever known. Not even the young Elizabeth Taylor, whom she resembled, was more beautiful. It was such a waste. She was so beautiful and so vulnerable.' Y'see how they all said *vulnerable*. They tried making her sound like some kind of weak-minded glamour girl. It's malarkey!"

"Well, thank you for reading each and every one, Happy," said Phineus with a slow shake of his head, which continued conspicuously as he nervously tapped his gold monogrammed Cartier pen on the hardwood, his crisp white shirt colored with patches of perspiration.

And then Happy was struck with a thought that caused her to collapse into the chair facing Phineus. "Hold on, I think I get it. Clare and Frida both wanted to make sure she would never be forgotten. That's it, Phinnie . . ."

A surge of memories rushed forth in Happy's sprightly little mind. As soon as she had read Hedda Hopper's column in November of 1938, she called her and asked breathlessly, "I saw that you wrote there's more to the story than meets the eye. I think so too. Who do you think killed her?"

"Everyone killed her, Happy," snapped Hedda. "Cholly, Harry . . . They killed her a second time. They ruined her good name."

"It's a tragedy!"

"Do you know what's a tragedy, Happy? The fact that heartless gossips pose as professional press, they get a few quotes and run with the story like Seabiscuit to the finish line. They're nothing more than conmen, salesmen, pitchmen, pompous men professing to be of public service—and they have the freedom to do so. There's no price to pay."

Happy responded with uncharacteristic silence as she scribbled down what Hedda had said.

"Of course, there are only a few bad apples in the basket," Hedda added hastily. "But—get this—I heard that she once told one of her friends, and I can't say who, but it's someone you know. Well, *she* said that *Dorothy* said the greatest honor you can bestow on a loved one is to keep their memory alive. Quite doable for her friends to bestow the honor, except . . ."

"Except what?" asked Happy, her eyes wide.

"Well, we can only hope they recall the other thing she said, that when she dies she wants to be remembered for . . ."

"For what? Remembered for what!"

"Something wonderful, Happy."

Hedda looked wistfully at the blank page on her typewriter. She could break the silence and erase the myth of Dorothy Hale without pointing fingers. She could write about the girl who lived out her grandest of dreams. But she knew that story wouldn't make it to the front page of papers or onto the tip of everyone's tongues. The wonderful ones rarely do.

EPILOGUE

October 21, 1995. I stood on the windowsill sixteen floors above Central Park South. An American flag waved at the north end of the park, the emerald crown of the Carlyle a faded green in the sunlight.

"So what do you think? 16E has one of the most enviable views in the city, dead center of Central Park," said Grace, one of the well-regarded realtors in town.

I had been there before, but only briefly. There wasn't time to linger. To get a sense of the place. To reimagine her brightest days and her last moments. After days and years living with her story, looking for clues, learning the personalities of those around her, it had consumed me. The characters followed me everywhere, inserting themselves into my thoughts, my conversations, my waking hours and dreams. This would be the final goodbye.

And where better to bid farewell than apartment 16E. There I discovered two of Dorothy's diaries, a gentleman's journal, and a young man's confessional note, hidden behind the bookcase. When she stood precariously by the window, he watched helplessly when he should have saved her. Taken the guy down. Exposed the lot of those rich thugs, he wrote. But he didn't name the killer.

You see what could happen when a housekeeper leaves a front door ajar, and a neighbor onto a story breezes in?

"Beautiful," I said, turning to face her.

"Only one owner in all these years. He bought it when the hotel transitioned to a co-op. I'm told he stayed here the night he signed the papers and never returned. He recently passed, and his family just wants to sell it."

"It sounds like a Huguette Clark story. Who was he?" I asked, holding the edge of the desk to climb down from the windowsill.

"Harrington. Wallace Harrington," she said. My hand slipped and I tumbled a little bit to the floor. Something in a slit under the cabinetry caught my eye. "Are you okay?"

"Fine, fine," I assured her. "Do you mind if I sit for a few minutes, just to get a feel for the place?"

"Of course, I'll be back in a little while," she said as she left, closing the door softly.

Immediately I lowered myself back to the hardwood planks, slid my arm below the cabinet, and took hold of the small object blackened with dirt. Rubbing it with a tissue, I felt its weight and flipped open the top. And there it was. The gold lighter, the initial *W* on one side and the face of a wolf on the other, the diamonds dull from dust. It *was* Ben Wolf.

And it was Wallace who wrote in the journal that I found on my last visit. Perhaps he returned before his death to leave another trail. At the bookcase by the window, I gently pushed on the wall of the bottom shelf. It swung open to reveal a stack of papers, causing my heart to race. Tucking them into my tote, it occurred to me that I should leave things well enough alone. And then Grace came into the room, we said our goodbyes, and I returned to my apartment a few floors below just as the sun was lowering in the sky.

Looking out to Central Park, the sky fading to black, the silhouette of grand towers glittering, the city silent, I find myself unable to turn my thoughts away from those papers. There's a lingering possibility the documents will reveal something that somehow contradicts the story I wrote, and I'm rushing to deadline like Seabiscuit to the finish line. No, no, it couldn't be. The evidence is there. Facts are facts. But what if the documents present more questions than answers? What if they reveal another unignorable story? It would take me back to a bygone era and keep me there indefinitely, when there's beauty and life in the here and now. *Ceuille le jour. Seize the day.* I have done enough by telling her story. Dorothy Hale can at last rest in peace.

Yet it seems there's little choice in this very mystifying matter, as I must know what was written and where it might lead. What else is one to do when presented so unexpectedly with such unlikely intrigue? You see how it's entirely unavoidable. It's a perfectly reasonable proposition to follow the course that Fate has rolled out before me like a red carpet, inviting me to step back to those years of laughter and scandal, champagne and cigarettes—indeed *Les Années Folles*—one last time.

ADDENDUM

Harry Hopkins was confirmed as secretary of commerce in November 1938. Two years later, he moved into the White House and made political history as FDR's closest advisor during World War II, and four years later, he married a glamour girl.

Gardner Hale is credited with reviving fresco painting in America and France, and his book, *Fresco Painting,* is still available today. His mural in the Chrysler Building's Cloud Club was removed during renovations; its location is unknown.

Margaret "Maggie" Case enjoyed a successful career at *Vogue* for more than forty years. In 1966, she allegedly jumped to her death from the sixteenth floor of her Park Avenue home, dressed to perfection.

Jane Kendall Mason was immortalized as the character of Helene Bradley in Ernest Hemingway's novel *To Have and To Have Not,* and as Margot in "The Short Happy Life of Francis Macomber." It was for Jane Mason that Hemingway wrote "A Way You'll Never Be." The epitaph on her tombstone reads "Talents too many, not enough of any."

Isamu Noguchi launched into the spotlight in 1938 when he unveiled his plans for his *News* sculpture in Rockefeller Center, which symbolizes freedom of the press and the journalistic pursuit of the truth. Today his work is honored at the Noguchi Museum in New York and the Noguchi Garden Museum in Japan, his home designs are sold across the world, and he is hailed as one of the great artists of the twentieth century.

Buckminster "Bucky" Fuller became one of the century's most influential innovators with twenty-eight patents, twenty-eight books, and forty-seven honorary degrees for his work toward a sustainable planet. His geodesic dome has been produced over 300,000 times worldwide.

Frank "Crownie" Crowninshield's *Vanity Fair* continues to thrive in keeping with his editorial mission: "To believe in the progress and promise of American life, and, second, to chronicle that progress cheerfully, truthfully, and entertainingly." His name as an original trustee and creator of the Museum of Modern Art remains on its wall today.

Frida Kahlo and Diego Rivera are regarded as two of the most significant figures of twentieth-century art. Today Frida is a pop culture icon who symbolizes female empowerment.

Clare Boothe Luce became a devout Catholic after Anne, her only child, died in a car accident. She served two terms as a US congresswoman, and President Eisenhower appointed her ambassador to Italy, thus making her the first female US ambassador to a major country. She later served on the US Intelligence Advisory Board, and in 1983, President Reagan awarded her the Presidential Medal of Freedom. Her plays have been revived on Broadway and adapted to the silver screen. She famously said, "Male supremacy has kept women down. It has not knocked her out."

Frida Kahlo's portrait entitled *The Suicide of Dorothy Hale* travels the world on exhibit, on loan from its final resting place beside the work of Diego Rivera at the Phoenix Art Museum in Arizona.

AUTHOR'S NOTE

L*ady Be Good* is based on the true story of Dorothy Hale and her coterie of friends. The fictional narrative was crafted around a framework of facts drawn from original research that I conducted over many years.

While great efforts were made to maintain authenticity to the people, timeline, and setting, adjustments have frequently been made in the interest of writing a fluid story. I endeavored to portray those who appear as main characters as accurately as possible, but in some cases, especially involving those for whom there is a dearth of information, I had to rely on imagination. My portrayals of Dorothy Hale and Clare Boothe Luce are based on research and fictionalized. It was necessary to create their conversations, motivations, and thoughts. I wrote a purely fictional portrait of Gaillard Thomas II with the exception of the newspaper articles and his family background. Also playing roles are fictional characters—most notably, there never was a Happy Longhorn, Wallace Harrington, or Ben Wolf, although there very well could have been similar personalities in Ms. Hale's circle of friends.

It is worth noting the following fictional elements. Dorothy and Gardner Hale first met in Paris where she was studying painting and sculpting, not at the Art Students League of New York. Claude Monet died in 1926; the fictional scene with him takes place in 1927. When art demands, history yields.

When I came upon the story of Dorothy Hale, I was immediately intrigued by her life story and those of her inner circle—the iconic figures of arts and letters, politics, and entertainment. What prompted me to delve into research, however, were the inconsistencies in the accounts about her. One of the first curious details I uncovered was that Ms. Hale's mother died sixteen years before Clare Boothe Luce commissioned the Kahlo painting, though Luce said it was a gift for Hale's mother and it appeared on the inscription.

I owe thanks to the authors and journalists whose work helped me recreate the world of the 1920s and 1930s and those who inhabited it. While the sources are too extensive to list here, I must point out a few. The archives of *Vogue*, *Vanity Fair*, *Time*, the *Daily News*, the *LA Times*, and the *New York Times* were especially valuable, as were the Clare Boothe Luce papers in the Library of Congress. You'll find numerous witticisms and bon mots from several people, used with attribution.

Time magazine was a solid resource for facts regarding news, politics, and personalities, and offers one of the most telling accounts about Maury Paul, who, to my knowledge, wrote the first indelicate column about Dorothy Hale after her passing. The line "Time magazine proclaimed him the 'fat, vain little Maury Henry Biddle Paul who coined the phrase Café Society and made a fat living insulting it'" is from his obituary in *Time*, dated July 7, 1942.

Frida: A Biography of Frida Kahlo by Hayden Herrera (Harper, 1983) and *Rage for Fame: The Ascent of Clare Boothe Luce* by Sylvia Jukes Morris (Random House, 1997) were quite helpful in providing information about Kahlo and Luce as well as the stories and anecdotes associated with the painting *The Suicide of Dorothy Hale* (see chapter "The Portrait of Dorothy Hale"), which have become legend. Examples include the commissioning and execution of the painting, the Bergdorf Goodman dress, and the identical press quotes from Clare Boothe Luce, Bernard Baruch, and Isamu Noguchi.

The Clare Boothe Luce papers proved a valuable resource as well. In addition to background information, it contains the letter she wrote to Nickolas Murray in 1939, the contents of which I excerpt in *Lady Be Good*. It begins, "I intend to have Noguchi, a great friend of both Dorothy Hale and Frida (Kahlo) Rivera, paint out the legend— that is to say the actual name of the unfortunate girl and my name."

The newspaper excerpt that Frank "Crownie" Crowninshield reads aloud ("She has much of the wit and some of the irony of Aileen Pringle . . .") was originally printed in the *Times Mirror*. Grateful acknowledgment is made to the *Los Angeles Times:* Quote from "Transfer May Alter Plays" in the *Times Mirror*, 1932, copyright © Los Angeles Times. Used by permission of the Los Angeles Times. All Rights Reserved.

Special thanks to the Phoenix Art Museum for permission to include a reproduction of Frida Kahlo's portrait. Frida Kahlo, *El suicidio de Dorothy Hale* (The Suicide of Dorothy Hale), 1939. Oil on Masonite with painted frame. Collection of Phoenix Art Museum, Gift of an anonymous donor, 1960.20.

Elsa Maxwell's autobiography, *R.S.V.P.: Elsa Maxwell's Own Story* (Little, Brown, 1954) was helpful in learning about Ms. Maxwell and her friends, as well as her parties and the guests who attended them. From her book, I drew the story about Cole Porter transforming a barge in Venice into a nightclub and the quote "to accommodate his guests, who had a wonderful time eating and drinking off his impeccably starched cuff."

In the 1920s, celebrated playwright Eugene O'Neill won three Pulitzer Prizes, and in 1936 he won the Nobel Prize for Literature. A deep bow to Mr. O'Neill for his quote: "Obsessed by a fairy tale, we spend our lives searching for a magic door and a lost kingdom of peace." It is included in the narrative of *Lady Be Good* as are the following lines from his poem "Free": "I know that I shall find surcease

/ the rest my spirit craves / where the rainbows play in the flying spray / 'mid the keen salt kiss of the waves." "Free" was printed in the *Pleiades Club Year Book* in 1912.

The Dorothy Parker quote "I know this will come as a shock to you, Mr. Goldwyn, but in all history, which has held billions and billions of human beings, not a single one ever had a happy ending" is thanks to Dorothy Parker, of course, for saying it, and Stuart Y. Silverstein, who included it as a footnote in the book *Not Much Fun: The Lost Poems of Dorothy Parker* (Scribner, 1996), for which he served as editor.

The section about the premiere of *Four Saints in Three Acts* at Hartford's Wadsworth Atheneum and the exhibition at the Avery Memorial Wing is in part derived from *Unfinished Business: Memoirs: 1902-1988* by John Houseman (Applause Books, 2000). He writes about Archibald MacLeish leading a chorus in Russian folk songs while Nicolas Nabokov played the piano and tells the anecdote I included about Salvador Dali, who was seated beside the wife of an affluent Hartford art collector. Houseman writes, "Salvador Dali gazed intently at the mother-of-pearl buttons on the bosom of her dress and inquired courteously, as I happened to walk by, if they were edible. ('Madame, ces boutons, sont-ils comestibles?')"

It is true that John Barrymore said these poetic words: "that lovely, lost look, that exquisite, forlorn look; that roseleaf cheek that is not quite a blush; that brightness in the eyes that is not yet a tear." Author Margaret Case Harriman, whose father, Frank, owned the Algonquin Hotel, quotes him in her book, *Blessed are the Debonair* (Rinehart Company, 1956).

It is also true that an actress, namely Margaret Mullen Root, said of Brock Pemberton "He has a face like that of a new baby, all bald and screwed-up into a frown." She said this in an interview with Charles R. Hill (March 27, 1969), which is documented in *The Emporia State Research Studies*, the graduate publication of the Emporia Kansas State College, Volume XXIII.

It was delightful to read Ione Robinson's admiring words about Dorothy Hale in her book, *A Wall to Paint On* (E. P. Dutton and Company, 1946), which is where I sourced the information that Dorothy Hale was present at Nickolas Murray's party.

A great deal of thought was given to writing about Ms. Hale's final hour. The narrative is meant to underscore the fact that we simply don't know what happened. The portrait by Frida Kahlo is a representation of Ms. Hale's last moments; yet in her time she was noted as a woman with joie de vivre who rose up and conquered each test of faith that life delivered and did so with magnificent aplomb. She made it to the other side of heartbreak. This part of her story was buried under headlines and lost to a legend that has endured for more than half a century.

ACKNOWLEDGMENTS

This book has been a long time in the making, and I appreciate all those who have supported me, a few of whom are mentioned here. To Kermit Roosevelt III, I owe a great debt of gratitude for his expert counsel and truly outstanding advice. It's with deep appreciation, admiration, and lavish applause that I thank Alexis Gargagliano for her skilled editing and remarkable insights. Hats off. And Timothy Rogers, the director and CEO of the Phoenix Art Museum, has made this especially momentous with his gracious endorsement.

To my steadfast friends who came with spirited support and have been an infinite source of inspiration over the years, I am ever grateful. Most notably are William Hall Wendel Jr., Ruth Fortunoff Cooper, Jackson Browne, and Corrina, Donald, and Marta Miller.

It's to my good fortune that the brilliant Richard Ljoenes of Richard Ljoenes Design LLC has been a vital part of my team, as is Carl Fospero of Made in the Shade Productions. To Richard and to Carl I say an enthusiastic thank you.

My heartfelt thanks to Bill Dedman, Pulitzer Prize winner and New York Times #1 bestselling author of *Empty Mansions*, for his generous words. And to the prodigious talents Ashley Longshore, Dennis McNally, and Andrea Cagan, for their beautiful quotes on the first pages of this book. Warm appreciation goes to the wonderful Karen Watson; *Wall Street Journal* special writer Brenda Cronin (special, indeed!); and former NCIS special agent in charge and author Mark Fallon for their encouragement. Those who tendered excellent advice include Marly Russoff of the Marly Rusoff Literary Agency and Pat Conroy Literary Center; Rose Solomon of the Mickey Hart music empire; and Ryan Fox of Lyons & Salky Law, LLP.

A wonderfully efficient group of people made it possible to include the images: Richard Ljoenes; the team at Condé Nast; Kerry Negahban of the Lee Miller Archives; Lisa Ballard of the Artist Rights Society; Adriana Milinic Fanning and the staff at the Phoenix Art Museum; and the gracious Michael Feldschuh of the Feldschuh Gallery, who was most helpful.

I must single out Jeffrey Blount, award-winning novelist and my former NBC News colleague, who led me in unexpected directions with an introduction to publisher John Koehler.

John Koehler believed in the work tout de suite and provided a splendid home for *Lady Be Good*. He's made the publishing process a joy. To him and to the staff at Koehler Books I say a special thank you.

Above all others I am grateful to my exquisite mother, Rose, who has retained the bright spirit of the Twenties era to which she was born and has kindly played the Dr. Watson to my Sherlock Holmes on this story for all these many years.